The
Land
Was
Ours

ALSO BY CHARLES W. BAILEY
(WITH FLETCHER KNEBEL)

No High Ground
Seven Days in May
Convention

The Land Was Ours

A Novel of the Great Plains

CHARLES W. BAILEY

Cornelia & Michael Bessie Books

An Imprint of HarperCollins*Publishers*

THE LAND WAS OURS. Copyright © 1991 by Charles W. Bailey II. All rights reserved. Printed in the United States of America. No part of this book may be used or reproduced in any manner whatsoever without written permission except in the case of brief quotations embodied in critical articles and reviews. For information address HarperCollins Publishers, 10 East 53rd Street, New York, NY 10022.

FIRST EDITION

Designed by Alma Orenstein

Library of Congress Cataloging-in-Publication Data
Bailey, Charles W. (Charles Waldo)
     The land was ours : a novel of the great plains / Charles W.
Bailey.—1st ed.
       p. cm.
     ISBN 0-06-039128-6
     I. Title.
PS3552.A365L36 1991
813'.54—dc20   90-55562

91 92 93 94 95 CC/RRD 10 9 8 7 6 5 4 3 2 1

For
Victoria and Sarah

The land was ours before we were the land's.
She was our land more than a hundred years
Before we were her people. She was ours
In Massachusetts, in Virginia,
But we were England's, still colonials,
Possessing what we still were unpossessed by,
Possessed by what we now no more possessed.
Something we were withholding made us weak
Until we found out that it was ourselves
We were withholding from our land of living,
And forthwith found salvation in surrender.
Such as we were we gave ourselves outright
(The deed of gift was many deeds of war)
To the land realizing vaguely westward,
But still unstoried, artless, unenhanced,
Such as she was, such as she would become.

—ROBERT FROST,
The Gift Outright

The
Land
Was
Ours

Prologue

Toward the end of his life, Dan's earliest memory came back clearer than ever.

He stood at the door of his family's sod house on the claim in Nebraska, looking down the slope, watching his father come across the creek and start up the hill. The slope was so steep and Dan so short that the wagon seemed to sink from sight; for several minutes Dan could only mark its progress by the sound of his father's voice as he urged Babe and Charlie up the slope. Then the horses' heads reappeared, and between them his father's head and shoulders, and then his hands holding the reins, and finally the whole outfit, legs and wagon and wheels and all. His father saw him across the farmyard and waved; Dan stepped out of the door and ran toward him.

"Pa, Pa. I saw you cross the creek!"

"Well, I saw you standing guard, looking out for your Ma." Henry Woods patted his son on the head. "Now, help me carry things into the house." He handed Dan the jug of molasses.

Dan turned toward the house, but it was gone. He looked back to his father, and he too had disappeared.

Chapter 1

EUDORA slid out of bed in the cold half-light. Shivering, she dressed before doing anything else, putting on all she could under her nightgown, then quickly pulling on her remaining underclothes and dropping her dress over her head. The hard dirt floor felt like ice through her stockings, and she shoved her feet into her stiff shoes and fastened them. She wrapped a shawl around her shoulders and went out to the privy.

The sun was not quite up yet, but the eastern horizon was brightening. In the farmyard the ground was bare, dry now but still rutted after the autumn rains. The buildings were all dirt-brown. The barn, like the house, was built of sod, but it was a dugout, set into the slope where the pasture began to rise. It had been their first home on the claim, so low-roofed that a tall man would have had trouble standing up inside.

The house also sat low, its back to the north as if anticipating winter. The door and one window were on the south side; a smaller second window was cut into the east end. The roof—rough pole rafters covered with brush, hay, and sod—slumped unevenly down over the top of the walls.

To the north, beyond the little cluster of buildings, the ground was carpeted with winter wheat, bright green against the dark earth. In the other direction, dry cornstalks and stubble still stood in the field that sloped down toward the patches of brush and trees along the creek.

Turning back toward the house, Eudora shivered again, not so much from this morning's chill as in anticipation of the cold months ahead.

She was just plain sick of it: sick of the wind that blew all the time, sick of the dank earth-smelling chill of the house, sick of the crowded little room where four people lived always all together with no privacy for anyone, surely not for a woman when she needed it.

She was sick of living in a dirty house. It smelled dirty, it looked dirty, it *was* dirty. You couldn't keep it even halfway clean, no matter how you tried; the sod walls and roof produced showers of dust in dry weather, globs of mud when it rained. The windows were so small that you couldn't really see to clean properly anyway.

Not that there was anyone to clean for; Henry never seemed to notice how things looked. As for company, Eudora often went three months without seeing another woman.

There were other visitors, such as the rattlesnakes. You always had to watch out for them. Eudora hated them, despised them, feared them more than any other living thing. They turned up everywhere, indoors as well as out, sliding through joints in the walls or dropping from hiding places in the roof. She had killed her share. Henry had taught her to fire the revolver, but she never could make her hands stop shaking when she faced a rattler. So she used a long-handled hoe they kept sharpened and standing by the door just for snakes.

Everything the family owned and everything it did were crammed into a single room, twenty-four feet long and fourteen deep. They all slept at one end, parents and children separated by nothing but curtains. Seven-year-old Emma and five-year-old Dan slept together in a trundle that pulled out from under their parents' bed; soon they'd need separate beds, and then it would be even more crowded.

The other end of the room was the kitchen, with stove and wood box, table, dry-goods boxes for cupboards, two chairs and more boxes to sit on, a water bucket and a washtub. All this and more filled the edges of the room and pressed in toward its center. With the kitchen at one end and the beds at the other, there was little space left for the "parlor": two chairs, one small table, one lamp, all set on a worn rag rug.

Eudora's face felt like old leather from the wind that blew and blew to drive you crazy. Her hair was dull and dirty and starting to go gray, and where once she had been smooth and soft she was now rough and hardened.

Above all else, she was tired, bone tired, tired from the moment she got out of bed in the morning until she finally lay down at night. Henry worked even harder, but that didn't make her any less exhausted.

Thinking these things made her feel confused and guilty. Her life was no different from a lot of other women's, no harder. What was a wife for, anyway, but to help her husband? And Henry was a good husband, sober and loving and gentle; he never raised a hand to her, as so many did to their wives.

Henry Woods had looked so handsome the first time she saw him, that July morning in 1860, his blue eyes bright in the dim interior of her father's gristmill in southern Minnesota.

Now there's a man, she had thought, feeling the telltale thickness in her throat. He was twenty-one and she was eighteen, and it was all over for both of them that first morning. They planned to be married the next summer; but then came the war, Henry enlisted in the First Minnesota Volunteers, and they decided to wait until his three months' service was over.

Three months turned into nearly three years, and when he did come home in late '63 he was on crutches. Still, he counted himself lucky: four out of every five men in his regiment had been killed or wounded in a desperate quarter-hour at Gettysburg, and Henry lay on the field for hours with a smashed leg before someone came for him. Through some miracle, the wound healed without the gangrene that killed so many others. Eudora helped him get over both his wound and his nightmares, and they were married that winter.

As an ex-soldier, Henry had a right to a free homestead. He couldn't find land that satisfied him close to home, so in 1866 he headed for Nebraska, where construction of the new transcontinental railroad was opening the country to settlement. It was a long, hard wagon ride for Eudora, pregnant with her first child.

They reached Grand Island, a booming railroad construction town, before Emma was born. That fall, while Eudora nursed her, Henry worked as a carpenter and went looking for the right piece of land.

He found it in early October, fifteen miles northwest of town, 160 acres of grassland sloping gently down to a creek that crossed its southern edge.

This is the place for me, Henry thought, dismounting and letting his horse drink. *That's something, a creek running this time of year. And there's a good stand of trees on the banks; looks like this is a year-round stream all right.*

He walked up the slope to a place where it flattened out in a kind of terrace.

Here's where we'll put the house. Dora can have her garden over there, handy to the kitchen. And the barn goes over there.

Henry stooped and picked up a handful of dirt. *Good soil, too.* He let it run through his fingers.

Rich soil, enough water, trees for firewood and fence posts, a protected place to put the house.

A man couldn't ask for more.

In the spring they moved to the claim, and for a little while life on their new farm was all they had hoped for, even if Eudora did have to live in a dugout until Henry got the sod house built. Their son Dan was born a year later, in the last week of April 1868.

But after that things never seemed to go quite right. It was like walking into the wind that blew all the time across these plains: you had to fight just to stay even, let alone go forward. Henry had known he'd have to borrow to get started, but he figured he could pay off the loan in a year or two. He couldn't. Even though he harvested good crops, he owed more each year.

Henry kept hoping their luck would turn. Now, in the fall of '73, after five years, he still hoped. His wife did not.

"I know it's hard for you," he said one night as they got ready for bed. "You've been awful good. I think we'll do a sight better next year."

She'd heard that before. *He's at it again, fooling himself.*

He seemed to read her mind. "No, Dora, I really believe we'll turn the corner next year. Things are bound to get better."

She wanted to believe, but she no longer could.

"Henry, there's too many ifs."

"What do you mean?"

"If there's enough snow this winter and enough rain next summer. If there's no 'hoppers. If hail doesn't ruin the wheat. If frost doesn't spoil the corn. If a horse doesn't come up lame. If . . ."

"Dora, don't worry so much." He interrupted her, then put his arms around her. "It'll come all right."

She sighed. "I hope so. I just wish I was as sure as you are."

She's cranky tonight, Henry thought. *Maybe she's tired. She's tired a lot these days.*

A few minutes later, outside in the cold stillness, he stopped to admire the clear night. The harvest moon rode high in the southern sky, washing the countryside with silver from horizon to horizon.

By God, he thought, *it looks just like it did the first night I spent here after I found this place. I knew right away a man couldn't ask for anything better.*

And now it's really mine, final proof all filed and published, all legal, signed and sealed. Good land, good as any around here, and a good crop this year too.

We'll do even better next year, and then I can pay that loan off. And then I can buy that quarter-section on the east, and when I do, they'll have to stand back and give us room to trot.

He turned back toward the house.

If only Dora was happier. She hasn't smiled in six months. Maybe she'll cheer up if we get some neighbors in the spring.

In the spring. But first there was another winter. Henry Woods shivered, feeling the chill of the turning season.

The really bad times began the next spring, just as Eudora was beginning to feel alive again after the long, dark months. March had been warmer than usual, and by the middle of the month the snow had gone. Henry got an early start on the field work, and by mid-April his oats were seeded and his wheat made a bright green carpet on the slopes north of the house. In the northwest pasture the grass was already starting to grow. Sloughs and bottoms were alive with songbirds, and migrating ducks and cranes crowded the larger streams.

The storm began late on Easter afternoon with distant thunder followed by gentle spring showers. It was raining hard by the time they went to bed.

When Eudora woke the next morning, the light coming into the house seemed strangely dim. It took her a minute to realize that the windows were completely coated with snow. Startled, she hurried to the door and pulled it open—to find snow packed in a solid drift halfway up the doorframe. Big, wet flakes were still being driven across the farmyard by a northerly gale.

"Guess I won't get in much field work today." Henry had joined his wife at the door.

Eudora felt sick to her stomach. They had never had so much snow so late—*My God,* she thought, *it's halfway through April!*—and the prospect of going back to winter's confinement was almost more than she could stand.

Henry sensed her despair. "Dora, this won't be so bad. I'll dig us out today, and at this time of year the snow'll be gone in a week or less. It won't hurt the crops, and the animals are all right." He bent to work the morning cramp out of his bad leg. "It's a good thing I put 'em in the barn last night. I'd hate to be looking for 'em today."

He was wrong about the shoveling; it was Tuesday before they had all the paths finally cleared, even with all four of them working. But he was right about the snow going fast: in ten days it had all but disappeared, leaving only a few stubborn drifts—and a lot of water—in the low places. The young grain was undamaged.

Still, it was a hard couple of weeks, and Eudora couldn't get over the spooky way the storm had crept up on them while they slept. It seemed to her a bad omen.

She had reason to remember her foreboding one day in late June when she looked out the kitchen door and saw a peculiar white cloud blowing in from the west, shimmering like snow in the sunlight as it moved across the creek and into their cornfield. She had seen that before: the grasshoppers were back.

She called Emma to help her—Dan was out with his father, shocking oats—and they ran to the garden. Eudora thought they might save a few of the vegetables she was working so hard to raise.

No more than three or four minutes passed before Henry reached the farmyard, his boots making ghastly crunching sounds as they trampled the layers of 'hoppers now covering the ground. But by then the garden was simply gone, potato plants eaten clean off, empty holes where onions had sat in the ground, everything consumed by the wave of struggling insects.

Down the slope to the south the cornfield was completely covered with the dark-bodied 'hoppers, thick as a swarm of bees, the sound of their feeding clearly audible as they stripped the cornstalks of everything edible. Another living, moving carpet crept across the fields to the north, eating the ripening wheat where it stood and clinging three deep to the oat shocks Henry and Dan had just stacked.

Less than an hour later, the 'hoppers left as suddenly as they had arrived. Henry and Eudora looked at the remains of their farm: where there had been a field of leafy green corn, there were now only bare, broken stalks. Raw earth was all that remained in the wheat field. In Eudora's garden, the only surviving plant was a single petunia, saved because she had covered it with an upended bucket that happened to be within reach. Every other green and growing thing was gone. Even leather harness and wooden tool handles had been chewed.

"Henry, what are we being punished for?" Eudora whispered. "What have we done?"

"We haven't done a damned thing, except work," her husband retorted angrily. He pulled himself up straight and pointed to the ravaged wheat. "I've always had bad luck with that stuff," he said. "I got shot in a wheat field. Maybe I should keep away from it."

Much to their surprise, the wheat field was at least partly green again two weeks later, putting out new growth under the stimulus of a couple of timely rains. It wouldn't make grain, but Henry thought it might make fall pasture. He salvaged what he could of the harvested oats, then replanted beans and turnips, hoping to get a crop before frost.

But then it quit raining and got hot. The temperature climbed into the nineties day after day, sucking all moisture from the earth, scorching the reborn wheat and the sprouting turnips, killing what little the 'hoppers had spared.

One day two wagons went by on the other side of the creek—heading east. One bore a crude sign painted on a torn sheet:

IN GOD WE TRUSTED
IN NEBRASKA WE BUSTED

"And that's about it," Henry told Eudora that night. "We're about busted, too. We'll have to buy food, and feed, and maybe kill the cattle so we won't have to feed 'em and so we'll have something to eat. Or sell 'em, if there's anyone left to buy. I don't know."

Eudora had already thought all that, and more. The children suffered even in an easy winter, always cold and shut up and lonesome, not getting enough good food to eat. This next winter would be worse—much worse.

Still, she couldn't be the one to say it.

[7]

"Henry, you'll have to decide."

He looked at her. She looked back at him, saying nothing. He got up and went out into the hot summer night.

Henry's younger brother really decided for them. Two years earlier, Benjamin Woods had moved to Dakota Territory and opened a dry-goods store in a little place called Falls City, just west of the Minnesota border. His letter reached them in early August.

Dear Brother Henry,

It has been hot here this past week. But there has been some rain and we escaped the worst hoppers last month. We hear of bad hoppers in Nebraska. I pray you are spared. I continue vy busy here, This store is more than I can manage myself so I must find help soon, if you get busted in Neb why not come here? You can partner me, there is enough trade to support us both.
There is a school here now. This is a booming place.

Ever your affec brother,
Benj. Woods

Henry brought the letter home from town and handed it to Eudora without saying anything. When she finished reading it she hardly dared breathe, let alone speak, but his voice was even.

"We'll leave as soon as I can settle things. I wrote Ben while I was in town. Saved a trip. There's no use putting it off any longer. We'd best get there and get settled before winter."

He stopped speaking and turned away abruptly. Eudora reached out to touch him, then was in his arms.

"Ah, Dora, don't." He touched the tears on her cheek. "It'll come all right."

He took it hard. On the trip from Nebraska across the dried-out plains, he hardly spoke. Late one morning they topped a rise and saw Falls City, tucked into a great bend of the river. Eudora and the children looked ahead eagerly at their new home, but Henry looked back at the plains they had crossed.

"It just doesn't feel right, moving to town," he said. "I'm a farmer. All I ever wanted was my own farm. Now I'll spend the rest of my life in a store."

Chapter 2

C LEMENT LOUNSBERRY walked from the dining room into the lobby of Willard's Hotel. It was barely eight in the morning, but the room was already full of men, voices, and cigar smoke.

Damnation, he thought, *I've only been in Washington one night and I already feel surrounded. There's just too many people. Well, why not? Bees swarm to honey, and there's plenty of honey in this town.*

He picked his way through the lobby and out onto Pennsylvania Avenue. The sun was well up over the Capitol, its first light reflecting off the storefronts and windows along the great avenue. The warmth of this late March morning was a pleasant change from the winter Lounsberry had left behind on the northern plains.

He was the editor of the only newspaper in Bismarck, the biggest town in the northern half of Dakota Territory. He had come to Washington to see Moses Armstrong, the Dakota delegate in Congress, and to deliver a message.

The farmers are in trouble, worse trouble than any time since the first settlers went West after the war. They're in trouble all over the plains, in Dakota and Minnesota and Nebraska and Iowa and Kansas. It's grasshoppers and drought and hard winters and debt.

And this time, the government has got to help.

Lounsberry had spent enough time around politicians—he'd been stationed in Washington when he was the youngest colonel in the Union army—to know that few if any in the capital would want to hear it.

Most of 'em wouldn't know a grasshopper from a green frog. And those that would are too busy stealing to pay any attention to people in trouble.

He wasn't even sure about Armstrong.

Mose Armstrong's a good man and I think he's honest. He understands.

But he don't cut much ice, being a Democrat—and not having a vote in the House because Dakota's not a state yet.

Lounsberry strode up the long slope to the Capitol. Armstrong was waiting for him on the steps leading to the House of Representatives, right where he'd said he'd be.

"Mose, how are you?"

"Why, Colonel, I'm well, I reckon. You look first-rate."

"Well, it makes a fellow's juices flow to get away from winter into this tropical climate. No wonder you wanted a second term."

"Oh, the weather's nice this time of year, but you wouldn't want to visit me in July."

Lounsberry laughed. "I know it gets hot. I was in these parts with McClellan the summer of '62."

The two men talked as easily as if they had last seen each other just the night before. In fact it had been six months earlier, when Lounsberry was starting his weekly newspaper in Bismarck and Armstrong was seeking his second term as Dakota's territorial delegate in Congress. Now the thirty-year-old newspaperman and the forty-year-old congressman amiably picked each other's brains for the latest news in both places.

"Seems like it's been a mean session of Congress," Lounsberry said. "There's an awful lot of stealing going on around here."

Lounsberry grinned. "I guess that's Washington. They get by with things here that we never could in the rest of the country."

"No, it's not just here," Armstrong responded. "It's the same all over. Everyone wants to get his bit on everything that comes along." He changed the subject. "What brings you here?"

Lounsberry got right to it. "What I really want to find out is what you folks are going to do for the farmers. They're in bad shape, you know. The grasshoppers ate 'em right down to the ground last summer, almost all over Minnesota and Nebraska, and most of Dakota and Kansas too."

"I saw what they did in the Territory last year." Armstrong fell silent for a moment. "But the government's not going to do anything for those people. You know, people here don't see the plains the way we do."

"What do you mean?"

"There's two kinds in Congress. Half of 'em think the plains are nothing but a big desert, all sand and scrub—just something you have to cross to get to California and Oregon. 'The Great American Desert,' they call it. They figure no one should try to live there, let alone farm it."

"And the other half?"

"They think just the opposite, that the plains are no different from what they know in the East: good land, enough rain every year, a long growing season, plenty of trees and ground water and rivers that run year 'round."

Lounsberry snorted. "Well, they're *both* wrong. It's no desert, but it's different from the East: you can't make a crop every year the way you can here. The weather's harder, it gets hotter and colder too. There's no pattern to it and no forgiveness in it."

"You and I know that. But people here don't, and they don't care, either. They figure that's just the way it is—farmers have always had some good years and some hard ones, some good luck and some bad, and always will."

"They don't use that rule on the railroads or the bankers, do they? They stuff money into their pockets every year, no matter what." Lounsberry was suddenly hot. "Mose, it's much worse this time. They were pretty deep in debt already, and then we had drought, and then the 'hoppers ate what little was left. Someone's got to help."

"Then you and your farmers had best talk to your governor. There's no help from here."

Lounsberry bristled. "Hell's fire! You know the Territory's got no money except what comes from Washington. And the states don't have anything but small change, either. What the farmers really need is more dollars in circulation, and that's up to you people down here."

"Well, this Congress and this president ain't going to do a thing for 'em. They reckon the government already did enough by giving 'em their land for nothing."

"That was little enough to do for men who soldiered. And anyway the speculators and the railroads got a lot more free land than farmers did. And it was the best land, closest to their tracks, so they could sell it for a fat price, while the homesteaders had to go into the back country and pick up the leavings."

"I know, you're right, Colonel." Armstrong shrugged. "I've tried to tell 'em if they don't play square with the farmers, they'll walk out of the Republican party. But most of 'em don't believe me, and those that do don't care."

"Well, the farmers don't care anymore which party wins, they don't think there's a damned bit of difference. You know, a farmer'd rather do anything than ask for charity, but they have to have help this time. And it has to come from here."

The two men went inside the Capitol. The corridors were already crowded, despite the early hour.

"My God, Mose." Lounsberry put his mouth close to Armstrong's ear, unconsciously mimicking the style of the conversations around them. "What's all this about?"

Armstrong smiled knowingly. "Why, this is just an ordinary morning in the place where the people rule."

Lounsberry looked at the freshly shaven faces, well-fitted and expensive clothes, soft hands, gold watch chains stretched across white waistcoats: all the outward signs of comfort and privilege. Armstrong identified some of them.

"There's the Pennsylvania Railroad; probably just keeping an eye on his people. . . . That tall fellow works for the mine owners, he's trying to get the silver purchase restored, and he likely will. . . . Over there, that's Jay Gould's man, wonder why he's up here, maybe watching the . . . Say!" Armstrong spoke aloud in his surprise. "There's Jim McLaughlin. You know him?"

Lounsberry did know James McLaughlin. He was the government agent for the Sioux Indians at Devil's Lake in northeastern Dakota, an honest man in a notoriously corrupt bureau. They pushed toward him.

"Jim, you're a sight for sore eyes in this place."

"Colonel! So are you! Hello, Mose." McLaughlin smiled under his ample mustache. "I was hoping I'd find you. Have you got time to see me today?"

"Always, Jim. Why don't you give me a little while to look at my mail and I'll meet you here? We can talk a bit then." He looked at Lounsberry. "You be here too, Colonel. I owe you some more time, and I'll get you into the gallery so you can watch us at work."

He winked and slipped away through the crowded hall. The two visitors went outside.

"I haven't seen you in, well, must be six months," McLaughlin said. "Your paper going well?"

"Yup. I'm just here for a few days. I'll be back in Bismarck next week, and none too soon, either. You can't run a newspaper by telegraph."

"No more than you can an Indian reservation," McLaughlin agreed. "But at least I know things will stay pretty quiet when there's snow on the ground and it's way below zero."

"That's what they need here—a blizzard, to slow down the stealing."

"Nothing slows *that* down. Some of the things I've heard would curl your whiskers."

Lounsberry was intrigued. "If you're not busy, let's have supper tonight," he suggested. "Come by Willard's at seven."

"I'll be there."

The lobby of Willard's was even more crowded at seven in the evening than it had been twelve hours earlier. "And every one of 'em wants something," McLaughlin said.

Lounsberry inspected the crowd of officeholders and office seekers, lobbyists and congressmen, businessmen and journalists, loafers and hangers-on.

"Well, we don't, so let's get out of here before we suffocate," he said. "Even your Indians wouldn't smoke such vile stuff."

They crossed the black-and-white marble floor, avoiding the brown splashes around the numerous spittoons. Outside, it was surprisingly cold; the day's warmth had gone with the sunset, a reminder that real spring was still a few weeks away.

"How did you get along with Armstrong?" Lounsberry asked.

"Not so well."

"Neither did I. I was trying to find out what they're going to do to help the farmers who got busted last summer. Mose says no one around here gives a damn."

"Well, that's about how I came out with him, too. You know there's a lot of talk about opening up the Black Hills to settlement."

"It's bound to happen."

"Well, I'm trying to get the government to play square with my Indians—for once." McLaughlin paused. "We signed a treaty giving the Sioux the Black Hills forever."

"What did Mose say?"

"The people who sent him here want the Hills, so he wants the Hills, and never mind the treaties."

"Look, Jim, there's timber there, and gold too."

They went into Wormley's Hotel, where the dining room was quiet and the food good.

"If we take the Hills, it would be the worst broken promise of all," McLaughlin said.

"Why?"

"Because that's their best hunting ground, and it's a sacred place for them, too."

"Jim, we have got to open up the Hills," Lounsberry, leaning across the table, spoke as the Dakota boomer he really was. "It's the only way we'll ever get railroads built across the southern part of the territory, and without railroads, we'll never get people to settle those lands."

McLaughlin pointed a finger across the table.

"Every Indian treaty has been made for the benefit of the white man, and every single one has been broken as soon as it inconvenienced the white man." It was his turn to be angry. "If the Sioux had any sense they wouldn't bother the settlers—they'd come down here and attack the Capitol."

"They don't have any sense. They kill women and babies."

"Hell's fire, I don't defend that. But the fact is that every Indian war has been caused by lying or cheating or stealing by whites."

Lounsberry shook his head. "I don't believe things are as bad as people say."

"I'll tell you how bad it is," McLaughlin said. "You know General Dodge, the man who built the Union Pacific?"

"Grenville Dodge? Sure. Didn't he go into Congress?"

"Only for one term, until he found something better. Now he's getting rich off the Indians."

"How's he doing that?"

"He had lots of friends in the government, from army days and from the railroad money he spread around. They gave him the contracts to supply food to the Indian reservations."

"Nothing wrong with that, is there?"

"Not if they'd put 'em out for bids. But there wasn't any bidding. He helped his friends in the government, and they returned the favor, just handed him the contracts. He's collected a million and a half already."

Lounsberry was startled at the amount. "How do you know that?"

"I still have a few friends here. Dodge got about a hundred and eighty thousand in '71, and more than half a million in '72. Then last year he collected over eight hundred thousand dollars."

McLaughlin chuckled at Lounsberry's look. "That's not all. Dodge applied for a veteran's pension last year, and now he's drawing thirty dollars a month."

"You either have to laugh or cry," Lounsberry said. "Thirty dollars a month is more to a Dakota farmer than that whole million and a half is to Dodge. They're breaking their backs to raise barely enough to eat, and they can't get a dime from people down here who get rich on other people's money."

McLaughlin finished his soup. "It all fits, doesn't it? Congress gives the railroads money, and a lot of free land, too, which they sell to farmers. In return, the railroads give congressmen free stock in their construction companies."

"So the congressmen give away public money and public land, and get back private boodle for themselves." Lounsberry picked up the tale. "The railroads make money selling land to farmers, then they make more money hauling what the farmers raise. And the farmers work like niggers— and get nothing but deeper in debt."

They fell silent as the waiter brought their dinner.

Chapter 3

Falls City, Dakota Territory, 1880

D AN SHIFTED on the hard schoolroom seat, watching the wall clock behind the teacher. Spring sunbeams fell warmly on Miss Blanchard's pupils, dozing over their books as the hour dragged to a close. It seemed to Dan that the hands of the clock were stuck tight at one minute before three.

"Daniel Woods." The teacher's voice interrupted his concentration on the clock. She was writing some numbers on the blackboard. "Come to the board and work this problem."

Dan stood up. He hadn't been paying the slightest attention, and had no idea how to work the problem. Fortunately for him, at that moment the minute hand finally moved and the clock struck three, ending the period and the school day.

Dan joined the crowd jostling noisily into the sunlit afternoon. Just three weeks past his twelfth birthday, he would have been delighted to spend the rest of the afternoon playing ball in the schoolyard; but he had garden chores to do and he knew he had to go straight home.

Well, almost straight. He decided he could take time to go an extra block or two to see his father, so he turned down Lincoln Avenue until he reached a two-story frame building with its white-painted false front lettered in black.

WOODS BROS
GENERAL MERCHANDISE
GROCERIES

Henry Woods was at the counter, assembling an order for a customer. Dan had seen the man in the store before: Mr. Harper, Amos Harper, that was his name. He was a farmer. He stood a bit over six feet tall and was thick through the body, with heavy forearms and hands. He was very strong—Dan had seen him pick up a whole hogshead of sugar—but his blue eyes were friendly as he smiled at the storekeeper's son.

Henry nodded at Dan too, but continued his conversation with the customer.

"Well, Amos, at least the ground's wet enough this spring."

"That's not the problem, for once." Dan thought Mr. Harper sounded angry, the way his voice came rumbling out of his belly. "Now if we could get half as good a deal from the railroads and the grain companies as *they* get from the government, we'd be well off."

Dan had often heard that kind of talk when they lived in the sod house on the claim. His father's anger was so strong that it was etched clearly in Dan's memory, even though he had only been a little boy then. Hearing the words now reminded him of sitting at the makeshift table in the dark, cold little house listening to his father's angry tirades.

But Dan hadn't heard him talk that way for a long time; in fact, he hardly ever said anything about those grim years. And anyway, Henry Woods wasn't much interested in politics—unlike Amos Harper, whose contempt for politicians was a legend throughout the county.

"I do miss the farm this time of year," Henry said. "Planting always makes a man feel good."

"That's so," Harper conceded. But he wasn't to be cheered up so easily. "That is, if your land don't blow away and your seed with it."

Henry had reason enough to know Harper was right, but the terrible times were behind him now, and he could laugh. "Amos, you won't believe you're in heaven when they hand you the harp. I never saw a man so set on being contrary."

"Except my big brother when he's in a bad mood." Benjamin Woods spoke up as he entered the room. No one with eyes could have failed to recognize him as Henry's brother: he had the same profile, the same sharp jaw below a beaked nose. But he lacked the pain lines etched in Henry's face, and there seemed more difference in their ages than the three years that actually separated them. Benjamin's hair was still yellow at thirty-nine; Henry's beard and hair were gray at forty-two.

Actually Benjamin thought Henry looked younger now than he had when he gave up on the claim and brought his family to Falls City six years before. *He works hard in the store, but he's not fighting blizzards and drought and 'hoppers and hail from before daylight to after dark, seven days a week. His limp is better, and if that leg still hurts it doesn't show. Not that he ever did complain, but a brother can tell.*

Dan edged around behind the counter to stand near his father as the three men talked. Henry turned to him for the first time, reaching out and dropping a hand on his son's shoulder. "Say, young feller, you've got chores at home, remember? Better get along or your mother'll wonder what happened to you."

Uncle Benjamin fished a couple of pieces of hard candy out of the big glass jar and handed them to Dan. "One's for your sister, remember."

"Well, if you're going to spoil my children, we may as well ruin that pretty Grace Harper and her little brother, too," Henry said. He reached into the jar, extracted two more candies, wrapped them in a twist of paper, and passed them to Harper. "Now you run along, Dan."

Dan wriggled out of his father's grip. " 'Bye, Pa. 'Bye, Uncle Benjy." Then, remembering as he went out the door: "Thanks for the candy."

He turned down Grand Avenue, dawdling past the last few store windows. The commercial district quickly gave way to homes, scattered comfortably across gently rolling fields. The house Henry had built was a half-dozen blocks further south, across the railroad tracks where the ground began to rise toward the ridge at the south edge of town.

Dan took a series of detours through backyards and alleys on his way home. He sniffed the apple blossoms; most people had a tree or two in their yard, and this week their fragrance masked the earthier aromas of stable and privy. In every yard there was a garden with peas, potatoes, green beans, and corn pushing tender sprouts from freshly turned earth.

Eudora Woods saw Dan coming, cutting across their own backyard and around the vegetable garden. She met him at the kitchen door.

"You've been a time getting home," she said. "Did you have to stay after school?"

"Aw, Ma, no. I stopped at the store to see Pa." He dropped his lunchpail on the kitchen table and looked around.

"There's nothing to eat. Now you get along and finish up the garden. Those weeds grow six inches every day."

"Right now, Ma?" Dan's instinct, as always when faced with weeding, was to seek a reprieve. "I got a lot of reading to do for school."

"Right now." She spoke crisply, but couldn't stifle a smile. "Weeding now, reading later."

Eudora marveled again at the change in her children since they had moved to town. Of course they were older, but that wasn't it. They had changed; they were *different*. On the claim both Emma and Dan had been wary and quiet, shy as deer, serious as any grownup. Now they were noisy and cheerful, and for the first time in their lives they were acting their age.

Eudora thought she knew why: *Here they have a decent house and other children to play with, instead of a sod hut miles from nowhere and their only company a pair of parents who were always dead tired.* Standing in the warm, sunlit kitchen, she felt again the chill that came over her whenever she thought about that house on the claim.

She shook off the memory.

"Snip-snap," she ordered, giving her son a little push toward the door. "Go along, now."

Dan headed for the garden without further argument, and in a few minutes was hoeing between the rows of three-inch-high corn plants. He did not hurry. He stopped to watch a pair of meadowlarks sporting in the bushes at the back of the garden. He took time to inspect clouds floating overhead. He spoke, or waved, to every passerby.

George Norton came walking by, on his way home from the bank where he worked. He was stocky, with legs a little too short for his body, and he bustled along; Dan thought he always seemed in a hurry.

At the store one day Dan had heard Harvey Harrison, who owned the bank, say that Norton was the smartest young fellow who'd ever worked for him. Dan was curious to know how someone that smart would talk.

"Hello, Mr. Norton."

"Hello, Dan. Nice day for working in the garden."

Dan was surprised Norton knew his name, but he didn't think he sounded so smart: *He wouldn't talk that way if he was the one doing the weeding.* Dan held up his hoe. "Want to swap?"

Norton's full mouth twitched. "No, thanks. Besides, you look like you're having a good time."

"I'm not."

"Why not? Don't you want to be a farmer when you grow up?"

"Gosh, no." Dan was emphatic. "We used to live on a farm, but we got busted. I don't want to do that. Not *ever.*"

"What do you want to do?" *This man sure asks a lot of questions,* Dan thought. *And he always stares at you when he talks.*

"Oh, I don't know. Maybe a . . . I don't know what. But I know I don't want to be a farmer."

Dan couldn't think of anything more to say. He leaned on his hoe, watching Norton as he walked away. *Why is he so serious about everything? I bet he never smiles.*

A farmer drove by, his wagon loaded with lumber, two sacks of flour, and other cargo. It reminded Dan again of the farm in Nebraska, when his father brought things from town in the wagon. Dan's memories of that time were episodic—he had been only six when they gave up on the claim—but he remembered a lot of hard work, even for a little boy, and hardly any fun.

And he knew he didn't like hoeing corn.

The meadowlarks sang again in the lilac bush. The late afternoon sun was lower now, but still warmed the new garden. Another farm wagon came by, wheels squeaking and harness creaking as the horse clip-clopped past.

Nosireebob, Dan thought, *I'll never be a farmer. Maybe I'll work in a bank, like that George Norton.*

He's kind of interesting, even if he is so stern.

George Norton was also making mental notes. *That's a bright boy. He'll make someone a good worker in a few years.*

Then he saw Eudora Woods through the kitchen window. *And his mother, now there's a handsome woman. Must be thirty-six, thirty-seven, but she doesn't look it.*

Bet she's still a nice armful.

Smiling a little over this pleasant fantasy, George walked on toward home, a block beyond the Woods house. Like most young single people in town, he lived with his parents.

George's father had always itched to see new places. Asa Norton moved from Maine to Minnesota in '55, when it was still a territory, and set up his blacksmith shop in New Ulm. When the homesteaders started to move into Dakota Territory in the '70s, Asa packed up his wife, his son, and his anvil and went along. George was glad to get away from New Ulm, where everyone seemed to be German, Catholic, or strait-laced—and sometimes all three. He liked Dakota: things were happening, life was interesting.

George finished school when he was seventeen and went to work running errands and sweeping out for Harvey Harrison at the Falls City National Bank. Most evenings he stayed home. He read every book he could lay hands on. He kept his eyes and ears open and his mouth shut, he worked hard, and he had steady habits. Three years later, when Harrison needed a new teller, George was the obvious choice. He was young, but he seemed mature.

He liked his job; after two years in it, he knew nearly all there was to know about who had money in town, who didn't, and why. George never talked about such things, of course, but he tucked them all away in his head. You never could tell when it might be useful to know who had what and where it came from.

Occasionally, with appropriate deference, he passed along something about a customer to Mr. Harrison: this one seemed a little concerned about meeting the interest dates on his note; that one was suddenly making a lot of money, to judge from the size and frequency of his deposits. Harvey Harrison soon learned his new teller's judgments were unfailingly acute.

Mostly, though, George was kept busy at the teller's window, where customers seemed to appreciate his competence and courtesy. Some of the ladies, in fact, seemed to time their approach to the tellers' windows so as to be helped by George. George liked women, and thought about them a good deal. He was gratified to discover that they seemed attracted to him.

It wasn't his looks; he was nice-looking enough, but not handsome.

[19]

Stocky and long-waisted, already just a bit heavy around the middle, he seemed shorter than he was. He had wavy light brown hair, a prominent forehead, hazel eyes, a long straight nose.

There was a hint of sensuality in this outwardly proper young man: the mouth a bit full, the smile a bit knowing, forearms a bit heavy, fingers just a bit too plump for his hands. He took good care of those hands. They were, after all, the part of him that every customer looked at, and he made sure they were smooth and the nails closely clipped. Small details made a difference; you never knew what a customer would notice.

When George reached home, he settled down to read the new issue of the weekly *Dakota News*. He read the paper carefully, storing up what might be useful in the future.

This week there was a good deal of news in the *News*. One story reported that construction would start next month on a third railroad line through the county. An editorial hailed the new line:

THE FINAL LINK

The new railroad will be the final link in the transportation chain binding the Cascade City to the world. The outlook is indeed encouraging . . .

It's not just railroads, George thought. *This whole town is booming. Population has tripled in the last five years. Now it's over two thousand, and they say it'll triple again in the next five years. This is going to be the biggest city in Dakota, no matter where they put the capital.*

An item in the paper provided evidence of the spring rush of immigrants bound for Dakota:

ST. PAUL—Two passenger trains of Dakota settlers left last evening over the Winona and St. Peter Railroad, and two trains on the Chicago, Milwaukee and St. Paul.

A longer story reported that the new Falls City Central School on Twelfth Street would be ready by fall, bringing to three the number of modern school buildings in the city. The same account said two more brick office blocks would be built in the business district.

Another item said that the owners of the new Cataract Mill promised to grind their first grain this summer, and would add more capacity next year.

There's more farmers every year, and more railroads to bring grain to town from farther away, so everyone thinks that new mill will turn a big profit. I'm not so sure. The best wheat country is farther north, and the good farmers hereabouts are switching to corn and livestock.

Those people at the mill may overextend. A lot of these fellows get greedy.

Greed. That's what made everybody want to speculate in Dakota farmland.

They're crazy. The big companies already own all the really good land. A little fellow can't trot in that class. He'd be better off selling things to the farmers who take up that land. That's a slower track, but it gets you to the finish line quicker.

George thought about the newspaper he'd been reading.

A man could have a lot to say about what went on in town if he owned the newspaper. The time isn't quite right yet, but pretty soon there'll be room for a good, solid, respectable daily paper.

Good, solid, respectable—and profitable.

Chapter 4

Falls City, Dakota Territory, June 1884

D AN WALKED along the Northwestern tracks by the river to the siding where the immigrant train was parked. Men, women, and children had spilled out of the cars into the fresh June morning. Some women were cooking over open fires; others washed clothes at the river's edge, sewed, or spread bedding to air. Men sat or stretched out in the sun, smoking, talking, or watching their children play on the riverbank and along the siding.

Dan listened hard, trying to identify the foreign languages that mingled along the sunny riverbank.

Those are Germans, he thought. *And there's some Norwegians, or maybe Swedes, I never can tell them apart. . . . That bunch there must be Russians. They say a lot of the immigrants this year are from there. . . . You don't hear too many talking English, unless it's some Irishman, and the way they talk it might as well be a foreign language.*

Thousands of new settlers—many organized into colonies and traveling together—were arriving in Dakota. The railroads put on special trains to carry immigrant homesteaders across the eastern half of the territory. There were so many of these trains that they often were held at places like Falls City to let regularly scheduled trains through, or to wait for sidetracks to open up further west.

This train was typical. It included four passenger coaches, a string of baggage cars packed to the roof with the settlers' goods, and a caboose to house the train crew.

Dan climbed into one of the coaches. Even with half its passengers disembarked it seemed crowded and stuffy. The stench of the convenience dominated one end of the car, while a communal cookstove filled the other end with the smell of frying pork fat, turnips, cabbage, and onions. Beds consisted of boards laid between the seats; blankets and clothing hung from

[22]

the overhead racks. Pots, pans, and other everyday utensils were piled everywhere, mixed with baggage of all kinds.

Something out of the past poked at Dan's memory. *Pots and pans, no room to move around, dirt and stink and stale air.* It took him a moment to remember the smell and feel of his own family's sod house in Nebraska on hot summer days. It was not a pleasant memory, and he hurriedly clambered down again from the crowded car.

Outside, a man with a concertina had attracted a group of singers. They sounded cheerful enough singing "In the Sweet Bye and Bye," but then they got onto "Home Sweet Home," and a wistful, melancholy quiet descended on the scene.

A full-bearded man jumped up in protest. "Stop it!" he shouted. "Ay heerd enough of t'at sad song. Sing somet'ing about t'e good country where we going to live."

The musician switched to a livelier tune, and the mood lifted at once. A few of the younger men and women started to dance, and others clapped their hands in time with the music. Everyone seemed happy.

The railroads and steamship lines tell 'em what a wonderful healthy climate we have out here, Dan thought, *how the soil is rich and there's plenty of rain and the winters are so mild that anything will grow. They don't have any idea at all what they're in for.*

Dan looked at the men relaxing by the riverbank.

A lot of those fellows aren't going to make it, and even if they do it's a hard country, it never lets up, never forgives a man his mistakes.

Two girls who looked about his own age had been watching him, and when he caught them looking, they giggled and blushed.

They won't laugh so much or look so pretty after a winter on the claim, cold and hungry most of the time.

I'm glad I'm not riding that train. I've been where they're going—and I don't want to go back.

Dan's visit to the train was part of his new job. He had finished high school that spring, and planned to go to college at the University of Minnesota; it was a good school and Dan could board with another uncle who lived in Minneapolis. But first he had to earn some money.

He had always thought it would be interesting to work for a newspaper, so he started his job hunt at the *Dakota News,* one of three weeklies published in Falls City. He had the good luck to arrive an hour after another boy had been fired for dropping a tray full of type, and so he became the printer's devil, doing a little of everything in the shop, cleaning up and sweeping out, setting type and helping feed the stubborn old press on publication day.

But he was most interested in what went on in the office of the editor, a nervous, grouchy young man named David Currier. Currier was perfectly willing to let this bright youngster help out on the news end, as long as he got his regular work done first and didn't ask to be paid extra.

So each afternoon when Dan finished in the back shop he'd spend another hour or so scouting out news. Soon he was a familiar figure on the downtown streets, walking in a long, unhurried stride, questioning and listening, letting people think he had nothing to do but listen to them, pausing between encounters to write in his notebook.

He tried to explain the technique to his mother. "Huh!" she retorted. "Sounds to me like loafing and gossiping. I can't imagine getting *paid* to do that."

Whatever it was, it worked. Dan discussed business and politics with the merchants; sports and social events and politics with the men who worked for them; crops and weather and politics with farmers who came to town. He went to the stations when trains came in from the east, and to the courthouse when court was sitting. He stopped at the grain elevator, the livery stable, the two hotels.

People soon got used to talking to this tall, gawky sixteen-year-old with dark eyes and rebellious black hair that stood up in front in a cowlick. They told him a lot. He found all of it interesting, and much of it wound up as short items in the paper.

This week's collection of "shorts" was typical.

LOCAL NOTES

—The immigrant train that was stopped in this city is only the first of many, according to railroad agents, who report seven more trains on the way to this section this week. It is estimated that more than 1,000 cars loaded with immigrant goods are now moving toward Dakota.

—John Gerald, a businessman from Connecticut, has purchased a lot at 11th and Union for a hardware store. He promises a first class stock always on hand.

—Attorney Christopher Todd has gone to Minneapolis on business. He will be away from this city for a week or possibly ten days.

—S. J. Morrow, photographer of Yankton, is in this city. He has been busy taking the faces of those who call on him for pictures.

—Paul Grew claims the brag team of draft horses. He recently drew 3200 pounds of lumber from Mitchell. . . .

There was a lot of lumber being hauled. The town was still growing fast, even after three straight years of expansion. Falls City was prospering in what they were calling the "Great Dakota Boom." George Norton told Dan one day that so much money was coming into the bank they needed shovels to get it into the vault. Dan wrote up George's remark, but David

Currier killed it, saying he didn't think Mr. Harrison would care to see that in the paper.

But such editing was rare. All in all, his new job was just fine. *It sure beats any kind of farm work you can think of seven ways to Sunday.*

In fact, it's hardly like working at all.

Minneapolis, Minnesota, December 1886

Dan climbed the stairs to Clement Lounsberry's office at the *Minneapolis Tribune.* Lounsberry wasn't there; he was probably in the composing room, making up tomorrow's editorial page. Dan dropped his schoolbooks and began searching the out-of-town papers for items worth reprinting. It was a routine but essential chore; like other papers, the *Tribune* used "pickups" to fill out its columns.

After two months he was still excited about working for Lounsberry, who had sold his Bismarck paper and returned to Minneapolis and the *Tribune* as an editorial writer and special correspondent. Lounsberry had made a national reputation by being the first to report Custer's defeat in '76; he had worked all over the Northwest and in Washington too, and he knew everybody and everything. Or so it seemed to Dan, whose luck had brought him to the *Tribune* just when Lounsberry was looking for an assistant.

Lounsberry had taken to the young Dakotan at once. At eighteen, Dan stood just under six feet, with his cowlick adding another inch or so no matter how hard he brushed it down. He was sturdy, though long arms and legs made him seem skinny. He had his mother's coloring—black hair, dark complexion, darker eyes—and his father's long nose and sharp jaw. The combination made him striking, if not quite handsome.

Lounsberry decided to try him. At first Dan was nervous, but after a couple of months he not only knew what his boss wanted but had begun to develop his own news sense.

That sense served him well one bitter December night. He was riding home from work, and as the horsecar trundled along Cedar Avenue two fire engines rushed past at a gallop, alarm bells ringing, and turned off the avenue two blocks further on. Through the frost that covered the car windows Dan could see a flickering light. He jumped off and ran toward the fire.

One look told him it was bad. On a block where three- and four-story wooden houses were packed in side by side, two buildings were already burning out of control, flames leaping from their windows. Dan knew the neighborhood; it was filled with rooming houses for day laborers and recent immigrants. Firemen were trying to get their hoses going, but in the below-zero cold the water froze as soon as it came out of the hose.

There's going to be a lot of people burned up, Dan thought. He reached for his watch. *Ten-thirty. Less than an hour to press start. Got to tell the paper.*

He ran back toward Cedar Avenue. There weren't many telephones in Minneapolis yet, but the *Tribune* newsroom had one, and if there was one somewhere around here.... Dan turned onto the avenue and saw what he was looking for: halfway down the block a wire ran from a telephone pole to a house. He rang the doorbell, pounding on the door for good measure.

After what seemed to Dan like an hour but was in fact perhaps a minute and a half, a man in a nightshirt opened the door. He was not happy.

"What do you mean, waking people in the middle of . . . My God!" He threw the door wide open. "What's going on down there?"

"Fire. Bad one. I need your telephone. Please!"

Dan looked past the stunned householder and saw a telephone on the wall of the front hall. He pushed in without waiting for permission, snatched up the earpiece, and spun the crank to signal the operator.

At the *Tribune,* the city editor answered. Dan told him who he was, reported the fire, and expressed his opinion that a lot of people would end up dead. The editor said he'd send a reporter right away.

"Thanks for calling, son." He was ready to dismiss Dan. "It's a big help."

"Hold on a minute," Dan said. He turned to the householder, now awake and aware that he was somehow at the center of major events. Dan tried to sound authoritative. "Sir, it's really very important that we maintain this connection. It would be a public service if you could stay on this line and keep it open for . . . for a while."

The man was impressed. "Oh, why, yes, certainly, that would be all right." He nodded firmly. "Glad to help."

"Thank you." Dan spoke urgently to the editor. "Look, it won't help to send a dozen reporters, there isn't time. I've got this telephone and I'll keep it open. I'll go out and find out what's happening, and I'll pass it to you. That way we'll get a story into the home edition. There's a lot of people dead over there. If you wait 'til someone gets here from the office, you'll never make it."

There was a long pause at the other end. Then the editor laughed.

"You know, you're right, Woods. I'll put someone on here to hold the line and you give him whatever you get. Don't worry about writing it up, we'll take care of that." Another pause. "And step lively. You're not working for the editorial page now."

Before he finished, Dan made five visits to the fire, which by midnight had burned out the entire block. Eleven bodies had already been found. Dan had provided enough material to produce a story that filled a full column on the front page.

It was not until he got home and took off his galoshes that he noticed his toes were frozen. It was even later when he realized he had ordered the city editor around as if he were a copyboy.

Fortunately the city editor had a sense of humor, and entertained the whole newsroom by telling how the kid from Dakota had taught him to handle the big story. (He also arranged for an extra five-dollar gold piece in Dan's next pay envelope.) People who had never before spoken to Dan now seemed to regard him as one of them.

But fame was fleeting, and three months later he was still sorting through the out-of-town papers. Today he was watching for one in particular: it was the day the *Dakota News* came in. When Dan found the paper he scanned the local news page, then read the lead story.

GRISLY DRAMA ON RANGES— MORE CARCASSES REVEALED

Melting Snows Disclose Horrid Sight of Cattle Killed by Snow & Cold

Late reports from correspondents in the north and west provide details of the terrible loss of livestock on the cattle ranges of Dakota and Montana Territories.

It is now established by reliable report that more than two-thirds of the animals in most herds were lost. In some, nine of every ten perished. The grim tally mounts each day as melting snowdrifts reveal terrible secrets in every coulee and slough.

Authorities ascribe the disaster to a combination of events. Northern ranges were overstocked with thin animals just off the trail last fall. Grazing was poor because of summer drought. Snow fell early and continued heavy through the winter. An ice crust prevented animals from feeding. Finally there was a long period of very low temperature . . .

Dan thought back to the last really bad winter, the one six years ago when the first snow fell on Falls City in October and never seemed to stop coming. Then the railroads had been completely blocked for months on end, clear into May; almost everybody ran out of fuel, and food was short everywhere.

But there had been no loss of livestock then to match this year's disaster, already being called "The Big Die-Up." There were predictions it would wipe out a lot of homesteaders and destroy the cattle industry—at least the many new outfits that had jumped into the business with lots of Eastern or foreign money but no experience.

Ma has it right, Dan thought, *when she says you should never argue with nature, because you always lose.*

Those Easterners and Englishmen didn't know what they were getting into, or what to do about it, and their cattle died for their stupidity.

Dan remembered the immigrant train that he had visited two years earlier, the men loafing in the sun, the pretty young girls giggling at him.

Even if they made it this far, they'll have lost everything now. They just had no idea what they were getting into, they wouldn't have known what to do to save their animals.

Then Dan thought of his own father.

But you don't have to be dumb. Bad luck'll do it, too. You can know what you're doing and still get beat down by nature.

The thought took him back to the grim winters on their Nebraska claim, when the wind never stopped blowing and the cold was a permanent presence in the sod house. Dan had been a very small boy then, but he remembered enough to be sure he'd never want to live that kind of life again.

"Hello, young man." Lounsberry strode into the room, trailing a handful of galley proofs. He noticed what Dan was reading. "What's the big story from home this week?"

"Well, Colonel, I guess it's this one." He indicated the article on livestock deaths. Then, pointing to a short item on the same page, he added: "But this is the one they'll be talking about."

HARRISON-NORTON.

Miss Mary Harrison, daughter of Mr. and Mrs. Harvey Harrison, was married Saturday at First Methodist church to Mr. George Norton, son of Mr. and Mrs. Asa Norton. A reception followed at the home of the bride's parents.

The bridegroom is Cashier of the Falls City National Bank. The bride's father is president of the bank.

After the reception, the couple took the cars for Chicago. When they return from their wedding trip, they will be at home at 14th Street and Union Avenue.

Lounsberry laughed. "You'll make a newspaperman yet, my boy. Of course you'd really have a story if he got the bank as well as the girl."

"That wouldn't surprise me," Dan said. "George Norton's got the best head for business of anyone in town, even if he isn't thirty yet. I think he aims to be the richest man in Dakota, and pretty soon, too."

Dan had heard that Norton saved every nickel he earned, and put his money into safe—and profitable—investments.

"They're going to live on a big block out in a new part of town. It has just the one little house on it," Dan mused. "I bet Norton bought the whole block, so he can build a mansion on it some day, or sell it at a nice profit."

"Sounds like you admire him."

Dan paused just a second before answering. "I do."

"But?"

"But . . . well, he's all wrapped up in business and so on. He's dead serious, always looks so stern. He almost never smiles."

"But you still admire him as a businessman."

"Yes. But I could never work for a fellow like that. I don't think he ever has any *fun*."

"Never say 'never,' young man. You may wind up as a teller in his bank. And anyway, now that he's married, he'll have more fun." Lounsberry grinned. "When are you going to get yourself a girl? Don't they have any at the university?"

Dan tugged at his cowlick in embarrassment. "What with studying and working both I haven't had much time for girls, here or at home. I'll think about that later."

"You can't plan those things. It'll be over and done before you know it."

Not me, Dan thought, *not by a long shot, nosireebob. And it sure wouldn't be someone like Mary Harrison. She's too fat.*

George Norton must be really interested in that bank.

An hour later, Dan had worked his way through the exchange papers. Lounsberry leafed through the stories his assistant had picked out.

"All right, some of these will do. . . . I can use this one tomorrow, it will go with what's on the page," Lounsberry said. "And we'll take that story about the dead cattle from your paper."

"Don't people already know about that?"

"People around here are so busy making money they forget where they came from. We'd best remind 'em. What happened out there is going to change what happens in a lot of places, including here."

At supper that night Dan repeated Lounsberry's prediction to his uncle. Albert Woods worked at the city's grain exchange, already one of the world's largest wheat markets.

"Uncle Bert, what do you think about all the cattle dying? Isn't that going to make it go hard for farmers—and for our store, too?"

"Oh, it won't hurt Henry and Ben. Long as those farmers can keep horses to work a crop, they'll grow wheat." Albert Woods's tone was patronizing. "I suppose some of 'em will be pinched because they have to borrow to replace their livestock. But I never did hear of a farmer who wasn't in debt, good times or bad. There's nothing new about that."

Dan's Aunt Maude looked up from her mending.

"Bert, you sound like some city fellow," she said. "Farmers don't like to owe money any more than anyone else. They just don't have a choice. Sometimes I think you forget where you were raised."

Dan said nothing, but he agreed with her. Farmers didn't want to be debtors, but they had to borrow. *It happened to Pa, and there are plenty more now in the same fix. They have to sell their grain for whatever the elevator will pay, and they get stuck going the other way, too: whatever they buy, they have to pay what the storekeeper asks.*

It's not fair. No wonder farmers get sore, even in good times, Dan thought. *And now that times aren't so good, I bet there'll be some real hollering out there.*

Chapter 5

WHEN Lounsberry came into the office, Dan handed him a story from an Omaha paper. "There's been two or three like this in the last couple of weeks."

ALLIANCE ON RAIL RATES

"Railroad discrimination and extortion constitute the question of the day. They have entered into the discussion of every farmers' meeting of this State for three years past."

Those were the opening words of a resolution passed yesterday at the meeting of the Nebraska Farmers' Alliance. The resolution continued:

"The railroad system is a system of spoliation and robbery. Its enormous bonded debt at fictitious values is absorbing the substance of the people in the interest of the millionaires.

"The railroads must not be allowed to issue bonds and stock amounting to many times the cost of construction and equipment, and then impose charges to cover interest and dividends on this enormous amount of bonds and stocks to enrich the eastern railroad manipulators."

The resolution calls for new laws to regulate rates, services, and profits of railroads.

"I'm not surprised." Lounsberry put down the clipping. "Part of it's the drought. Nebraska and Kansas about blew away last summer, so it's no wonder they're mad. But railroad rates have been a sore subject for a long time."

"When I was home this summer, that was all the farmers wanted to talk about," Dan said. "We had some drought, too, but it seemed to me it was mostly Alliance people stirring things up."

"They've been stirring, all right. The only thing that surprises me about this story is they didn't complain about the elevators, too. The Alliance claims the railroads connive with the elevators and the traders to keep grain prices down."

"I can't figure the right of it," Dan said. "I hear from farmers at home and then I listen to Uncle Bert—you know he works at the grain exchange—and they don't see anything the same."

The older man laughed. "You'll get used to that if you stay in this business. Hardly anyone ever admits the other fellow might be anywhere near right."

"But who *is* right?"

"Oh, both of 'em partway, I guess." Lounsberry gathered a handful of copy and proofs and headed for the door. "I can't sit around and talk. But I'm going over to see Jim Hill on Thursday, and if you like you can come along. He'll tell you what it's all about."

James J. Hill was already a legend throughout the Northwest, admired and feared in equal measure. He had come to St. Paul thirty years earlier without a dollar; now, at forty-nine, he had almost finished building a railroad empire stretching from the Great Lakes to the Pacific.

Hill's office was plain and unassuming; the man himself was overwhelming. He was not tall, but he was powerfully built, with a heavy neck and bull chest, thick arms and big hands. His massive head was topped with a tangle of long gray hair; his one good eye—the other had been blinded in an accident—was dark and intense, staring out over a bristling beard.

Dan was awestruck, but Lounsberry was completely at ease; he and Hill had been friends back in Lounsberry's early Dakota days, before Hill went into railroading. The editor got down to business at once, quizzing the railroad man about his plans.

"Your men laid track this year at a great rate," Lounsberry said. "More than six hundred miles west from Minot, wasn't it?"

"Six hundred and forty-three miles, Minot to Helena. A long, hard summer's work." Hill did not add, as he could have, that it was also a record-breaking summer's work. "A great many people call it my folly."

"Not folly," Lounsberry said. "But you will have to get some people to move into that country before your new lines will pay out."

"It does not require a genius to see that," Hill rasped. "We have no government land grants in Dakota or Montana, as our competitors do. So we must make our money building and operating a railroad, not by land speculation. We are going to settle the country. But meanwhile we'll have track finished to Butte next year, and I mean to have the carriage of the copper from there."

There was cold certainty in Hill's voice. "Soon there will be coal to be hauled from Montana, too, and we will haul it. And when we cross the

[32]

mountains, there will be timber. The forest is almost gone from Minnesota and Wisconsin, and demand for lumber keeps growing."

The railroad man banged a large fist on his desk. "There are not many farmers out there now, but we will bring them in, and help them, and teach them. They will grow wheat, and we will carry it."

Lounsberry nodded. "And if what I hear is right, you'll be able to carry that wheat right through to the Great Lakes, and on to the East."

"Precisely." Hill's good eye blazed. "We will carry wheat from the West to our own elevators and docks at Superior. We will have our own ships, we will be able to offer low rates all the way to the mills at Buffalo. That will be good for the farmer—and good for us."

"Jim, that's not the way the farmers see it. They don't think you're any different from the others. They blame *all* the railroads for their troubles." Lounsberry pulled out the paper Dan had given him the day before and showed it to Hill.

Hill scanned the story of the Nebraska farmers' rate protest. "That's nonsense."

"It *is* true that rates are higher west of Chicago than in the East."

Hill shook his head. "Yes, but it costs more to serve the West—coal costs more, and it's almost all one-way traffic, so westbound we haul a lot of empty cars."

Lounsberry conceded the point. "That may be true. But still, it's plain as an old maid's face that the railroads—maybe not yours, but the rest—charge as much as they can get away with."

Dan, listening to the two older men, spoke without really intending to. "Where there's competition, rates ought to go down. But that doesn't seem to happen. We've got four lines serving Falls City, but the rates are high as ever."

"They'll go down when we finish our new line through there next summer," Hill snapped. "I promise you that. We always set rates as low as we can, not as high as we could."

Lounsberry intervened. "You do, but there's plenty who don't, and there's other ways they squeeze the farmers, too. Look at the country elevators. The railroads want to keep out competition there, and they do, because they generally own the only elevator in town."

"That's just good business." Hill spoke abruptly, but his tone was matter-of-fact.

"I don't know about that, Jim," Lounsberry replied. "But I do know everybody's making money—except the fellow who grows the grain."

Hill yielded an inch, no more. "Maybe a few railroads and elevators take advantage of some farmers. That's stupid of them, it won't pay in the long run. But even if they didn't, what the farmer gets for his grain and livestock is always going to be decided by someone else. That's what

[33]

railroads and elevators and exchanges are for, and they do the job pretty well."

"Maybe so, Mr. Hill." Again Dan forgot to defer to the rail magnate. "But if that's true, farmers will find some other way to take care of themselves. Maybe they should get more into politics."

"They will." Lounsberry laughed as he waved the paper with the Nebraska protest story. "They already are."

"If they do, they'll lose," Hill growled.

Later, riding the horsecar home through the early darkness of the November afternoon, Dan mused over the day's conversation. He'd heard enough last summer, at the family store and around Falls City, to know that Lounsberry was right: the farmers were starting to go into politics in a big way.

Then he recalled Hill's last remark—and the menace in his tone as he predicted the farmers' defeat.

It's coming, all right, and there's going to be hell to pay.

Minneapolis, January 1888

The papers were full of it; more bits and pieces of the story trickled in each day. But even after a week, Dan still knew nothing about what had happened to Falls City in the great blizzard. The *Tribune* telegraphers tried every day to contact the operators there, but they got no answer; the wires were all down. And of course Dan had no mail from home—the railroads were shut down by deep, wind-hardened snowdrifts all across southern Minnesota and Dakota. So Dan worried about his family as he read accounts of the storm that had savaged the countryside all the way from the Canadian border to Kansas.

The second week of January had been a season out of season throughout the northern plains. A warm south wind blew for three days, melting much of the snow cover. Then the wind died, and by the morning of January 12, the air was moist and warm, with patches of fog in low-lying places.

The warmth turned out to be the worst of it, because it fooled people into leaving home that morning without their usual heavy winter clothing. It felt, as so many said later, more like April than January.

Lincoln County, Dakota Territory, January 1888

Grace Harper arrived early at the sod schoolhouse that morning. She was young—just eighteen—and as a brand-new teacher she felt better if she got a little head start on her students. It wasn't all that hard for her to get there early; the schoolhouse stood at a corner of her father's land, less than a mile from their house.

The morning was so balmy that she didn't bother to make a fire in the schoolhouse stove. As children drifted in, wearing light jackets, many without hats or mittens, they chattered cheerfully in the unaccustomed warmth of the morning. But they settled down soon enough, and the seventeen pupils worked well through the sunny morning.

At noon, boys and girls alike played outside without coats. Some of the bigger boys, including Grace's fifteen-year-old brother Charlie, went a little way off on the prairie to play baseball, shouting their pleasure at this unexpected taste of spring.

Grace, eating her lunch outside the schoolhouse, noticed an odd thing off to the northwest, toward Falls City: under an otherwise clear blue sky, something that looked like a gray cloud was moving along at ground level. She thought it might be a fog bank, but all at once it seemed to grow in size and speed, becoming a whirling gray blur that filled the sky as it rushed toward the schoolhouse, preceded by the crackling of static electricity.

Grace suddenly realized it was a blizzard, rolling toward them with the speed and sound of an express train. Some of the smaller children, frightened, ran to her. She pushed them inside, grabbed the school bell, and rang it as hard as she could to call the others. The baseball players, farther off, looked at the sky and came running; they barely got inside ahead of the storm.

Grace and the older children managed to close and latch the windows before the wind struck the building, shaking the solid earthen walls and nearly lifting the roof off despite its double layer of heavy sod. The door blew open, filling the room with blowing snow; Charlie Harper held it shut while another boy jammed a chair against it.

The roof creaked as a particularly hard gust hit. Snow filtered in around window frames and under the door. Grace noticed the smaller children were rigid with fear, sitting stock-still, eyes wide, watching her. She must distract them.

"We will clean our desks this afternoon," she announced. No one moved. Then she realized they could not hear her over the noise of the storm. She stepped closer and cupped her hands to her mouth.

"WE WILL CLEAN OUR DESKS NOW!" This time they did hear. Books and papers were pulled out to be sorted and straightened. Once or twice drafts from particularly strong gusts of wind sent papers flying across the room. Grace tried to make a game out of sending children to retrieve them.

By the time she had the stove going well, the desk cleaning was finished, and Grace had to think of something else. This time she organized them into two lines and marched them around the room, singing. It seemed to be getting much colder; she put them through exercises to warm them up. Then she had them put on whatever outer clothing they had.

Grace tried to look and sound cheerful, but she was scared. It was going to be a long night, and before morning the room would be terribly cold. There wasn't much fuel in the schoolhouse, and nothing to eat except the scanty leftovers from lunch. But the children couldn't leave in this storm, and she was sure no parents would dare come to take them home, either. They were there to stay.

The three oldest boys came to her with an idea. They would tie themselves together, go outside, and get enough coal from the shed to keep the stove going all night. Grace was nervous about letting them go—one was her brother—but she knew they had to have more fuel. The boys tied themselves together with scarves and belts and the long rope from the water bucket. They hitched the end of the rope to the doorknob, then fought their way outside and along the outer wall of the schoolhouse to the shed at the corner.

They had to give up after three trips because their faces and hands had begun to freeze. But the coal bin by the stove was chockablock full, and Grace rubbed snow on the dead-white spots on their cheeks and fingers until they regained their circulation.

She scraped the frost off one windowpane to look at the thermometer outside. It registered near zero. It had fallen fifty degrees already, and she knew it would go much further. The inkwells were freezing, and the room was brutally cold despite the coal fire. She made them move the benches close to the stove, and kept the smallest children closest to the heat. It didn't seem to help much.

As darkness closed in, Grace lit the single kerosene lamp. It gave so little light that it almost made the room seem darker and colder. Soon some of the little ones were complaining of hunger, but Grace wanted to hold off as long as possible before handing out the little food there was.

Suddenly, just as full darkness closed in on the schoolhouse, there was pounding at the door. They released the brace and opened it to admit an apparition: a tall, husky man, wool cap pulled down over his ears, coat collar turned up, face hardly visible behind the ice and snow that caked his eyebrows and beard. He was carrying two loaded sacks. As he shook off the snow, Grace realized it was her father.

Amos Harper spoke quietly to his daughter. "This storm is the worst I ever saw. You'll have to keep them here all night. . . . Those little ones wouldn't last a minute outside. We thought you'd better have something to eat. Mother put up some meat and cornbread."

"Pa, you shouldn't have come out," Grace said. "It's just not safe."

"It wasn't bad." Amos wiped melted snow from his face and neck. He pulled off his mittens and kneaded his big hands, stamping his feet hard to restore circulation. "I came on the mule, and we stayed right up alongside the fence. Lucky thing it runs all the way from the house to here. I would never have found you otherwise. . . . You can't see a thing going into that wind."

"Maybe you should stay here instead of trying to go back."

"No, it'll be easy as pie going home, the wind'll be behind us this time. Anyhow I'd trust that little mule to get me home blindfolded." After warming himself at the stove for a few minutes, he bundled up again and left.

Grace lined up the children and shared out the food, chunks of cornbread and boiled beef. They were more cheerful after eating, and eventually most huddled around the stove and fell asleep. Grace, cold and worried, stayed awake.

At first the storm seemed actually to gain strength, but after midnight the wind began to drop. At half past four she scraped a windowpane clear and could see a few stars. The next time she checked, a little after six, the sky was full of stars. The storm was over. The thermometer read 34 below zero.

Minneapolis, January 1888

"We finally got some news from Dakota," Lounsberry said as Dan came into the office two days later. "Your paper came, too, and it's got all kinds of stories."

"They must have got the trains running," Dan said. "I got a letter today, too. Ma wrote they're all safe, but she thinks it was very bad out in the country."

Dan picked up the *Dakota News*. The headlines echoed his mother's guess:

TERRIBLE BLIZZARD

**NEARLY 100 DEAD
ALREADY KNOWN**

**MANY OTHERS LOST & FEARED
PERISHED IN HUGE STORM**

Little Ones Lost Returning from
School; Brave Teachers
Save Many Others

Dan scanned the long story that followed. It was full of detail:

> . . . Just as children were preparing to start home from the rural schools, the blizzard struck in blinding fury. In Turner County alone 28 children were frozen to death, while in Bon Homme County 19 young ones lost their lives.
>
> In many schools teachers saved the lives of their pupils by keeping them overnight. One such in this locality was Miss Grace Harper, 18 years old, teacher in the Foley Township school 5 miles southeast of this city, who cared for her students throughout the icy night.

Once again Dan felt the chill of winter in the sod house on the unforgiving Nebraska plain. He thought of his sister, a teacher these past three years in the Falls City schools. *I'm glad Em's in town and not in one of those soddy schools way out in the country.*

One of the saddest cases was that of Mrs. M. R. Brown and her 12-year-old son in Wayne Township. Her husband had gone out to repair the windlass on their well. When he did not return, she went to search for him. When neither father nor mother returned, the son went out to get them. The father stayed alive by digging into a haystack. After the storm he found first his wife and then his son, both frozen to death.

That could have been Pa and Ma—and me, Dan thought, *if we were still out there on the claim. Maybe it's a good thing he got busted.*

The thought produced a wave of guilt; he shouldn't ever think that way. It made him feel disloyal to his father.

But it's true, dammit. If we'd still been out there we might all be dead now, and for sure we'd be frozen and hungry.

He was about to put down the paper when he noticed a small item near the bottom of the local page:

BANK PRESIDENT.

George Norton, cashier of the Falls City National Bank, has been named president of the institution.

Harvey Harrison, president of the bank since its foundation, announced the change. He will devote his attention to his many other business and civic interests in this city and county.

Dan pointed out the story to Lounsberry and reminded him of their talk almost a year earlier. Lounsberry chuckled. "Well, well. I was just talking that day, but you knew it was no josh, didn't you? Will he do a good job?"

"I think so. He's pretty shrewd in business."

"And at picking a wife. Well, more power to him. But I think the editor should have reported the family connection."

"Everybody in town already knows that."

"Sometimes the editor has to print something everybody already knows, just to show he's his own man. One of those times is when he's writing about the biggest banker in town. Try to remember that when you have your own paper."

Dan looked at Lounsberry. *By God, he thinks I might make a newspaperman.* He felt himself blushing. *Makes you feel like you've got the world by the tail and a downhill pull.*

Chapter 6 '

Falls City, South Dakota, 1889

T HE NOISE began at sunrise with a thirteen-gun salute. Actually it was thirteen salutes from one gun, since that was all they had, but by any calculation it was an emphatic beginning for the biggest Independence Day observance in the twenty-year history of Falls City.

By the time the Grand Parade started a few hours later, every man, woman, and child in the whole county seemed to be somewhere along the ten-block route of the parade through downtown. American flags flew from every building, red-white-and-blue bunting fluttered in the morning breeze, firecrackers popped, children shouted, babies cried. The sky made a bright blue arch over Lincoln Avenue. Later it would be hot, but at midmorning the air was still fresh.

Dan stood on the flat roof of the newspaper office and looked down the avenue. The two-story *Dakota News* building was at the corner where the parade would turn toward the city park by the river, so his vantage point gave him a view of the marchers both coming and going. As he waited, he heard the first notes from the Cascade City Silver Cornet band, turning from the assembly area onto Lincoln Avenue half a mile away.

Just about everybody in the city had a part in the day's program, which this year saluted not only the nation's birth but also the long-delayed coming of statehood, finally approved by Congress in February after years of partisan political maneuvering. So it was a good story, whose every detail—and most of all, every name—must be in the next issue of the *News.*

The cornets blared "Marching Through Georgia" as the band swung around the corner. Behind it marched the mayor, the members of the county board, and an assortment of other politicos. The volunteer fire company followed, pulling its new hose cart.

Great applause greeted the next unit, a horse-drawn float carrying no fewer than forty little girls and one handsome young woman, all costumed and arranged to depict the Goddess of Liberty attended by the states and territories of the Union. Dan didn't recognize the striking blonde who was cast as Miss Liberty, though she looked vaguely familiar. She smiled up at him as the wagon went by.

Got to get her name for the story.

Now another brass band came by, setting the cadence for the local encampment of the Grand Army of the Republic. The commander was mounted, his horse dancing nervously at the corner where spectators stood thickest. Nearly a hundred G.A.R. members, many in their faded blue service uniforms, marched in two files; Dan spotted his father, limping a little from the wound he had suffered twenty-six years ago that week.

The parade ended with a procession of carriages, wagons, buggies, buckboards, and other horse-drawn conveyances of every kind. Some, sponsored by businesses or civic organizations, carried signs, bunting, and an occasional tableau; many more belonged to individuals showing off a team or a rig—or just joining for the sport of it.

From the first band to the final stragglers, the parade lasted nearly an hour. Dan watched the last wagon turn the corner, then closed his notebook and climbed down.

"You're the man on the roof." Waiting in line for a plate of food in the Methodist Ladies' tent, Dan turned around and found himself looking into a pair of amused female eyes.

"Yes, ma'am." Dan blushed and ran his hand through his hair, but managed a reply. "And you're the Goddess of Liberty."

Up close she was even prettier than she'd seemed from the roof. She was tall, with dark blonde hair the color of ripe wheat, a wide mouth, and a straight nose with a little dent at the tip that gave it an uptilted look. But what really got his attention were the eyes, wide and very light blue and appraising.

Dan tugged at a dim memory. Had she been in high school when he was? She must have been two or three classes behind him; she couldn't be more than nineteen now. Then he recognized the man standing in line behind her. He was husky and middle-aged, his sunburnt face and neck contrasting with a pale forehead: a farmer. Dan had last seen him marching beside his father in the parade.

"Hello, Mr. Harper." Dan looked back at the girl. "And you must be Grace, Grace Harper. We were in high school together. I'm Dan Woods."

"Oh, I know who you are." *He's not quite handsome,* she thought, *but he's nice-looking. I like the way his hair stands up in front.* She smiled, widening her eyes a little. "But I didn't think big boys in school paid any attention to the little girls, Mr. Woods."

"Only to a few. Besides, now I'm not so big and you're not so little, Miss Harper." He was surprised to find himself enjoying this exchange.

[40]

They moved past the serving table, each taking a plate loaded with beans, slaw, a slice of ham, and a chunk of bread. Dan tried to think of something to say. He remembered a newspaper item he'd read eighteen months ago.

"Don't you teach school now?"

"I started last year, out in the country."

That was it, all right: she was the teacher in that newspaper story about the great blizzard. "That was a fine thing you did in the big storm."

"Oh, Mr. Woods, we country girls are used to weather. Anyway, I just sat there. Father brought us hot food through the worst part of the storm. He was the one who really did something." She laid her hand on Amos Harper's arm, and Dan surprised himself again: he wished the arm were his.

Stumbling for conversation, he switched to Amos Harper. "You're going to be one of the speakers this afternoon."

Amos Harper's voice came rumbling up. "Yah, they probably want a little fun after the Republicans and Democrats talk, so they asked a farmer."

Dan thought the invitation probably had more to do with the large and growing number of farmers who were joining the Farmers' Alliance, of which Harper was an official. But before he could say anything, Grace spoke again.

"Pa, you know Mr. Woods works for the newspaper, so he must be very interested in your speech today. I'm sure he wants to talk with you." She smiled and ducked her head a little, raising her eyebrows as she looked up at Dan. "It was nice to meet you, Mr. Woods."

Then she was gone, across the tent and into a gaggle of other girls. Amos Harper watched with amusement: *She must be taken with him.* He had seen his daughter flirt before, but he'd never seen her go at it so hard—and with such effect. Henry Woods's son looked as if he'd been hit on the head with a hoe handle.

A couple of hours later, Dan found a patch of shade by the corner of the speakers' stand and settled down. He'd stood in the sun listening to the windy self-congratulation of Republican and Democratic orators each taking full credit for statehood, and he decided to take the Alliance rhetoric sitting down.

The mayor did not think much of the Alliance, and his introduction of Amos Harper was unenthusiastic; but for the first time in the long hot afternoon the farmers in the crowd applauded, and there was a small stir of anticipation as Harper stood up.

The other speakers had been dressed up in stiff black suits and neckties, but Amos Harper wore bib overalls and a plain shirt open at the neck, as if to emphasize how he earned his living. He looked every inch the farmer—and a good deal more comfortable than the others on the sun-baked platform.

"Thank you, Mayor Johnson," he began. "And thank you, too, for reminding us of the constitutional convention that begins today. We had best watch that convention." He paused, then waggled a big finger. "We know the railroads will."

A murmur floated from the audience.

"And the banks, and the loan sharks, and the elevator companies. They'll all be there, every day and every night, in the hotel rooms and the hallways.

"That is why we need to join together to return control of the people's government to the people. This is a fitting day to think about that. This is the time to look out for the people's interests in South Dakota, because right now we are building the government of our new state, starting from scratch.

"We don't have to fight any longer against dictation by appointed federal officeholders. But now we have a harder fight—against the dictation of the interests, and of all the interests, the railroads are the worst."

He looked around at the crowd. "Everybody here knows what railroads do." There was a rumble of agreement from the farmers in the crowd. "They tell us what rates we must pay—and they set rates sky-high. When we want to ship grain, they tell us where we must deliver it. And they own the elevators, so they not only decide how much we will pay them for shipping but also how much they will pay us for the grain itself."

There were scattered calls of "That's right!" and "You tell 'em!" Harper's voice rose.

"The old parties lied to us. They told us that we should go to work and raise a big crop, and we plowed and we planted, and the sun shone, and the rain fell, and we got a big crop, and what did it bring us? Ten-cent corn."

There was a throaty stir of agreement.

"And ten-cent oats." Harper was building up; his listeners responded again.

"And ten-*per*-cent interest!"

He waited while applause splashed around the platform. "Now they tell us we're overproducing." This time there was a roar from the farmers in the audience. When it quieted, Harper shifted to an almost conversational tone.

"I'll tell you what the real problem is, and it's not too much wheat. It's too much money, in too few pockets—too many millionaires and too many poor folks."

Dan, scribbling notes, was startled when Grace Harper slipped down beside him in the little angle of shade by the platform.

[42]

"Hello there," she said quietly. "You've got a good spot. Can I sit here?"

He nodded and mumbled, trying to pay attention to Grace and listen to her father at the same time. It didn't work very well, and he stopped taking notes.

"Which speaker do you like the best?" she asked him.

"Well . . ." Once again he was having trouble thinking of something to say. He was overwhelmingly aware of her being beside him. "You know as a . . . a journalist, I'm supposed to keep out of politics, not take sides."

Grace half-stifled a laugh. "Oh, come on, nobody believes that. You just don't want to admit your politics."

"Well, I guess . . . I always figured I was a Republican, come down to it, like my Pa. Still, I agree with your father that the farmer gets the short end of things. But I don't . . . I mean, how're you going to change that just by walking away from a political party?"

Amos Harper finished his speech. He was rewarded with heavy applause from the farmers in his audience—and heavy silence from the rest.

"If you'd listen more to my father you'd know the answer to that question, Mr. Woods." Grace stood up, Dan scrambling to get up with her, as Amos Harper came down off the platform and his daughter spoke to him. "You were just fine, Pa."

Harper smiled. Dan noticed his eyes were the same light blue as his daughter's. "Thank you, child. And what did you think, Dan?"

Grace gave Dan no time to reply. "Oh, Mr. Woods doesn't have an opinion, Pa. He says his calling forbids it."

Dan flushed in frustration. He could hardly get a word in edgewise with this girl, and when he did, it seemed to be the wrong one.

Just then George Norton came up, his full face ruddy and his shirt clinging damply to his neck and chest in the afternoon heat. Dan started to introduce him to Harper, but they greeted each other before he could finish.

"A very interesting talk, Mr. Harper," said George, fanning himself with his straw hat. "You make a persuasive case."

"But you don't agree with it," Harper replied good-naturedly.

"Well, actually, no, I don't," George said. "I'm a Republican, first, last, and always. But I know a good speech when I hear one."

"At least you have an opinion." It was Grace. "Unlike some people."

George looked at Grace, measuring her. He touched his black bow tie and ran a hand over his hair. "I don't think I've had the pleasure," he said.

"This is my daughter, Grace," Harper said. "Grace, this is Mr. Norton, George Norton. He runs the bank. He's a Republican, but he's all right to do business with."

George laughed. "And your father's an Alliance man, Miss Harper, but he's a good farmer and a good customer." He looked at Grace. "And the father of a most attractive daughter."

Dan felt completely shut out of the conversation; he might as well have been clear across town as far as the other three were concerned. He decided that flight was the only course.

"Well, I have to get back to my office to write up this story," he said. "Will you excuse me, Miss Harper?"

"Of course, Mr. Woods." Grace hardly seemed to notice him. She turned to George Norton. "Which bank did you say you worked at, Mr. Norton?"

Dan was in the back shop one morning in August, helping make up the local page, when David Currier came into the room with George Norton.

"This will only take a minute, I know you're all busy," Currier said. "Some of you already know George Norton. All of you are going to know him better, because he is now the owner of this paper."

Dan and the print-shop crew exchanged startled looks. There'd been no hint that Currier was thinking of selling the paper. Dan glanced at Florence Berdahl, the bookkeeper, who had also come into the shop; she shrugged and shook her head to signal that she, too, had known nothing.

"I imagine you're all surprised," Currier continued. "Well, I was too when Mr. Norton first spoke to me about buying the *News.* I had no idea of selling. But after we talked it over, and I thought about it, I decided to accept his offer."

Currier smiled uneasily. "He asked me to stay on as editor, and I have agreed. He'll take over all the business side. We hope you'll all stay on too. Mr. Norton?"

The new publisher's suit coat was buttoned despite the midsummer heat, and his necktie was knotted snugly under a high, starched collar. He fixed each of his new employees in turn with a steady stare. When he spoke, his words were measured and careful.

"Well. David is right. I believe we will keep things pretty much as they are, at least for now, and that goes for the staff, too. This is a good paper already; that's why I bought it. I hope we can make it better as we go along. This city should support a daily paper soon, and I want the *Dakota News* to be that paper."

Norton stopped and looked around the room again.

"Now, some people will want to know about our politics," he continued. "I didn't buy the paper to get into politics. Of course the *News* will support every Republican candidate. But the best way for a newspaper to have influence is to be trusted by its readers, so we will keep our news pages completely fair and open to everyone. We will express our political opinions only on the editorial page."

Dan listened intently. Norton was proposing something very unusual:

[44]

almost every newspaper shaped its contents—and usually its staff as well—to suit the political prejudices of its proprietor.

The new owner of the *Dakota News* lifted a hand as a signal that he was finished. "I won't keep you any longer today, I just wanted to meet you all."

He moved around the room, picking his way carefully and just a little awkwardly through the unfamiliar, grimy spaces of the print shop, shaking hands with each worker. When he reached Dan, Norton stopped for a moment.

"David says you're a big help this summer. You must be getting a lot out of college."

"Well, I've probably learned more at the *Minneapolis Tribune*," Dan replied. "I've been working there part time ever since I started at the university."

"Oh." Norton considered this information. "Who do you work for there?"

"I did some reporting for the city desk last semester. But mostly I work for a man named Clement Lounsberry. He runs the editorial page. He's the man who—"

"I know Colonel Lounsberry." Another pause. "Are you going back to school this fall?"

"I have one more year."

"Oh." Norton seemed about to ask him something more, but did not. He looked around, then turned and left the shop. Dan wondered what the unasked question was.

He found out a month later. A few days before Dan was to leave for Minneapolis, Norton came into the shop as he was finishing work and proposed that they walk home together.

Before they had gone a hundred yards, Norton spoke up.

"I wanted to talk with you privately, Dan, away from the office."

Once again Dan felt an unasked question hanging between them, but this time Norton didn't make him wait to find out what it was.

"Are you sure you want to go back to college this year? You're doing very well at the paper, and I think you're ready to be a regular reporter."

Dan was taken aback. Of course he was going back to finish school. David Currier had never mentioned a full-time job to him. "Did Mr. Currier say that?"

Norton didn't hesitate. "We haven't discussed it, but I'm sure David would like to have you."

That's not an answer, Dan thought. He tried to sort things out as he replied.

"Well, I have planned all along to finish college, get a degree. . . . I don't know if I should stop now. It's only one more year. But I never thought about a regular job here."

"Well, you think about it for a day or two. You ought to look at the long run. Doing this might help you more than the last year of college. It's a good job—and I'm sure you'd have a chance for a more responsible place at the paper before too long."

Dan was startled again: *Is he trying to tell me something? On this little paper there's only one job "more responsible" than being a reporter.*

Norton came at it from another angle. "And you'd be starting in a place you already know, where you know the people and the town." He gave Dan a confiding smile. "I'm not just thinking of the job, either. Aren't you keeping company these days?"

"Well, not exactly." Dan blushed. He hadn't realized his attentions to Grace Harper were so well known; he'd been calling on her since mid-July, but she lived out in the country.

Norton smiled. "I'm just joshing you, Dan. But seriously, think about it."

He did think about it—for twelve hours. When he talked to his parents that night, they were divided in their counsel. His mother wanted him to finish college, but his father told him to settle for the three years he had—"more than most ever dream of"—and take the job while it was there for the taking. The next morning, Dan decided to do that.

He started to tell Norton when he got to the office, but the publisher put him off, again suggesting quietly that they talk on the way home.

"Well, what's your decision?" he asked Dan as they stepped from the *News* building into the oven heat of late afternoon in August.

"I'd like to stay and try the job," Dan said.

"Fine. I'm glad." Norton seemed to file the matter away like a letter he'd finished reading. "Now, I think it would be better if you didn't say anything about this to David until I've had a chance to talk with him."

Dan felt vaguely uneasy. *That's funny. Sounds like Currier doesn't know Norton offered me the job. But it's Norton's newspaper now, I suppose he can decide what to tell people who work for him.*

"Sure, if that's how you want it."

"I think that would be best. I'm sure David will be talking to you in a day or so about the new job. It'll be good to have you on the regular staff." Norton affected a man-to-man tone and winked at Dan. "And I'll tell you something else: if I weren't a married man, I'd give you a run for your money with that Grace Harper. She'd make anybody daffy."

The editor called Dan to his desk the next day.

"Dan, I was wondering . . . I want to . . ." Currier started again. "Have you ever thought about staying on here instead of going back to school this fall?"

Dan could give a straight answer to that one. "Yes, I have thought about it, some."

Currier seemed pleased, as if an awkward corner had been turned. "Well, then. I've been thinking, too, about what I'd do for help when you left, and I wondered if you would be interested in staying on here."

Dan was uneasy with this charade, but figured he'd better play his part. So he waited a moment, as if considering the offer, before answering.

"I think I'd like that. I have thought about it." Just in time, he remembered something Norton hadn't mentioned. "What would the pay be?"

"Oh." The editor hesitated. "Well, there might be a little more than you're getting this summer. Of course, not much to start. Mr. Norton wants us to tighten our belts. But I think I can find a dollar or two."

"Well, I'd like to stay, then."

Currier smiled and held out his hand. "Well. Fine. I know you're going to really help us. I'm glad I was able to talk Mr. Norton into this."

Dan took Currier's offered hand. "I'll do my best," he said. He wanted very much to get away.

Chapter 7

Falls City, Fall 1889

BY LATE SEPTEMBER the dimensions of the drought had become painfully clear. Things were bad enough nearby, but further west it was much worse, drier than it had been in years. So once again many farmers, unable to pay off their loans because they had no crop to sell, simply packed up and headed back East.

Dan stood on the sidewalk with George Norton, watching one of the eastbound families drive through town. Two scrawny mules hauled an old wagon crammed with household goods, tools, a farmer, his wife, and three children. The whole outfit—team, wagon, possessions, people—looked dead tired and used-up. It reminded Dan of the trip up from Nebraska in '74, his father silent the whole way, the heat and dust baking them in the crowded wagon.

You can beat a lot of things, but you can't do anything when it quits raining. A lot of these farmers, they get one wet year and they forget all the dry ones, Dan thought. *But it's like Ma says, nature's going to have her way, no matter how hard you fight.*

Pa never did learn that.

"There goes the Dakota Boom," Dan said. "I guess it's hard times coming."

Norton snorted. "The boom was over two years ago. People who don't understand that are just deluding themselves, and that's the worst mistake you can make in business. Never argue with the facts, Dan. Two or three big mortgage companies have already failed, and more are going to. People don't realize how many farms have been abandoned already."

"That doesn't sound too good for the paper."

"In the short run, it's not. But now's the time to lay a foundation for the long haul. We'll have to make do for a while with less, keep a tight hold on spending, do without some equipment we need. But there's two things that matter more than any of that."

He stopped. Dan was getting used to George Norton's habit of pausing in the midst of a conversation, inviting some response from his listener. If he didn't get it, he usually continued, as he did now.

"We have to keep up the quality of the paper, and we have to hold onto our readers. Do the one and we'll help the other, they go together."

"But if times get hard, won't people stop buying the paper?"

"They'll stop a lot of other things first. Newspapers don't cost much. And if they stop paying, well, we'll barter where we can, and carry 'em as long as we can. Especially advertisers. That way they'll be there when things get better, and they'll stay hitched."

Norton went on to tell how a farmer had come into the bank several weeks earlier with no cash to pay his note, and had offered to turn over his only milk cow as payment.

"I told him he had no business taking milk away from his children. Then I extended his note, and forgave this year's interest, and he went away happy."

"I should think he would. That was pretty decent of you."

Norton shook his head. "No. It had nothing to do with being decent. It was a straight business proposition. If he goes under, his land isn't worth anything the way things are today. The bank can't use the cow, and there's no market for them, either. If he fails, I lose the whole loan. This way he'll pay all he can as soon as he can, and he'll never use any bank but mine.

"Same thing goes for the paper, for readers and advertisers. That's what I mean by getting 'em to stay hitched."

Norton stopped, and this time Dan didn't wait. "But I'm not sure that'll work for newspaper subscriptions. People don't think we're that important to them."

Norton pounced. "That's because we haven't given them reason to think so. Why, newspapers come and go around here so fast you can't keep track, and most of 'em are full of stuff that's of no real value to the fellow who buys the paper. We've got to make people believe they need us."

Dan was fascinated. *This man has really thought about things, hasn't he? It may be a rough ride around here for a while, but it won't be dull. I'm glad I signed up for it.*

By the time President Harrison finally signed the statehood proclamation in November, there had been so much politicking that even the newspapers were tired of the subject.

"Well, that foolishness is over, I hope," George Norton said as he looked over the *Dakota News* special statehood edition with Dan and David Currier. "Now we can start building something besides political castles in the air."

[49]

"I don't know." Dan smoothed his cowlick as he thought. "I think there's still going to be lots of politics, with the drought, and the farmers so angry. The Alliance is coming on strong, and now there's even talk about a new party. The Republicans are going to have a lot of trouble in this part of the country."

"At least we have a Republican president again," Norton said, "and Republican majorities in Congress."

"But if the Republicans are in charge, they'll get the blame," Dan insisted. "The things the farmers are mad about aren't going to go away just because there's a new man in the White House."

Currier, who until now had been silent, disagreed. "You pay too much attention to those crazy farmers, Dan. Most of them don't know the first thing about real politics. Why, they don't even know what they like."

Dan figured Currier probably said that to please Norton, and he responded sharply. "Well, they know what they don't like, and they know *who* they don't like. They're already starting to put people out of office. And next year they might get control of some legislatures and elect some governors and congressmen, even senators."

"What do you fellows think will happen here?" People joked about the way Norton always asked questions, but Dan guessed he did it not only to find out what you knew, but whether you'd tell him what you really thought—or only what you thought he wanted to hear.

Currier was quick to answer. "The farmers will make a lot of noise, but when people vote they'll come to their senses and stick with the Republicans, the way they always have."

The editor's tone was condescending, and Dan was suddenly enraged. Once again he saw his father's face as he looked at a cornfield ravaged by grasshoppers; he saw his mother weeping at the sight of a blizzard in April. He remembered driving away from the Nebraska claim, household goods piled in the wagon and no one able to look back at the drab little sod house they were leaving.

His face was flushed with anger, but he managed to control his words. "I don't think that will happen at all. I think the Alliance is going to get a lot of votes. They're on the rise, and not just here."

Norton sighed. "I really hope you're wrong. They scare off business with all their wild talk. They make it sound like a bad place to invest, and we don't need that just now."

"But it's not just wild talk." Dan knew he was contradicting the publisher, but he didn't care. "I watched my father ruined, never mind that he worked so hard. It was no fault of his own, but he thought it was, and he still blames himself. And there are plenty like him."

Dan's voice shook. "And I watched my mother get old. I was just a little boy, but I could tell. She stopped singing and she stopped smiling, and after a while she couldn't hide it when she hurt."

His temper was cooling, but he went on to make his point. "They may be wrong, but they really hurt. People have to understand that."

"Politicians can't make it rain, or repeal the law of supply and demand," Currier objected.

"I know that." Dan shook his head in frustration. "But somehow farmers have got to be treated better. The country has changed and everybody else is better off, but farmers are worse off and nobody seems to care out East."

Norton stared at his young employee, measuring the passion in Dan's voice and face.

"I understand what Dan is talking about, and he's quite right," the publisher said. "The only question is *how* to do it—and whether it helps any to disrupt the political system, tear things apart."

Saying that seemed to remind Norton of some other things.

"You fellows decide what goes in the paper, of course, but I hope we won't just write about the problems and the angry people. We should always pay attention to what's good for this community, because what helps Falls City is going to help the *Dakota News.*"

Dan's anger drained away as Norton moved the conversation to this less contentious topic.

"The important thing is to build soundly, so we'll have business here to smooth out the big ups and downs when farm prices drop or there's a drought, like now. We'll always have those things, but we can offset them if we have things to sell that people need, good times or bad."

Dan had never heard Norton say so much at one time, and he wasn't finished yet.

"It isn't just manufacturing. There's other kinds of business that you might not think of right away. If we can get schools and colleges—give them land or even cash to locate here—they'll bring people and jobs and customers. We need to improve the streets, and build a street railway to the edge of town, make it worthwhile for people to locate here, just like we did for the railroads."

And all that would be good for the newspaper, too, Dan thought. *He thinks about three things at once, and he always looks at the long pull.*

He's an odd one, and cold. I don't think I could be like that. But mostly he's dead right.

Dan had another chance to measure his publisher's judgment a couple of months later. It was a Wednesday, publication day, and he had been left in charge by David Currier when the editor went home sick to his stomach. Dan was in the editor's cubicle, trying to finish the local-page layout that Currier had started, when the back-shop foreman came in and shut the door. He was visibly agitated.

"What's the matter, Bill?" Dan asked.

"I know I should take this to Mr. Currier, but he's out sick, so I guess you'll have to do."

Dan managed a small smile. "Try me. It can't be that hard."

"It is." The printer handed Dan a composing stick with a two-inch chunk of type in it. "But I thought you had to know. Mr. Norton came back a few minutes ago and took this story out of the page form. He didn't say anything to anyone."

Dan tilted the metal container so the type caught the light as he read it backward. The two-paragraph item reported the arrest of a young man on charges of being drunk and disorderly and assaulting a policeman. Dan knew about the story: the arrested man was the son of the owner of the Meyers Packing Company, the biggest business in town.

Dan looked up. "I got that from the police register. David wrote it; he said we should use it, even if it caused trouble."

"Well, I guess it did." The foreman sighed. "What do you want to do?"

Dan thought hard. *The editor should deal with this. But the editor isn't here, and there isn't time to go ask him, and anyway he's sick. And he left me in charge, so I guess it's up to me to decide what to do.*

He thought maybe he should ask Norton why he had taken it out of the form.

I already know why he took it out.

Maybe he should decide what to do and then tell Norton what he had decided.

No, that'd just give him a chance to order it out again.

It was a news decision, and Norton was always saying his editors were the ones who made the news decisions. And he knew what this one should be.

I'm going to make someone mad, that's for sure. Oh well, I can always go back to college.

He tried to sound confident. "Put it back in the page—" He glanced at his layout sheet. "—at the bottom of column three. If anybody asks about it, tell them I . . . I ordered you to do it."

The two men looked at each other across the desk, and then the foreman suddenly smiled. "I never knew Mr. Norton could read type," he said.

"Neither did I," Dan replied. He returned the type stick. "You learn something about people every day, Bill."

The foreman looked hard at Dan. "Yes, you do."

Currier was aghast when Dan told him about the incident. He told Dan he should never have countermanded Norton's action, and he made it clear he would not have done so himself. But he could hardly come down too hard on Dan, since Norton never mentioned the matter to either of them.

* * *

Life wasn't all work for Dan, thanks to Grace Harper. He had been calling on her as often as she'd let him since midsummer. They enjoyed each other's company, intellectually as well as physically, and by fall, companionship had ripened into something more than mere affection.

Grace was still living on the farm, though this year she was teaching school in town. Dan drove out to the Harper place so often that the horse soon knew every foot of the route, and Dan hardly had to touch the reins, day or night, going or coming.

The two of them were regulars at spelling bees, church socials, literary evenings, the dramatic society, the dance club, and other less formal gatherings. They acted in charades. They attended musical evenings, Dan's harmless drone and Grace's bright soprano joining in "Annie Laurie," "Nellie Gray," "Dixie," and "Spanish Cavalier." They often ended with a mock-sentimental favorite:

I am looking rather seedy now while holding down my claim,
And my victuals are not always served the best,
And the mice play slyly round me as I lay me down to sleep,
In my little old sod shanty on the claim.
Yet I rather like the novelty of living in this way,
Though my bill of fare is always rather tame,
But I'm happy as a clam on the land of Uncle Sam,
In my little old sod shanty on the claim.

Dan and Grace didn't always stay to the very end of an evening's program. This led to winks and nudges, but they weren't the only ones who sometimes left early—and it *was* a long ride out to the Harper place.

Those rides under the harvest and hunter's moons seemed made of magic. They would leave the lights of town behind as the buggy came over the hill and into the valley. Across the river, the plains lay still and silvered in the moonlight, punctuated here and there by the dark mass of a clump of trees around a farmhouse. There was no sound but the horse's hoofs on the road. Sometimes they talked, sometimes they sang, but mostly they just sat and watched the countryside slip past.

Moonlit October evenings gave way to chilly November nights, and then winter laid an iron hand on the country. For fifteen bitter days after Christmas the thermometer never rose above zero. There was no more driving through the country for fun; a buggy ride in such conditions was an endurance test.

In the coldest months Grace boarded in town during the week, so she and Dan could see each other more often, though they had less privacy. In the evenings they sat in the parlor of the house where she boarded—or at the Woods house, where Eudora and Henry made her welcome and fed her regularly.

Grace had strong opinions and rarely let Dan escape without argument when he said something she differed with.

They had one particularly deep disagreement. Dan had never paid much attention to Indians, and he saw them as most Dakotans did: shiftless, troublesome, untrustworthy, unable to take care of themselves. Grace, on the other hand, viewed them as victims of the white man's greed, robbed of their lands and reduced to depending on a hostile white government.

Dan and Grace got onto the subject in February, when the federal government opened a huge chunk of the Great Sioux Reservation in western South Dakota to white settlers. Dan accepted the proposition that much of the reservation was not needed by the Indians, and should therefore be offered to homesteaders even though it had been granted to the Indians by treaty. Grace rejected this, utterly and scornfully: to her, it was one more proof that whites would break any agreement with the Indians if it suited their convenience.

"Twenty years ago they forced the Sioux out of eastern Dakota, and they gave them a treaty that promised they could keep everything west of the Missouri *forever*," Grace said. "Then they found gold in the Black Hills, so they took them away; never mind the treaty, they just rewrote it. Now the speculators want the land between the river and the Hills—so they tear up what's left of the treaty."

"The Indians agreed to both those changes," Dan objected.

"Oh, I know that." Grace's voice was chilled with sarcasm. "And both times the government made it plain that if the Indians didn't agree there'd be no more food, no more blankets, no more cattle, no more payments, no more anything. It was simple: give in—or starve and freeze."

"Grace, that's not how it was."

"That's exactly how it was, and you know it. Remember that Indian agent, that man McLaughlin that you met in Minneapolis with Mr. Lounsberry?"

"Yes, and he said he'd told the Indians they should agree."

"And you told me he said he did it only because he knew that if they didn't agree, Congress would completely cut them off."

"Well, maybe so. But—"

"But nothing!" Grace stood up and turned toward him, ready to continue. She stopped when she saw how upset he was.

"Dan, listen to me. I don't like to fight with you."

"A fellow would have a hard time figuring that out."

"But I have to be honest with myself, and say what I think." She took a deep breath. "And I want you to be right about things. So if I think you're wrong, I have to say so."

[54]

Because I think I'm going to be with you for a long, long time, Dan Woods. And I care too much about you to let you be wrong—about anything.

Grace was indeed coming to the conclusion that she wanted Dan. He was intelligent and articulate, gentle and affectionate. If she sometimes found him just a little predictable, she also found him more than a little attractive: something always stirred inside her when they were close, and she returned his embraces as ardently as he offered them.

As for Dan, he was simply lost, hopelessly in love with this tall, amusing girl with the saucer-sized blue eyes. He thought she was the most beautiful thing that ever walked on two legs. And if she occasionally argued with him, well, she was right more often than not. So, in slightly different ways, they enjoyed each other as winter turned finally to brief spring and then suddenly to summer.

At the end of June a dozen young people drove out to spend the weekend at a lake cottage fifteen miles from town. Mostly they were married couples, among them George and Mary Norton, but a few were unmarried. Dan and Grace were the youngest in the crowd.

As soon as they had unloaded their buggies and wagons, the weekenders changed into old clothes and headed for a swim before attacking the picnic supper they had brought along. At that time of year it was still light at ten o'clock, and they lingered outside, eating and talking, watching the lake, its surface smooth except where fish rose to feed in the twilight.

They sang a few songs. Then someone suggested a dance, and they trooped down to the water's edge. Harold Larimer had brought his harmonica, and they paired off on the hard-packed sand, their energetic activity keeping the mosquitoes at bay.

After a few minutes they changed partners, and Grace found herself dancing a polka with George Norton. As he swung her around he moved them to the edge of the group, away from Dan, who was fully engaged guiding the ample Mary Norton.

George looked down at Grace. She was surprised he was that tall; because he was long-waisted, he seemed shorter than he really was. His wavy brown hair fell over his forehead as he swung her around to the music. He put his mouth close to Grace's ear—closer, she thought, than was absolutely necessary.

"This is some fun, isn't it?" He pulled his head back and looked hard at her. She looked back, watching coolly as his eyes flickered downward to the open throat of her dress; she felt his hand press harder on her waist, his fingers moving, pulling her closer as they spun around.

"Why, it surely is." She pulled back just enough so he'd notice. He relaxed his hold just enough so she'd notice.

"Your Dan is a lucky man, I hope he appreciates that." Again he spoke into her ear. "There's others would if he doesn't."

[55]

Again his hand pressed on her back, this time a little lower, and this time she didn't pull away.

Look out, Grace, you're fooling with fire . . . but it's sort of fun.

The idea made her giggle. George, misreading the giggle, moved his hand again. Grace twisted reflexively and her eyes opened so wide he could see white all around the blue. Just then the music stopped.

"I can't play this thing and slap skeeters at the same time," Harold Larimer announced. "Let's go inside where we won't get eaten up."

They all trooped up the little hill to the cabin, George and Grace rejoining Dan and Mary Norton. There wasn't room for dancing inside the cabin.

That night they slept the deep sleep of the young—men wrapped in blankets on the living-room floor, women jumbled three apiece in the beds in the bedroom. The next day they fished and swam and walked, talked and ate, swam again and dozed in the sun. It was a halcyon day.

Finally, after supper and one final plunge, they threw their wet bathing clothes in the back of the wagons and drove home.

"That was fun," George said, speaking to the group in general but looking straight at Grace. "We should do it again."

I wonder what kind of man he really is, Grace thought. *I ought to keep clear away from him, he's nothing but trouble.*

But he's interesting.

Chapter 8

Falls City, August 1890

GEORGE NORTON stood in front of the *Dakota News* building watching the stream of farm wagons headed across the river to the fairgrounds.

One came past carrying a group of young men and women. As they passed the newspaper office, they burst into song.

> My country 'tis of thee,
> Once land of liberty,
> Of thee I sing.
> Land of the millionaire,
> Farmers with pockets bare,
> Caused by the cursed snare,
> The Money Ring!

Most of the wagons carried homemade signs or slogans. The messages, stitched or painted on bedsheets, proclaimed the owners' disillusion with the traditional political parties.

WE VOTED WITH OUR PARTY NO MATTER WHERE IT WENT.
WE VOTED WITH OUR PARTY TILL WE HAVEN'T A CENT.

MORTGAGED—OUR HOMES BUT NOT OUR VOTES.

NOT VESTED RIGHTS, BUT HUMAN RIGHTS.

"Huh! This is no parade," Norton grumbled to David Currier, standing beside him. "This is a revolution."

Dust rose over the fairgrounds in a thickening cloud as wagons kept arriving. By midday there were hundreds of them, from Minnesota and Iowa as well as South Dakota, bringing thousands of men, women, and children to the great rally of the Farmers' Alliance.

Most had started before dawn to get here; some had driven all night to make sure they would get a good vantage point for the day's program. Now they waited quietly and ate the lunches the women had packed the night before.

Dan stood by the corner of the speakers' stand, watching the wagons arrive and taking notes. *It's for sure the biggest parade I've ever seen—maybe the biggest I ever will see.*

A strange tide was running, running hard. The men who had always controlled politics, men who owned things and sold things and loaned money, were suddenly afraid. They masked their fear behind ridicule and scorn, but secretly they trembled at the sounds from the countryside.

Throughout the Great Plains, farmers were testing their strength, feeling political power grow like corn in the hot summer nights. It was a new feeling: farmers had never put much faith in a political system that ignored and oppressed them, but now they were trying to seize the very machinery that had ground them down. It was heady business, half Sunday-school picnic and half holy war, and they brought to it the mingled anticipation and uncertainty of a bridegroom on the wedding night.

Amos Harper was on the platform at the Falls City rally—in recognition of his prominence in the state Alliance—but he would make no speech today. The major oratory would be provided by two well-known figures: Mrs. Mary Lease, the oratorical heroine of the movement, and Leonidas L. Polk, a former Confederate soldier from North Carolina and president of the National Farmers' Alliance.

Mary Lease was the wife of a failed Kansas homesteader. Physically, she was unappealing: too thick in the waist, too thin in the shoulders, too long in the legs. Her black hair contrasted with dead-white skin, and heavy eyelids drooped over her blue eyes.

But when she started to speak, people forgot how she looked. Her deep contralto voice instantly captured the full attention of everyone within earshot.

This time she began by identifying the enemy.

> Wall Street owns the country. The West and South are bound and prostrate before the manufacturing East. Our laws are the output of a system which clothes rascals in robes and honesty in rags. The parties lie to us and the political speakers mislead us.

Dan was struck by her presence. Taller than many men, she was dressed as always entirely in black. A single emerald pinned at her neck was the only jewelry she wore. She spoke in short, muscular sentences.

The common people are robbed to enrich their masters. There are thirty thousand millionaires in the United States. Go home and figure out how many paupers you must have to make one millionaire with the money in circulation only ten dollars per capita.

There are thirty men in the United States whose aggregate wealth is three and one-half billion dollars. There are half a million men looking for work. There are sixty thousand soldiers of the Union in poorhouses, men who wore the blue and dyed it red with their blood in the country's defense.

Now she drew her audience into her argument: "Tell me one law," she challenged, "that has been passed which directly benefited the common people."

A man shouted back from the crowd: "The Homestead Law!"

She smiled. "The people got the law—and the railroads got the land!" The farmers roared their agreement.

The great common people of this country are slaves, and monopoly is the master. Money rules.

We want the accursed foreclosure system wiped out. We will stand by our homes and stay by our firesides by force if necessary. We will not pay our debts to the loan shark companies until the government pays its debts to us.

She ended with a line that had become the Alliance battle cry since she first shouted it at a Kansas meeting:

"You farmers need to raise less corn—and more hell!"

Leonidas Polk was the last speaker. It was late in a long, dusty afternoon, but he brought the crowd up shouting.

Will you tell me who has a better right in America to go into politics than the farmers?

I will tell you what you are going to see. You will see arrayed on one side the great magnates of the country, and Wall Street brokers, and the plutocratic power. And on the other side you will see the people.

Wall Street, Wall Street, Wall Street, Dan thought. *That's the enemy in every Alliance talk I've ever heard.* There was an approving roar from the big crowd, and Polk turned to another subject.

Some people have stirred up sectional feeling and have kept us apart for twenty-five years. They've been teaching little children to hate. The man who has waved the bloody shirt knows that if we get together and shake hands and look each other in the face and feel the touch of kinship, their doom is sealed.

There shall be no Mason and Dixon line on the Alliance maps

of the future. The farmer of North Carolina, Georgia, Texas, South Carolina is your brother.

I stand here today, commissioned by hundreds of thousands of Southern farmers, to bid the farmers of South Dakota to stand by them.

There was another shout of approval. *He may not have the right of it,* Dan thought, *but those farmers sure think he does.*

Amos Harper had a good deal more political experience than most farmers. He had helped organize the Alliance in South Dakota and he knew many of the leading Alliancemen in other states. So he was both a local leader and a player on the larger stage, where the Alliance was trying to provide strategy and strength for a rural movement that some were already calling the "People's party."

Amos took pains to explain the Alliance to Dan. He liked the young reporter—and reckoned that as long as he was courting his daughter, Dan would give him a fair shake in his paper.

"It's really pretty simple," Amos said one day when Dan was at the farm. "There's different ways of saying it, but we all support the same few basic things."

He signaled each item by raising one of his big fingers. "The government should own the railroads . . . we need free coinage of silver . . . get rid of the national banks and have the Treasury issue paper money, plenty of it . . . make it illegal for foreigners to own land . . . make it against the law to speculate or trade futures in grain and stocks."

"That can't be all you want."

"Of course not. There's direct election of senators, the secret ballot, the graduated income tax. And there's others. But these are the most important, the ones we all agree on."

"Some of the others sound pretty strange," Dan said. "I even read that some of your people want the government to build a ship canal from the Great Lakes to the Gulf of Mexico."

Amos smiled confidingly. "If you set up a big tent and invite everybody to come in, you're sure to collect some strange characters. But that kind of talk is just hot air."

He grew increasingly confident as the fall wore on.

"It's going real well right now," he said one October afternoon. "We'll elect a lot of our own people—and people we support. But that's only a start, and it's the easy part, too. The hard part will be to turn this into a real political party."

"Why do you want a new party?" Dan asked. "I don't think people will take to that. They're used to the two we've got."

The big man stirred, squinting his blue eyes against the setting sun. "Because neither of 'em gives us a fair shake, and neither of 'em ever will.

But the biggest reason is that this thing has got a life of its own now. You can organize and you can talk all you want, but when people take over, everything changes. We couldn't keep these farmers in the old parties now if we wanted to."

Dan paid attention to Amos Harper. Perhaps because he was such a big man, he never seemed to get as excited as other farmers. He rarely raised his voice except when making a speech. Like his daughter, he was cool and detached; like her, he kept his passions so much to himself that when he did reveal them they seemed all the more intense. One of those passions was for the land and for its proper care. Amos had no sympathy with farmers who overworked their fields or ignored the imperatives of nature and then complained that the world was unfair.

David Currier was unhappy with both the tone and the content of Dan's report on the big Alliance rally. He came into the back shop, where Dan was helping make up a page, brandishing a proof.

"Why do you pay so much attention to these damned fools?" the editor scolded. "The way you've written it up sounds like it came right out of some Alliance pamphlet. It'll have to be done over."

Dan had expected that sooner or later Currier would grumble about treating the Alliance as the equal of the Republicans. But now the editor was accusing him of actually favoring the insurgents, and he didn't like it.

"I don't want it to sound like I'm supporting the Alliance, David," he said, trying to keep his voice even. "So if you think it does, show me how to fix it. But we need to report what those people are saying and doing. It's important."

The editor was insistent. "You should remember what Mr. Norton said last fall, how the Alliance drives away business with its fool talk."

"I remember," Dan said. "I also remember he said we should keep our news pages fair and open to everyone, and keep our opinions on the editorial page. The Alliance is the biggest story around here this year, and everybody knows it. It's news."

"You don't know much about news, young fellow. This is a *Republican* paper."

Dan was angry, and for once he let his anger show. "You're the boss. If you want it changed, you change it. I like it the way I wrote it."

Currier was also enraged. In fact the two men were so intent that they didn't notice George Norton until he was standing beside them. Neither Dan nor Currier had any idea when he had come into the room—or how long he had been listening. Norton gave no hint when he spoke.

"David, it occurred to me . . . I just thought I'd make a suggestion . . . Of course, you will decide what goes into the paper." He directed his usual disclaimer solely to the editor; Dan might as well have been somewhere else.

"But I hope we continue to give thorough coverage to politics, even things like . . ." He hesitated, as if searching for an example. ". . . like that Alliance meeting the other day. I want our readers to know what those people are saying. That will show our fairness. Then I want you to write a good, strong editorial. We must make clear what our editorial position is." He put just the slightest emphasis on the word "editorial."

Currier fought a brief rearguard action, then retreated. "Personally, I wouldn't give those people a stick of type, but if you think it's best, George . . . Woods, be sure to let me have a full story on that circus. I'll handle the editorial, and there won't be any doubt where we stand."

The editor left abruptly. Dan thought over the incident: George Norton hadn't mentioned the argument between editor and reporter, but Dan was sure he had heard it—and had gone out of his way to signal his agreement with Dan, even though he'd been careful not to criticize Currier in front of a subordinate.

Norton cleared his throat. "I'll look forward to reading your story on the Alliance . . . ahem . . . circus," he said. Dan saw the hint of a smile come and go on the publisher's otherwise impassive face.

Currier was as good as his word. His editorial, published in the same edition that carried Dan's long story on the farmers' rally, left no doubt about the paper's opinion of the Alliance.

FARMERS' FOLLY

The latest Alliance meeting showed clearly that this organization is destined to go the way of all such "movements." No party based on so preposterous a program as that proposed by Alliance speakers can possibly appeal to sensible men; therefore no party that advocates such a program can long survive.

There is probably no class of presumably intelligent men less able to deal with the complex subject of public finance than those who live and work far from the centers where the mechanisms of trade and exchange are shaped. The schemes proposed are among the wildest and most fantastic ever seriously put forward by apparently sober men. . . .

The morning after this editorial was published, early arrivals at the *Dakota News* building found a crude gallows erected in the middle of the street. From it dangled a dummy, stuffed with straw and clothed in a shabby Prince Albert coat, striped pants, and an old top hat. A sign hung on its chest.

EDITOR
Apparently Sober.
Presumably Intelligent?

[62]

On election day, the farmers had their greatest political success. In South Dakota they seized the balance of power in the new state legislature, and so would be able to name a U.S. senator. In Minnesota, Alliancemen joined Democrats to control the legislature. In Nebraska they elected a governor, controlled both houses of the legislature, and chose all three congressmen. And in Kansas, the Alliance virtually took over the state: it won 91 of 125 seats in the state legislature—thus guaranteeing the defeat of a Republican senator—and elected its candidates to all five seats in the House of Representatives.

"It's setting one group of people against another, and that's something we've never had in the West. People came out here to get away from that, and we don't want it here. It's bad for the state."

George Norton waggled a plump finger at Amos Harper as he spoke. It was a raw, gray Saturday afternoon in late November. Amos, in town to do his weekly shopping, had spotted George through the window of the *Dakota News* office. When Dan came into the office a few minutes later, the farmer and the businessman were deep in political talk. Amos's heavy frame overflowed the chair beside Norton's desk, but he seemed completely at ease as he replied to the publisher's complaint.

"Well, you may be right about that," Amos said. "But if that's going on, I know how it began: people started calling farmers lazy and ignorant, or worse, when we started asking for a fair shake." Amos spoke quietly, as usual, but there was resentment in his voice. "They said we were fools and hayseeds, and if a woman spoke up, they called her a whore. That's not exactly sweet reason."

"People get carried away." George's tone was conciliatory. "There was some of that on both sides. I didn't like what your folks said about bankers, either. But what really worries me is that people may really think it's class against class. That's wrong." He hitched himself forward in his chair and stared at Amos. "The banker can only do well if the farmer does well, and vice versa. The banker loses if the farmer defaults on his loan, and the farmer loses if his banker fails."

"I know that's what *you* believe, that's why you have my account." Amos seemed a bit embarrassed to say it; he paused and tugged at his gray-flecked blond beard. "But the rich people out East, the Wall Street bankers and the railroad presidents and industrialists, they're getting a lot richer, and faster than before, too. There's more distance all the time between them and the rest of us. Including you, George."

"Oh. I suppose you think I should join the Alliance."

Amos was not interested in joking. "No, listen a minute. Some things have changed and we've hardly noticed it. The free land is gone. The easy credit is gone, too—all those loans the mortgage companies pushed on us. A farmer can't make it anymore with a quarter-section and one horse and his own sweat. He has to have more land and a lot of machinery. So he's always in debt."

"But that doesn't mean we have to have some kind of class war," George argued. "You talk about things the way they really are, and I won't dispute you. But your Alliance friends mostly talk about dreams, not facts."

Dan interrupted. "I'd say you're both right." He spoke tentatively, not sure he'd be welcome in the discussion. "Seems to me if both sides could quiet down some, they might be able to work things out."

Amos shook his head. "I don't think so. That might work if the political parties still cared about this part of the country, but neither of 'em does and I don't think they ever will again. So the only thing left for us is a new party."

"But how can a new party—a farm party—win?" Dan pursued the argument. "More and more people live in cities, in the East, every year. And business is getting stronger all the time."

"All the more reason why we can't count on the old parties. The Democrats only care about the South and the cities—and the votes they get from the immigrants. And the Republicans!" Amos was derisive. "The Republicans used to be our party, the little fellow's party, the old soldier's party, the farmer's party. Now they only care about big men, big business, big money. We may not make it on our own, but it's by-God sure there's no other way to get our share."

George banged a fist down on his desk. "It won't work! You'll tear the country apart, and you'll end up losing, too. You'd be better off making your fight inside the Republican party."

Amos smiled, but his words were grim. "George, we tried that, and we got nothing. We might as well try something else." He stood up. "I've got to go see Dan's father. Lydia gave me a grocery order and I'd best fill it before I forget it."

He shook hands with both men and left. George thumped his fist on the desk again, this time not angrily but with an air of resignation. "They'll keep on, all right. They've had a taste of politics, and they'll not stop now. They've gone too far to turn back."

Chapter 9

AFTER the clamor of the summer and fall, winter seemed even quieter than usual. The arguments of autumn were heard only occasionally, and then only as distant echoes. If there was now a new hardness to political discourse, a certain edge not previously noted, at least for the moment it was muted. As temperatures dropped and snowdrifts rose, politics slipped down to its customary place on the scale of things, somewhere between the price of corn and the latest local gossip.

One topic of conversation around Falls City at the end of the year was a familiar one: Indians. In late November, federal troops were sent to round up a recalcitrant Sioux band that refused to come in to its regular winter camp. The Indians were angered by the reduction—in violation of specific promises—of their government meat ration; delays in delivery of even the reduced amount had left them near starvation. They were further outraged in mid-December when Sitting Bull, their legendary medicine man, was shot and killed while being taken into custody.

Two weeks later, near a place called Wounded Knee, Sioux warriors fired on soldiers who were disarming them under an agreement reached the previous day. Instantly, a strong force of troops surrounding the Indian camp opened fire. A few minutes later, more than a hundred Sioux men were dead or dying. So were more than two hundred women and children, cut down by explosive shells and rifle fire as they fled in panic across the frozen plain.

Dan tried to put together a full account, but it was hard. The news came back slowly from the remote reservation, and what came was mostly the army's version. In any event he got no encouragement from David Currier, who told him to forget the whole thing: "No one cares if a few squaws get shot. Teach 'em a lesson."

Dan reported the remark to Grace. "I'm not surprised," she responded. "What did you expect?"

"I know." Dan shook his head. "You were dead right in what you said last winter. About whites and Indians. The government broke its word again. And I think the troops were green and just went berserk."

"But you can't write about it." Grace's tone was acid.

He stood up, and when he spoke, there was a hard sound in his voice she had not heard before. "Not the whole story. Not yet. But I'll get it sooner or later."

"When you do, can you get it into your paper?"

"I'll worry about that when the time comes." Dan put his hands on her shoulders. "Thank you for making me think about it."

Grace was gratified, but as usual she masked her appreciation behind a mocking reply. "It was my pleasure, Mr. Woods." She moved toward him. "But wouldn't you really rather think about something else?"

As the long winter wore on they thought about many things—including their future. Dan seemed to assume that someday they'd be married, but he never quite said so. Grace shared the assumption and looked forward to the event, but she felt a little frustrated, and more than a little irritated, by Dan's failure to take decisive steps toward the altar.

In fact he was often preoccupied that winter. He didn't feel right about things at the paper; David Currier was consistently cool, at times almost hostile. Currier seemed to go out of his way to emphasize Dan's youth and relative inexperience, and when he edited his copy, he was routinely sarcastic.

"He obviously thinks you're a danger to him," Grace said one night. "He's afraid you're going to take his job away from him."

"Oh, come on, Grace. I'm ten years younger than he is, and I haven't had anything like his experience. How could he think that?"

"Dan, you're so much better than he is already, never mind if it was fifty years instead of ten." Grace's voice was impatient. "You're good. You always have been. I'm sure Norton thinks so, too, the way he sided with you in that argument last fall. You could run that paper right now, and you'd run it a lot better than David Currier."

If you'd just make up your mind to do it, she thought. *And do some other things too, slowpoke.*

Dan recalled Grace's comment two months later on a May morning, when George Norton called him into his office and closed the door.

"Dan, I believe it's time for you to take on more responsibility here." Norton never was much for small talk. "I've decided you should be the editor of the paper."

Dan was too startled to speak.

[66]

"I want to go to daily publication this year, and you're the right person to do that." The publisher's words were measured, matter-of-fact. "David is a fine man, but he's a little set in his ways. I think a younger man with more energy will do better, and I'd like you to get into the job now so that you'll be ready to take us daily in the fall."

Dan found his voice. "Well, I'm certainly . . . I'm not sure that I could . . ."

Norton ignored him and went on. He could have been reading from a report card.

"You've gotten yourself an education. You've done well in your work. You're a reliable reporter. You write things straight, even when you have strong opinions. I like it that you *do* have strong opinions. You accept responsibility. You are able to persuade other people—sometimes even publishers." The poker face relaxed into a half-smile. "I should have expected all that. Lounsberry told me you were an exceptional young man."

Dan was surprised. "You talked to the colonel about me?"

"He was your last employer, and he has a good reputation. He knows newspapering, and he thinks you're ready to run a paper. So do I. The *News* can be the most important newspaper in this state if it's built up the right way, and now is the time to do it."

Dan wasn't sure. "Business isn't so good right now."

"That's exactly why we should do it," Norton said. "The others are cutting back now, and we can take advantage of that."

Dan knew he was right; their two rivals, the *Falls City Journal* and the *Lincoln County Gazette,* had recently cut back the size of their weekly editions.

"We'll fill the gap and get the jump on them," Norton continued, "and if we manage things right they'll never catch up."

Dan was listening to Norton but his mind was on another track.

What do I owe to David Currier? The man is my boss, and even if he's a grouch, he's a fair man and a good teacher. How can I take his job?

Norton said nothing, waiting as if he could hear the words rushing through Dan's head.

He's going to get rid of David one way or another. If I don't take the job, he'll get someone else. It's not as if I could save it for David by turning it down. He's going into the hellbox anyway.

So why not take it? I can do it. And by God I want to do it, too. Run my own paper. I can't say no to that.

As if he had heard those final words, Norton held out his hand. Dan took it silently.

"I'm delighted," Norton said.

Dan thought: *I should get a few things straight before I agree to do it. Now is the time to ask, when he wants me to say yes. But what should I ask?*

Again Norton seemed to read his mind. "I'll take care of the business end, so you won't have to worry about that. You'll have full responsibility over the news side, full authority," he said. "I don't know anything about news. I'll stay out of it. You'll decide those things."

I hope it works out that way, Dan thought. *I don't think he really means it. We may have trouble about that.*

Norton brought up another matter. "Of course you'll get a good raise. What do you think would be fair?"

Dan relaxed and replied with a new certainty. "You said you'd take care of the business side, George. You figure out what you want to pay and we'll see if it's enough."

"I'll work something out," Norton said, secretly pleased that his new editor had forced him to make the first offer. "One thing I'll promise, it'll be enough so you can afford to get married."

Dan was thrown into confusion. "Oh. Well, I'm not sure . . ."

"You better not wait too long, someone will steal that Harper girl away from you." Norton smiled and winked, but his voice was serious. "Take my word for it."

Dan thought, as he had before, that for a respectable married man George Norton sure paid a lot of attention to girls. Well, they seemed to like him, too.

Even Grace. She flirted with him the first time she ever met him. And she sure seemed to enjoy dancing with him that night at the lake last summer.

It occurred to Dan that it was just as well Mary Norton was expecting in a month or two. Having a baby might make George think more about his wife—and less about other women.

Dan tried to clear his head. There was a lot to think about, a lot to do. Some of it had to be done right away. "George, when are you going to tell David?"

"I already have."

I was right. He was going to drop David anyway.

"I told him he could stay on the payroll for now, but I said of course it would be up to you whether you keep him." Norton waved an admonitory finger. "Don't be in too big a hurry to decide that. And don't feel that you have to keep him on if you don't want to."

I sure hope he never decides that I've gotten too set in my ways, Dan thought. *I think I just hired on with a hard man.*

Currier said he'd stay on temporarily while he scouted for another job. He turned out to be unfailingly helpful, offering advice only when asked, and soon he was much more relaxed and cheerful than he had been when in charge. Dan sometimes felt uneasy giving orders to an older man who had been his boss, but Currier seemed to bear no ill will; within a couple of months they reached an understanding that he'd stay on permanently.

[68]

The Norton baby, a girl they named Lucy, was born at the end of June. It was a difficult delivery that kept Mary Norton bedridden for weeks and left her much weakened. In October, just after the paper went to daily publication, the baby sickened. In three days she was gone, dead of some sudden infection that overwhelmed her tiny body. Mary Norton collapsed at the funeral service and returned to her bed, her emotions frayed by all that had happened to her since spring.

Her husband simply closed himself up, showing no emotion to anyone at the paper or elsewhere. He was never seen to weep in public. He accepted condolences gravely, politely, but remotely, as if from a great distance. When he returned to work after the funeral, he plunged into his job with almost savage energy, as if to blot out everything else.

Energy was certainly in demand at the newly renamed *Dakota Daily News*. It seemed to Dan that everything that had been smooth and familiar was now suddenly cranky and strange, full of surprises and prone to accident. Tired employees made mistakes or, worse, fought with each other. The printing press developed a whole new set of complaints, as if to protest being forced to run five days a week instead of one.

Dan found he had to work late into the night to have a paper ready for the press each morning. David Currier, though pitching in with a will, couldn't turn out enough copy, let alone handle the added editing and makeup work. So Dan hired the two brightest high school boys he could find to help with the "locals" and in the back shop. He signed up several women to turn out weekly social notes.

It was helter-skelter, but somehow they got out an edition every day, and by the fourth week they were getting papers to the railroad stations on time.

Norton insisted on that, right from the start. The first job, he said, was to gain circulation; he thought the key to that was the small towns. He reckoned the secret of selling newspapers in those towns was reliable delivery, and the way you achieved that was to get the paper onto trains.

Fortunately, Falls City was served by more rail lines than any other community in South Dakota. Norton could tell you when each train left, where it went, and when it got there. Within a couple of months, bundles of newspapers were thumping onto station platforms up to a hundred miles from Falls City. From there they went into post-office boxes, to be picked up with the mail by people who had never before been offered a daily newspaper.

Soon Dan was looking for ways to collect and publish local news from distant towns where significant numbers of new readers lived. He turned that problem over to Currier, who built a network of correspondents, paid by the column inch for what they got into the paper. Currier organized a schedule of deadlines, edited all the copy, and tutored the growing number of stringers.

With circulation coming along nicely, Norton turned his attention to advertising. As a weekly, the paper had enjoyed fair advertiser patronage, but had to share the revenue with the two other weeklies in the county. Now the combination of daily publication and increased circulation gave advertisers a chance to reach more people more often, and Norton was able not only to sell more ads but also to raise his rates.

Their competitors reacted in differing ways. The *Gazette,* the weaker of the two, simply gave up and went out of business when most of its advertisers, and many of its readers, switched to the new daily.

The *Journal,* on the other hand, met Norton head-on, not only going to daily publication but also cutting its subscription and advertising rates.

Norton rejected suggestions that he match the cuts. "If we do our job well enough, readers and advertisers will be glad to pay," he said. "Cut-rate goods are usually second-rate, and people know it. Besides, if we cut rates now, we'll have to raise them later, and people will only remember the raise, not the cut."

By New Year's Day of 1892 Norton was working full time at the newspaper. He resigned as president of the bank, explaining that "there's a good man there to take over, and I'm needed here at the paper." Dan suspected the truth was that George, at thirty-three, was bored with banking and excited by the challenge of the new daily paper.

Whatever the reason, Norton now brought all his restless energy to the *Dakota News.* He not only put in six ten-hour days a week, but fell into the habit of coming in after church on Sunday. He said it gave him a chance to read his mail; in fact, he snooped through the entire building.

As for Dan, he too was completely absorbed in his work. All through the winter and early spring of 1892, he was at the office full time and then some, early and late, day in and day out, week in and week out.

There was a price to pay. One night in early May, almost a year after he became editor, he arrived late—very late—to call on Grace. It was not the first time it had happened that year, but this was once too often, and she exploded the moment he stepped onto the porch.

"Do you know what time it is? I'm beginning to wonder whether you care anything for me at all," she said. "I really believe that newspaper is the only thing that means anything to you."

"Please, Grace." Dan was not surprised; he had felt the storm coming for days.

"No, I mean it." She was not to be coaxed this time. "Just tell me. Do you care for me—or for the paper?"

"Don't make me choose. Of course I care for you. I care very much." Dan stopped, then plunged on. "Dammit, I love you, Grace. But don't set it up as some kind of competition. You were the one who said that I should be editor of the paper."

Grace opened her mouth, then shut it. *He's right, I did. Oh, God. And I'm going to have to share him with that paper all my life—if I want him at all.*

She wondered about that swap. She felt trapped, and that made her not only angry but frustrated as well.

I don't really have a choice, do I? I've seen so much of him, and only him, for so long that now there's no one else.

But he's the only one I want.

Grace's mood wasn't improved by Dan's travel plans for the next couple of months, either: he was going to attend both the Republican convention in June and the first convention of the new Populist party in July.

Dan was excited by the prospect. Grace was not.

"You'll be gone for over a month, then."

"I'll only be away a week each time," Dan said. "And I'll be home almost a month in between."

She was not to be soothed. "You'll be home just long enough to get your washing done, then you'll leave again."

Dan shrugged. "If you want to see it that way, there's nothing I can do. But it's my job, you know."

"I know. That's the trouble. It's always your job. Sometimes I think it would be better if you didn't like your job so much."

If you were bored with your job, you might pay more attention to me. Oh, Dan, I do love you and I want to spend my life with you, but I wish you'd get a move on.

"Look, it's a while before I leave." Dan was suing for peace. "And it'll be better after these two trips, I promise."

You may believe that but I don't. I could tell when you kissed me tonight, your mind has already left. Grace looked appraisingly at Dan. *I'll have to find something to do this summer, because I'm not just going to sit on the porch and wait.*

Minneapolis, June 1892

Dan stepped off the train in Minneapolis into the sticky heat of early June. By the time he reached his hotel, his shirt was stuck to his body and his collar was limp.

Clement Lounsberry had fixed him up with a room at the West Hotel, where all the important Republicans were stopping. After getting settled, Dan made a beeline for Lounsberry's office at the *Tribune*. The colonel was entertaining a half-dozen visiting newspapermen, but he made a fuss over his former helper, interrupting the conversation to introduce Dan around the room. Most of those present were political reporters from New York, Philadelphia, and Washington.

"Now here's a fellow you ought to get to know," Lounsberry said, waving at a sandy-haired young man in a white suit. "Will White, from Kansas. You'll get along famously. Unless I miss my guess you're almost exactly the same age, and you both blow the horn for the small towns."

White was plump and short, almost six inches shorter than Dan, his forehead beaded with sweat. His blue eyes twinkled as he pumped Dan's hand vigorously.

"You're a lucky fellow," White said. "Got your own paper already."

"It's not really mine," Dan demurred. "I don't own it. I'm just the hired editor."

"All the better. You have the fun and get someone else to take the risk. You'll have to tell me how to do it."

The talk reverted to politics; Dan listened hard, hoping to learn what was going to happen. Lounsberry's guests agreed that the party would renominate President Harrison—there seemed no real alternative—but the consensus was equally strong that he stood little chance of reelection if the Democrats put up former President Grover Cleveland, as they seemed sure to do.

There was more interest expressed in Governor William McKinley of Ohio, a popular former congressman who was to be chairman of the convention, and in Mark Hanna, a Cleveland businessman who was McKinley's manager and a rising Republican figure.

"That Hanna is one of a kind," Lounsberry said. "He's a rich man, not that you'd guess it from talking to him. He's been in a half-dozen businesses and made money in every one. Now that he's in politics, he's treating it like any other business."

"What do you mean?" Dan was intrigued.

"Well, he started out small, in Cleveland, about ten years ago. Organized something called 'The Cleveland Business Men's Marching Club.' You know, one of those Republican social clubs, except Hanna took it seriously. Pretty soon he was running the party in the city, and then he took up McKinley and built up support all around the state. He got a big campaign fund from his business friends in Cleveland, and last year he ran McKinley for governor—and won."

One of Lounsberry's guests chimed in: "He's the best money raiser the Republicans ever had. He just walks in on the big bugs and tells 'em they need the Republicans to keep tariffs high and money sound, and they'll have to pay for it, and they cough up the mazuma—in big chunks."

"So now he's pushing McKinley for president?" White asked.

"Not really," Lounsberry said. "Hanna doesn't want to run McKinley this time—he figures it's a Democratic year, so he'd rather save his horse for the next race."

White leaned over and whispered to Dan. "We ought to try to get to know Mark Hanna."

Dan nodded. *This fellow White might be fun to work with. And Hanna sounds interesting; I should meet him.*

But not right away. That evening Lounsberry was taking Dan to dinner, and the next day they all had to attend the opening of the convention in the new Industrial Exposition Hall by the great falls of the Mississippi.

The arrangements were not perfect. Sticky drops of pine pitch, squeezed by the heat from the unseasoned pine ceiling of the just-completed building, fell onto the hair, clothes, and chair seats of the assembled delegates. This contributed to the already sour mood of the Republicans, who could smell defeat as well as pine pitch in the air. They managed to whip up some enthusiasm for James G. Blaine, the party's "Plumed Knight" of 1884, and there was surprising support for McKinley, who got votes from twenty-five states despite his appeal to delegates not to vote for him; but when the cheering faded, they glumly renominated Harrison.

Dan and Will White finally managed to meet Hanna shortly after the convention's final session. They got back to the West Hotel just as McKinley's carriage pulled up. He was surrounded and shoved by enthusiasts as he entered the hotel. A formal, reserved man, he was considerably rattled and took refuge in his room. Dan and White followed McKinley upstairs and were standing outside the room when Hanna arrived to join him a few minutes later.

Hanna was a stocky man with a heavy head, a full face, and large ears. As he strode along the hallway, sweat ran down his thick neck into a wilted collar. He glared at the two young reporters, snorted at their request for an interview, and brushed past them into the room.

Dan and White were about to leave when a pair of waiters came down the hall carrying trays with pitchers of water, chunks of ice, and glasses.

White pulled a five-dollar gold piece from his pocket and held it up between thumb and forefinger.

"Gentlemen," he said to the waiters. "Allow us to bear your heavy burdens into the room."

It took only a moment to strike a deal. Dan and White shucked off their coats and slipped on the waiters' white jackets. They knocked on the room door, identified themselves as from room service, and were admitted to the sanctum.

Dan never forgot the sight. McKinley lay on the bed, stripped to his underwear. On a nearby sofa was Hanna, equally unclothed. Hanna was speaking.

"My God, William," he said, "that was a damned close squeak."

Then he turned his head and saw the two bogus waiters unloading glasses, ice, and pitchers. He swung himself up off the sofa. For some reason Dan noticed his feet; despite his heavy body, they were small, almost delicate.

"Didn't I just see you in the hall and tell you 'no'?" Hanna growled. Then he smiled. "Look, boys, I'm sorry to disappoint you, but I don't have anything to tell you, and it's too hot, and anyhow I never give interviews in my drawers."

White was speechless, but Dan thought of something to say.

"Whatever you say, Mr. Hanna. But my name is Woods, Dan Woods, and if you ever come to South Dakota with your britches on, I hope you'll see me."

Hanna laughed out loud. "Son, it's a deal." He pointed to the door. "Now get out of here. And don't forget to tip the real waiters—I can't afford the reputation of a miser."

Dan didn't go to the Democratic convention in Chicago ten days later. But he did cover the convention of the newly minted People's party; it was so clearly of interest to their readers that George Norton urged him to go despite the publisher's personal dislike for the Populists.

Dan didn't lack for company on the train trip down to Omaha; a number of local farmers, including Amos Harper, went as delegates. Amos took his wife along to watch the doings and have a little holiday. "This time you can see some of these fellows without having to cook dinner for 'em," Amos had said. "Grace can take care of the place. Charlie can do the chores, and she'll have plenty of time on her hands with Dan away."

Falls City, July 4, 1892

George Norton had thought about Grace off and on for a year, ever since that weekend at the lake. Now, as he sat at breakfast with his wife, he thought of Grace again.

Mary Norton was five months pregnant and feeling it. In fact, George thought gloomily, she hadn't been much company—in bed or anywhere else—for the last year and a half, what with two pregnancies and a nervous breakdown in between. Now the doctor had ordered her to stay home, so she couldn't even go out for a ride with him. The medicine the doctor prescribed for her nerves seemed to shut her off from other people; now she sat silently at the table, wrapped in her thoughts and her ailments. George thought he might as well go to work.

Then he remembered that he didn't have to go to the office today; it was a holiday, Independence Day, and there'd be nothing but crowds and noise downtown with the parade and all. So why not take a drive out in the country by himself . . . and maybe swing by the Harper place? With her folks away in Omaha, Grace would be taking care of the farm, so it wouldn't be a bad idea to make sure she was getting along all right. And with Dan at the convention, she might be glad to have company.

Maybe take a buggy ride, and maybe go for a swim.

Maybe she'd like that. She might be kind of lonely.

George hitched up the horse, threw a shirt and trousers in the back of the buggy to wear swimming, and drove off. He didn't tell Mary where he was going, and she didn't ask. He chose a roundabout route; there would be less traffic, and anyway where he went was nobody's business but his own.

When he pulled up at the Harper house, Grace came to the door. If she was surprised to see him, she didn't let on; as usual, she was cool and self-possessed. It turned out she was alone, brother Charlie having gone to town to take part in the holiday high jinks. A couple of minutes later George was sitting on the porch with a glass of cold buttermilk in his hand, jacket off and collar loosened, making small talk.

It was all very easy and amiable, and when he suggested a drive Grace agreed without hesitation. She went to fetch a sunbonnet and gloves. When she returned, George had another suggestion.

"What would you think about a swim, too? We might get a little warm driving around in the sun. In fact, you know, I brought some old clothes along because I thought I might stop for a dip. D'you think that would be fun?"

Grace sensed adventure. It did sound like fun, the more so for seeming just a little wicked. That was a feeling George seemed to evoke—a feeling she enjoyed, one she didn't often get from Dan. And anyway, why should she sit out here all alone when Dan was enjoying himself in Omaha?

"Why, I think that would be nice, George. It *is* a warm day, and it might cool us off." She went back in the house and got an old dress for a bathing costume.

They rode for a while, not saying much, through the early-summer lushness of the prairie. The grass was still green, and it was filled with wildflowers—yellow and light blue, red and purple, all mixed together. They passed cornfields heavy with the earthy smell of early July, pale tassels trembling above wavy-edged green stalks. Under a hazy sun, distant clumps of trees faded into varying shades of blue.

George broke the silence. "I thought we might go over to Round Lake. There's a little sandy beach there and pretty nice water. You know it, don't you?"

"Oh, yes, we used to go there sometimes." Without quite knowing why, Grace went on: "I know another place, and I bet you've never seen it. It's on the river where it crosses our land. The water's nice and deep, and there's a little grove of trees."

She added, again without conscious purpose: "And there won't be a lot of people there, because not many from town know about it."

[75]

That last comment drew a quizzical look from George. "Why, that sounds good. You just show me how to go."

She told him to head back to their farm. There she directed him across a strip of pasture and down into a little grove of cottonwood trees shading a bend in the stream. When she stole a glance at him from under the brim of her bonnet, he was looking at her, too. Neither of them spoke.

They changed quickly—Grace behind a clump of small trees—and splashed into the water. A duck and ducklings, paddling around the edge of the stream, swam away. It hadn't rained for a week, so the water was relatively clear.

Grace swam back and forth in a determined way; George paddled intermittently and floated on his back, watching her. After a few minutes they stood up, she shoulder-deep in the current that shaped the high-necked dress she was wearing. It felt good to let the water tug at her clothes.

"Feels fine, doesn't it?" Grace shook the water from her head as she spoke, the drops glistening in the sun as they landed around her.

"Oh, yes." George squeezed water from his face. "And it feels good to be having a good time. I haven't had much of that recently."

"Oh?"

"Well, you know, Mary's been sick a lot, and more than that she's been unhappy, kind of closed off. She hasn't . . . it hasn't been a very happy household, I guess is one way to say it."

Grace realized that George was staring hard at her, and he seemed to be standing awfully close. Suddenly she felt hot under her cool wet dress. Confused, she splashed off to swim some more.

This time he simply stood and watched her for a long minute, then dove under the surface. He came up beside her, and without a word, lifted her and carried her out of the creek and up the bank under the trees.

Water ran from her face and arms as he stood her up and held her at arm's length. "I never knew a girl could look so pretty wringing wet." His voice was thick in his throat. "You look just the way you did last summer at the lake."

His hands moved behind her, unbuttoning the dress, and a small voice called to her from a great distance, telling her that it was time to stop. She shut out the voice so she wouldn't hear it any more, and then there was only the sound of her own pulse. It, too, seemed to speak to her.

Shouldn't . . . shouldn't . . . shouldn't . . . shouldn't . . .

George managed the last button. The top of the dress fell forward, and she shivered as the cool air raised goose bumps on her bare wet skin. George's mouth found the hollow of her neck.

Shouldn't . . . shouldn't . . . shouldn't . . .

With a great effort she managed to speak. "Someone could come along anytime."

[76]

He lifted his head just long enough to dismiss the idea. "They're all in town, celebrating the Fourth."

Why, that's right, she thought, *it's Independence Day.*

Afterward, lying beside him under the trees, her pulse was slower.

Shouldn't have . . . shouldn't have . . . shouldn't have . . .

She moved drowsily in the mingled sunlight and shade. The sun was almost directly overhead, and she closed her eyes against its brightness. An intermittent breeze brushed her body. It was midday in midsummer, and the world seemed suspended in humid heat.

. . . But I don't care. It was nice. I wanted to.

Grace knew what she had done was wrong, but she also knew that it wouldn't happen again with George. Even as they lay side by side, still touching, she felt the distance between them grow.

Now that he's been with me, he won't come around again. I won't seem as sweet to him. And he's a very careful man. He doesn't care for me, not a bit. . . . He wanted me, that's all.

She knew the same was true for her: she had wanted him, just for a moment, just once, and that was all.

A cloud crossed in front of the sun. She stretched again and opened her eyes, then sat up, arms around her knees. The breeze sprang up, stronger and cooler, pulling her back from the place she'd been.

She stood up and walked over to the little clump of trees to retrieve her clothes.

Next time I come here I'll be with Dan.

Chapter 10

FROM THE MOMENT Dan stepped off the train in Omaha he was caught up in a continuous swirl of people. The Populists flooded railroad stations, trolley cars, streets, sidewalks, auditoriums, stores, restaurants, hotel lobbies, stairways, hallways, elevators—and any other place where two or more people could be squeezed together. There was no escaping the crowd: it oozed, it flowed, it surged, it steamed.

Dan carried his suitcase the three blocks to the Millard Hotel. By the time he arrived he was wringing wet with sweat and numb with noise. When he finally got his room key, there was no bellboy to be found, so he hauled his bag three flights up the crowded stairway to his floor. He could hardly breathe the close, stale air.

Why do they have conventions in this weather? he wondered. *I'll bet the people who decide have never been to Omaha in July.*

In his room at last, Dan pulled off jacket, tie, collar, and shirt, then splashed cold water over his face and neck. Temporarily refreshed, he walked over to the window and looked down on the street.

What struck him most was the difference between these delegates and the Republicans he had seen a month ago in Minneapolis. There, faces had been well barbered and sleek; here most were bearded and sunburnt, with the contrasting pale forehead that is the farmer's trademark. The Republican delegates favored plug hats and well-polished shoes, while this crowd ran to slouch hats and rough boots. Most of the men sweltered in dark wool suits; the women wore cotton or homespun dresses and poke bonnets. They worked with their hands and lived in the country, in marked contrast to the people who had dominated the earlier convention.

It wasn't just their looks, either. For many, perhaps most, the People's party was a first venture into politics, and their energy and optimism were untempered by previous disappointment or acquired cynicism. Everything was new, anything was possible.

Dan walked downstairs into the packed hotel lobby, where waves of excited talk were punctuated by outbreaks of laughter and even bursts of song.

> The old party is on the downward track,
> Good-bye, my party, good-bye.
> Picking its teeth with a tariff tack,
> Good-bye, my party, good-bye.
> With a placard pinned upon my back
> That plainly states "I will never go back";
> Good-bye, my party, good-bye.

Edging around the lobby, hoping to find someone he knew, Dan ran into a couple of the Eastern reporters he'd met at the Republican convention; to judge from their jokes about "crackpots" and "hayseeds," they weren't taking this one too seriously. One of them, a large, amiable fellow from the *Boston Globe* named James Morgan, quizzed him.

"What do you think, Woods? Will the farmers go for Gresham?"

There was a fundamental split among Populists—between the "fusionists," who believed the only way to win was to broaden the party's political base, and the "middle-of-the-roaders," who believed any ties to the old parties would sap the party's moral authority and doctrinal fervor.

The fusionists proposed nominating Walter Gresham, a respected Indiana judge, a Republican who had split with his party on the tariff question and had influential Democratic friends—in short, a man who could draw support from outside the Populist ranks. The favorite candidate of the middle-of-the-roaders was James B. Weaver of Iowa, a Civil War general and a veteran of protest politics who had been the Greenback party's presidential candidate in 1880.

Dan didn't hesitate in answering Morgan.

"Jim, I just can't see it. I don't think these people will vote for a man who's never been in the party or worked for what they believe in."

Morgan snorted. "Huh! What *do* they believe in, besides having the government take over the railroads and print money to give to people who won't work?"

"I'll tell you one thing they believe, and that's that the two old parties don't give a damn for farmers." Dan was irritated by Morgan's gibe, and his voice revealed it. "That's the root of it all, they're just plain fed up. Everybody takes a bite out of the farmer, until he's nibbled to death."

His temper faded as he went on. "At least that's how they see it. What they believe in is the St. Louis platform—the one they adopted in February. Unlimited silver coinage, more money in circulation, an income tax, foreigners not allowed to own land, the government taking over the railroads: that's about all there is to it."

This last remark sent Morgan into a fit of laughter. "Oh, is that all?" he finally spluttered. "Just a few minor changes, eh?"

Across the lobby, a group of Texans in identical white cowboy hats announced their arrival with a chorus of Comanche war whoops. From around the big room came an answering chorus of coyote hoots, rebel yells, whistles, and shouts. The reporters grinned at each other and shook their heads, acknowledging the impossibility of further conversation. Dan went to convention headquarters on the second floor to pick up his press badge—and to collect the latest rumors about the nomination.

A couple of Chicago reporters came in and said Weaver had just agreed to nominate Gresham. But an Iowa editor brought word that Weaver had denied it and demanded that Gresham state whether he would accept a Populist nomination. Then Ignatius Donnelly of Minnesota strode into the room and said no offer should be made to anyone unless the convention knew it would be accepted.

"We can't afford to give such a prize away to have it hurled back into our faces," Donnelly told a crowd of reporters. "And the nomination should go to some man whose record on the platform to be adopted is without question."

Middle-of-the-road Populists shared that view. "The man we choose must stand on the St. Louis platform with his toes and heels down," Amos Harper told Dan. "He should at least have warmed the seat of his trousers in the new party."

The dispute over the nomination didn't seem to bother the Populists jammed into the headquarters hotel. That night, at an impromptu mass meeting in the multistory lobby of the Millard, more than a thousand voices bellowed out "Glory hallelujah" and cheered a string of Populist orators who spoke from the landing of the main stairway.

The star of the evening was Mary Lease. As always, her voice was like old gold, deep and burnished and rich, and she used it to seize her audience by the throat.

> I want to speak of monopoly of land. Never in the history of
> the world has landlordism assumed such proportions as in America
> today. And not the land alone; the oil, the coal, the roads, the water,
> are owned by the soft-handed dude, the idler who has never
> produced an ear of corn or any other needed thing in all the world.

It was raw meat to this crowd, and an answering growl filled the lobby. Mary Lease fed the anger:

[80]

Thirty-five percent of the farmers of Kansas have become
tenants. Ah, you say, those Kansas farmers! Lazy! But listen:
Thirty-seven percent of the farmers of rich Ohio are renting from
landlords. And meanwhile the government still labors to decrease the
currency!

There was more applause from the floor and stairways and balconies
where men and women stood packed together. Mrs. Lease went on, lowering her voice almost to a whisper as she closed with a string of biblical
phrases.

God has sown in our souls the seeds of his millennial harvest.
We have a high and holy mission to perform. Ours be the mission to
blaze the path down which all nations of the earth shall walk till
they feel the fatherhood of God—and the brotherhood of man.

She stopped, and for a moment there was no sound. Then a shouted
"A-men!" came from somewhere in the crowd, and the hall erupted with
applause.

Dan, standing on an upper balcony, felt the surge of emotion in the
crowd. *It's like a revival meeting: they believe, but they don't know exactly
what they believe in,* he thought. *That's all right in church, but it might not
work too well in politics.*

It was midnight before the hotel quieted enough so that Dan could
get to sleep.

Dan clambered to his seat in the press section Monday morning. No one
expected real political fireworks on this first day; only a couple of hundred
delegates were present when the convention chairman banged his gavel for
order. But the atmosphere changed as more delegates poured in. By the
time the hall was two-thirds full, they were alive, buzzing, expectant,
waiting for an excuse to erupt.

It came on a relatively minor matter—a resolution deploring the
refusal of railroads to give Populists the same special fares they had offered
delegates to the Republican and Democratic conventions.

Little, white-haired Marion Cannon of California climbed up on a
chair to speak. "All we asked was the same privilege granted to the bankers," he shouted. "They refused. Well, we will not humble ourselves so
much as to again ask this reduced rate." The crowd applauded; Cannon's
voice rose.

"We want it distinctly understood," he said, bearing down on each
word, "that we will . . . *own* . . . and . . . *operate* . . . that Pacific line!"

The hall exploded in cheers and shouts. Men jumped up and down,
embraced each other, threw hats in the air; women waved handkerchiefs.
Cannon's thin, tired voice had touched a central nerve: they hated the

railroads, and they deeply believed in a government takeover. This was not anger over a single incident; something deeper was driving these men and women to an emotional frenzy. Dan, standing on a bench to look out over the crowd, noticed that even people in the outer lobbies were joining the uproar.

Dan looked around the floor. Everywhere he saw rage, naked anger, even hatred. *They really hate the railroads, don't they? All those years of frustration and failure, of getting pushed around and cheated and exploited, all busting out right now.*

But even knowing all that, even amid the shouts and cheers, Dan wondered about these farmers.

Sure, they're right about the railroads, but a lot of it's their own fault. They don't handle their land right, they plant the wrong crops, they won't face facts about the weather.

He looked around. *There are damned few here like Amos Harper. Most of 'em do it wrong, and fail—and blame everyone but themselves.*

Like my Pa.

Dan returned to the hall after lunch, his stomach complaining about the stale bread, dry cheese, and lukewarm beer that had made up his midday meal. *I have a lot to learn about politics,* he mused, working a toothpick, *but one thing I already know: Conventions are hard on the belly.*

When the platform committee reported at midafternoon the delegates were ready to holler again. They cheered almost every sentence of the document as it was read. The plank on railroads drew the most fervent response:

> The time has come when the railroad corporations will either own the people or the people must own the railroads. . . .
> Transportation being a means of exchange and a public necessity, the government should own and operate the railroads in the interest of the people.

But the cheers were almost as loud for other planks.

> We demand free and unlimited coinage of silver and gold at the present legal ratio. . . .
> We demand that the amount of the circulating medium be speedily increased to not less than fifty dollars per capita.
> We demand a graduated income tax. . . .
> We demand that postal savings banks be established by the government for the safe deposit of the earnings of the people. . . .
> The telegraph and telephone, like the post-office system, being a necessity for the transmission of news, should be owned and operated by the government in the interest of the people.

[82]

There was an edge of anger in the roar that greeted the platform's provision on land ownership:

> The land, including all the natural sources of wealth, is the heritage of the people, and should not be monopolized for speculative purposes, and alien ownership of land should be prohibited. All land now held by railroads and other corporations in excess of their actual needs, and all lands now owned by aliens, should be reclaimed by the government and held for actual settlers only.

By the time the reading was done, the hall was in almost continuous uproar. Several dozen men shouted motions to adopt the platform, and when the chairman banged his gavel and declared it done, the crowd erupted again.

Behind Dan, a reporter for the *Omaha World-Herald* dictated a running story to a telegraph operator, who worked his key steadily to transmit it in time for the paper's late edition. Dan leaned back a little to hear the reporter, who was shouting into the operator's ear to make himself heard over the din:

"Spontaneous comma electrifying comma almost menacing comma deep from the lungs it came stop. It had none of the qualities that mark the enthusiasm of the old parties stop. It did not even have the ring of triumph stop."

The reporter paused to let the telegrapher catch up. Dan marveled at their smooth teamwork as the reporter resumed without missing a beat.

"It was the shout of desperate men who were marching to battle comma and who comma though uncertain of the outcome comma were prepared to fight and fall by what they considered right stop."

"No hired claque was there to stretch the applause out to a desirable length stop. Irresistible as the shriek of pain that follows long and silent torture was this terrible cheer of men who were in that convention for an idea stop."

Great stuff, Dan thought, *and he hasn't even got it written down, he just dictates it off the top of his head. I wonder if I can ever learn that?*

The *World-Herald* man waited again, then went on.

"These men were not concerned with office stop. They were not shouting because they hoped for spoils stop. They were crying for liberty to work and to win the natural results of toil stop. They were asking for a right to live stop."

Jim Morgan of the *Boston Globe,* sitting in front of Dan, turned around and pulled him closer.

"I think you're right, kiddo." He was shouting, too, but Dan had to strain to make out what he was saying. "This is the damnedest convention I've ever seen. They're hollering about ideas, for God's sake!"

[83]

Dan grinned and nodded agreement. "Now you got it!" he yelled back at the Bostonian. Dan noticed most of the national reporters who had been snickering at the people and ideas of this convention were now frantically scribbling notes.

The convention band played its whole repertoire—"Dixie," "Marching Through Georgia," "Yankee Doodle," "Maryland, My Maryland," and, again and again, "The Girl I Left Behind Me."

State standards bobbed up and down as they were carried around the floor. A growing procession of delegates and spectators followed the standards; Dan was startled to see Amos Harper bouncing along behind the South Dakota standard and bellowing out the words to some song. *Grace will never believe it.*

The sound would fade a little, then burst out in some distant corner of the hall, spreading until it seemed that every one of the ten thousand people present must be shouting. Finally, after thirty-seven minutes, the chairman's gavel began to take effect.

Dan could feel the emotion drain away like water from an emptying sink, swirling and receding until the last remnant gurgled away, leaving only exhaustion.

The nomination that night was an anticlimax. When it was over at midnight, Weaver had nearly four times as many votes as his nearest competitor. Dan finished his story at four o'clock in the morning, handed the final page to a telegraph operator, and walked back to the hotel in the last hour of darkness.

He had never experienced anything remotely like it: ten thousand people caught up, exalted, moved, lifted by nothing but *ideas.*

Falls City, July 1892

Grace and her brother Charlie drove in to meet their parents when they came home from Omaha. She was on the platform, chatting with her mother, when Dan stepped off the same train and came up to them.

"Dan has been such a help," Lydia Harper said. "Why, he just explained so much to me about what was happening. I wouldn't have had half so good a time if he hadn't been so thoughtful."

"It wasn't anything, really," Dan told Grace. He looked at her and knew he was home. *Hello, Grace. I missed you. I'd like to show you how much. Right now.*

Grace, reading his look, tried to return it in kind. "I'm sure you were a big help. I wish I could have been there."

He looks good. A door snapped shut in her mind. *That's over and done with, and it doesn't have anything to do with us. We're all right.*

"Maybe I can come out and see you this weekend," Dan said.

[84]

"Maybe." Grace ducked her head and looked up mockingly at him. "If you can spare the time."

"Oh, I think I can steal an hour or so." Dan's tone was light too, but he turned toward Grace for just a moment and spoke softly but urgently under the station clatter. "I love you."

Grace felt a catch in her throat and mouthed a silent response, but when she spoke she kept up her offhand tone. "I'd be glad to have you come, if you can get away from your newspaper, and your politics."

Dan certainly could get away from his newspaper, and that night on the Harper porch not a word was said about politics.

September–October 1892

It was hard to get very far from politics that autumn. Dan heard plenty of public argument, but he also had a front-row seat for something better: the private debate between George Norton and Amos Harper. The clash between businessman and farmer—the central struggle of this campaign in the Dakotas—was on display right there in Norton's office, usually late on Saturday after Amos finished his weekly shopping.

"No, no, *no,*" the publisher was saying one September afternoon as Dan came into his office. "You seem to think the government can just create money out of blank paper with nothing to back it up."

"Why not?" Harper was equally insistent. "The government's already done it. They lent the Union Pacific railroad fifty million dollars, and then gave it more millions worth of land it could sell to cover the loans. Now all the land has been sold, and not one penny of the fifty million has been paid back. That's creating money out of nothing if I ever saw it."

The farmer leaned forward, hands planted heavily on his knees. "And so is letting the moneylenders charge so much interest that they collect in one month what the money costs them for a whole year."

Norton shrugged. "Look, Amos, I know some of those Eastern bankers are greedy."

"The farmer who's getting strung up doesn't care who's doing it. He just wants it to stop."

"He wants it to stop so much that when some patent medicine salesman takes a gill of fact and passes it off as a gallon of grievance, your farmer swallows it all," George growled. "The fact is, what's good for my bank or Woods Brothers store is good for you and the other farmers too. You ought to be telling your people to think things through instead of swallowing that socialist nonsense about taking over the railroads."

"They *have* thought, and that's why you Republicans are so scared." Amos thumped the publisher's desk. "Look, George, these people aren't fools or loafers. They've worked hard for a long time and they can't get ahead. All they want is a fair return on their work. If that's socialism, you're for it, too."

George laughed. "That's a point for you, Amos. You're getting to be quite a debater. Too quick for me."

"That'll be the day." It was Harper's turn to laugh. "You're as quick as it's safe to let anyone be."

"Well, I'll tell you one thing," Norton said. "I'm quick enough to comprehend that taking over the railroads is the short route to tyranny. Three-quarters of a million men work for the railroads, and if the government took over the companies, the party in power would have every one of those men. And then that party could never be put out of office."

Amos roared with laughter. "Now, come on, George, that's plain preposterous. You must have got it out of some Eastern paper."

"Maybe there's some truth in those Eastern papers," George said. "Dan says they had first-rate men at the conventions."

Amos winked at Dan as he answered Norton.

"I know how those fellows work," he said. "Some street-corner windbag in Omaha talks to ten people and gets written up in the local paper because it's a slow day. By the time the story gets into the papers in the East, it's turned into a mass meeting that started a whole new movement. That about right, Dan?"

Dan wasn't about to get caught between the two older men. "I'll let you two argue about it. Most of those fellows are good reporters, but once in a while they do stretch a story out a bit."

"Which *you* never do," Amos shot back.

"Never!" George spoke before Dan could open his mouth, and the editor noticed an unaccustomed twinkle in the publisher's eye.

He's sticking up for me and having fun doing it, Dan thought. *He isn't usually this lively. Come to think of it, I've never heard him laugh before.*

"I know your people aren't all crackpots." George was serious again. "But Amos, they have to learn to think harder. Who's going to benefit from making a lot of new silver coins? Why, the men in Boston and New York who own the silver mines, that's who. Not the little business people around here. Certainly not the farmers. So make them *think.* Set out the facts and let common sense go to work."

Norton was into one of his favorite speeches about politics—and newspapers: lay out the arguments on all sides, let people make their own decisions, and they'll mostly come out right. Dan had heard the sermon often enough to know it by heart. He excused himself and went out onto the sidewalk.

As he looked back through the window Norton and Harper were waggling forefingers at each other, deep in argument again.

★ ★ ★

At the big Populist rally at the new fairgrounds, the candidates faced a grandstand crowded with five thousand people. Several hundred more stood or sat in the bright October sunshine around the speakers' platform.

Grace settled down beside Dan in the front row of the grandstand.

"I must say you newspaper people get good seats." She spoke softly. "I don't think I'm supposed to be sitting here."

"There's lots of room," he said. "Don't worry, nobody'll mind. Just don't talk to me when I'm trying to take notes."

He thought he'd be taking lots of notes; General Weaver was the main speaker, and Weaver's managers were counting on this single appearance in Falls City to carry the state.

But Weaver gave the friendly crowd nothing more than his standard stump speech, attacking Eastern moneylenders, bankers, railroads, "gold bugs"—the Populist litany. The candidate used old-time oratory to attack modern business:

> That struggle is still on, and now it is thundering at our gates with renewed energy. It will not down, though the Trust heap Ossa upon Pelion. The people will rise and overturn the despoilers, though they shake the earth by the displacement.

There was a salvo of applause. Grace spoke to Dan under the cover of the crowd's noise.

"Is he promising an election—or an earthquake?"

Dan smothered a smile. "It's old stuff," he muttered. "He sounds tired to me."

"Well, his talk certainly is."

Again and again the crowd shouted agreement with Weaver's words. But Grace shook her head, and Dan recalled something her father had said back in July: it was too bad the Populists couldn't find someone who wasn't shopworn. Weaver seemed to have nothing but old answers for new questions, an old response to a new opportunity.

November 1892

It wasn't good enough. The Populists elected ten members of Congress and enough state legislators to control the election of U.S. senators in five states. But in the presidential contest they fell far short. Weaver polled more than a million votes, but he failed to break old-party habits: in the West, the Republicans held onto Minnesota, Iowa, Nebraska, and South Dakota; in the South, the Democrats held every state, and Grover Cleveland won back the White House.

Dan sat with Amos Harper and George Norton as they talked it over on the Saturday afternoon after election day.

"George, your face is so long you could eat oats from a churn," Amos said. "You should be happy. You've got Grover Cleveland, and he's a gold bug, like you."

"I'm a Republican. Cleveland's not." Norton's voice was flat, his eyes unblinking, but he couldn't quite suppress a smile. "But I guess he'll do. What happened to your man, anyway?"

Amos shifted his big body. "Oh, three-four things." His tone was analytical, dispassionate. "We couldn't get enough farmers to break away from the old parties when it came time to vote for president. And things have been a little bit better this year. Prices are still low, but the crop was pretty good, and when things are even halfway good, farmers forget awful fast."

Norton smiled. "You mean they're like other people."

"No, they're worse. Something about farming makes a man forget ten years of trouble when he gets one good crop." Harper paused. "Actually I believe the Populist party is in bad shape."

He smiled at the surprise on the faces of his listeners, then cracked his knuckles as he continued. "We have to face facts. We didn't do well enough in this part of the country, we lost the whole South, we were never even in the race in the East, and the states that did go for us did it because of silver, not because they're Populists."

Norton shook his head. "Everybody else tells me the Populists did very well, got a million votes the first time out, showed they're stronger, gaining ground, that kind of thing. I reckoned we'd have an even bigger fight next time."

"That may be, but if we do, the Populists won't be leading it." He spread his heavy hands in a helpless gesture. "Look, our new party's barely born and it's already being taken over. People just don't realize it."

"I don't understand what you're talking about." Dan, fascinated, broke in.

"Why, it's simple enough." Amos shrugged. "The silver people got their nose under the tent this year, so now they'll push even harder. A lot of farmers think silver means cheap money, and that sounds so good to them that they forget what the party really stands for, things that really matter most."

Amos took a deep breath. "What's worse, the Democrats will likely take up silver as *their* issue, and the Populists . . . well, we'll be sucking hind tit."

"What are you going to do, Amos?" Dan was struck by the certainty in the farmer's voice.

"Oh, I'll go back to being a farmer. I haven't been taking very good care of the place these last few years. It needs attention." Harper sighed. "And I might have a little more time with the family, get to know my wife again, teach Charlie how to run the farm."

He looked at Dan, and the blue eyes twinkled. "I might even spend some time with Grace—while she's still around the place."

Chapter 11

AMOS HARPER may have had more time to spend with Grace, but Dan did not. Mary Norton delivered a baby boy a week after election day, and her husband was so delighted that he virtually disappeared from the office. That left Dan to put out the paper and keep an eye on the business side, too—a double handful that occupied him early and late.

He did take time, at the publisher's urging, to inspect the baby. He turned out to be large and active, with a fat face and a voice that rattled windows.

Dan searched for something to say that would pass for a compliment. "He sure is . . . energetic, isn't he?"

"Oh, yes indeed," George said. "And smart, too. Isn't he, dear?"

Mary Norton smiled and nodded. She spoke slowly, and her voice seemed to come from a distance. "Oh, yes . . . like his father."

Looking at her, Dan thought: *It's like she's asleep. I haven't seen her for a while, and she has surely gained weight. Her face and hands are all puffy. She's always been plump, but now she's plain fat.*

"Take a good look at him, Dan," Norton went on. "Won't be long before you're teaching him how to put out the newspaper."

Dan laughed. "Isn't it a little soon to be choosing his career? He might want some say in that."

George was dead serious. "No, you're looking at the next publisher of the *Dakota Daily News,* make no mistake about it."

Dan glanced at Mary Norton again. She seemed completely oblivious to the conversation. *She's acting funny. There's something really wrong with her. . . . I wonder if she's still using that nerve medicine.*

"Well, George," he said, "you may be right. He may turn out to have printer's ink in his veins. But let him be a little boy first, will you?"

"Of course." Norton's tone told Dan that subject was closed, but he remained in a genial mood. "You've been carrying a double load this past week, Dan. I'll come in early tomorrow and catch up. I want you to take a few days off."

Dan promptly took him up on that offer; he had something he wanted very much to do. That business was the reason he was waiting with a horse and buggy outside Central School the next day when classes ended. Students poured out first, then teachers, including Grace and his sister, Emma. He waved at them as they emerged into the cold, blustery afternoon.

"How about a ride, ladies?"

They were surprised. Emma glanced at Grace. "Thank you, Dan, but I'm going straight home. I may as well walk."

"No, hop in, we'll drop you off. Grace and I are going for a drive."

"Oh, are we?" Grace didn't like having other people make her plans for her, even when the other person was Dan. "It so happens I rode my horse into town today. And what are you doing gallivanting around in the middle of the day?"

"We'll hitch Punkin in back of the buggy." Dan was brisk. "And I took the afternoon off because the publisher thought I'd been working too hard. Now hop in, both of you."

He handed the two women up into the buggy and drove over to the livery stable at Tenth and Main to collect Grace's horse. Then they climbed the hill and dropped Emma off at the Woods house.

"Now, Mr. Woods, what's this all about?" Grace asked as they started away.

"Why, Miss Harper, I thought this might be the last day nice enough for a ride in the country," Dan said. He was silent for a moment. "And I want to talk to you."

Grace had an odd feeling, a sudden shortness of breath, but she couldn't resist taking a dig. "Really? I'd never have guessed it, the way you've been staying away from me."

"Stop that, Grace." His abrupt tone startled both of them, and he was silent for several minutes while they drove up over the height of land and out onto the farm fields that sloped gently toward the river and the Harper place.

When he spoke again his voice was gentler. "Grace, I've done a lot of thinking the last few weeks. I think it's time we thought about getting married."

She felt as if she'd burst, but she wasn't going to make it easy for him, not after he'd made her wait so long. "Well," she said, trying to sound matter-of-fact, "what do you think we should do after we think about it?"

"Grace." There was that tone again; Dan wouldn't be teased today. "Grace, listen to me. I love you, you know that. Will you marry me?"

She started to say something, but found she could not speak. Then her arms were around his neck, and his cheek was wet with her tears.

After some little time Dan retrieved the reins and slapped them across the horse's rump. "We better get a move on," he said. "I have to talk to your father."

Amos Harper gave his consent instantly. He expressed his reservations later to Grace.

"I like him fine, Gracie. But you're marrying into a family of failures. I hope Dan does better than his father and his uncle."

"He will."

Her voice was cool but her eyes were intense.

"And if he doesn't, you'll straighten him out, is that it?" Amos laughed and swept his tall daughter into a hug. "He'll be all right."

"To the happy couple, and God bless." Henry Woods lifted his glass. Amos Harper echoed the toast.

The two families were at the Harpers' for Thanksgiving dinner. Lydia had agreed to let Eudora bring the pies; Henry produced wine for a celebratory toast. Charlie Harper and Emma Woods made it eight at the cheerful, noisy table.

Now, with dinner over, Henry and Amos were alone at the table. Their wives were in the kitchen; the four young people had bundled up and gone off for a ride. Amos undid the top button of his trousers to ease his midsection as Henry mused about Dan and Grace.

"Makes a man feel a little old to see his child getting married." Henry stretched his stiff leg to ease a cramp. Amos, noting the movement, thought again that Henry wasn't looking so good these days.

They listened for a minute or two more to the kitchen sounds. Then Henry stood up. "I don't know about you, Amos," he said, "but if I don't get some fresh air I'm going to fall asleep right here in this chair."

They walked down toward the river in the fading light of a cold, gray afternoon, past cattle scavenging through the stubble of the previous month's corn harvest.

"You can almost feel it getting ready to snow," Amos said. "It just kind of hangs up there in the clouds this time of year. Seems like the animals and the land feel it too."

"Your place looks good, even at this time of year," Henry said. He both envied and admired Amos, who not only had first-rate land but also took better care of it than any other farmer around. *That's why he comes through the bad years that bust a lot of other men,* Henry thought. *Like the year that busted me. What does he do that I didn't? Or was it just bad luck that got me?*

"You have to take care of the land," Amos said, as if answering Henry's unspoken question. "That's what a lot of these fellows don't know, or forget. They plow every acre every year, never let the land rest. The soil can't stand that, any more than a man can go without sleep."

He waved a big hand at his well-tended farmland. "Keeping up soil fertility will do more for South Dakota farmers in the next hundred years than any new machinery anyone could dream up."

"You keep an awful lot of land in grass," Henry said.

"That's what the Almighty meant for this country. You can grow wheat and corn in good years, but this land's really meant for grazing. Keep plowing it, it'll dry up and blow away."

Amos shook his head.

"Some of 'em never learn. The land is always there. It rewards them that use it right—and breaks the ones who don't. Stay in harmony with nature, you survive, maybe even prosper. Go against it and you lose every time." To himself, Amos added: *The way you lost that place in Nebraska.*

Henry Woods was looking across Amos's rich fields, but he too was thinking of that hardscrabble homestead he had abandoned nearly twenty years before. When he spoke again, his voice seemed to come from that other time and place.

"That's what Dora used to tell me down in Nebraska. She was mostly right, too."

Amos watched Henry out of the corner of his eye. *The bullet he took in the war wasn't the only thing that left a mark on him,* he mused. *He fought the Rebels and he won, but when he went up against nature he lost. He's stubborn. That kept him alive at Gettysburg—but it beat him on the claim. He didn't do right by nature, and nature broke him.*

They turned back toward the house. A few snowflakes, big as goose down, began to drift down.

February 1893

Lydia and Eudora suggested a summer wedding, but Grace and Dan wouldn't hear of it: they didn't want to wait another week, let alone six months. So families and friends crowded into the Harper parlor on a bright, cold February afternoon. Dan stood stiffly in a new suit, his cowlick momentarily under control; Grace dazzled everybody; afterward there was plenty to eat and drink.

Dan and Grace spent the night in her upstairs bedroom. A dozen of their friends, bundled to the eyes against the iron cold, stood under the window and serenaded them with bells, whistles, and much banging of pots and pans. Then they were alone, oblivious to anything beyond the compass of their own embrace.

"How was I so lucky as to catch you?" Dan whispered, some time later. Grace snuggled down into the warmth of the bed and put her lips to his ear.

"You were ripe," she murmured. "All I had to do was spread my apron and kick the tree, and you dropped right into it." *Of course I had to kick pretty hard.*

Grace woke up once, in the middle of the night. She slid out of bed and pulled back the window curtain. The moonlight fell across Dan's face as he slept.

It's certainly true about still waters running deep. She reached over and touched his cheek with her fingertips. *Oh, Mr. Woods. It's all right now. Oh, my, yes.*

Three months later, Dan and Grace were still all right, but a lot of others were not. By late spring, the Panic of '93 had the country in its grip. The stock market dropped, dropped again, then collapsed in early May. More banks and businesses were failing every week. There was talk of the government running out of gold; the Treasury's reserves were shrinking at an alarming rate.

Closer to home, there were the beginnings of drought, and George Norton noted the early signs of a real depression: subscriptions unpaid, accounts overdue, merchants cutting back or even eliminating their ads.

"It's the same at the bank," George told Dan. "There's more loans in arrears every week. More people are coming in trying to borrow, but money's drying up. We're in for a bad time."

Dan thought the publisher's tone was almost cheerful, as if he was looking forward to the fight.

"We'll have to go at it hard to come out whole," George continued. "But it's a great chance for us if we do things right. If we can get through the next three years—"

"Three years!" Dan was shocked at this estimate of the duration of the depression.

"Yes, this is going to be a bad one. Probably the worst since the war. But it'll be a great chance for people who take sensible risks. We're going to do that, and watch the other fellows run for cover, and when it's over we'll be ready to rip."

"What do you want me to do?"

"Just keep putting out a paper that people think they can't do without. We've gotten a lot of new subscribers in the past year or so, and it's up to you to hold 'em. I'll take care of the business side."

"Can we keep the new people we've hired?"

"We're not going to lay people off. We may come to that, but it's the last thing we should do, not the first. We need more news, not less, especially now. But . . ." George stopped.

Dan took a chance. "But what?"

"But please don't make anybody mad except on purpose," the publisher said. He looked at Dan with his hard, flat stare. "We're going to need all the friends we've got. You may have to make some enemies, but don't do it without good reason."

Lounsberry's letter arrived at the end of July.

> Dear Dan:
>
> I am going out to Washington next month to see what they're doing about the Panic, gold, &c. I thought you might like to come along. It's time you got to know the place, what they do there is more & more important to us here as time goes on. I can promise you some good eating.
>
> Your friend, C. L.

Dan showed the letter to Norton. "I do need to learn how things work in Washington," he told the publisher. "And he's right, there's a lot happening now." Cleveland had called Congress back in special session to deal with the Panic and the gold problem.

"You editors always want to go somewhere," Norton grumbled. "We've got to save money."

Dan sensed a lack of real urgency in his publisher's objection. "I know, George. But you're the one who told me we need more news, not less, especially because of the Panic. And this story is the most important one to our people right now. We'd be the only paper in the state to have someone on the spot when they vote."

"Oh, I know, but—"

"If we just use what comes over the wires it won't make sense to our readers. But if I find out what's really going on, I can explain it so it will make sense to people."

Norton stared at Dan. "Well, maybe at least it'd teach you not to swallow all this silver nonsense. All right, go ahead. But don't stay too long." His look changed, and Dan saw the ghost of a smile. "And don't spend too much of my money on that good eating."

Washington, D.C., August 1893

Dan had never been so hot in his whole life. Dakota summers were scorchers, but in Washington just breathing made you sweat, and if you walked a block you were soaking wet. Dan envied the local residents in their white cotton suits; at least they *looked* comfortable.

Dan and Lounsberry spent most of their time in the labyrinthine hallways and chambers of the Capitol, watching the first skirmishes of a new political war.

"They say it's a fight between gold and silver," Lounsberry mused as they waited to see a congressman. "But that's only the top layer of it. The real fight is between lenders and borrowers—between those that own money and those that have to borrow it."

"But the fight is over this bill that Cleveland's put in," Dan protested. "The one to stop making silver dollars."

"I know. But it's the borrowers, the debtors, who want to keep putting out more silver dollars. And it's the lenders who want to stop that."

Lounsberry gestured as he tried to explain.

"Look, it's like this: people who lend, the bankers and mortgage companies, they want the government to stop making silver dollars, so there'll be fewer dollars in circulation and each one they take in will be worth more than it was when they lent it out."

This is awful hard going, Dan thought, *but I've got to get it straight. Thank God for the colonel.*

Lounsberry went on. "But borrowers, farmers with mortgages and so on, they want the government to make even more silver dollars, because that would lower the value of the dollar. Then the fellow who owed money could pay back his loan in dollars that were worth less than the ones he borrowed."

"I think I get that," Dan said, groping. "So it's really rich against poor?"

"More or less. That's why most of the Republicans in Congress seem to be for Cleveland's bill, even though he's a Democrat. And why so many Democrats are against it, like the fellow we're waiting for."

Lounsberry looked across the room. "And here's Mr. Bryan now. Let's see how he tells it."

What Dan noticed first about William Jennings Bryan was his striking manner. The Nebraskan seemed younger than his thirty-three years. He was slim, with a full head of dark hair above a high forehead. His face compelled attention with its long straight nose, strong chin, wide mouth, and intense eyes. And when he spoke, even in casual conversation, it was immediately clear that his voice was an extraordinary political asset.

He was so unassuming in private conversation that Dan was startled at the force of his public manner. He was first exposed to that contrast a few days later when Bryan spoke in the House against Cleveland's bill. Dan had never seen a speaker so completely capture an audience. He was supposed to speak for an hour; he spoke for three, his silvery baritone filling the cavernous chamber, his delivery and gestures flawless.

Why, Bryan asked, were farmers in the West upset? Because they had mortgages—and because the shrinking money supply meant "the mortgage remains nominally the same, but the debt has actually become twice as great."

If a Nebraska farmer were to loan a neighbor a 100-pound hog, he said, and demand to be paid back with a 200-pound hog, he would be called dishonest,

> even though he contended that he was only demanding one hog—just the number he loaned. The poor man who takes property by force is called a thief, but the creditor who can by legislation make a debtor pay a dollar twice as large as he borrowed is praised as the friend of a sound currency.

Bryan waved one arm as he continued.

> On the one side stand the corporate interests of the nation, moneyed institutions, aggregations of wealth and capital, imperious, arrogant, compassionless. They demand special legislation, favors, privileges, and immunities. They can subscribe magnificently to campaign funds and, to those who fawn and flatter, bring ease and plenty.

He gestured in the opposite direction.

> On the other side stands that unnumbered throng which gave a name to the Democratic party and for which it has assumed to speak. Work-worn and dust-begrimed, they make their sad appeal. . . . Their cries for help too often beat in vain against the outer wall, while others less deserving find ready access to legislative halls.

Dan shivered as applause swept the great hall and echoed in the corridors outside. Members crowded around Bryan to congratulate him. His success was more a matter of style than of substance: Dan noticed that when people talked of the speech they usually asked not "What did he say?" but "Did you see him?"

That did not diminish his political success, however, and Dan left Washington sure that he had made the acquaintance of a rising star.

Chicago, October 1893

Two months later, Dan took another trip—this time with Grace, to Chicago and the great world's fair on the Lake Michigan shore.

He hadn't been sure they should go, but she insisted. She hadn't had a proper wedding trip; he could get free passes from the railroad; they could put up at a boardinghouse instead of one of those expensive hotels he usually stayed at. And he could write some articles for the paper about the fair.

So there they were, wandering and wondering, alternately amused and bemused, proud that this great display was in Chicago instead of New York or Philadelphia. It was really a coming of age for the West, and Dan and Grace felt that.

The fair commemorated the past—the four-hundredth anniversary of Columbus's discovery of America—but in fact it was a celebration of the future, a window onto the next century and onto the more complicated, more urban, more sophisticated society that had grown up almost unnoticed in recent years.

By the time the fair closed, more than eleven million people, one in every six Americans, had seen it. For most, it was an introduction to a world they barely knew existed, a world of art and architecture and industry and, above all, of science.

It was that kind of an experience for Dan and Grace, too, and they tried to see it all, hurrying from one huge pavilion to another. They were swallowed up in the vast Manufactures building, a third of a mile long and two hundred feet from floor to ceiling. They were fascinated, and more than a little frightened, by the Palace of Electricity, with its man-made lightning, Thomas Edison's kinetoscope pictures that moved, and all kinds of other electric devices—including one that fascinated Grace: an iron heated by electricity.

"Look at that!" she exclaimed. "Why, that's just magic. You can do all the ironing with just one iron, and you don't have to keep the stove going all day to heat it up, either."

It's a new world, Dan thought, *a million miles away from the old one.*

Again he remembered the sod house, his mother carrying buckets of water and struggling with the old stove, his father wrestling with the plow handles as he limped behind his team.

Ma and Pa were born too soon. They got no help from all these new things that are going to make life easier for Grace and me. Once again Dan felt the familiar mixture of anger and guilt. *Farmers are getting left behind again. These inventions are going to benefit the cities and towns pretty quick, but they'll be a long time getting out to people in the country.*

Of course the fair wasn't all serious. When the inevitable moment arrived each day, when they knew they couldn't absorb one more fact or look at one more scientific wonder, they headed for the Midway. There they gawked at Chinese and Algerian theaters, Persian sword dancers, and Dahomey villagers. They ate Vienna sausages in the Austrian Village and watched lions ride horseback in Hagenbeck's Arena. They had their picture taken perched uneasily on a moth-eaten camel at the Arabian Village.

They were on the Midway again their last afternoon at the fair, listening to the brass band at the German Village.

"I don't think this is much fun." Grace pouted as she tugged at Dan's elbow. "I want to see Little Egypt doing her hootchy-kootchy dance."

"Oh, come on, Grace. That's no place for a lady."

"That's just what a man would say. Maybe I'm not such a lady." Grace squeezed Dan's arm and nudged him with her hip. "Besides, I might learn something."

"You know enough already." Dan grinned at her. "Come on, we're going to ride that Ferris wheel before we go even if we have to stand in line for an hour. Maybe if I get you 250 feet up in the air you'll quiet down."

Falls City, November 1893

Dan was reading galley proofs one gray November morning when the delivery boy from the grocery burst into his office, breathless and scared.

"Your uncle says for you to come quick! Your father's sick!"

Dan ran the four blocks down Lincoln Avenue and over to the Woods Brothers store on Grand. Inside, Henry Woods was on the floor, his face gray and sweaty, his head pillowed by a folded blanket, his brother Benjamin beside him. He barely stirred when Dan grasped his hand. It was cold and clammy.

"I've sent for the doctor, and someone's gone to fetch your Ma," Uncle Ben said. "I think it's his heart. He said he had an awful pain and then he just collapsed."

"He looks awful," Dan said. "Send the boy over to school to fetch Em, too. And hurry!" He put his mouth near his father's ear. "Pa, can you hear me?" He waited, then gently shook his father's arm. "Pa! Pa!"

Henry's eyes slowly focused on Dan's face. "I saw you, standing guard, looking out for your Ma." Dan had to bend close to hear. "Now help me carry things into the house."

Dan saw his father driving the team up the slope and into the Nebraska farmyard after a trip to town, and he knew he was back there now.

Part of him always stayed there on the claim, Dan thought. *That land grabbed hold of him the first day he saw it, and it never let him go, not even when he gave up and left, and it's holding him still.*

The next time Henry Woods spoke he was in a different place.

"They'll come get us after dark. Got to stick it out. . . ." His face twisted with remembered pain. "Damned leg. . . . Stopped them, anyway . . . but no one's left."

Again Dan knew. "He thinks he's back at Gettysburg, out there in that wheat field." He spoke urgently to his father, pleading with him. "Pa, it's going to be all right. The doctor's coming."

Henry shook his head feebly. "They can't come till dark." He tried to swallow. "Thirsty . . ."

Someone brought a dipper of water. Dan started to give him a drink, but then his mother was there, on her knees, taking the dipper from him, cradling her husband's head, helping him take a sip.

Henry recognized her. "Dora . . . turn the corner next year . . . bound to get better." Eudora put her hand on his forehead, trying to quiet him, but the words kept coming, urgent though increasingly faint.

"I know . . . hard for you . . . been awful good. We'll—" There was

[98]

a long pause, and when he spoke again only his wife could hear him. "We'll do a sight better . . . next year."

Eudora put her head down on her husband's chest, holding him tightly. He spoke once more.

"Best get settled before winter." His lips were barely moving now. "Ah, Dora, don't. . . . It'll come all right."

Lydia Harper, Grace, and Emma were in the kitchen with Eudora, washing up and putting away leftovers, but mostly just keeping her company. The friends and neighbors who had come back to the Woods house after the funeral were gone, and the family was alone for the first time since Henry's death.

"Dora, you should be pleased," Lydia said. "The church was so pretty, with those green boughs and all. And it was full right up. Why, I even saw Mr. Norton and his wife."

"I didn't really see who was at the church." Eudora was in a daze. "I do remember George Norton coming by here after. But I didn't see Mary."

"She didn't come," Grace said. "He must have dropped her off after the service. She doesn't go out much, you know."

"She did look kind of far away in church, but I didn't think anything about it," Emma said. "I was listening to Mr. Robinson's eulogy. I believe he really made people think when he talked about how Pa was hurt so bad in the war that it was just as if he had given his life for his country."

"That was just poppycock!" All at once Eudora Woods was angry. "It wasn't the war that killed him. It was drought and grasshoppers and blizzards, and hailstorms!"

They stood amazed at her outburst.

"No, not the war, not anything that men did!" Eudora was almost shouting now, emphasizing her words by banging her fists on the drainboard. "Mr. Robinson . . . just . . . doesn't . . . understand! No one who's town bred *can* understand!"

She spoke with a terrible intensity, her rage pouring out in a great release. "Nature killed Henry, that and him thinking he could beat it like he did that bullet. That's the real trouble, and he isn't the only one that has it. Men just don't—*won't*—realize they have no power over the sun and the rain, and the cold, and the pests . . . all those things."

Eudora stopped and looked at Lydia. When she resumed her voice was softer, but bitter. "You're lucky. Amos is one in a million, the way he knows how to live with the weather and care for the land and all. The rest of them, even my Henry—"

Saying the name, she faltered.

"—they all think they can beat it. They just can't understand, not any of them, and they won't learn, so when they get beat down they think it's somehow their own fault. Men don't bend."

She looked down at her hands, still clenched into fists on the kitchen counter. "They don't bend, so they break. They break themselves, and blame themselves. Even a man smart as Henry."

Eudora turned to face the other women, and now the tears came slipping down her cheeks as she spoke to Grace: "So please take care of my son. Don't let him break himself."

Then, for the first time, she sobbed aloud as Grace embraced her.

Walking home later, Grace thought about Eudora's despairing plea.

She's right, most men don't know when to bend, so they hold out—and they break.

But Dan's different, I think. And he's never going to be a farmer anyway, so what's she worried about?

Dan was silent, and she slipped her hand into the crook of his elbow as they walked through the early evening darkness. "Don't be too sad, darling," she said.

"Actually I wasn't thinking about Pa, I was thinking about the newspaper. We have problems." He lapsed into silence again for a few steps. "But I guess I should let George worry about that. It's his money—and he said he'd take care of the business. I better stick to putting out the paper."

That's fine, she thought, *as long as George lets him "put out the paper." If that ever changes, we're in for trouble, because Dan won't bend on that.*

Maybe that's what Dora was worrying about.

She clutched her husband's arm more tightly, and not only because of the cold.

Chapter 12

Falls City, 1893–1894

G EORGE NORTON was as good as his word: he took charge. He came in at seven in the morning, stayed until seven at night, and kept the *Dakota Daily News* afloat through the great depression. As Dan had suspected, Norton took the crash as a personal challenge, and he met it with a single-mindedness that bordered on obsession.

Once, when the publisher looked particularly worn, Dan urged him to take a day off. Norton stared at him, then gestured toward the front office and the print shop. "What would happen to those people out there if I couldn't keep this paper going?" he said, and turned back to his figures.

He insisted on approving every bill, no matter how small, before it was paid; he personally signed every payroll check; he checked everyone's arithmetic, calling on his banker's ability to scan a column of figures and tell at a glance if it added correctly.

But at the heart of his strategy, as always, was circulation. "We need more circulation to get more advertising to make more money to make a better paper to get more circulation," was the way he put it. But in those hard times, the immediate need was to keep the subscribers they already had—and to keep them paying.

First, Norton changed the way he delivered the paper. He already had a small network of delivery boys in Falls City itself; now he extended that system to every town where the paper was sold, ending his reliance on the post office. He required the delivery boys to collect in person for the paper; it was a lot harder for a subscriber to "forget" to pay when a neighbor's son came to his door.

Then Norton switched from monthly to weekly billing, which made each payment smaller—but at the same time changed to pay-in-advance, which guaranteed that everyone who got the paper paid for it.

When the new system was firmly in place, Norton began to use it to sell the paper as well as deliver it. The boys were assigned the task of getting new subscribers, and were awarded prizes or cash bonuses if they did well. Now it was in their interest to add new customers as well as hold old ones.

Norton didn't rely on incentives alone. He kept the pressure on, stressing the need for on-time, reliable delivery.

"Subscribers are like other people, they hate to be disappointed," he said in a letter to all the delivery boys. "When they expect the paper to land on their porch at 5:30 P.M., it hurts their feelings if they have to wait until 6:10. But a good newspaper delivered promptly every day within easy reach of the front door can't shake off its subscribers with dynamite."

Grace reacted without enthusiasm when Dan explained Norton's new circulation schemes. "He's not risking much," she pointed out. "Now he's got a lot of little boys to sell his paper, and deliver it, *and* collect for it. And he doesn't have to put a single one of them on the payroll."

"They make money, too," Dan protested.

"Not much. Probably no more than he's been paying the post office, and certainly not as much as he'd have to pay grown men. It's a bargain for George."

Grace paused a moment and looked at her husband. "You know, he only does things he thinks will help get him something he wants. He never does anything just to be nice, or just to help someone else. You'd best keep that in mind as long as you work for him."

Dan bristled. "Well, I hope that's a long time. George is going to have a first-rate paper and I plan to put it out."

Grace laid a hand on his arm. "Of course you do. Just try to remember that he's getting more out of you than he's paying for. He's a good publisher, but he's not a saint."

Dan watched Norton leaven sympathy with self-interest in handling the other major problem the depression created for the *Dakota Daily News:* advertisers who didn't pay their bills.

Norton kept after them, but varied his tactics to fit differing circumstances. Some got extra time to pay. To others, he offered settlements: pay half the bill and he'd write off the rest. A few were encouraged to "trade out," paying for advertisements in goods or services—from potatoes to train tickets—that the paper or its employees could use. A handful were told they'd have to pay in advance from now on to get their ads published.

"It's not complicated," he told Dan. "There's no point pushing a man to the wall. If he hasn't got the money, he can't pay, and if he goes broke, he'll *never* pay. So I try to work something out to get us as much as possible, one way or another."

"Don't you lose a lot when you settle for half?"

"Maybe some think so, but it only looks that way. We only do it when it's that or nothing. We get a carload of good will, and I'll collect on *that* in better times. Maybe he'll give us all his advertising instead of only part of it."

Norton would have to wait a while for those better times; for now, there seemed no bottom to the depression, in Falls City or anywhere else. Across the country six hundred banks failed and closed. The financial panic shattered business confidence, which led to wage cuts and layoffs as more and more plants closed, which in turn led to less buying, which lowered business expectations even further. Two out of every five industrial workers were out of work. In big cities, thousands marched in protest, and as spring advanced, tramps fanned out into the countryside, looking for food and work.

All of that worried the well-to-do and the middle class, but what really scared them were the strikes. One hundred seventy thousand coal miners walked out and stayed off the job for almost two months. Then, in May, strikes began on the railroads; by July 60,000 men were off the job, one-third of them in Chicago, the hub of the country's rail system. President Cleveland finally called in federal troops to break the strike.

Dan argued long and hard with his publisher over what stand the *Daily News* should take on the strikes. Norton pretty much kept his promise not to interfere with the handling of news, but when it came to editorials, he was not at all reticent.

"These strikes are nothing but anarchy," he announced. "And there's only one way to deal with them: call in the troops."

"That's what Cleveland did in Chicago, George, and the result is there are people dead and wounded." Dan tried to reason with his angry publisher. "There's got to be a better way than shooting men and women like sitting ducks."

"Serves them right." George wasn't interested in cooling off. "They were trespassing on private property."

"George, it was the place where they worked. Look, if men don't get violent, and don't destroy company property, they ought to have the right to strike for better wages and conditions."

"No, no, no!" the publisher retorted. "Every strike, even if it's peaceful, is a violation of an individual's right to manage his own affairs as he sees fit."

Dan shook his head in despair. "I'll agree with you that if it comes to violence, or if the public health is threatened, or essential services—"

"Like the mail trains being stopped in Chicago."

"Well, I think we could get along without mail for a day or two."

"Oh, do you?" George pounced, and Dan knew at once what he was going to say. "I suppose as editor of the *Dakota News* you wouldn't mind if our mail papers didn't get delivered for 'a day or two.' "

"Well—"

"But it's not just business." Norton pressed his advantage. "Every strike is an attack on the whole idea of private property—on the whole society. That's why it's anarchy."

In the end, editor and publisher could agree on only one proposition: when a strike turned violent, or threatened the public health or essential services, government had an obligation to stop it—by force if necessary.

The editorial that resulted from this debate satisfied neither man. Norton insisted on his antistrike position and had his way, but he thought Dan's editorial was a pale, watered-down version of his views. As for Dan, he knew he had written something he didn't believe in. So both men wound up angry and frustrated.

Grace addressed Dan's irritation head-on.

"You've got to work something out with George," she said. "Obviously neither of you is happy with this kind of editorial, and it's bound to come up again. Think of two years from now, when there's an election."

"That won't be a problem." Dan was perched on a kitchen stool as Grace cooked supper. "I'm a Republican, and so is he."

"You're not nearly so much of a Republican as he is," she retorted. "And anyway that's no help on things like strikes or silver—things that aren't party matters."

"We won't agree every time. But it's his newspaper. He owns it, so in the end he can decide what it stands for. Fact is, he almost always lets me decide, and he always listens to my arguments. I think that's all I can ask for."

"The things he won't let you decide will be the most important things. Is that going to be good enough for you?"

Dan hesitated, but when he did answer his voice was sure. "Yes. It's only fair. It's his newspaper."

You're bending, Grace thought, remembering Eudora's outburst after Henry's funeral. *You're bending so you won't break.*

That's just fine.

Except that someday George may try to tell you what to put in the paper—and then you'll find out that you think it's your newspaper, too.

And then you may not be able to bend any more.

Amos Harper had resumed his Saturday visits to George Norton's office, and the debate between the two men quickly resumed where it had stopped after the last election.

"I think you're wrong about the strikes, George," Amos began the week the editorial appeared. "But—"

"Surely you're not in favor of violence and anarchy?" the publisher interrupted.

"Of course not. That's not the point." Amos snapped his jaw shut. "I was going to say, I think you're entitled to your opinion in your paper, and anyway I don't think that's as important out here. Farm prices and interest rates, those are things that really matter to us. I wish you'd print some editorials about them."

"If I did I'd remind you that you'll get better prices when business recovers and people have money to spend. That's why you ought to be for sound money, and gold, instead of this silver nonsense."

"George, hard money's the problem, not the answer." Amos sighed. "Even when they got free land, farmers had to borrow money to get started, for horses and machinery and seed and breaking sod and all."

He reached for a pencil and paper to illustrate his argument. "Let's say a fellow borrowed a thousand dollars at ten percent interest, when wheat was selling for a dollar a bushel. That meant his debt amounted to about a thousand bushels of wheat, and his interest amounted to a hundred bushels a year.

"But now when his loan comes due wheat is down to fifty cents, so he has to raise *two* thousand bushels to pay off that thousand dollars. His debt has doubled. And his interest payments have doubled, too: he's still paying ten percent, but now he has to sell two hundred bushels of wheat every year just to pay that interest, instead of one hundred when he started."

"Amos, you can't just go around writing off legal debts, and that's what cheap money would do. The country would collapse."

"You talk about cheap money." Harper was insistent. "I'm talking about money that will buy the same amount of wheat now that it did when the farmer borrowed it. That's only fair."

"You set class against class with that kind of socialist nonsense." Norton glared at his friend.

"You sure worry a lot about class war, George, you've been talking about it for a year now. Well, I'll tell you what sets class against class." Harper's eyes were equally angry. "It's foreclosing on mortgages that have suddenly doubled so a fellow can't pay them off. It's stuffing the pockets of J. P. Morgan and his friends by selling them government bonds at a special discount. It's using federal troops to shoot down workmen who only want a job and a decent wage."

"Most of those workmen in the big cities are just an ignorant rabble, a mob of illiterate immigrants."

"Somewhere back there we're all immigrants, George." Amos Harper took a deep breath, then spoke quietly. "I hate to hear a decent fellow like you talk that way."

Norton's sigh seemed to acknowledge the rebuke. "Oh, all right. I suppose there's something in what you say."

"You're not *always* wrong, George." Harper stood up and extended a big hand. "I've got to go. See you next week."

"I'm caught right in the middle," Dan told Grace one night. "I agree with both of them. I know it's hard times for the farmer, and a lot of it is unfair, and I think your father is one of the smartest men I ever met. But George understands farmers and respects them, too, and I think he knows more about business and banking than Amos does. And I think those things are just as important as farming, maybe more important."

"Nothing, *nobody,* is more important than the farmer." Grace's eyes were wide with sudden anger. "Oh, he's way off in the country, hundreds of miles from the cities, and people there don't even know he exists, let alone care. But they couldn't live without what he raises."

"I know all that. And he's damned tired of politicians telling him how important he is—and then turning their backs on him when he's in trouble." Dan shook his head. "But it's not simple. You can't just print a lot of money to wipe out debts. The whole country would collapse."

Grace spoke carefully. "You decided when you were still a little boy that you didn't want to live on a farm. If I'd lived on that claim in Nebraska, I'd probably feel the same way. But anyway you shut that life out. You grew up a town boy, and you've come to think like one."

"And you don't."

"No, I don't. I lived on the farm 'til the day I married you, and I think like a farm girl, and I guess I always will. I think the farmer supports everybody else in this country, and ought to get fair pay for it. So if I could vote, we'd go different ways."

"I think that same argument, that same split, is happening to the whole country." Dan smoothed his cowlick absentmindedly; it stood up again. "The country's changing and it's going to change even more and even faster. We could see that at Chicago. One way or another, we have to go ahead. We can't keep still."

"No, I suppose not," Grace said. *He's been doing some thinking, and I'm afraid he's right.* "And you've decided to go along for the ride."

"You put it that way, yes."

"Well, I'll come along too." Grace pointed a finger at her husband. "But don't expect me to agree with you all the time. Someone's got to remind you where you came from."

South Dakota, October 1894

There was no doubt about it, Dan decided: William McKinley might be short, but he was a fine figure of a man. He stood in the observation car at the rear of the special train, Prince Albert coat unwrinkled, white vest snug and spotless, black tie perfectly knotted, trousers perfectly pressed.

His manner, as he welcomed yet another group of Dakota Republicans to the train, was as polished as his appearance.

The avowed purpose of this "swing around the circle" was to help local Republican candidates in the West. But McKinley had a more compelling, if unstated, mission: to advance his own candidacy for the presidential nomination two years hence.

The local politicians had only a few moments with the great man, but he was far more available to the press. Most reporters, like Dan, boarded the train for a day or two as McKinley passed through their states. Dan had several chances to talk with him; McKinley invited his questions and chatted easily—though when Dan went through his notes later, he realized he hadn't really said much.

Dan hadn't seen him since that hot June day in 1892 when he and Will White were expelled from a Minneapolis hotel room by Mark Hanna. Dan didn't remind McKinley of the incident, and the governor obviously had forgotten it. But Hanna, riding along on the special train, recalled it the moment they met.

"Falls City, eh?" The manager gave Dan a long look and his wide mouth curved up in a smile. "I remember you. This time you caught me with my clothes on."

Dan was flattered to be remembered. He decided to make the most of it. "Well, since you're not in your underwear, maybe now you can give me that interview."

"This isn't a very good time for that," Hanna said. "I've got to talk with all these local fellows. But I did promise, didn't I?" He thought a moment. "Tell you what: we're stopping overnight at Aberdeen."

"I'm leaving the train there," Dan said.

"Well, stay and have dinner with me. We'll go off somewhere and talk."

Dan agreed at once, trying not to show his surprise and delight. The train lurched as the engineer began to brake for the next stop.

"Where are we?" Hanna asked.

Dan looked out the window. "Coming into Watertown."

Hanna pulled out a schedule sheet and inspected it. "He's going to talk here. Say, he's going to talk farming, and you know more about farmers than I do." He grinned confidingly. "Maybe more than he does, too. So hop out and listen, and tell me what you think tonight."

The local party leaders had done their work well; a couple of hundred men and boys stood in the bright autumn sun on the station platform, while a five-piece brass band played "Hail! The Conquering Hero Comes." It switched to "Beautiful Ohio" as McKinley emerged onto the rear platform.

When he talked about the farm situation, he seemed to be groping for a way to deal with the free-silver sentiments of Western farmers.

He started with the price of wheat: that was determined "by the law of supply and demand, which is eternal." He went on:

> Gold has not made long crops or short crops, high prices or low prices. Gold has not opened up the wheat fields of Russia, India, or the Argentine Republic—nor will free silver in the United States destroy them.

What really pushed wheat prices down, he said, was increased production at home—and increased competition abroad. That led him to his main argument: that the lowering of the protective tariff—sponsored by a Democratic president and enacted by a Democratic Congress—left the farmer unprotected against rising foreign competition.

> Depression in agriculture always follows low tariff legislation. The farmer is suffering today because the number of his competitors has increased, and his best customers are out of work.

McKinley was shifting the argument away from silver and onto traditional Republican ground. He liked talking about the tariff, and he had obviously used his closing lines many times before.

> We stand for a protective tariff because it represents the American home, the American fireside, the American family, the American girl, and the American boy—and the highest possibilities of American citizenship.

McKinley delivered these platitudes as if they were revealed truth, and the crowd cheered. The brass quintet swung into "Columbia, the Gem of the Ocean"; the local guests were hustled down the rear-platform steps while McKinley disappeared into the car. The reporters scrambled aboard as the train moved out of the station toward Doland and Aberdeen.

Dan headed for the baggage car that had been set aside for the reporters to work in. His story had to be handed down to the telegraph operator at Doland, and they'd be there in less than an hour.

"That's pretty good hash." Hanna put down his knife and fork after swallowing another big mouthful. He and Dan were off in a corner of an otherwise deserted hotel dining room. "It isn't as good as I make myself, but it'll do. Now, tell me: What do you think? Will that line go over with the farmers?"

The question made Dan uneasy, despite Hanna's cheerful informality and the glass of whiskey he'd had before dinner. He was used to asking questions, not answering them. "I'm not really in the business of giving political advice," he said.

"Oh, come on," Hanna grumbled. "This is just between us. You won't print that I talked to you—and I won't repeat what you tell me. But you'll print what you think in the paper in a day or two anyway, so why not tell me now?"

"Well, if you put it that way." Dan relaxed and thought a moment. "I think it may work for now, as long as times don't get worse again. But he didn't even mention the thing that's most important to most farmers."

"And what's that?"

"Debt. That's the biggest problem around here. Most farmers are up to their necks in mortgages. That's why they're for silver. They think it would let them pay their debts with cheap money."

Hanna grunted. "We can't run around the country promising to wipe out everybody's debts. Besides, it wouldn't work. We've got to stay on the gold standard."

"I didn't hear McKinley say *that* today."

"No, and you won't if I have anything to say about it. We're trying to get nominated for president, and we aren't about to antagonize every Republican west of the Mississippi."

"Sooner or later he'll have to say he's for gold."

Hanna started to reply, then stopped and held up a warning finger. "This is just between us, not for your paper, remember."

Dan nodded. Hanna went on. "Somewhere down the line we'll yield gracefully to widespread popular demand." He smiled benignly. "And when we do, we'll get something in return."

"Such as?"

"Oh, I don't know." Hanna stuffed another forkful of hash in his mouth. "Maybe just good will. Maybe the last few delegates we need to get the nomination. Maybe something else. Whatever it is, it'll be better than making a lot of people mad now before they're committed to us.

"Besides," he added, "I think we ought to campaign on the tariff. I can't believe silver will be the big issue. I don't think you can really stir people up with something that's so hard to understand."

"I think you may be wrong. You'd be surprised how hard these farmers are studying on silver. They read a lot, and they're stirred up."

"There are other people who vote besides farmers." Hanna's voice for the first time turned cold, and Dan felt the steel in the man. "But it doesn't make any difference. It's organization that wins elections anyhow. It's just like business—you have to figure out how things work, and devise a system, and invest enough to make it run right. All this fuss about silver and cheap money's just going to make it easier to convince businessmen they better get back on the Republican side—and pay their dues."

Now there's a man who knows what he wants—and how he's going to get it, Dan thought. *He intends to make McKinley president, and I wouldn't bet a nickel against him.*

* * *

As Amos Harper had predicted, the Democrats increasingly looked to "free silver" as an issue that could win back popular support. So did a lot of Populists; silver seemed the only good issue they had left, and they began talking with silver Democrats about a possible alliance.

One of those they contacted was William Jennings Bryan. Bryan was busier than ever, traveling the South, Midwest, and West—preaching free silver and, like McKinley, making new friends wherever he could. He visited South Dakota twice in 1895, and Dan spent most of a day with him when he came to Falls City.

Bryan at thirty-five was still slim and darkly handsome; in fact, he looked even younger now that he had shaved off his black beard. And, in private talk, Dan found him as direct and unassuming as he had been a year and a half earlier. But in public, Bryan sounded different: he now defined political issues either in moral terms or as class struggle.

He talks about silver as an issue, Dan mused after his day with Bryan, *but he doesn't really want to think about it. He just wants to use it to stir people up.*

The depression came close to home at the end of the year when Benjamin Woods lost the grocery store. It never had been a great success, but as long as Henry Woods was alive, they turned a small profit. When he died, however, his brother couldn't handle things alone. He liked to gossip with his customers, but he never cared much about selling to them, or stocking what they needed—or collecting his bills. In the two years following Henry's death, the business simply dried up. The customers vanished and Ben Woods went bankrupt.

"He's going to work for Anderson's Hardware. Not much of a job, but it's a bad time to look for work," Dan told Grace. "Kind of funny, isn't it?"

"What's funny?"

"Uncle Benjy's winding up just like Pa—going bust and having to work in another man's store."

Father was right, Grace thought, *there are a lot of failures in that Woods family.* She changed the subject.

"Now I won't have to shop at two grocery stores."

"What do you mean?"

"For the last year or so, most of Benjy's stock wasn't fit to eat. So I only bought things that wouldn't spoil from him, flour, sugar, stuff like that. I did most of my marketing at Peterson's. I'm sure Benjy knew, but I never could bring myself to say anything to him—or to you."

"That's all right." Dan thought a moment. "But you know, we owe Uncle Benjy a lot."

"We do?"

"If he hadn't written to Pa just when he did, and offered him that job, we'd've never come here."

The thought took him back to the house on the claim in the summer of '74, the crops ruined by 'hoppers and drought, and his father bringing the letter home and saying it was time to give up.

And Ma crying. She was crying because she was going to be free of that place, free at last.

And that was the last time I ever saw her cry until the day we buried him.

Falls City, 1895

Despite the depression, the *Dakota Daily News* was alive and well. George Norton's unflagging efforts produced steady circulation growth; his shrewd business sense and his relentless watch over every penny spent brought the paper through the worst times in remarkably good shape.

That was definitely not the case with the competition. The *Falls City Journal* had never caught up with George Norton, despite its price-cutting tactics and its effort to match his daily publication. The *Journal* struggled through two years of the depression, losing more money each month, until its owners finally gave up and ceased publication.

"That ought to make your life easier," Dan suggested to the publisher on the day the opposition folded.

"Not a bit of it." Norton rejected the thought. "Now that we're the only daily, people will expect more of us. We'll have to do better."

They were doing pretty well already. When Dan became editor four years earlier, circulation had been less than 3,000, with almost all of it in Falls City and the nearby area. Now it was over 8,000, with nearly half those papers going out to the widening circle of communities served by Norton's delivery network.

When Dan was hired, the news staff consisted of two: himself and David Currier. Now it was up to seven, including four reporters, and the publisher had just approved adding another reporter to cover news around the state. In addition, two dozen stringers now reported from outlying towns, and a "society editor" wrote a twice-weekly column on the doings of Falls City's first families.

There had been similar growth in other areas. In the front office, Norton now directed a circulation manager and an advertising salesman, as well as the office manager and another young woman who divided her time between the front counter and stenographic duties. The back shop had also grown to include a foreman, a pressman, three printers, and two part-time high school students.

At first Dan had been involved in every aspect of the newsroom, but now Currier, with the help of an assistant, handled almost all the routine editing chores, "putting out the paper" each day. So though Dan was responsible for a larger staff, he found himself able to spend more time writing, reading, and thinking. He enjoyed that. He wrote editorials, talking with Norton when he knew or suspected that the publisher would want to have a say before Dan put the paper on record. Almost always, even when he disagreed with Dan, Norton let him make the final decision, contenting himself with raising questions and urging a moderate tone. "You can't convince a man by lecturing him," he said. "We should try to persuade people, not shout them down."

It wasn't all smooth sailing. For one thing, George Norton occasionally forgot his promise not to interfere with the handling of the news. One morning he approached Currier as the editor was planning the layout of the day's paper.

The publisher said he understood that Carl Hansen, a prominent local real-estate speculator, had declared bankruptcy that morning. "I just wanted to be sure you knew about it. Of course we should have a story about it." He hesitated. "You'll decide, of course, but if I were doing it I think I'd put it inside, maybe on page three. Probably with a one-column headline."

Norton left without waiting for a reply. Currier headed straight for Dan's office.

"Where were you planning to put it?" Dan asked.

"On page one. Where it belongs. With a two-column head."

"Well, put it there. I'll talk to George."

Dan walked across the hall to Norton's office and poked his head through the door. "I told Currier to put the Hansen story on page one."

George Norton stared at him. Dan stood at the door, stock-still, staring back. He knew he must outwait the publisher. Finally Norton sighed and spoke.

"Well. Of course, you fellows have to decide those things."

"That's what you've always said." Dan drew a deep breath, started to leave, then turned back. "That's what makes this such a good place to work."

He walked over to Currier's desk. "Put the Hansen story on page one, below the fold," he said, using newspaper jargon for the lower, less prominent half of the page. "With a one-column head."

Currier gave him a quizzical look. Dan explained: "Remember what Grant said at Appomattox: 'Let them keep their horses. They will need them for the spring plowing.'"

Despite the outcome—or maybe because of it—the encounter with Norton bothered Dan all day. He was still preoccupied with it that night.

"What's on your mind?" Grace asked. "You're miles away."

He sighed and told her. She looked at him fondly. "You are something, Dan Woods. You stood up to him, but you didn't embarrass him. You handled it just right."

Dan shook his head. "I don't know about that."

"Well, I do," Grace fired back. "He knows you were right, and he'll respect you for it. And you'll never have that kind of problem with him again. Never."

Dan had another kind of problem with his publisher that spring. Mary Norton was pregnant again, and George was apparently using that to justify a renewal of his tomcatting.

Norton's appetites were well known to his male friends, and any attractive woman who worked for him soon learned not to let him stand too close behind her. But until now he had kept up appearances, outwardly remaining the soul of rectitude, every inch the strait-laced Methodist deacon.

This time, however, he had not been discreet. Dan heard from his Uncle Benjamin, who heard one customer in the hardware store tell another what he had heard from his neighbor: George Norton had been seen on two occasions coming out of Mollie Doyle's high-class whorehouse on the edge of town.

Dan was troubled. What George did in private was his own business, but if it got to be public knowledge it could hurt the paper. For one thing, sooner or later they were going to have to campaign for closing the whorehouses, and it wouldn't strengthen the case if the publisher was identified as a customer.

He wrestled privately with the problem for a day or two; finally, as usual, Grace decided it was time to find out what was bothering him.

"All right, Dan. What's on your mind this time?" He was drying the supper dishes as she washed up.

"Nothing."

"Come on."

"I don't want to talk about it."

"You'd better."

"No, not this one."

"Daniel Woods. Whatever it is, you *know* you need to talk about it, and it's obviously something you can't talk about it with George or anyone at the paper."

"Well, I sure can't talk to George about it. Or maybe I have to talk to George. That's the trouble." He hesitated. "It's about him . . . and women."

Another pause, longer, before he spoke again. "It's hard for me to talk about that with you."

Dan was too embarrassed to look at Grace as he spoke, so he didn't see her stiffen, didn't notice her flush. She fought to maintain her composure, staring down, hands pressed against the bottom of the dishpan, pulse pounding, a roaring in her ears. She could barely hear him as he continued.

"I mean, it's pretty sordid stuff. Not the kind of thing a fellow likes to talk about around his wife."

She breathed. *Oh, God,* she thought, holding on, *maybe it's not that. Maybe it's all right.*

Very carefully, Grace washed a plate, rinsed it, and put it in the drainer. She had to repeat the process before she could trust her voice.

"I think you better tell me about it." Then she had an idea, a happy idea. "You're worried about the paper, aren't you?" All at once she was sure. "That's why you're upset."

"That's right," he said, and went on to tell her about Uncle Benjy's report. "Everyone knows George has always had an eye for the girls—even you must have known that. But this is different."

He said "even you."

Her voice was steady now. "Different? How?"

"Well, what happens when we go after the whorehouses, if it's common knowledge the publisher is a regular customer? Where does that put the paper? And where does it leave me when I have to write editorials about it?"

"That would be a problem. We'll have to think about it." She tried to think, but then she looked at him and something turned over inside her and she couldn't think anymore. She emptied the dishpan and pulled the towel out of his hand.

"Those things can dry themselves. You close up, I'm going upstairs." She started for the door. "Don't take all night."

As it turned out, Dan didn't have to deal with Norton's behavior. When he got to the office the next morning there was a message from the publisher: he wouldn't be in that day because Mary had gone into labor.

A few hours later they got more news. Dan allowed himself a little license when he wrote the short for the next day's paper:

> Mr. and Mrs. George Norton of this city announce the birth
> of a second son, Harrison Norton. Mother and son are reported
> doing well. The father may recover in due course.

Norton behaved just as he had when his first son was born: he peacocked around town, distributed cigars, ignored his business, and lavished affection on his wife.

Chapter 13

D
AN ARRIVED in St. Louis on a Saturday, three days before the
official opening of the Republican National Convention. He immediately went looking for Mark Hanna, who had ended their
dinner-table talk a year earlier by inviting Dan to come see him at the
convention. Dan found McKinley's manager in his office at the Southern
Hotel, checking his delegate count on a tally sheet. He was in an amiable
mood, recalling the day they had spent together in South Dakota and
joking once again about their first encounter in Minneapolis four years
earlier.

He sounds like he hasn't a care in the world, Dan thought. *He must like
the numbers on that sheet.* But Dan knew he might be invited to leave any
minute, so he got right down to the most important question: Would Hanna
support a specific endorsement of the gold standard in the party platform?

Hanna pushed the question aside. "I'm here to get my man nominated. We're too close to the nomination to risk it in a pissing match with
that stuck-up little Boston snob." Dan knew Hanna was talking about
Henry Cabot Lodge, the blue-blooded senator from Massachusetts and
self-appointed leader of the gold forces.

"But won't you have to go for the gold standard?" Dan asked. "Seems
to me I remember you saying last year you're for it yourself."

Hanna was silent for a moment, tugging at one of his large ears.
"Woods, if you use this I'll never speak to you again."

"All right."

"Of course I'm for gold. And when it's all done, it'll be there, and no
trimming, either. I approved the plank last night. Hell, I cleared it with
McKinley ten days ago. But you can't print that. It's too soon to talk about
it. By the time this convention opens, there'll be an overwhelming demand
for a gold plank." Hanna smiled. "And we'll yield gracefully."

"And let Lodge take credit?"

Hanna laughed, a short, barking, mirthless laugh. "Sure. He can take the credit; I'll take the nomination."

Dan remembered what Hanna had said over dinner a year earlier. *He said he'd go for gold when he could get something he needed in return— something like "the last few delegates we need to get the nomination."*

Monday morning Dan and a dozen other reporters were back in the corridor outside Hanna's office, drawn by word that Lodge was on his way to see him. The senator came briskly down the hall and turned into Hanna's rooms.

He didn't stay long, and he came out steaming. There was a rush of questions. Lodge's slight figure leaned forward, and he bounced like a boxer dancing in the ring as he answered them.

"Mr. Hanna seems to want a fight. Well, we shall oblige him, and we will win. . . . No, he flatly refused to consider it. . . . I found him rude in the extreme."

There was a rush for the stairs leading down to the press workroom off the lobby. Dan thought about filing a story, but decided he'd be better off staying where he was and trying to learn more.

He didn't have to wait long. In ten minutes a man emerged from Hanna's office and hurried down the hall. Dan recognized him as one of Hanna's assistants; he followed him at a distance, turning the corridor corner just in time to see him go into the Massachusetts headquarters.

Dan returned to Hanna's office and sent in his card, first scribbling "One minute?" on it. He was surprised to be admitted at once to the back room; he was astonished to find Hanna completely relaxed and bubbling with good humor.

"I don't know why I waste so much time talking to you." The Ohioan chuckled and leaned back, his small feet tucked under his swivel chair. "Comic relief, I guess."

Dan didn't take the bait; Hanna could say anything he wanted as long as he continued to see him. "What's going on? Lodge was in a perfect rage when he came out."

"Oh, really?" Hanna smiled the smile of a deeply satisfied man.

"He said you turned them down cold, and were rude to boot."

Hanna threw his head back and guffawed. "Takes one to know one." Then he added, coldly: "He didn't give me a choice, I had to turn him down. So he said they'd take it to the floor, and then I lost my temper. Told him I didn't give a damn where he took it, and he could go straight to hell."

"No wonder he was mad. So there will be a floor fight after all?"

Hanna pursed his lips. "Look, you can't use any of this until tomorrow. All right?"

It was Dan's turn to laugh. "That's all you ever say to me. What about it?"

"Won't be a fight."

"Why?"

"Wait and see."

"Because the word 'gold' will be in the plank the committee approves," Dan said, using Norton's tactic of stating a question as fact. "That's what you just sent your man to tell Lodge."

"You're pretty smart for one so young." Hanna winked. "Now go, I've got work to do. Remember, you can't use it until tomorrow."

Dan proposed an amendment: "Unless Lodge puts it out today."

Hanna grunted. "Fair enough. Now please, Dan, get out of here. And use the back way, will you? I don't want every reporter in St. Louis to know what an easy mark I am."

Dan went out the back door and down a service stairway. He had it all now.

Hanna's giving Lodge and the goldbugs exactly what they want, but Lodge doesn't know it's also exactly what Hanna wants, too. He's going to let them think that they forced it out of him. He's going to let Lodge take credit for it. The silver people will think Hanna only agreed because he had to, when he really approved the final version Friday night—two days before Lodge even got here.

Dan went back to his hotel room to write. When he had finished, he walked over to the Southern and handed his story to a Western Union operator in the press room. As he turned to leave, he was surprised to see William Jennings Bryan come in. Dan greeted the Nebraskan, reminded him of their encounter in Falls City the previous autumn—Bryan claimed to remember it, too—and asked him what a Democrat was doing in this nest of Republicans.

"Oh, I'm not here as a politician," Bryan replied easily. "I'm an editor now, you know, just like you. I'm just trying to find out what's going on."

Dan was inwardly angered by this assumption of journalistic camouflage by so prominent a politician. *Editor my foot,* he thought. *If you're an editor, I'm a presidential candidate. Everybody knows the silver lobby bought that paper in Omaha so it could pay you a salary while you go around making speeches.*

But he couldn't pass up a chance to quiz Bryan, so he hid his irritation. "There's no contest here," he suggested. "But you Democrats might manage one. Who's going to get your nomination?"

Bryan's strong jaw and wide mouth were set and his dark eyes fixed on Dan. "Well," he said in a matter-of-fact way, "I believe I have as good a chance as anyone."

As far as Dan could tell, the man was dead serious. *When they get that fever, it doesn't matter how smart they are, it just rots out their common sense.*

Nothing happened during the first two days of the convention, but when Dan walked into the convention hall Thursday morning, he sensed a change. The platform was finally ready to be read and debated, and for the first time both delegate and spectator sections were full.

The chairman of the platform committee began to read the document. When he reached the section on money, the hall was hushed; most of the delegates hadn't seen the language, and they wanted to hear it.

> The Republican Party is unreservedly for sound money. It caused the enactment of the law providing for the resumption of specie payments; since then every dollar has been good as gold.
> We are unalterably opposed to every measure calculated to debase our currency or impair the credit of our country. We are therefore opposed to the free coinage of silver except by international agreement with the leading commercial nations of the world, which we pledge ourselves to promote, and until such agreement can be obtained the existing gold standard must be preserved.

Each mention of the word "gold" drew loud cheers.

Now the leader of the silver faction, Senator Henry Teller of Colorado, came to the podium. Somber in his customary black suit, erect despite his sixty-six years, he warned that adoption of a gold plank would force him to "sever my connection" with the party he had helped found forty years before. There were cries of "No! No!," but when the roll was called, the plea for silver was rejected overwhelmingly.

Teller shook hands with the presiding officer, stepped down from the platform, and walked slowly up the center aisle. Only a handful of delegates, perhaps two dozen, joined him. The rest watched coldly; the old man's speech had been a gallant gesture, but walking out of the convention, deserting the party, was quite another matter. Hisses, boos, then a crescendo of hostile shouts followed the bolters.

"Go! Go! Good-bye!"

Dan heard one voice rising above the rest. Mark Hanna was jumping up and down, shaking his fists, yelling for all he was worth. First his Ohio colleagues and then the entire hall took up his chant:

"Go! Go! Go!"

Hanna's voice was harsh, but he had a beatific smile on his face. His strategy had worked. The silver walkout was contained, confined to fewer than two dozen delegates, and now for a few minutes he was letting go, relaxing, enjoying himself.

"Go! Go! Good-bye!"

The triumph was complete a few hours later. New York, Pennsylvania, and a few other Northeastern states held out to the bitter end, but

Hanna had all the rest tucked in tight. Of 906 votes cast, McKinley got 661. No one else had more than 84.

The next day, the Republican National Committee elected Hanna as its new chairman. He went home to Cleveland, confident that McKinley had clear sailing for November.

That same day William Jennings Bryan, who had watched with particular interest as the silver men walked out, visited the editor of the *St. Louis Post-Dispatch*. The editor was drafting the platform for the Democratic convention, and he was glad to accept Bryan's proposed wording for the money plank.

Bryan did not linger in St. Louis. With less than a month remaining before the Democratic convention, he had a great deal still to do.

Chapter 14

Chicago, July 1896

WILLIAM JENNINGS BRYAN had espoused the cause of silver coinage before he knew what it was all about.

"I don't know anything about free silver," he told a campaign meeting in 1892. "The people of Nebraska are for free silver, and I am for free silver. I will look up the arguments later."

Bryan's silver advocacy so angered Grover Cleveland that the Democratic president ordered the purging of the young congressman, and he was denied renomination. But he still had an issue—one that he sensed could soon dominate the nation's politics. His new friends in the silver-mining industry circulated a million copies of his 1893 speech; they also bought control of the *Omaha World-Herald* and installed him as editor to give him an income and pay his expenses.

Bryan spoke all over the West and South in 1895, making acquaintances and allies, preaching silver, silver, nothing but silver. It did not seem to occur to the public, nor to most Democratic leaders, that Bryan was running for president; he was considered a crusader, not a candidate.

He just kept working. He wrote hundreds of letters in the spring of 1896. Bryan sent a proposed silver platform plank to all state Democratic chairmen, urging them to adopt it at their own state conventions. After each state meeting, he wrote again, asking for the names of delegates to the national convention; many of them then got letters from Bryan. In this way he promoted both himself and a platform he could run on.

If Bryan did not trumpet his candidacy, he did not hide it, either. He told a former House colleague, Champ Clark of Missouri, "I will get the nomination." He said almost the same thing to reporters who asked him to guess the Democratic nominee. The "logic of the situation," he explained, gave him "as good a chance as anyone."

Politicians and reporters alike dismissed the idea, but by the time the Democratic convention opened, the silver men had a solid majority of delegates.

Dan reached Chicago on Independence Day. It was hot, and the smell of firecrackers couldn't quite mask the pervasive stench of the stockyards. Though the convention would not open for three days, the lobby of the Palmer House was already jammed with hangers-on and fouled with cigar smoke.

Dan found the press room and canvassed his fellow newspapermen. The consensus was that Richard Bland of Missouri—nicknamed "Silver Dick" for his long advocacy of silver coinage—was the leading candidate.

"He has by far the best organization," a Chicago reporter said. "Lots of literature, banners, badges, bands, and all the rest. He's way ahead."

But Dan sensed an uncertainty about the Bland candidacy. Much of his support seemed more a matter of sentiment than of enthusiasm. "He's an old man and his pants bag at the knees, and he looks like a hayseed," Jim Morgan of the *Boston Globe* argued. "Besides, his wife's a Catholic, and he's from Missouri, which most people think is part of the South."

Several other silver Democrats were jockeying for position, but none stood out. It looked as though the party had an issue, but no leader—so it might be Bland by default. Dan asked his Eastern colleagues if they had heard any talk of Bryan; he was surprised to find that many had hardly heard of him, and none thought him a candidate.

The Nebraska delegation arrived on a special train the next day. Dan went to see Bryan in his unpretentious room at the Clifton House. Bryan was in his shirtsleeves, helping his wife unpack. He was relaxed and cheerful, black hair falling over his high forehead, the mouth and jaw that set so firmly in public relaxed and loose. His large brown eyes shone as he talked.

Dan reminded him of their talk in St. Louis a month earlier. "What do you think of your chances now?"

"Well." Bryan paused, but only for a moment. "I still think I have as good a chance as any. None of the present candidates can be nominated. If I am able to address the convention at the right time, I believe I will get the nomination."

Dan was taken aback both by the forecast and by Bryan's matter-of-fact confidence. Later, back at the Palmer House, he reported the conversation to his colleagues.

"My God, young man," said a *New York Times* reporter in a condescending drawl. "You're not suggesting that windbag is a serious candidate?"

"I'm not sure whether he is or not," Dan replied, "but he's nobody's fool, and he seems to think he's got a good chance." The *Times* man laughed, but Jim Morgan did not.

"You know, that ties in with something I heard," Morgan mused. "I've got a friend from Illinois, a man who's close to the big fellows, and he told me to keep my eye on William J. Bryan. He wouldn't explain why. Do you s'pose Altgeld is working for Bryan?" John Peter Altgeld, governor of Illinois, was widely regarded as the most powerful man at the convention.

"Altgeld says he's for Bland, all the way," Dan said.

"So do a lot of people," Morgan retorted, "but I don't think one in ten will stick with him if they think someone younger and stronger is available."

"Well, I hope you didn't file that Bryan stuff," the New York man scoffed. "Your office would think you'd gone 'round the bend."

Morgan smiled. "I didn't write it. But I did tell the desk to be sure they have a picture of this fellow Bryan, just in case."

When the convention convened on Tuesday, the silver forces won the first test easily, installing one of their own as chairman and confirming their control of the convention.

"That nails the silver plank into the platform," Dan muttered to Morgan, sitting beside him in the press section. "Now let's see if Bryan can find a way to make that speech he's counting on."

That proved astonishingly easy. Bryan was Nebraska's representative on the platform committee; when the committee finished its work on Wednesday, the chairman sought him out. He said he had a sore throat that would prevent his being heard in the big hall, so would Bryan be willing to manage floor debate on the platform?

Bryan could hardly believe his ears. This was exactly what he wanted: to address the convention on its only major issue, just before the nominations for president. He accepted instantly, then by careful negotiation made sure he would speak last. He had known for weeks what he would say, but now he went over it in his mind again and again.

The papers were all predicting that Bland would be nominated on the third ballot at the latest; there seemed no substantial support for anyone else. As for Bryan, few correspondents even mentioned him in their dispatches.

It will have to be some speech, Dan thought. Then he remembered the first time he had heard Bryan, nearly three years ago, in Washington. *But if anyone can do it with a speech, he can. There'll be some action tomorrow.*

The doors to the hall were opened at 9:30 A.M., and a half-hour later every one of the thirteen thousand spectator seats was occupied. Delegates were slower to arrive, but eventually their section too was full. Hundreds of newspapermen crowded onto the press benches. Altogether, close to twenty thousand men and women were packed into the hall, aroused by the prospect of debate on the platform and eager to hear, at last, from the party's stellar orator.

An hour after the doors opened, the chairman finally brought his gavel down to begin the platform debate on the silver issue. Tension and anticipation built up as other speakers came and went, fanning the crowd's passions as it waited for Bryan. He sat with the Nebraska delegation, listening intently and sucking a lemon.

As the applause for the last of the other speakers faded, Bryan jumped up from his seat and literally ran up the steps to the speaker's platform. As Bryan came to the center of the platform the whole audience—spectators and delegates alike—rose and cheered.

Bryan stood stock-still, one foot set ahead of the other, his left hand on the lectern, his right hand raised in acknowledgment, the handsome head up, dark eyes intent above the aquiline nose, the wide jaw set.

"He'll have to be good," Morgan shouted into Dan's ear. "The gold-bugs have had the better of it so far."

"That's no matter," Dan said. "Silver's got the votes. But he's ready for this. It'll be a barnburner."

Bryan let the applause roll on. Slim and straight, he was a study in black and white: black hair, pale face; black alpaca coat and vest, white bow tie; a single black stud in a white shirt. After five minutes, the crowd quieted enough for him to begin.

He had the audience completely in his grasp. He talked smoothly, without apparent effort, without seeming to raise his voice at all, but every word reached clearly to the far corners of the hall. He spoke precisely, biting off the ends of his words, sounding the consonants distinctly, making the most of his great instrument. Unaided by any mechanical device, his voice filled the vast chamber. It was not just that it carried better than others; there was a musical quality to it. It was a light baritone, not sharp but penetrating, and he spoke with a rising inflection to make sure everyone could hear the end of his sentences.

> I would be presumptuous indeed to present myself against the distinguished gentlemen to whom you have listened if this were but a measuring of ability. But this is not a contest among persons. The humblest citizen in all the land, when clad in the armor of a righteous cause, is stronger than all the whole hosts of error that they can bring. I come to speak to you in defense of a cause as holy as the cause of liberty—the cause of humanity.

He paused; the crowd burst into applause. He held up his hand; the crowd fell silent. The biblical phrases rolled out as he recalled the growth of the silver movement.

With a zeal approaching the zeal which inspired the crusaders who followed Peter the Hermit, our silver Democrats went forth from victory unto victory until they are now assembled, not to discuss, not to debate, but to enter up the judgment already rendered by the plain people of this country.

Again Bryan paused. Again applause. Again the slightest signal with his hand; again silence. This time he addressed the business interests of the East.

When you come before us and tell us that we shall disturb your business interests, we reply that you have disturbed our business interests by your course.

He was interrupted by cheers, but pressed on. Most of this speech he had used many times before, but he had devised this section for this occasion, and he emphasized it with his slow, intense delivery.

We say to you that you have made too limited in its application the definition of businessman. The man who is employed for wages is as much a businessman as his employer.

The attorney in a country town is as much a businessman as the corporation counsel in a great metropolis. The merchant at the crossroads store is as much a businessman as the merchant of New York.

The farmer who goes forth in the morning and toils all day, begins in the spring and toils all summer, and by the application of brain and muscle to the natural resources of this country creates wealth, is as much a businessman as the man who goes upon the Board of Trade and bets upon the price of grain.

Now the audience seemed to Dan to be acting just like a church choir: rising in unison at each pause, shouting its approval, then falling silent and sitting down again when Bryan resumed.

It is for these that we speak. We do not come as aggressors. Our war is not a war of conquest; we are fighting in the defense of our homes, our families, and posterity.

There was an outburst at every sentence now.

We have petitioned, and our petitions have been scorned. We have entreated, and our entreaties have been disregarded. We have begged, and they have mocked, and our calamity came.

We beg no longer; we entreat no more; we petition no more. We defy them!

[124]

This produced the greatest uproar so far. Everywhere Dan looked, he saw a blizzard of waving white handkerchiefs and red bandannas. Applause, cheers, and shouts blended into an avalanche of sound. The hall literally rocked from the pounding of canes and boots on the auditorium floor. When the crowd subsided several minutes later, Bryan resumed, speaking now of the arguments of the gold men who had preceded him.

> And now, my friends, let me come to the great paramount issue. If they ask us why it is that we say more on the money question than we say upon the tariff question, I reply that if protection has slain its thousands, the gold standard has slain its tens of thousands.
> If they ask us why we do not embody in our platform all the things that we believe in, we reply that when we have restored the money of the Constitution all necessary reforms will be possible; but that until this is done there is no other reform that can be accomplished. . . .

They were listening intently now as Bryan went after the Republican nominee.

> At St. Louis . . . Mr. McKinley was the most popular man among the Republicans, and three months ago everybody in the Republican party prophesied his election. How is it today? Why, the man who used to boast that he looked like Napoleon—

Cheers and derisive laughter rolled across the hall.

> —that man shudders today when he remembers that he was nominated on the anniversary of the battle of Waterloo. . . .

The crowd roared, but Bryan had a point to make.

> Why this change? Ah, my friends, is not the reason for this change evident to anyone who will look at the matter? It is that no private character, however pure, no personal popularity, however great, can protect from the avenging wrath of an indignant people a man who will declare that he is in favor of fastening the gold standard upon this country. . . .

Repeated, almost continuous cheering made it impossible for Bryan to go on. Finally, he raised both hands and got enough quiet to plead that he had only ten minutes left. That worked.

> You come to us and tell us that the great cities are in favor of the gold standard; we reply that the great cities rest upon our broad

and fertile prairies. Burn down your cities and leave our farms, and your cities will spring up again as if by magic. But destroy our farms and the grass will grow in the streets of every city in this country.

Now he was nearly done. If the Republicans dared to defend the gold standard as a good thing, he said, Democrats would fight them to the end.

Having behind us the producing masses of this nation and the world, having behind us the commercial interests and the laboring interests, and the toilers everywhere, we shall answer their demand for a gold standard by saying to them:

Bryan raised his hands above his head, spread his fingers, and pulled them slowly down onto his forehead.

You shall not press down upon the brow of labor this crown of thorns.

He spread his arms straight out from his shoulders.

You shall not crucify mankind upon a cross of gold.

Chapter 15

South Dakota, 1896

DAN STARED out the window at the countryside. Farmhouses, barns, cornfields, and cattle drifted past as his train chugged westward across Iowa. But he wasn't paying attention; he was trying once again to sort out how Bryan had won the nomination at Chicago.

Of course it never would have happened without the speech. But he could never have won it with the speech alone, either. Everybody thinks that was all there was to it, but they're wrong. He'd been working on that nomination for two years, and he had a hundred delegates before he ever opened his mouth.

Still, even after all that hard work, and after the speech, when the voting started Bryan had solid support in only five states. "Silver Dick" Bland had almost twice as many votes on the first ballot.

Bryan was ready, but it's just as important that when they really got to looking, there wasn't anybody else. They laughed when Bryan said that before-hand, but he was right. He knew Bland's people wouldn't stay hitched if they had an excuse to bolt.

And that was where the speech had made a difference: Bryan so thrilled and overwhelmed the convention that when Bland started to slip, Bryan was the obvious—indeed the only—alternative, and he won going away on the fifth ballot.

It was no accident. He planned and he worked, so when the brass ring came 'round, he could grab it.

Dan swayed in his seat as the car crossed a set of switches where a siding led to a grain elevator. The jolts shunted his mind back to a question he'd been weighing since he left Chicago: Which man was he for?

He knew who George Norton would be for. There was never any question that Norton—and his newspaper—would back McKinley. Dan also knew who Amos Harper would be for, and he guessed Grace would go the same way: for Bryan. But Dan hadn't made up his own mind.

It's all come down to silver, and that's too bad, because it's not the real problem. You could mint all the silver money in the world and it wouldn't do one damned thing to control the monopolies, and they're what hurt the farmers. It's monopoly that holds down the price of grain, and it's monopoly that pushes up the price of things they have to buy.

Everybody agreed that the "free," or unlimited, coinage of silver would cut the value of the dollar by about one-half.

I can see how farmers with all their debts think cheap money would be good for them. They've gotten the short end of the stick from the moneylenders for years. No wonder they think silver is a cure-all.

But it wasn't. Cutting the value of the dollar might seem to help debtors, but whatever farmers gained that way would be offset by higher prices for what they had to buy.

And there was the problem of confidence.

There isn't so much talk about that, but it may be more important than anything else. This country needs to get going again, and that's not going to happen until business people think things are settling down. Bryan sure doesn't give them that feeling.

However long he thought about it, Dan kept coming back to a belief that you couldn't make the country work better by setting one group against another, one section against another, and that was what Bryan seemed to be trying to do.

Of course there was truth in the argument that the East was exploiting the West. The East had the money; the West borrowed it. Everything of value in the West—railroads, elevators, banks, farm machinery companies, and a lot of the land itself—was owned by rich men in the East. The price of everything the West bought and sold was dictated by the East.

But even if you could win the election by putting class against class and East against West, Dan thought, *it would be bad for us, because the Eastern cities are growing a lot faster than we are out here.*

This isn't the same country it was when Pa and Amos homesteaded, and it won't ever be like that again. And if the people out here are going to survive they've got to accept that. You can't turn the clock back.

Dan had made his choice.

George Norton had certainly made *his* choice, as Dan discovered the minute he walked into the *Dakota Daily News* office.

"I hope you had a good bath when you left that zoo in Chicago." Norton's voice was hard. "I was afraid the boy demagogue might have infected you."

"I take it you didn't admire Bryan's speech?" Dan said.

"No." Norton's stocky body was tense and he stared at his editor. "Did you?"

"I never heard anything like it," Dan said, hedging a little. "I don't agree with him about silver, but in that speech he wasn't trying to make that case. He was trying to stir them up, and he certainly did that."

"Huh." Norton swiveled back to his desk, picked up a pair of scissors, and began to trim his fingernails. Dan knew it was a sure sign that he was angry. "Damned rabble-rouser, that's what he is. Dangerous. Appeals to the worst element."

"Come on, George. Some of your friends are for him."

"Former friends." He snapped the scissors.

Oh-oh. It's going to be a long season, Dan thought. *I better get a few things settled right at the start, or it'll be nothing but trouble. But best give him a little time to cool off first.*

"I went through the papers at home last night," Dan said. "Looked to me as if David and his people did a good job while I was away."

"Yes. They did well. And I thought your stories were splendid." Norton's voice was calm again; he even managed a small smile. "Even though the contents made me sick."

Dan changed the subject. "How are the boys doing?"

Norton's smile was broad this time. "Just fine. James is playing with bigger boys now. He's quite the athlete for a three-year-old."

"And Harry?"

"Well, he turned thirteen months while you were away. He's not walking yet, but he's the most curious child I ever saw. He wants to find out about everything."

Dan laughed. "There's the newspaperman."

The Populists had purposely delayed their convention until after those of the two major parties, gambling that both would endorse the gold standard and thus drive silverites of all parties into the Populist fold. But it didn't work out that way: as Amos Harper had predicted four years earlier, the Democrats preempted the silver issue and named a presidential candidate who seemed sure to skim off a great many Populist votes.

"We put him to school, and he wound up stealing the schoolbooks," Ignatius Donnelly complained to his fellow Populists at their convention in St. Louis. "But that doesn't mean we have to turn the teacher's job over to a slow student."

Old-line Populists like Amos Harper saw their party and its program being sacrificed to expediency. But the party leaders sniffed victory and wanted to share in the spoils, and the prospect of winning proved more compelling than the preservation of ideological purity. Besides, they had no credible candidate of their own. So they endorsed Bryan.

Dan went into the publisher's office at the end of the month. "I thought you might have some ideas about the campaign," Dan said. "I've got to make plans for the rest of the summer and fall."

"It's a very important election." Norton spoke deliberately. "Of course you fellows will decide what to put in the paper. But we should do whatever is necessary for our readers to understand the real issues."

Norton stressed the word "real." Dan didn't like the sound of it. He ran his long fingers through his hair, then leaned forward as he spoke. "We'll print all the arguments on both sides," he said steadily, "and we'll keep our own opinions where they belong."

"Of course, of course. I won't interfere, you know that." Norton sounded defensive, as if he'd been caught out. He stared unblinkingly at Dan. "But this is a very, very important election, and it's very, very important that the country chooses the right man."

"And it's going to be very, very close in this state," Dan replied. "We're not talking about a little bunch of lunatics, you know. We're talking about half the people, give or take a few. That's why it's so important that we be absolutely fair."

"Huh." Norton stirred. "Don't be *too* fair. We should let people know where we stand. I want strong editorials."

"I'm talking about the news pages. We've got to put up a fence between news and editorials, and it's got to be hog-tight." Dan leaned back in his chair, stretched his legs and locked his hands behind his head. "I still remember what you said the day you bought the paper."

Norton took the bait. "Well, I don't. What did I say?"

"That our influence would depend on the trust of the readers, and that meant we had to keep our news pages fair and open to everyone, and keep our opinions on the editorial page. This election will really test us on that." Dan knew he had to win this one. He looked hard at Norton. *"All* of us."

Norton stared back for a moment before responding. "Of course. I want people to believe we're fair, too."

"I know you do. And if we are, we'll be the only paper in the state that is. The others are all so partisan no one believes anything they print. So if we follow your rules, we'll look all the better."

Dan sensed an opening. "And if people think we're fair, they'll subscribe to us instead of someone else. That will make a big difference as we reach out further, into other papers' circulation areas. It'll help that Sunday paper we're going to have. And it'll mean more advertising." He paused. "It's just good business."

Norton's reply was tart: "Your logic is irresistible." Then, as if dismissing that issue, he changed the subject. "What *are* your plans for the campaign?"

"Well, I thought I'd spend a few days with McKinley and Bryan, try to get some measure of each campaign. I'm sure Bryan will be around here, but I'll have to go to Ohio for McKinley; he's staying home. We'll use the wire services for the everyday stuff. And we'll put a reporter pretty much full time on the governor and attorney-general campaigns."

Norton interrupted. "I'm not concerned about the local offices this year. I'm worried about the presidency. That's the one that's dangerous for the country." The publisher paused. "Who's going to write the editorials?"

"You—if you want to. I always figured that was the owner's prerogative."

Norton frowned. "That's a safe offer. You know I can't write a lick. No, I meant you or David, which of you will do them?"

"I will."

"Why?" Norton was obviously not pleased.

"Because I'm the editor. I'll take the heat for what we say, I might as well choose the words." He tried a light touch: "And David's already been hung in effigy once. I never have."

Norton was not amused. "David's a lot more of a Republican."

"I'm enough of a Republican. And I'm for sound money."

"The way you were talking the other day about Bryan's speech, it sounded to me as if you were in favor of free silver."

"I'm not." Dan was emphatic. "Bryan's a good man and he made a great speech, but he's pushing a bad idea. As long as he makes that the issue, I have to oppose him."

Dan stopped. *That's enough, keep quiet now. Wait him out and it'll come all right.*

Norton looked at him, then shrugged. "It's up to you. Of course I'll have some thoughts for you from time to time. Just suggestions." He repeated what he had said earlier: "I want to be sure we take a strong stand. A *very* strong stand."

"I think you're out of your mind." Grace and Dan were sitting on their porch. Her temper had risen as she listened to Dan's account of his talk with Norton. "I've said it before. You shouldn't try to write something you don't really agree with. Certainly not when it's this important." Her words came tumbling out. "I know you, it'll just eat you up."

"I'll be writing what I believe."

Grace could tell, from the way he gestured with his long arms and tugged at his cowlick, that he was irritated, but she kept on.

"You mean you're for McKinley?" She was incredulous. "All I've heard you talk about since you got home from Chicago was what a wonderful speech Bryan made and what a good politician he is."

"That's all true. But he's wrong about the most important issues." Dan sighed. He hated arguing politics with Grace; she shared not only her father's beliefs but the force with which he advanced them.

"Such as?"

"Such as silver, mostly." Dan wanted to keep this conversation short and avoid a row. "I've thought a lot about it. Bryan's a great talker, but

[131]

he doesn't face up to it. If we start coining too much silver we'll cut the value of the dollar in half. And that would make a terrible mess of things."

"Maybe for the bankers and the moneylenders." Grace wasn't letting him off the hook. "Not for the farmers who're getting strangled by low prices and big mortgages."

"If farmers got higher prices for what they sell, they'd have to pay higher prices for what they buy, too. They won't get ahead that way. Farmers are the only people who sell at wholesale and buy at retail. When they sell, they take what is offered, and when they buy, they pay what is asked."

Dan, warming to the argument, leaned forward for emphasis. "Prices aren't the answer—markets are. Farmers have to have someone to sell their wheat to, and their cattle and hogs and all, and if business is bad, city workers lose their jobs, and then they can't buy things. That's what happened after the Panic."

Grace shook her head. "No, what happened after the Panic is that Cleveland turned the treasury over to J. P. Morgan and his banker friends. He thought they would straighten things out." She was really angry now. "They made a killing, and the rest of us got no help at all."

Dan held up his hands. "We better stop. We're not going to agree, so we better leave it where it is."

Grace started to speak, then bit her lip. "All right. But still, when it comes to the editorials, why not let George do them? Let him be the one people get mad at."

"Grace, you know better than that. He's never done it, he isn't going to start now, and he's right: he can't write a lick."

"Well, then, why not David Currier?" Grace would not be put off. "George is right about him—he's a lot more of a Republican than you are."

"That's exactly why I don't want him doing editorials. I know the way he thinks and writes, he overstates everything, he's so partisan, and he sounds . . . well, mean. We can't afford that this year. People are too stirred up already, we shouldn't make it worse."

Grace would not give up. "But at least he's a real Republican."

"Well, I'm a Republican, too. At least this year." Dan jumped up from his chair. "But it's more than that. Bryan and the silver people aren't a bunch of radicals or anarchists. They're wrong, but they're good people—people like your father. David thinks they're all loafers or lunatics, or worse. If I write the editorials, I can keep *us* from sounding crazy. That's pretty important for the paper."

"And I guess it's important to you, too," she snapped. "You're turning your back on your own people, and you want to make it sound sweet and reasonable."

She's right, he thought, *I am turning away from my people*. The thought made him feel uneasy, guilty, but then those feelings were overtaken by anger.

But damn it, those farmers have got things all mixed up. They're looking for some miracle, some patent medicine to cure everything that's wrong with them. Some political Lydia Pinkham's.

Dan glared at his wife. "They may be my own people, but when they're wrong, I have to say so. I wouldn't be much of an editor—or much of a man—if I didn't."

Grace saw the rage in his eyes. She stood up and went to where he stood by the porch rail, and this time she spoke quietly.

"Of course you have to say what you believe. But you're always worrying about the paper, so someone's got to look out for *you*. I'm not going to let it eat you up."

She sighed. "It's going to be a long season, isn't it?"

Chapter 16

Canton, Ohio, 1896

DAN STOOD on the station platform in a crowd of boisterous Republicans. He had come to take a look at William McKinley's stay-at-home campaign, traveling down from Cleveland on one of the special trains bringing delegations to Canton to meet and hear the candidate.

This group called itself "First Voters of Cleveland." Most were in their early twenties, though Dan spotted a few whose first votes must have been cast at least two decades earlier. Young or middle-aged, they were all having a good time.

A tall man in cavalry boots and a uniform stepped forward and introduced himself to the group's leaders. Then he turned and said something to another uniformed man, who mounted a waiting horse and trotted off. Other riders encouraged the visitors to form a marching column on the street beyond the depot. They lined up four abreast, swinging decorative canes and checking the gold-colored badges and ribbons pinned to their lapels. The leaders were escorted to a carriage at the head of the column; the band of Canton Post No. 25, Grand Army of the Republic, struck up "Marching Through Georgia," and the column moved off, several hundred strong, more or less in time with the music.

Dan tagged along, lugging his bag and making mental notes. Everybody in town seemed to be standing in the bright September sunshine, applauding the visitors as they marched past.

I'd clap too, if I lived here. This campaign must be a bonanza for Canton. Two or three thousand visitors a day, ten or twenty thousand on Saturdays. Think of the money they spend here.

A few blocks further along, a white-painted arch spanned the street, topped by a portrait of McKinley. Here the mounted escort halted the column while one rider went on ahead. He was back in a couple of minutes.

[134]

"All set, gentlemen," he said to the men in the carriage. "Major McKinley's previous guests have left and he's ready to receive you." The march resumed. A few hundred yards farther on, they came to a white frame house on a large lot, set back from the street under tall oak trees. The marchers broke ranks and scrambled across the hard-packed, dusty yard, crowding up to the porch that ran across the front of the house.

Dan, standing at the back of the crowd, noticed a half-dozen men lounging on the porch. Something in their manner—a casually proprietary air—told him they were reporters. He'd wait until this crowd left before he tried to join them.

A burst of cheering drew his attention to the front door of the house as McKinley emerged, accompanied by the First Voters' leaders. He was as Dan remembered him: well-tailored, dignified, his neatly combed dark hair contrasting with pale skin, a determined look on his smoothly handsome face. He looked friendly, if a bit distant.

When the cheers faded, a spokesman for the group read a brief statement. Then McKinley climbed on a chair.

"I congratulate all of you upon having reached your majority," he said, the steady, sincere voice reaching out across the crowd. "I congratulate you upon having entered into full possession of sovereignty in the best government of the world."

The listeners cheered, happy to applaud themselves, and McKinley went on to remind them how fortunate they were:

> You have lived in a period of the greatest opportunity for moral and intellectual growth and enjoyed most favorable conditions for forming right opinions.

He left no doubt what kind of opinions would be right on election day.

> No young man will want to place weights upon his own shoulders, or raise barriers to his own progress which hitherto have never impeded the progress of the industrious, honest, clean, ambitious young man.

Then McKinley turned to one of Bryan's favorite arguments—that the Republicans cared only for the rich and powerful:

> Away with caste and classes! Such a doctrine is un-American and unworthy to be taught a free people. He who would inculcate that spirit among our people is not the friend but the enemy of the poor but honest young man whose soul is fired with a worthy ambition for himself.

He closed with an all-purpose appeal.

> May your votes, young gentlemen, be always given to preserve
> our unity, our honor, our flag, our currency and our country, and to
> save our blessed inheritance always from lawlessness, dishonesty, and
> violence.

The crowd gave three cheers for the candidate. He reached forward
to shake hands with a few of those closest to the porch, then disengaged
gracefully and waved as he disappeared back inside the house.

That's pretty smooth, Dan thought, moving toward the porch as the
Horse Guards herded the First Voters away from the house. *They think he's
talking just to them, but he's not. The reporters will send out that crack about
class and caste, so he'll get in a lick at Bryan in every newspaper in the country
tomorrow. And he doesn't even have to go downtown to do it—just stand on
his own front porch.*

When Dan reached the porch, he was delighted to find a heavyset, round-
faced correspondent named Mark Matthews, political writer for the *Cleveland Plain Dealer* and a friend from convention days. Matthews had been
covering McKinley for a month.

"They don't leave anything to chance," he explained as they sat
waiting for the next delegation. "Did you notice that fellow *read* his little
speech to McKinley? Every one of those has to be approved ahead of time
by the candidate himself, and he rewrites half of 'em. That way nobody
says anything to embarrass him. And he writes out his own stuff to get it
just the way he wants it for every talk. That way, each delegation thinks
it's only them he cares about."

"Isn't it awful hard to keep track of 'em all, with so many coming and
going?"

Matthews waved toward the rear of the house. "They have an office
out back. Every time a train comes in, one of those Horse Guards trots over
from the depot to let 'em know who's just arrived. They pull out a paper
with all the information about that group and the remarks that have been
prepared, and McKinley studies it over for five or ten minutes and then
goes out and delivers it word-for-word. He's something."

"What happens to them when they leave?"

"Oh, that's all taken care of, too. They form 'em up and march 'em
back downtown, and if there's time they feed 'em lunch." Matthews chuckled. "And then they turn 'em loose to distribute their money to the merchants of Canton."

"Seems like the whole town is part of it."

"That's about right. Everybody makes money. Why, when the delegations get backed up they even have 'em wait on the street where the brewery is. They've never sold so much beer."

"No wonder the citizens stand on the sidewalks and applaud." Dan shook his head. "Who thought it all up?"

"Well, in a way it just happened," Matthews said. "The day he was nominated, four or five trainloads of people came here, from Alliance and Massillon and Minerva, places like that, to cheer him and celebrate. He was up most of the night. They say fifty thousand came and went by morning."

The Cleveland reporter warmed to his tale. "A day or two later, they were planning the campaign, and McKinley said he wouldn't try to match Bryan as a speaker and a traveler, 'cause he couldn't do the one and wouldn't do the other, and that was that. Someone got to talking about what happened here the night of the nomination, and McKinley said why not *bring* people here? Hanna got the railroads to help with special trains and fares so low you can hardly afford to stay home. And there you are."

Dan grinned. "And here *you* are, for the season."

"Well, it's not so bad. You sleep in the same bed every night and the food's pretty good at the hotel," Matthews said. "I guess it's different if you have to cover the Silver-Tongued Orator of the Platte. I've heard some terrible stories."

"I'll bet. I haven't done that yet, but I'm going to, and I'll send you a report." Dan stood up and hefted his bag. "Now I better go get a room. Where'd you say you were putting up?"

Through the afternoon and evening and into the next day, Dan watched delegations come and go, worshiping at the Republican shrine.

McKinley talked sound money to every group. He told three thousand workers from the Carnegie Steel Works in Homestead, Pennsylvania, that the issue was

> whether we shall have the same good money we now have and have had for more than sixteen years past, or try the hazardous experiment of engaging in the independent free coinage of silver, an experiment that has worked disaster everywhere and is bound to work it here if ever tried.

In contrast, Dan noticed that the candidate talked about farmers only once in two days. When he did, he said exactly what Dan had heard him say two years earlier in South Dakota.

> It does not require a great effort of the mind to comprehend that if you increase the quantity of wheat in a single year

enormously, with about the same number of consumers as before, the prices will come down.

The price of wheat is fixed by the law of supply and demand, which is eternal. Gold has not made long crops or short crops, high prices or low prices. Gold has not opened up the wheat fields of Russia, India, or the Argentine Republic, nor will free silver in the United States destroy them.

McKinley scorned Bryan's familiar charge that Eastern bankers exploited the hard-pressed farmers of the West and South. He said it was "absurd" to argue that the gold standard was hurting the farmers of the West.

The new and promising states of North and South Dakota, Kansas, Nebraska, and Minnesota are certainly young giants of the West, and their growth in population from 940,000 in 1870 to 4,490,000 in 1890 demonstrates to any fair-minded man that however much they have suffered by drouths and poor crops, they are still reasonably vigorous and in no great danger of being abandoned or bankrupted.

The sarcasm invited—and won—laughter and applause from the audience, but Dan found it neither amusing nor valid.

He uses 1890 as the year to measure. That lets him ignore the drought and the depression and all the farmers that have given up and left since then. Maybe McKinley is trying to put down the East-West argument because he thinks it's beginning to cut.

There is nothing the matter with any of the states, Eastern or Western, except their people have not now the full occupation at full wages which they formerly enjoyed. The great trouble in this country is that we have not enough for our people to do.

That's a funny way to say that thousands of people are out of work, Dan thought. But the visitors ate it up.

McKinley never missed a chance to let his listeners applaud themselves. Dan could hardly believe his ears as the candidate lathered up some friendly Ohio newspaper editors.

To be a real, capable, and worthy journalist, wise, honorable, and efficient, is to attain the highest plane of human opportunity and usefulness. To love and proclaim truth, for truth's sake; to disseminate knowledge and useful information; to correct misimpressions; to enlighten the misinformed; to feed an expectant and anxious people with the occurrences of the world daily—indeed, almost hourly; to discover and correct abuses; to fairly and honorably advocate a great cause; in short, to mold and direct public opinion, which is always the mission of journalism, is surely the noblest of professions.

Two days of such stuff left Dan bemused, his mind dulled by pompous generalities. But he had to admit that it seemed to work. McKinley was clearly a strong and self-confident candidate who knew exactly what he wanted—and how to get it.

On his way home Dan stopped at Chicago to see Mark Hanna. He found the manager in a small office at Republican headquarters, tucked away behind rooms filled with mountains of pamphlets, letters, booklets, and posters.

Workers bustled in and out, bundling and addressing stacks of literature. On one wall a large map of the United States bristled with colored pins.

"What's that?" Dan asked Hanna.

"Pretty, ain't it?" The manager chuckled. "Each color pin is for a different Republican speaker. We're like any other business with something to sell—we have to keep track of our traveling men, make sure we don't miss any promising territory."

Dan reported on his visit to Canton.

"I'm glad that's going well," he said. "It makes for good party spirit and newspaper stories. But *this* is what's going to win this election." Hanna gestured at the tables loaded with literature ready for shipping. "On this money issue you have to educate, educate, educate. Billy Bryan's talking nonsense; we're going to give people facts and let 'em decide for themselves."

"That's going to cost a pretty penny."

"I was in New York last week. Mr. James J. Hill and I visited with some folks there. It was slow going at first, but after he explained, they understood."

Hanna offered no details; he didn't discuss Republican finances with reporters—even those he liked. Dan tried a different tack.

"Out our way, Bryan's pretty strong. I believe he'll carry South Dakota."

"Wouldn't surprise me if he did, and Nebraska and Kansas too," Hanna replied. "But if he keeps talking nothing but silver, we'll carry the East and the old Middle West. That'll win this election."

Dan grinned at Hanna. "You may be right. But if you don't mind, I think I'll take a look from Bryan's side of the fence before I write that."

Chapter 17

MORE THAN ten thousand people came to Falls City to see the handsome young Democrat whose barnstorming campaign had captured the nation's attention. Despite a steady rain, South Dakota's biggest city swelled to nearly twice its normal population. People crowded around the depot, lined the parade route, and overflowed the grandstand at the fairgrounds where William Jennings Bryan would speak. Bryan, sheltered under a big umbrella, rewarded their endurance with a rousing stump speech.

Dan stood with Grace among the reporters traveling with the candidate. He thought Bryan looked tired; there were shadows under his eyes, and he seemed to have lost weight since Dan last saw him in Chicago. But the mellow baritone voice was strong and steady, and he struck a defiant note.

> People tell us we cannot succeed because the financiers, the businessmen, those who have great property interests are against us. My friends, money talks, but money don't vote.
>
> They tell us we cannot succeed because some of the great newspapers are against us. Why, my friends, editors only vote once.
>
> We would like to have all the newspapers on our side, but we would far rather have the people with us than the newspapers, and it is almost true that there is nobody on our side but the people.

Grace giggled. She tugged at Dan's sleeve and whispered to him: "He put that in just for you, to welcome you aboard." Dan was joining Bryan's train for the swing through the Dakotas and Minnesota.

"No, they all run against the newspapers," Dan muttered. "Bryan's no different. He gets along fine with the reporters. He only says that because he knows people don't like editors telling them how to vote."

Bryan advised his listeners to go home and dry off so they could "stay healthy to vote." Dan swung his carpetbag up into the wagon set aside for traveling reporters and turned to his wife.

"I'll miss you."

"Huh!" Grace retorted. "You'll have too much fun to miss me, and you know it." She reached out, turned up his coat collar, and buttoned the top button. "Try to keep warm and dry. You'll be out in this weather, and you won't do the paper any good if you get sick." Dan, embarrassed by this public display of domestic concern, kissed her hastily and climbed up into the wagon as it started along behind the candidate.

The Bryan train steamed northwest through the raw, darkening afternoon. It was raining so hard at the little town of Salem that Bryan spoke from the back platform of the train for only five minutes before sending his audience home.

The weather was better at Huron, and though Bryan was two hours behind schedule, there was a big crowd at the depot and another at the speaker's stand.

By the time he finished that speech it was dark, but the day's work was far from done. The reporters were astounded, on arriving at Aberdeen at one o'clock in the morning, to find nearly ten thousand people still waiting to hear Bryan.

Bryan rewarded them with a full oratorical dose—and then spoke to two more meetings. It was nearly three o'clock in the morning when he finished in Aberdeen, and they had to wait an hour longer to change to another train for the next leg of the trip. So no one had more than a couple of hours' sleep, and that on the unyielding seats of a day coach, before the new train reached Wahpeton, a little North Dakota town on the Red River.

It was just after six o'clock in the morning, but the weary reporters stumbling out into the first light of day found several hundred men and women, many bundled in bearskin coats, waiting for Bryan. The candidate came out rumpled and unshaven to greet the faithful, though for once he didn't produce a speech. Dan, shivering sleepily in the predawn chill, massaged a crick in his neck and thought glumly of Grace's parting remark about the fun he'd have on the Bryan tour.

As the train rattled north toward Fargo and another long day of campaigning, Dan recalled his visit to Ohio the previous month. *This isn't much like sitting on McKinley's front porch. I hope we have time for a decent breakfast before we have to get back on the train.*

While Bryan napped in Fargo, Dan guided his fellow travelers to a hotel dining room where they devoured steak, bacon, eggs, hotcakes, and fried apples. The food—and the coffee that went with it—brought the weary reporters back to life.

"Is every day like this?" Dan asked. "I don't see how you stand it."

The Associated Press man drained half a cup of coffee at one swallow. "Pretty much. He makes a dozen speeches a day, plus all those little back-platform talks. Anytime he finds two or three people in one place, he makes a speech."

"I don't see how he keeps going," Dan said.

"Well, he can sleep anywhere, for one thing," the Associated Press man explained. "I've even seen him sleep standing up, leaning against a wall. And he eats a lot."

"And he takes care of his voice," the United Press reporter added. "He really loves what he's doing. He'd rather make a speech than anything."

Bryan had plenty of chances that day to do what he liked best, starting with a half-hour speech at Fargo, where ten thousand people waited in the morning mist of the Red River valley. He kept the message simple:

> The maintenance of the gold standard means a continuance of low prices and hard times. If anybody likes hard times, he ought to vote the Republican ticket.

Around Fargo, the rich fields of the Red River valley were as flat as a billiard table, but as the train headed south into Minnesota the country began to change. Dan felt a stirring of recognition, and all at once he realized these rolling plains looked a lot like the Nebraska homestead where he was born.

At Breckenridge 1,500 men and women were at the depot. At Herman, a smaller place, several hundred farmers and their families crowded around the back platform of the train. At Morris, the biggest crowd since Fargo. At Benson, 1,500. At Willmar, 2,500.

Dan noticed that in every talk, short or long, Bryan raised the idea of conflicting class interest. On one side he saw "a handful of millionaires" with "great aggregations of wealth," the "holders of fixed investments." On the other side he put everybody else—particularly the "toiling masses," farmers and workers who were the "producers of wealth," those who earned their living by hard physical work.

At the little town of Waverly Bryan made the class argument more explicit:

> If you sympathize with the struggling masses of the people you will vote for bimetallism; but if your sympathies are with the capitalistic classes, you will vote for the gold standard.

He may be talking about money, Dan thought, *but he's setting section against section, have against have-not, even farm against city.*

That kind of argument still troubled Dan, who thought Bryan's talk of "struggling masses" and "capitalistic classes" sounded almost alien.

As if in reply, Bryan noted at his next stop that he was being accused of "arraying one class against another."

> Well, let us divide society into two classes; on the one side put the nonproducers, and on the other side put the producers of wealth, and you will find that in this country the majority of the laws are made by the nonproducers instead of the producers of wealth.
>
> My friends, that is the only class that we raise; and if to tell the people who produce wealth that they have a right to make the laws so as to secure to themselves a just portion of the wealth they produce is raising class against class, then I am willing to be called an agitator.

The farmers cheered, and Dan had to admit it made some sense—especially when he remembered Hanna describing how he and James J. Hill had rattled the doorknobs on Wall Street for campaign funds.

Maybe it's true in the cities, Dan thought. *People are different in the cities; the rich are richer and the poor are a lot poorer than in the country. So maybe it's natural to set people against each other in those big cities out East. It still doesn't seem right around here.*

He'd have to think about it when he wasn't so tired.

St. Paul, Minnesota, October 1896

If Bryan was tired, he didn't show it that night. He made three speeches in St. Paul, and the excitement in the packed halls and along the city streets seemed to energize him, as if he drew strength from the more demonstrative big-city crowds.

Eight thousand people jammed every space in the Civic Auditorium, with some even perched on the rafters. The band played him in to "El Capitan," the Sousa march that had become his campaign theme song. Bryan responded with a fiery talk that hit hard at the Wall Street bankers.

> We have had hard times in this country and yet, my friends, you cannot convince the Morgan syndicate that we have hard times in a country where they can make several million dollars out of one bond issue. These men first make it necessary to have the country saved, and then save it at so much per save.

Bryan closed his final St. Paul speech that night with a prediction.

> I believe the people are awake at last. I believe the people are aroused to action, and that they are about ready to express

themselves. And if you don't want to hear vigorous language, you had better keep cotton in your ears when the election returns come in.

The great answering roar of the crowd woke Dan, sound asleep on the press bench.

Minneapolis, Minnesota, October 1896

Lounsberry took a long swallow of beer, set the stein down on the table, and wiped his mustache. Dan was winding up his account of Bryan's triumphal evening in St. Paul.

". . . and I kept falling asleep, and the crowd kept waking me up." Dan smiled ruefully in the dim light of Schiek's restaurant. "He really had 'em going, Colonel."

"He'll get an even bigger welcome here tonight. But it doesn't mean he'll carry the city. Minneapolis always turns out when a big bug comes to town."

Dan recalled the remark an hour later as he and Lounsberry entered the Exposition building beside the Mississippi River. Minneapolis had certainly "turned out": twelve thousand excited people were packed into the hall, and the candidate, refreshed by a Sunday rest, rewarded them with a stemwinder.

Bryan reminded his city listeners how they depended on the farmers.

> Here is a great city and across the river is another great city, the Twin Cities of the Northwest. These cities rest upon the broad and fertile plains. Make it impossible for the farmer to buy, and I ask you how the merchants of Minneapolis and St. Paul are going to sell to men who cannot buy.
>
> It is your farmers who are going to buy the things you produce, and you had better take care of them instead of making legislation to suit the financier.

"You know, there's one thing I don't like about him," Dan said to Lounsberry as they walked back across the new Mississippi River bridge. "He keeps setting class against class, farmer against banker, West against East."

"Well, that's the way things are," Lounsberry replied. "Look, I'm not voting for him, but he's dead right on that one. Things aren't what they used to be, when what was good for one man was good for everyone. Nowadays you've got a big working class in the cities, a lot of them foreigners, and there's more separation between them and the fellows who hire them. That's bound to change politics."

Lounsberry gestured back toward the Exposition building. "You

[144]

could see it tonight. I looked at the men on the platform; damned few of them were the ones you usually see at public meetings. The businessmen, the professional men, the leaders, they're all against him."

Dan shook his head. "I don't think there's that kind of split at home. And I hope it doesn't go that way, either."

His friend and mentor took him by the elbow. "Dan, it's going that way in the small places as well as the big ones. It probably already has in your town, and you haven't seen it because you don't *want* to see it. But it's there."

I'm afraid he's right, Dan thought. *And maybe Bryan's right, too. Maybe the reason that class war talk upsets me is because I know that it's true.*

Falls City, November 1896

On election day the voters ended the argument with an avalanche of nearly fourteen million votes, by far the greatest number ever cast in a presidential election.

As expected, Bryan won most of the West and all of the South, while McKinley swept every state in the Northeast. The election was decided, as Hanna had predicted, in the Midwest: McKinley carried every state from Ohio across to Iowa and Minnesota, with North Dakota thrown in for good measure. Altogether he defeated Bryan by half a million votes; by carrying all the big states, he rolled up an even wider margin in the electoral vote.

After all the sound and fury, the citizens of Falls City accepted the results quickly and quietly. Civic discourse quickly regained its normal civility.

Amos Harper appeared in the *Daily News* office on the first Saturday after the election and sat down beside George Norton's desk.

"How've you been, George?"

Norton stared at his friend, then relaxed into a tentative smile. "Oh, pretty well, Amos. Little Harry's started to talk."

"And he takes after his father—"

"I like to think so."

"—so he won't stop talking except to eat." Amos laughed and, in a moment, George joined in. Dan, listening from his adjacent office, knew the two friends were again comfortable with each other; Amos's sally had swept away whatever animosity remained from their political disagreements. Dan poked his head through the door to greet his father-in-law.

"Come in here, Mr. Editor," Amos said. "Maybe you can tell us what happened on Tuesday."

"Bryan lost."

"Now there's a piece of revealed truth." It was George's turn to try a witticism. "I sometimes wonder about newspaper men."

Dan grinned. "All right. But actually that's really the story: Bryan lost—everywhere."

"Not in South Dakota," Amos reminded him. Bryan had carried their state by the narrowest of margins, 183 votes out of almost 83,000 cast.

"Not quite. But he only carried the states he couldn't lose, in the South and the West. He lost the Midwest, the cities and the country both, and that's what beat him."

"What beat him," George suggested, "was that he was wrong about silver and cheap money, and everybody knew it."

"Well, you're partly right," Amos mused, scraping out his pipe. "He lost the argument."

"He deserved to lose it," George insisted.

"Maybe, maybe not," Dan said. "He passed up a lot of other good arguments to talk silver. When he did attack bankers and Wall Street and the trusts, people cheered. He should've done more of that."

"How could anyone fall for that stuff?" George said.

"I watched them in St. Paul and Minneapolis," Dan insisted. "They ate it up. City people. Bryan needed city votes—and he didn't go hard enough for 'em."

"I'm afraid you're right." Amos puffed to fire up his pipe. "I hate to admit it, but farmers can't do anything anymore unless they join up with city people."

"City people? A bunch of ignorant immigrants, anarchists, foreigners!" George was scornful. "Why would you want to join up with them?"

"Because there's more to connect us than there is to split us," Amos said. "And there's a whole lot more of *them* than there are of *us*. We've tried to do it alone—in '90, '92, this time—and it won't work. Farmers don't have the power anymore."

"Actually, Bryan didn't do so well with farmers." Dan had been studying returns all week. "He almost lost this state—a state that's all farmers, no big cities. And he did lose every farm state east of here."

"They knew they'd be better off with McKinley and the Republicans," George said. "Bryan couldn't fool 'em."

Amos pointed a big forefinger at George. "You think the Republicans won, don't you?"

"Are you trying to tell me the Democrats won?"

"Nope." The other two men waited as Amos relit his pipe. "Neither of them won. The really big fellows won, the rich men, the railroads, Wall Street, the trusts—the ones that don't care which party gets in as long as they're in charge. That's what Mark Hanna's all about."

Dan listened hard. *He's saying what Bryan said, only he makes more sense. It's not a matter of party against party at all.*

"You think the Republicans are the party of business, don't you?" Amos continued. "Well, that's not good enough for the really big interests.

[146]

There's too many different kinds in the Republican party—workers, farmers, all kinds of little fellows with interests of their own.

"The big men have only one political goal: to make the government work for them, protect them from interference, so they can go on skimming the cream. And they don't care which party does it. Cleveland's no different from McKinley to them."

"That's just hogwash," George sputtered.

"No, it's not, and you know it's not." Amos jumped up and leaned across George's desk, thumping it to punctuate his argument. "The grain companies get together in Minneapolis every day and set the price they'll pay for grain, and they send out orders to their elevators in the country, and it's the same everywhere, and that's that." *Thump.*

"No competition, no bargaining, take it or leave it—and farmers have to take it because they have no other place to sell their grain." *Thump.*

"You're exaggerating," George grumbled.

"No, I'm not, and you know it." Dan had never seen Amos so visibly angry. "And price is only the start. You know perfectly well that elevators give short weight, too, and set low grades on the grain they buy—so they can make an extra profit when they sell it at the true grade later. The farmer loses five or ten cents on every bushel, but he can't do a damned thing about it because the government just ignores it."

"Nobody's ever proved that kind of thing. It's just gossip."

"Some things you *know* are true, even if you can't prove 'em," Amos said. "And there's more. The railroads—"

He suddenly stopped and stepped back, raising both hands in a gesture of apology. "I didn't mean to blow off steam like that. The point is that the really big fellows have a different kind of political party."

George tried to lighten the mood. "That sounds like the kind of party I'd like to join," he said. "Where do I apply?"

"You can't," Amos answered quickly. "You're not big enough or rich enough. You're too honest—and you don't think money is the most important thing in the world."

"Well. Well." George seemed embarrassed, as if he had been caught doing a good deed. "If it isn't, it'll do for second best until something better comes along."

Dan came back to Amos's idea. "If that's the way it is, then Bryan had it right when he talked about class against class."

Amos nodded. "Yes, except he missed the point. He thinks it's farm against city, East against West, and so on. But it's really the richest, the biggest, the most powerful, against everybody else—farmers, workers, merchants, Democrats, Republicans, *everybody.*"

"So what's the answer?"

Amos smiled his knowing, weary, forgiving smile. "Bright young fellows like you have to persuade the old parties to adopt the Populist

[147]

program from 1892. Remember the Omaha platform? The one you thought was so radical? That's the way to get the rich men's hands off your throats. Just about everything you need is in there."

"Huh!" George Norton couldn't contain himself. "And a whole lot we *don't* need, too."

"Now, George, all you remember is silver, and taking over the railroads." Amos spoke quietly now. "Stop hollering for a minute and think about some of the other things in that Omaha platform: Secret ballot. Eight-hour day. Initiative and referendum. Direct election of senators. Commonsense things like that."

"You won't get me to call that common sense."

Amos sighed. "Don't pay any attention to him, Dan, even if he is your boss," he said. "Just remember what I'm telling you. One of the parties, probably both, will come back and steal that platform, one plank at a time. Until they do, Mark Hanna and his friends are going to run this country for their own benefit."

Dan wasn't sure about that. But he was sure about one thing: for the first time in an election, the country had divided along class lines, and it wasn't just Bryan's doing. Mark Hanna and his helpers had made precisely the same argument—to the rich.

Chapter 18

"MRS. NORTON, Mrs. Norton, wake up!"
Mary Norton struggled to come awake. The voice came from a long way off. Her head felt as if it were stuffed with cotton, and she let herself slide back into the comforting darkness.

"Mrs. Norton. Please!" The voice, she realized, belonged to the hired girl. It was reinforced by a series of sharp knocks on the bedroom door. "The baby's sick. Please come."

The urgent words penetrated the fog. *Oh my God, what time is it? Where's George?* She reached across the bed. Nobody there. He must have gone to work. She made herself sit up.

"I'm sorry, Anna. I must have overslept again. I'll be there in a minute."

A splash of cold water on her face helped. Mary pulled on a robe and went across the hall to the baby's room. Four-year-old James was standing by the door.

"Is baby Harry real sick, Ma?"

"I don't think so, dear. Don't you worry about it." Mary's hand stroked his blond hair. "Did you see Father before he left for work?"

"Yes, at breakfast." James giggled. "He made Anna sew a button on his coat."

Mary remembered: last night she had promised George she'd do that first thing in the morning, before he left for work. "Oh, Anna, I'm sorry. I said I'd do it and then I forgot."

The maid was a husky Norwegian girl from a farm outside of town. "That's all right, Mrs. Norton." She gestured toward the baby's crib. "But he wouldn't touch his breakfast, and he don't look too good."

Mary leaned over the crib. Little Harry was flushed and listless, and his forehead was hot. She made an effort to concentrate.

[149]

"Is John here?" John was the hired man-of-all-work.

"No, he took Mr. Norton to the office in the buggy," Anna replied. "It was too cold for him to walk, way below zero and the wind's awful. But he should be back any time now."

Mary made herself think clearly. "When . . . when he gets here, send him for Dr. Lewis. I don't think the baby's real sick, but it won't hurt to have him take a look. I'll take care of him for now."

"All right, Mrs. Norton." Anna glanced at Mary Norton, then collared James as she started for the stairs. "You come with me, Jimmy. Your mama's busy with the sick baby."

Mary picked up Harry. She carried him into her bedroom, climbed back into bed, and laid him down beside her. She sank back into the pillows, shutting her eyes tight to stop the tears that pressed against her eyelids.

I am not going to cry again. I won't. I just won't.

But it was no use: today was going to be like yesterday and the day before and the day before that, and tomorrow would be like today, and the day after tomorrow. . . . It had been that way ever since she lost her first baby, her precious little girl. Why had Dr. Lewis told her she'd feel better when she had other babies? He shouldn't have said that, it wasn't so.

Now she was angry, and the buzzing began again, filling her head and making her arms tingle. She reached into the drawer of her nightstand and found the little silver box. She took out a pill and swallowed it with some water. Then she looked into the box.

Only four left. When the doctor's here I'll get some more from him. They're the only thing that makes me feel better.

George Norton stood by the front-office stove, swinging his arms and rubbing his hands. The short ride from the house on Union Avenue to the *Dakota News* had left him chilled clear through.

He was deep in thought, but not about the cold or his moody wife. He was thinking about the Sunday edition of the *Dakota Daily News*.

Now we can do it. Before, we couldn't; there was no way to deliver a paper on Sunday, because there was no mail service on Sunday.

He turned around to warm his backside. *But now we have our own carriers six days a week in every town, and there's no reason why those boys can't work Sundays too.*

And the time is right. The depression's letting up, business is improving.

Warmed both front and rear by the potbellied stove, Norton headed for Dan's office. As usual, he wasted no time on small talk.

"What will it cost to produce the Sunday paper?" he began. "I mean for added news material. I can figure the production costs; what will you need?"

Dan was startled. The publisher had talked to him about a Sunday edition as long as two years ago, but he had told him not to discuss it with anyone else, and he hadn't mentioned the subject in over a year. He certainly had never committed himself to a Sunday paper; now he was talking as if Dan knew a decision had already been made.

In fact Dan had thought about it months ago, daydreaming through a slow afternoon, and had even made some notes. But he had stuck them away and forgotten them until now.

"Well, I've thought some about that," he said, trying to sound as matter-of-fact as his boss. He dug the old notes out of a desk drawer. "It was a while ago, and the figures are a little rough, but they'll give you an idea."

He showed Norton the sheets and explained each item: a new feature service, more money for local correspondents, the extra cost of taking the Associated Press news wire seven days a week, an added illustration service, and the other nuts-and-bolts costs of expansion.

"You don't have any new people on this list." Norton, as he often did, phrased his question as a statement.

"I figured we could get by with what we have, at least to start."

"Would you rather start out strong?" Now the publisher made a statement by asking questions. "Would that make it easier to sell new subscriptions?"

Dan thought a moment. "Is this going to be mostly a city edition?"

"No, no, no. We'll deliver in every town in our circulation area." Norton spoke crisply, as if it were an accomplished fact. "We'll use the carriers."

"Then we'll need news from the whole area, and we will need some new help—at least one more reporter to do regional stories, and we really should put somebody full time at the statehouse. And maybe another to cover farm news. And—"

"Whoa." Norton managed a frosty smile. "You're not running some big-city paper. And I won't pay anyone to loaf around the governor's office. But you can add one man, to do regional stories and cover farm news." He thought a moment. "Farm news. I like that idea. That'll sell papers in the country."

"But George, we can't deliver to farmers on Sunday. We don't have carriers out in the country, and there's no mail service on Sundays, even with rural free delivery."

Norton smiled. "People won't buy a *daily* paper if it comes a day late. But with a *Sunday* paper it doesn't matter. You'll put out one they can read all week long. It'll stay fresh until the R.F.D. delivers it on Monday."

"I think that'll be hard to put across."

Norton nodded. "Maybe it will, at first. But I'm in this for the long run. Someday we'll be able to deliver to farms on Sunday, and when we do, we'll go over the whole state. Sooner or later, we'll have a lot more country circulation on Sunday than on weekdays. Farm circulation can make the Sunday paper our big earner."

Dan was again struck by the contradictions in his publisher. Behind that noncommittal banker's face was a gambler—a man who calculated the odds with great care, but was willing to put in his whole stack at the right moment.

"I'll check those figures over today," he told Norton. "Get 'em up to date."

"Good." Norton was through with this subject for the moment. "I want to start Sunday publication by the first of September."

By evening the baby was feeling better; it was apparently no more than a minor stomach upset. Mary Norton was feeling better too—partly because Dr. Lewis had replenished her supply of nerve pills.

She knew she shouldn't take so many of them, but sometimes they were the only thing that helped her through the bad times when all she could think of was little Lucy.

Of course she loved James and Harry too, but that didn't keep her from thinking about her first child, the beautiful baby girl God had taken away. It still made her feel guilty—*I must have done something terrible to be punished that way, what could it have been?*—and when the sadness and guilt got hold of her, and the buzzing began, and the tingling, the pills were the only thing that could make her forget.

She never talked to George about it. *He wouldn't understand.* And he was so busy with his work at the newspaper, he even went back to the office at night sometimes. *He shouldn't work so hard.*

February 1897

Norton did work hard, but that wasn't always the reason he went out after supper.

David Currier slid into Dan's office late one afternoon. He had an uneasy half-smile on his face as he closed the door behind him.

"Why, Dan," Currier began, "I ... ah ... wondered if you knew about something."

He stopped, and Dan thought: *Here comes a juicy piece of gossip.*

"Can't tell you if I know when I don't know what it is I'm supposed to know," the editor said, grinning.

"Well." Currier hesitated again, then leaned forward across Dan's desk and spoke in a half-whisper. "It's about George ... Mr. Norton." He raised his eyebrows. "And a woman."

Dan's smile faded abruptly. "Tell me about it."

Once started, Currier told the story readily: there was a young widow. Dan recognized the name; she was a handsome woman. Her late husband had done business at Norton's bank. The unfortunate man, making a will at the time of his marriage, had named Norton executor of his estate. The man was so young that no one thought anything of it—until he died of the infection caused by a burst appendix.

"Nothing happened for a year or so," Currier continued, "until about a month ago Mr. Norton apparently concluded that she might be interested in, well, more than business. So instead of meeting her at the bank the way he usually did, he went to her house one evening."

Apparently Norton had guessed right, Currier said, because in the last four weeks he had visited the lady at her home, in the evening, no fewer than seven times.

"I thought you should know about it," Currier said. "Of course I don't like talking about such things."

Of course not, Dan thought. *That's why you're practically drooling.*

"You seem to have a lot of details."

Currier allowed himself just the shadow of a smile. "Well, I try to keep my ears open. And I have a couple of friends who work at the bank. They know when papers are taken out of the vault, and things like that."

"Of course you've said nothing to anyone but me."

Currier hesitated only a second or two. "Of course not."

Dan got him out of his office as soon as he could. *David's got a little sly streak; he really enjoyed telling me that. Still, he was right. I should know about something like that. It could affect the paper. It will for sure if this goes on much longer.*

But what can I do about it?

As it turned out, he didn't have to do anything. Norton's evening conferences with the widow provided pleasant sport through the dark midwinter weeks; but soon, as was his habit, he began to disengage. At about the same time, the lady decided she should look for someone younger—and someone available for marriage. So it all ended quietly and amicably.

Dan was vastly relieved. For his part, Norton seemed unconcerned about any potential scandal, and unembarrassed in his domestic affairs: in fact, Mary Norton was soon pregnant again.

Still Dan had an uneasy feeling. *Sooner or later George will have to learn to keep his britches buttoned—or there's going to be hell to pay.*

Dan came half-awake in the gray light of early morning. He was dimly aware of Grace turning over in the warm hollow of the bed.

Was it time to get up already? No, it was Sunday.

He let himself slip back toward sleep, but her fingers were on his face, tracing the line of his jaw, brushing his lips.

"Wake up, sleepyhead." The touch of her hand was just enough to bring him fully awake.

"It's Sunday. Can't a fellow get some sleep on his day off?" His grumbling was amiable. "Your hands are cold."

"I woke up and I was lonely. I've been lying here thinking."

Dan felt her smoothness through the flannel nightgown. "Thinking? What about?"

"That's for me to know—and for you to find out." They moved closer to each other, arranging their bodies, and after a moment Grace sighed. "There you are."

Later Dan pulled a blanket up, reaching over to make sure Grace was covered too. It was April, but the mornings were still cold. He propped himself up on one elbow and repeated the question he had asked earlier.

"What were you thinking about?"

"You." She traced the line of his jawbone again. Then her finger stopped, and she giggled. "About how you better enjoy yourself while you can."

Dan smiled down at her. "I wasn't planning to leave."

"Well, I'm certainly relieved to hear that, Mr. Woods." She shifted to her familiar mocking tone. "But you won't be playing any more games in the morning after November."

"Why not?"

"Because after that one of us will always have to get up to look after the baby."

Grace's pregnancy brought no immediate change in their life, aside from Dan's tendency to fuss over her health and comfort. His concern was needless. She continued to teach her tenth-grade high school class; the school year would be over before her condition became obvious, she said, and besides she felt fine.

Dan didn't have any extra time to worry about his wife, in any event. Deadlines were closing in for the start-up of the new Sunday paper, and a lot remained to be done.

George Norton wanted something clearly different from the daily editions—something that would proclaim, as he put it, that "Sunday is a different day." With that in mind Dan planned a sort of weekly magazine: lots of pictures, a page devoted exclusively to news of statewide interest, another page of national news, and—at Norton's suggestion—a third page about foreign countries and faraway places.

"We should bring the world to our reader," the publisher said. "Not just a lot of froth, either, but solid news and information. People need to understand that what goes on in other places affects us."

Norton didn't want it all heavy; he prescribed plenty of lighter stuff, too. "I don't believe in publishing a highbrow newspaper, or one that wears a minister's collar," he lectured Dan and David Currier. "I do believe in a tolerable deference to the interests of the reader."

So Dan ordered several of the new "funny papers," made room for lots of sports news, and looked for features on readers' special interests. (He recruited the secretary of the Falls City Wheelmen, for example, to write a weekly column for bicycle riders.) And he reserved several pages for "society" news—which could include anything from wedding announcements to pickle recipes, so long as it was aimed specifically at women.

It all added up to a lot of new material to be handled every week. So much, in fact, that Dan finally went back to Norton and asked for one more new hire: an editor to deal with all the Sunday copy. The publisher's reply surprised him.

"I thought you'd need somebody like that," he said. "So when I figured the costs I put in enough to pay him."

Norton surprised Dan again when he suggested that Dan write a weekly column for the Sunday editorial page. "That's the place for you to talk about politics and so on," he said. "You know a lot about those things, and you ought to let our readers in on it. Besides," he added, displaying a rare smile, "people like to read things they can disagree with."

Dan wasn't sure he needed to go out of his way to collect critics, but the idea appealed to him—especially when Norton added that it would help the column, and the paper, if Dan traveled more and got down to Washington at least once a year.

Norton, as promised, took care of the rest. As spring turned to summer he began coming back to the office after supper, driven by his compulsion to check every detail of every decision. He worked so hard that Dan, who of course should have known better, finally suggested he let up.

The publisher replied as if he were speaking to a not-too-bright child. "At an early age I knew that I would never have money given to me. And I knew I would never be helped to get jobs, so it would be up to me alone if I succeeded in business. I still operate on that assumption." And that was the end of that.

George did it all. He contracted for more newsprint, he directed the overhaul of machinery so it could be run seven days a week, and he drew up delivery schedules. He supervised the sale of advertising for the new edition, and made the most important sales calls himself.

As always, he gave the most attention to building circulation. He took personal command of an all-out effort to sell advance subscriptions to the Sunday paper. He did a lot of traveling that summer to exhort the carrier boys, whose work would be critical to the new venture. He urged them not to limit their efforts to people who already bought the daily paper.

"We'll get those people anyway unless we beat them off with a stick," he told one meeting. "Our job is to get the people who *don't* take the paper now. If we can sell them the Sunday paper, and hold onto them, pretty soon they'll want the daily too."

Norton made the youngsters feel important: "The paper that holds every subscriber it signs up has won the hard part of the fight. The way to hold subscribers is to give them good service, and for that we depend entirely on you."

His timing was just right. After years of business depression and bankruptcy, low farm prices and foreclosures, in the summer of 1897 town and country alike were booming. Business prospered, paychecks grew fat again. Farmers harvested a bumper crop of wheat—and for once, they got high prices at the same time, thanks to a massive crop failure in Russia that brought European buyers rushing into the American market. Wheat prices rose sharply, to almost a dollar a bushel.

When Norton's young salesmen knocked on doors, they found people with money in their pockets—and willing to spend a little of it on a new Sunday newspaper. Advertisers, too, were ready to risk at least a few dollars in the new publication.

On a Saturday afternoon in September Norton and Dan stood in shirt-sleeves and watched the first issue of the *Dakota Sunday News* come off the old press. They had to start the run in the afternoon in order to get papers to the most distant towns for Sunday morning delivery. They would stop the press later and revise—"make over"—a few pages to get late news and sports into papers that would be delivered in or near Falls City.

Now, standing by the clanking, rumbling press, the two men relaxed for the first time in months. Dan felt completely drained after the last-minute rush to get the new paper ready on time. Norton turned to his editor.

"Remember when you told me not to work so hard?" he shouted over the noise of the press.

Dan nodded.

"Well, it's my turn. Get out of here. I'll watch the store. You've done a wonderful job. Go home to Grace!"

He reached out, and they grinned like schoolboys as they shook hands in the noisy shop.

The Sunday paper was a success from the start. Circulation grew steadily; so did advertising, though not as fast as Norton would have liked. He was unruffled: "When we get circulation up, advertisers will come along. They'll need us more than we need them." He revisited all the major towns, encouraging the carriers to redouble their sales efforts.

And everywhere he went, Norton also asked questions: What did people think of the new paper? What did they particularly like? What more was wanted? He discovered one constant: readers liked pictures, especially pictures of people, and wanted more of them.

He reported his findings to Dan and urged him to meet the demand. "Let's have a picture page, maybe more than one," he said. "Get well-known people in. Kings and queens, J. P. Morgan, baseball players, that kind of person. And foreign lands, you know, China, Turkey, places like that." He paused and then, to Dan's astonishment, he added: "And plenty of good-looking women."

Grace laughed when Dan reported the conversation that night. "That's George, all right," she said. "He may be a Methodist deacon, but he knows how to sell newspapers: print a lot of news—and show a few pretty ankles."

Everyone knew George Norton had a long memory. Now it turned out he had a sense of humor, too. He volunteered to write the item about the birth of Dan and Grace's baby in November. After spending a few minutes in the back-copy file, he produced this squib:

> Mr. and Mrs. Daniel Woods of this city announce the birth of a daughter, Abigail, yesterday. Mother and daughter are reported doing well. The father may recover in due course.

Three weeks later it was Norton's turn to be the subject of a similar item when his wife gave birth to a baby girl. They named her Margaret, and to Mary Norton she seemed a sign that God had finally forgiven her for letting little Lucy die. For the first time in six years, she had a happy Christmas; she was so cheered up that she didn't need her nerve medicine nearly so often.

On the day after Christmas, Dan took care of some long-unfinished business. At breakfast he handed Grace the editorial page of the Sunday paper. "This is something I promised you a while back. Read the column."

POINT OF VIEW
By Dan Woods

> Seven years ago this week, on December 29, 1890, there occurred in South Dakota a massacre of three hundred Sioux Indians, two-thirds of them women and children, near Wounded Knee Creek on the Pine Ridge Reservation.
>
> At the time the truth was concealed, and before the facts could be ascertained, public attention turned elsewhere. But now an official and authoritative account has been published in the Annual Report of the U.S. Bureau of Ethnology.
>
> The tragedy came about as a band of Sioux was being escorted back to the reservation by the army. The Indians had fled

because of grievances over the government's failure to provide food and winter clothing as promised.

The report states that on December 28, 1890, the Indians camped as ordered near Wounded Knee Creek so they could be disarmed the next day. Soldiers, supported by four Hotchkiss guns, surrounded the camp. The report states there were 470 soldiers and no more than 106 Sioux warriors.

A little after 8 o'clock the next morning, as troops began to disarm the warriors, one Indian fired his rifle at a soldier. The troops instantly replied with a volley into the crowd of warriors, and a sharp fight broke out.

The report tells what followed: "At first volley the Hotchkiss guns trained on the camp opened fire and sent a storm of shells among the women and children, who had gathered in front of the tipis to watch the unusual spectacle of military display. The guns poured in 2-pound explosive shells at the rate of nearly fifty per minute, mowing down everything alive. . . .

"In a few minutes 200 Indian men, women and children, with 60 soldiers, were lying dead and wounded on the ground, the tipis had been torn down by the shells and some of them were burning above the helpless wounded, and the surviving handful of Indians were flying in wild panic, pursued by hundreds of maddened soldiers and followed up by a raking fire from the Hotchkiss guns. . . .

"There can be no question that the pursuit was simply a massacre, where fleeing women, with infants in their arms, were shot down after resistance had ceased and when almost every warrior was stretched dead or dying on the ground. . . . The bodies of the women and children were scattered along a distance of two miles from the scene of the encounter. . . .

"The whole number of (Indians) killed on the field, or who later died from wounds and exposure, was probably very nearly 300. According to an official statement from the Adjutant-General, 31 soldiers were killed in the battle. About as many more were wounded."

We publish these facts, not to stir up old grievances but merely to complete the record of a sad event in our state's history.

Grace looked up at Dan when she finished reading.

"Remember I promised you I'd find a way to print that story?" he said. "Well, I forgot all about it until one day this fall when Jim McLaughlin came into the office. He's the Indian agent at Standing Rock; you met him one time when he was here."

"I remember him. You said he was different because he was honest."

"That's the one. He told me the government had finally published the true story about Wounded Knee. So I sent away for a copy of the report."

Grace looked up at her husband. "That's really something. It was so long ago that I'd forgotten, but you remembered."

Dan covered his embarrassment by running his hand through his cowlick. "When I was reading that report I got to thinking that the government nowadays treats farmers just the way it used to treat the Indians. Farmers treat Indians worse than almost anyone does, but they're really, well, sort of white Indians. I thought this might make a few of 'em think."

"I think it will."

Dan shook his head. "I don't think too many people around here give a damn about Indians."

He was right. There were a good many snide behind-the-back comments, just loud enough for Dan to hear. There was a fair amount of unpleasant mail, especially from the Black Hills area. And that Sunday night, someone threw a brick with a handful of feathers tied to it through the front window of the *Dakota News* building.

"That's one we won't have to wash this year," George Norton said cheerfully as he inspected the damage on Monday morning. "By the way, I thought the column was splendid."

Falls City, January–March 1898

"He's at it again," Dan informed Grace one night in January as they sat down to supper.

Grace glanced at her husband. "George has found another girl?"

"Yup. Only this time it's not just a 'girl.' She's almost his own age. Supposed to be quite a looker. She's here getting a divorce."

"Oh? How'd he meet her?"

"I think he was at the bank for a directors' meeting when she came in to open her account, and one thing led to another." Dan paused. "He could get into a real mess, getting involved with a divorcée."

Grace glared at her husband. "Who do you think you are, the keeper of community morals?"

"What?" He was stunned.

"It's the way you say 'divorcée.' It was all right for George to get mixed up with a girl almost young enough to be his daughter, but it's not all right with a woman who happens to be divorced."

Dan protested. "I didn't think it was 'all right' then, either."

Grace ignored him. Her temper was rising.

"There's a double standard in this town. Divorce is *legal,* but it's not *respectable.* At least not for a woman. All your merchants and lawyers and hotelkeepers are glad to have women come and spend money here for three months, but they sneer at them—except when they sleep with them."

South Dakota law required only three months' stay to establish legal residence and qualify for a quick divorce. Falls City, as the largest and most accessible city in the state, attracted "Dakota Divorcées" from all over the country.

Now, in her anger, Grace personalized the argument.

"You and your respectable friends are hypocrites. You take money from these women—and then you treat them like prostitutes. I never hear you criticize a divorced man."

Dan didn't like being tarred with that brush. "I don't think I'm a hypocrite. I don't have anything against this woman. What I worry about is what it could do to the paper if there's a scandal."

Grace looked at him for a moment before answering. "All right, fair enough. Just don't coat it up with a lot of pious moralistic mush."

"You needn't worry about that," he growled.

"Good," she snapped. "Grateful for small favors."

Grace had pushed Dan as far as she could, but she knew he was right about the potential damage to the paper. Dan was startled at Grace's vehemence, but he knew she had a point.

They finished supper in silence.

A few days later, Dan and George Norton, bundled in heavy winter coats, stood on a snowy hillside in the bright noonday sun. Dan, seeking total privacy for his showdown with Norton, had asked the publisher to come with him during the lunch hour to inspect a lot Dan was considering buying to build a new house on.

Below them the city stretched away to the north, locked in a glistening coat of snow and ice. There was no wind. Vapor trails rose straight up from every furnace chimney; fatter puffs of steam traced the comings and goings of railroad switch engines across the river. The distant sound of freight cars being coupled carried faintly but distinctly through the frigid air, but the packed snow muffled the sound of wagons and sleighs on nearby city streets.

They admired the scene for a minute or two. Then Dan took a deep breath and changed the subject.

"George, there's something I have to say to you."

"Oh." Dan's choice of words and tone of voice seemed strained, and Norton's defenses went up instantly. "Yes?"

"It's about . . . about this woman."

"What woman?"

Dan took another breath. The cold air burned in his throat, and he exhaled a plume of vapor into the still midday air. "Let's not play games, George. This is hard enough as it is."

Norton was furious, but Dan kept his own voice steady. "I'm not trying to preach; I don't have a license to do that. But you're risking everything you've built up all these years—your standing in this town, your influence, your bank, your chance to build, your money." He hesitated. "And your family."

Norton fixed his eyes directly on Dan's. "It occurs to me that my personal life is nobody's business but my own."

Dan was shaken, but it was too late to pull back now, and he plunged ahead.

"Maybe that's true for some people, ordinary people," he said. "But it's not true for George Norton. You've reached a place where a lot of other people have a stake in what happens to you and your life."

"My life is my affair." Norton was defiant. Then he added, almost wistfully: "I've never met anyone like her."

Dan ignored that. "I'm not talking about your wife . . . or your children. That *is* your affair. I'm talking about people that depend on you, whether you like it or not.

"You once asked me what would happen to the people who work at the paper if you couldn't keep it going. But it's not just those people, it's the paper itself, and the people who depend on it."

Norton was incredulous. "Are you trying to tell me I owe something to people who just *read* the paper?"

"Yes, I am. And you've done it to yourself. You've made the *Dakota News* important to the whole community. That raises the stakes quite a lot. You just can't risk all that. It's not even yours to risk."

"I still don't see why anyone else should tell me how to conduct my own business."

Dan thought he heard the first intimations of retreat in the publisher's voice, and he kept talking. "A newspaper is more than a piece of private property. It's more than just a business. A lot more. God damn it, George, you *know* that."

Norton's response was tentative this time. "I don't see how a purely personal matter could put the paper at risk."

Dan played his high card. "George, you know that sooner or later the owner of a good newspaper in this kind of town will have to deal with the worst kind of pressure. If you keep getting mixed up in this kind of thing, you won't be able to resist that pressure—you'll either have to fold, or have a scandal spread all over the state. Either way the paper's ruined."

Dan stopped. He had never given so much advice all at once to anyone, let alone his boss, and he knew it was time to quit.

The two men stood side by side, still and silent, for several minutes. When Norton broke the silence, his voice was calm and matter-of-fact.

"I'd say this is a prime building site. The town's coming this way, and this will be a mighty fine neighborhood in five years. I reckon any bank would lend you whatever you needed to build." He looked at Dan; his face revealed no emotion. "Even the Falls City National."

Then he turned and walked down the hill, stocky body thick in the heavy winter coat, head pulled down into the turned-up collar, shoulders hunched, alone.

[161]

In the end, it finished quietly enough. Dan knew it was over when Norton's habits reverted to normal and he went back to putting in eleven-hour days at the office. The publisher never said another word to Dan, either about the affair or how it ended.

In fact, though he had reluctantly decided to take Dan's advice, the lady showed him the door first. He had hardly begun to suggest they must part when she announced that she had never considered him anything more than a temporary diversion. She was going to be remarried as soon as she returned to Minneapolis; that was why she was getting the divorce.

"Honey," she added gently, "you just happened along at the right time. I was lonely and needed a man and there you were. But I knew all along that's all it was ever going to be."

That left him feeling that he had been taken advantage of—*used*—by a woman. It was an unfamiliar sensation, one he didn't care for at all.

The affair had also changed the relationship between publisher and editor, as Grace pointed out to her husband.

"You made him admit that he was wrong; you made him back down," she said. "You took it upon yourself to pass judgment on him, and he accepted that judgment, but he'll never forgive you."

"Forgive me for what? I don't think I had a choice."

"That's as may be. But things can never be so easy or so close between you. And someday he'll throw it right back at you."

"What do you mean?"

"I mean you've appointed yourself the guardian of the paper's reputation, and he's accepted that. But the first time you do something that he thinks could harm that reputation, he'll let you know that he remembers every word you said."

Dan laughed. "I guess I better behave."

"You better had." She was not amused. "You mark my words, he'll get even someday."

And when he does, look out, darling—because you'll think a whole load of hay has fallen on you.

For the moment, Dan was too busy to worry about the future. For months it had been obvious that they needed a new plant. It wasn't just the Sunday edition; even before that, the old Lincoln Avenue building had outlived its time. There was no room for the new press, typesetting machines, platemaking equipment, and office space they would need to produce and sell more newspapers, with more pages, more days a week.

They also needed more room for people. Dan's news staff was already badly overcrowded even before the addition of an editor and reporter for the Sunday paper. Now that they had full-time copyeditors they needed a proper copy desk. Dan, trying to manage a full-sized staff that seemed sure to keep on growing, needed a bigger office where he could sit down with three or four people in at least partial privacy.

The same was true elsewhere in the building. Circulation and advertising were separate departments now, with more people, and they too needed more space. Even the frugal publisher admitted he'd like a slightly bigger office.

Norton, as usual, was prepared for the moment. Almost three years earlier, when land prices were still at depression levels, he had quietly bought half a city block at Union Avenue and Eighth Street. Now, in the space of a few weeks, he had plans drawn, new machinery ordered, a builder hired. Construction would start as soon as the frost was out of the ground: he wanted to be in the new building before the end of the year, and he took personal charge of making that happen.

The new plant was not the only building project on Dan's mind. He and Grace decided to go ahead and build a new house, and Dan bought the piece of hillside property that he had showed to Norton. It was a perfect location: close enough to Eudora's house, far enough from Norton's, and within walking distance of the new office.

"Besides," Grace said one February afternoon as they stood on the lot, "you'll be able to look out the window and see the whole downtown from up here." She struck a heroic pose, hand shading her eyes: "The editor, watching over his people."

Why, she's right, you can see it all from up here, he thought. *Maybe that's why I liked it so much.*

Dan jumped as her thumb dug between his ribs and her mocking laugh rang across the hillside.

Chapter 19

D AN HAD the same feeling he always did coming home from Washington: riding the night train out of Chicago, he awoke amid the endless fields of northern Iowa. The land was flat and treeless, the scattered buildings gray and weathered. The contrast with Washington was especially marked this time because it was spring: the capital was at its most beautiful, warm and blooming, while the Midwest was still drab, cold, and gray.

Out here there aren't any trees, there aren't any hills, he thought. *Everything is flat and square and often as not plain ugly. And in Washington there's four seasons in the year; here there's only three, no spring at all.*

I ought to take Ma down there sometime, let her see what a real springtime is like. The anger rose again in his throat as he thought of Eudora's existence in the sod hut.

This country is God-awful hard on people, but it makes them strong, too. Then he thought of his father: *That is, the ones that don't kill themselves fighting it.*

These conflicting thoughts were on Dan's mind as his train came into Falls City in the late afternoon.

Washington's a beautiful place to look at, but the politics are awful dirty. Here it's the other way around: The country's not so pretty but the politics smell a whole lot better.

Oh, this is hard country, all right. And not much to look at this time of year, that's for sure. As the train slowed and the familiar landmarks slid by, he stood up and swung his bag down off the rack.

But I guess I belong here, it's my country.

It's home.

★   ★   ★

Dan had visited Washington just as the long dispute with Spain over its rebellious Cuban colony turned into a crisis. President McKinley had sent the battleship *Maine* to Cuba in January to show that the United States could—and would—project its power in Cuba. The Spanish authorities were friendly, and the ship had been anchored in Havana harbor for three weeks when it exploded and sank the night of February 15. Two hundred and sixty men were killed.

McKinley tried to avoid a war that everyone else seemed to want. He urged calm, arguing that the cause of the explosion was not yet known. The advice was drowned out in an uproar from press, politicians, and public.

To Dan, the political climate seemed all the more harsh in contrast to the capital's gentle springtime. All his life he would remember how it felt when he got off the train in Washington: though it was still March, the afternoon air was balmy, buckets of daffodils brightened the carts of flower sellers along Pennsylvania Avenue, and horses' hoofs clattered on the cobblestones. Dan realized he hadn't heard *that* sound since the first snow fell at home four months earlier.

Dan sought out Mark Hanna. McKinley's manager, now a U.S. senator from Ohio, greeted him cordially enough, but when Dan asked him about Cuba, he shook his head gloomily.

"We're sliding down the slope, and I don't see any stopping. My distinguished Republican colleagues want war." He grimaced as he bit the words off. "They forget that we sent the damned ship to Havana in the first place. They don't care that we risk losing everything we've done to make this country prosperous again. They don't care that the Spanish are looking for accommodation. They just . . . want . . . war."

"There's plenty of war talk," Dan ventured.

"Oh, sure, there's talk." Hanna gestured in disgust. "Half of it's from old men who've forgotten what war is like, and the other half's from boys too young to know."

"Can't the president do something?"

Hanna shook his heavy head. "He thinks if he keeps quiet and delays, he may be able to keep us from going to war over the *Maine.*"

"Do you think he's right?"

"Huh." Hanna grunted uneasily. "Just between us? No, I don't, and I've told him so. People have already decided who's to blame for blowing up that ship, and they don't think it was an act of God. Congress is likely to declare war without waiting for him to ask."

Within a fortnight, Congress had forced a declaration of war on a reluctant president. Two weeks later the U.S. Navy won the war's first victory, half a world away from Cuba, when Commodore George Dewey steamed into Manila Bay and destroyed a Spanish fleet without losing a single American life.

Hardly anyone in Falls City knew where Manila Bay was, and even the president confessed he had to look at a globe to locate the Philippine Islands. But Dewey's victory produced a burst of national euphoria. Two months later U.S. forces in Cuba won well-publicized victories at Santiago and San Juan Hill, and the war was over less than four months after it began.

And yet . . . in South Dakota it wasn't over, not by a long shot. At the end of the summer a thousand soldiers of the First South Dakota Volunteer Regiment were still abroad. They had signed up to fight in Cuba—but they had been sent to the Philippines. In Falls City and across the state, people wondered what their boys were doing there. They certainly weren't fighting the Spanish, who had surrendered. That left only the Filipinos, and weren't we on their side?

"The country's changed," Amos said gloomily. "I can't quite explain it, but it's not the same place any more. This war's put us in the world to stay, and there'll be hell to pay sooner or later."

Falls City, October 1898

Dan heard it from Grace, who had heard it at the dry-goods store. A worker at the Meyers Packing Company—Falls City's biggest employer, with more than four hundred workers—had slipped on the bloody floor of the hog-slaughter line. He lost his balance and fell in front of the worker beside him just as that man swung his cleaver downward toward a hog carcass. The razor-sharp blade, driven with the full force of a strong man, smashed into the falling worker's left arm just above the elbow. His life was saved by coworkers who improvised a tourniquet; but he lost the arm.

"He has a wife and four little children," Grace said. "Benjy says they told him at the plant they have no jobs for one-armed men." She seized Dan and shook him, her eyes wide with anger. "You've got to *do* something! That's . . . that's *criminal!*"

It wasn't the first incident of its kind; meat-packing plants were nightmarish places at best, and slaughtering was inherently dangerous work. But this incident troubled Dan, and not just because of Grace's rage; he had a feeling there were more and more accidents at that plant these days.

He was troubled for another reason, too.

That fellow Meyers, he's getting rich off the land, really—and off the farmers. They run the risk. They go up against nature, they take their chances on the weather and the price of corn. And they have to sell their hogs to him for whatever price he sets, because they've got nowhere else to go. He's got the only slaughterhouse in fifty miles.

Meyers and his kind don't do anything, really, except take what comes from the land and turn it into money. Seems like the least he could do is try to make it safe for the people that do his dirty work, that make all that money for him.

The next morning Dan called in his best reporter and told him what he'd heard and what he suspected.

"I don't know for sure that there's a story there, but it smells like it," Dan said. "Take a few days and nose around, talk to people, and tell me what you find out."

The reporter came back three days later. He had talked to several dozen men who worked at the plant, checked records and interviewed staff members at the city hospital, and talked to several doctors. Dan was right. Accidents were on the rise at the Meyers plant, and he had figures to prove it.

He had also discovered a plausible reason: increases in the speed of the machinery that carried hog carcasses past the line of workers who cut them up. "The cutters say the company speeded up the line three times in three months when it got a lot of big orders during the war," he said. "They claim it's a miracle there haven't been more people hurt."

Dan told him to prepare a story, including a list of other accidents on the hog line in the past year and the dates of the speed-ups.

"And get in all the quotes you can from workers, about the accidents and the speed-ups, and any other safety problems."

"They won't let me use their names."

"Afraid they'll lose their jobs?"

"Scared to death."

"You know the names?"

"Sure."

"Will you give them to me?"

"If you insist."

"I won't." Dan grinned. "I just wanted to be sure you would if I did."

When the story had been written, checked, and rechecked, Dan instructed the reporter to go see the president of the company and ask for his comment. Then he spoke briefly with George Norton, had a few words with David Currier, and sat back to wait for the visitor he knew would come.

It took less than an hour. Bob Meyers was a big man, not tall but heavyset, with a thick neck and a round, bald head. He came striding into Dan's office and slammed the door shut behind him.

Dan invited him to sit down, and opened the door again. Meyers eyed him coldly.

"Woods, I hope we're not going to have a misunderstanding."

"I certainly hope not, Mr. Meyers. What would it be about?"

Meyers's fuse was short. "Don't get fresh with me, sonny. You know damned well what the problem is. Some smart-aleck kid on your staff is running around trying to invent a story about accidents at my plant."

"Oh, that." Dan studied Meyers's face. "Actually, I asked him to do that. We're planning to publish the story, and we'd like to have your comments as part of it. That's why I asked our reporter to call on you."

"Well, it's a good thing you did, because now I can do something to stop this foolishness."

"I'm not sure that's how it works, Mr. Meyers." Dan spoke slowly and carefully, raising his voice just a little. "We find it works best when we rely on our own judgment in deciding what to put in the paper. I believe our readers expect us to do that."

"Well, I'm a reader, and I don't want that kind of trash in my paper."

"I can promise you we checked the facts very, very carefully."

"That's not the point, Woods. This kind of story shouldn't be printed at all. It'll get people all stirred up, it'll give our workers crazy ideas. And it will encourage outside labor agitators to come in here and make trouble. You'll hurt every legitimate business in Falls City."

Meyers shook his finger at Dan. "You know, some people in this town, if you printed that kind of stuff about their business, they'd send a couple of men in here to break both your arms."

Dan waited until his own anger abated. Then he said: "I don't respond very well to threats."

"I'm not threatening anybody." Meyers put his hands on the arms of his chair and leaned forward. "But you should understand that if that story or anything like it appears in your paper, I will have no choice but to do whatever I can."

Dan smiled bleakly at the angry businessman. "I'd be surprised if you didn't, Mr. Meyers. I've always been impressed by your energy and . . . determination."

"Well, are you going to print that horse manure?"

Dan thought a moment, then pulled a sheet of paper from his desk drawer and picked up a pencil. "Maybe it would be easiest if I took your comments right now. That way we wouldn't have to bother you again."

"God damn you." Meyers had lost his temper. "I'll have nothing to say about your filthy story."

". . . Nothing to say . . . about your . . . filthy . . . story." Dan repeated the words as he wrote. He held up the paper. "Would you like to check this?"

Meyers was on his feet. "I'm not going to waste any more time on you. I'll talk to George Norton. He'll kick some sense into you."

"His office is just around to the left as you go out the door." Meyers strode out; in a minute David Currier slipped in.

"My God," Currier whispered. "He's a bad apple."

"Did you get good notes?" Dan smiled at his worried lieutenant. "You may need them if I turn up with a couple of broken arms. I'm glad you took the trouble to learn shorthand."

* * *

George Norton stared unblinking at Robert Meyers. "Bob, it's just this simple: I don't interfere with news decisions. Period."

"You own this business. It's just like any other business. It's yours, so you have to run it. You're ducking."

"That's your opinion, and you're certainly entitled to it," Norton said. "But that's not the way a newspaper works. It's a business, yes, but a special kind. Its only stock in trade is trust; it only succeeds if people believe it, and they believe it only as long as they are convinced it's completely independent."

"Don't you put on airs, George. You're just a businessman like the rest of us. If you print this trash, every anarchist and labor agitator in the Northwest will be in here making trouble—for all of us, for you too."

"I don't like unions any better than you do. But you don't stop unions by trying to hide what goes on in a plant where four hundred people work."

Meyers crossed his arms on his chest.

"I hoped it wouldn't come to this, George. We've been friends for a long time. But you leave me no choice. If you print that story Meyers Packing will have to close its account at your bank."

"I'm sorry to hear that," Norton replied. "I'm not positive, but I think it's our biggest account."

"I assume so. That's a lot of business to throw away."

"I hate to lose it. But as you put it, you leave me no choice."

There was a moment of silence in the little office. Then Meyers hitched his chair closer to Norton and lowered his voice.

"There's one other thing. If this story is printed, there may be another story printed. One that involves you." He looked hard at Norton. "And a certain person with whom you had an . . . ah . . . close relationship last winter."

Norton favored the meat packer with a frosty smile. "I wondered when you'd get around to that. I'm surprised it took you so long."

Meyers started to say something but Norton went on, his voice rising.

"You won't do that. You won't do it because you can't afford to get into that kind of a pissing contest, and I guarantee you that's where you'll be if you try that gutter stuff on me. Now please get out of my office and off my property."

When he described the conversation to Dan a few minutes later, Norton did not mention either of Meyers's threats. The publisher told his editor to use his own judgment.

"Of course you'll decide." Dan often joked about the overworked phrase, but it had never sounded so good to him as it did now. "But I will say I believe we must run that story, though I'd be much happier if we didn't have to."

[169]

Dan nodded. "I understand, George. Sometimes we make life hard for you. Thank you for backing me up."

Norton stared at him. "No, I should thank you."

Dan was astonished. "Why, for God's sake?"

"Never mind." Norton kept the answer to himself: *Because this proves you were right about that woman. If I hadn't played a hunch and run a pretty good bluff on Bob Meyers, I might be on the way to looking like a damned fool—or worse.*

The story was published the next day. Everybody in town read it and talked about it, and not one question was raised about its accuracy. But as Dan noted ruefully to Norton a few weeks later, neither did it change the way the packing plant was operated.

"After all that struggle and strain, we didn't accomplish anything," the editor said.

Norton leaned back in his chair. "No, you're wrong. Running that story was good business."

Dan was startled. "What?"

"The more honestly a newspaper is conducted, the more successful it will be."

Dan nodded and turned toward the door, only to be brought up short by the publisher.

"But please don't do it any more often than you have to."

A couple of months later, Dan heard that the Meyers Packing Company had closed its account at the Falls City National Bank. George Norton never mentioned it to him.

Thanksgiving Day, 1898

Amos was waiting on the porch when Dan drove up.

"Well, Dan, here you are—with a whole load of females!" He threw back his head and laughed at the sight: Dan's wife, year-old daughter, mother, and sister were all in the wagon. Amos winked at Eudora and held out his hand. "Come on, Dora, age before beauty."

Eudora took his hand and climbed down. "Flattery will gain you nothing, Amos," she said, then hugged him as the others laughed.

They had come from town, as usual, for Thanksgiving dinner on the Harper farm. Grace, Eudora, and Emma disappeared into the kitchen to help Lydia Harper; Amos amused himself with his granddaughter Abigail while Dan turned the horse out in the pasture.

After dinner Amos, Dan, and Charlie Harper walked down the road toward the river. Pale sunlight slanted across the well-kept fields.

"You had a good year, didn't you?" Dan asked. "The place looks fine."

Amos shrugged. "We didn't have a bonanza like some did. We don't plant so much wheat, and it was wheat really boomed this year, with the foreign market so strong."

"We did well enough, Pa." Charlie Harper, at twenty-five, was even bigger and taller than his father; his voice had the same solid sound. "I'll settle for a little less in a year like this if I can come through all right in a year when most folks get blown away."

"I wonder where you got that idea," Dan said. "Seems to me I've heard it around here before."

"Well, it's worked for me up to now." Amos looked fondly at his son as he spoke. "Treat your land right and it'll treat you right. Some of these fellows get greedy and overwork their acreage, never give it a chance to rest or store up moisture. They do fine when it rains, but they pay an awful price in a dry year."

He dropped a big hand on Charlie's shoulder. "Besides, I owe it to this one to keep the place up. I'm fifty-one, I can't run this farm forever. I figure it's up to me now to get it in shape and keep it that way."

Amos, looking at Dan, remembered the Thanksgiving afternoon six years before when he and Henry Woods had walked down this same road after dinner.

It's just as well Dan didn't go into farming. Henry wasn't that good a farmer to learn from, and besides, he was unlucky. No matter how smart you are, you can't control weather and bugs and such. You need good luck, and Henry didn't have it. He was a born loser. So is his brother; look how he lost that store.

But Dan's different. He likes what he's doing, and he does it well. And he's making my Grace happy, there's damned few could do that.

The wagon track ended at the river, in a little grove of cottonwoods. Below the bank, in a bend of the stream, a few fallen leaves floated on a clear, dark pool.

"Remember when you and your sister were little and we brought you down here to swim?" Amos asked Charlie.

"Sure do. Fact is, I still come down here sometimes on hot nights. Water's deep enough so it stays cool." He turned to his brother-in-law. "You should try it next summer."

For the moment, Dan had no time to think of next week, never mind next summer. In December they moved the *Dakota News* into its new building, and though it was only four blocks away it might as well have been a hundred miles.

They had to get the new plant up and running before they closed the old one at Ninth and Lincoln. The front-office force wasn't too much of a problem; people, desks, files, and all could be moved over a weekend when the office was closed anyway. But the production side was another matter. Workers had to be trained to use new devices in the new plant while still putting out a paper with old ones in the old plant. And some older machines—those they would continue to use—had to be moved literally between one edition and the next.

George Norton personally managed every detail of the transfer. He drew up schedules for moving every person, every function, every piece of machinery and furniture. He drafted David Currier to oversee the move. Currier's passion for detail made him an ideal choice for the job, but it also meant that Dan had to take over his daily editing chores.

At last, on a Saturday morning in mid-December, the final daily edition was run off at the old plant; that afternoon, the first Sunday edition rolled off the press at the new plant. The front page carried an announcement:

NOTICE TO PATRONS.

The Dakota News takes pleasure in announcing that the improvements in the paper which were recently promised are now being put into effect. Today the News is published for the first time from its new building. The plant is the most complete and well-appointed, and is provided with a Hoe Perfecting press, the first to be introduced in this state, with three Mergenthaler Linotype machines, a full stereotyping outfit and all other facilities required by a modern newspaper.

As soon as practicable, but no later than January 15, we shall enlarge the paper to seven columns, giving 10 columns more of reading matter, shall increase our editorial force, shall considerably extend our telegraph, state news and market services, and shall aim to give our readers a first class modern newspaper, the equal of any outside newspaper circulating in this state.

G. Norton, Publisher

An important side effect of Norton's twin moves—starting a Sunday paper and building a new plant—was to foreclose any effective local competition. The *Dakota News* was already the only daily paper in town; it soon became the dominant paper in the entire state. George Norton had gained such advantages in circulation, production, and advertising that no one could ever seriously challenge him again.

Chapter 20

Sioux Falls, South Dakota, May 1900

AMOS HARPER sat in a folding chair under the musty canvas of the big circus tent. Sunlight filtered wanly through the tent roof, and the smell of drying mud was everywhere.

The People's party is dying, he thought, *right here in front of my eyes.*

Behind him stretched row after row of empty seats; in front of him, a few hundred people clustered around the speaker's platform, where the governor of South Dakota was reading a welcoming speech.

Populist leaders had advised the people of Sioux Falls to be prepared for the thousands who would come to their national convention in May. Merchants stocked up, restaurants hired extra help, saloons ordered extra whiskey, hotels set up extra beds, and thrifty housewives prepared to rent extra bedrooms.

Almost nobody came. There were perhaps four hundred delegates, fifty or so newspapermen, and a few hundred friends, relatives, and hangers-on. Even adding everyone else who turned up—political supporters, pickpockets, bunco artists, confidence men, farmers looking for an excuse to come to town, and the merely curious—you still couldn't count two thousand souls.

Sitting in the nearly empty tent, Amos realized it wasn't just a matter of numbers; there was a tired tone to the Populist rhetoric, too. Where only a few years ago the party had proclaimed a vision of the future, it now evoked the past. Amos felt as if he were at a funeral, not a political convention, as he listened to Governor Andrew Lee.

> There was a place for Populism in the politics of the country; it was and is a political necessity. It has filled its place as advance guard to the army of the people with conspicuous ability, courage, and patriotism.

[173]

It has lived to see some of its ideas embodied in the laws of most of the states, and to witness the general acceptance by nearly all the people of its fundamental doctrines.

He makes it sound like there's nothing left that needs to be fixed, Amos thought. *Guess he never read the Omaha platform.*

Amos recalled the zeal and idealism of the delegates at Omaha in 1892. By contrast, this gathering seemed almost meaningless—a tiny island of people in a sea of empty chairs under a circus tent.

Bryan and the Democrats took up silver, and we went along for the ride—fat, dumb, and happy. Now all that's left is for the other parties to steal our platform, plank by plank.

But Amos knew it wasn't just silver.

We've had two-three years of good weather and good crops and good prices, so farmers think they're well off and bound to stay that way. They forget awful fast, even the good ones, the ones that take care of their land.

They forget that nature's going to come back and hit 'em in a year or two with a drought or hail or 'hoppers.

Amos thought of the song the Populists sang in 1890 to celebrate their new party. The words seemed ironic now:

> The old party is on the downward track,
> Good-bye, my party, good-bye.

Philadelphia, June 1900

Will White had met Theodore Roosevelt in 1897, and from that moment, he had been a Roosevelt supporter. White himself couldn't be at this Republican convention, but he provided Dan with a letter of introduction.

Dan wanted to meet this New York governor who was being described as the likeliest choice for vice president. So as soon as he arrived in Philadelphia he went around to Roosevelt's hotel and sent White's letter in.

After a few minutes the door swung open and a stocky figure bustled into the reception room. Theodore Roosevelt was not a particularly big man, but his handshake rattled Dan's teeth.

"Woods? Come in! Glad to see a friend of White's; splendid fellow. What may I do for you?" He didn't wait for an answer. "From South Dakota? Falls City, eh? Tell me, what's the situation out there?"

Dan started to reply, but Roosevelt kept talking.

"I know that country, old man. Had a ranch on the Little Missouri, out in the Badlands. Had to give it up after the big die-up in '87. Frozen out."

Dan was struck by Roosevelt's mannerisms. He squinted through rimless pince-nez glasses, grimaced as he talked, and clicked his jaws to punctuate his staccato phrases. His voice was not particularly pleasant, but he exuded so much energy that a listener didn't really notice the high-pitched, nasal tone.

Dan steered the conversation around to the vice presidency. Roosevelt responded with a shower of negatives: he had unfinished work as governor and wanted a second term. Powerful interests wanted him out of Albany, and he would not have people think he was ducking a fight. Nor would he have it said he was making back-room deals with the bosses. The vice presidency was an empty office. And so on.

He said everything—except one thing, Dan realized. *He never did say he wouldn't take it.*

Dan paid a call that same day on Mark Hanna. Hanna looked a lot older; he'd had heart trouble earlier in the year, and he was painfully hampered by rheumatism. But he was cordial as ever—until Dan mentioned that he had been to see Roosevelt. Then Hanna's mood turned frosty.

"His clothes are full of pinholes from the medals he hangs on himself, but these fool delegates may make him vice president, and the president won't let me do a thing about it. I can't understand it."

By Monday morning, Hanna was seething. Dan, waiting in his outer office, heard him shouting: "I am not in control! McKinley won't let me use our power to defeat Roosevelt. . . . He is blind, or afraid, or something." He was apparently on the telephone, for there was a pause before Hanna shouted again. "Don't you understand there'd only be one life between that madman and the presidency?"

He's beginning to slip, and not just physically, Dan mused. *His power's beginning to drain away. No one really cares about the vice presidency. The game's not about this year, it's about next time. And they're already playing for keeps.*

Dan and Jim Morgan stood in the crowd of reporters outside Hanna's office. Finally the door opened and Hanna limped out to read a statement.

> The administration has had no candidate for vice president. It has not been for or against any candidate. It has desired that the convention should make the candidate and that has been my position throughout.

There were a few snickers. Hanna glared in the direction of the sounds, and they stopped.

> I have within the last twelve hours been asked to give my advice. After consulting with as many delegates as possible in the time at my

disposal, I have concluded to accept the responsibility involved in this request.

This time the laughter was general. Hanna glared again, but his mouth twitched in the suggestion of a smile as he resumed reading.

In the present situation, with the strong and earnest sentiment of the delegates from all parts of the country for Governor Roosevelt, and since President McKinley is to be nominated without a dissenting vote, it is my judgment that Governor Roosevelt should be nominated with the same unanimity.

As Hanna turned to go back inside his office, Dan caught his eye. The old politician's face was weary and expressionless, but he twitched one eye in a fleeting wink as he went through the door.

He's a professional, all right, Dan thought. *He fought as hard as he could as long as he could, and he won't sulk over losing.*

But he won't be Roosevelt's friend, either.

Roosevelt was the star of the campaign. He attracted huge crowds every-where he appeared—and he appeared almost everywhere. When he came to South Dakota, Dan got on his train to "swing around the circle" with him.

Roosevelt was so animated that he seemed taller than his five feet eight inches, sturdier than he really was. His blue-gray eyes snapped behind the glasses he always wore, and his prominent teeth chopped off his phrases in distinctive fashion.

Dan was captivated. The New Yorker was a reporter's dream—vibrant, accessible, quotable, and more personally attractive than any other politician he had ever met. Dan also found himself responding to the themes Roosevelt stressed: the need for honesty and courage in politics and life; the abuses of big business and the trusts; the conservation of natural resources; the virtues of hard work.

By contrast even Bryan, again the Democratic nominee and a man who only four years earlier had himself seemed young and exciting, now seemed faded and middle-aged, though he was in fact the younger of the two.

For the first time, Dan felt drawn to a political figure. *He's for all the right things,* he thought, *and he talks straight, he's no trimmer. No wonder the Rough Riders took that hill in Cuba, with a leader like that.*

He didn't agree with everything Roosevelt said. He was, for example, disappointed in his message to South Dakota farmers:

I don't wonder that four years ago there should have been doubt and hesitation. I don't wonder that under the pressure of accumulating bad years there should have been a tendency to grasp blindly at anything that promised a remedy. But now we have the right to ask you to compare the prophecies made by the two sides four years ago with the actual result.

He should know better, Dan thought. *If he learned anything out there on that ranch, it had to be that good years and bad years don't depend on what politicians do. Those things depend on whether it rains or not, and how bad the winter is, and whether you get hit by hail or 'hoppers.*

Roosevelt's a different kind of politician, but he's just like the rest in one way: he doesn't know anything about farming, and maybe doesn't care.

For all the sound and fury, there was never much doubt about the outcome. Hanna got what he wanted: a victory so overwhelming as to insure Republican dominance for the foreseeable future.

"It was a first-class landslide." George Norton, sitting in his office on the Saturday after election, allowed himself to gloat a little as he talked with Dan and Amos Harper.

"You're right," Amos said. "People were so surprised to find themselves still alive and well after four years of McKinley that they lost all hold on their common sense."

Norton laughed. "Still alive! You just won't admit how well the country's doing—and how wrong you were about Bryan's crazy silver ideas."

"Well, George, no candidate's perfect. But Bryan isn't the only one who lost. In the long run, so did Hanna and the people he looks out for. The real winner was Roosevelt. He's next."

"You're right about that." Dan had heard enough from Will White to know that Roosevelt was already working for the presidential nomination in 1904. "He's ahead of everyone else for next time."

"Huh." George Norton wasn't impressed. "He's a windbag. All noise and no substance. And what few ideas he does have are wrong."

"You better get used to them, George," Amos said, "because he's going to be the next president. The Populists are dead, much as I hate to say it, and the Democrats are sick, and as for your Republicans, why, Hanna's finished and so are his friends. So get ready for Teddy."

Get ready . . . for what? Dan thought. *Roosevelt's a fascinating man, he's all energy, a great campaigner. What would he do if he got to be president?*

If I was a farmer I'd be worried: he's city born and bred, never mind those two years he played at being a cowboy.

But he's different. He's not in it for patronage or boodle, like most of 'em are. He's—he makes you think he's actually in it to serve the public interest, for God's sake.

Amos stood up to leave. "George, pretty soon you and I will be singing the same song. You better learn the words." As he reached the door he turned and, in his rumbling bass, softly intoned the old Populist refrain:

> The old party is on the downward track,
> Good-bye, my party, good-bye.

Chapter 21

T HE HOTEL registration clerk was apologetic. "I'm sorry, Mr. Woods, we don't have a double room as we promised you. There's been a mix-up."

Dan started to protest, but the clerk hastened to placate him. "The manager has reserved a suite for you instead." He leaned forward and murmured discreetly: "At the regular double room rate, of course."

Upstairs, Dan and Grace explored their windfall, which included a sitting room, a lavishly outfitted bathroom, and a bedroom with a huge double bed.

Grace sat down on the bed, bounced a couple of times, and laughed. "They've given us the bridal suite."

Grace stretched lazily as they lay in bed the next morning.

He's a different man when you get him far enough away from the newspaper, she thought. *When he's home, no matter what time of day or night, he's always got that paper on his mind.*

I guess I can't complain. I knew before I married him it was going to be that way.

But this is sure a lot more fun.

"Come on, Mr. Woods, it's time to go to the fair." She stretched again, and her body moved against his.

They had come to Buffalo on vacation to see the big Pan-American Exposition. It was Grace's first trip away from home in three years, and they made the most of it, sleeping late, going wherever their whim took them, laughing and joking, flirting and holding hands in restaurants, wandering through the fairgrounds.

"It's almost as good as Chicago," she told Dan on the evening of the third day. Along with thousands of others they were watching the grand illumination and fireworks display in honor of President McKinley, who had interrupted his vacation in Ohio to visit the fair.

They stood entranced as thousands of electric lights were switched on, outlining buildings, towers, and broad avenues. Then the fireworks were touched off: a line of set pieces depicted battleships firing their big guns. A replica of Niagara Falls gushed liquid fire instead of water. The final display was a pyrotechnic portrait of the president with the legend WELCOME TO MCKINLEY, CHIEF OF OUR NATION.

The next afternoon, Dan returned to the exposition to watch McKinley shake hands with the public at a big reception in the Temple of Music.

He suggested to Grace that she come along. "You may think you have to work on this trip," she said, "but I don't."

Well, I had him for three whole days, she thought. *It was nice while it lasted.*

"Don't get too interested in that McKinley," she said. "Remember you're taking me out for dinner."

It was a hot, sunny afternoon, the kind that makes September feel like midsummer, but it was cool and comfortable inside the cavernous music building. Dan showed his press card and was admitted to a roped-off area next to the platform where McKinley was to greet people as they filed past.

Promptly at four o'clock the sound of cheering outside signaled McKinley's arrival. He was escorted into the packed auditorium by John G. Milburn, president of the exposition. Uniformed police and plain-clothesmen lined the aisle down which people would walk to shake hands with the president, and a detachment of soldiers stood nearby. On the platform close to McKinley were three secret service agents. The affair had been planned as a purely symbolic gesture; McKinley was to spend only ten minutes shaking hands.

People began to file past. The president reached to his left as each person approached, took the offered hand, and pulled it across toward the right, trying to keep the line moving briskly.

Dan, standing with the other reporters a little to one side, saw a short, slim man approach McKinley. Clean-shaven and dark-haired, he wore a plain black suit. What caught Dan's attention was his right hand: it was wrapped in a handkerchief.

McKinley reached over to greet him, but the man shoved the president's hand aside and fired two shots from a pistol wrapped in the handkerchief. He was so close to the president that the sound of the shots was muffled; to Dan they seemed no louder than a cap pistol, but he knew instantly and beyond doubt what had happened.

For one second, perhaps two, a sickened silence held the great hall as the president and his assailant stared at each other. Then, as McKinley staggered, two secret service agents jumped on the gunman. As the struggling men fell to the platform, a cursing soldier kicked the pistol out of the assassin's hand.

The crowd broke out of its trance. People surged forward, shouting and screaming. Soldiers and detectives struggled to hold them back. The little platform was surrounded by pushing, shoving people.

Two aides half-carried McKinley to a chair on the dais. Dan was no more than six feet away, close enough to see that the president's vest and shirt were speckled with powder burns.

McKinley slowly put his hand up to his chest and felt inside his shirt. When he withdrew his hand, the fingers were smeared with blood. He seemed puzzled. He looked at his fingers, then let the hand drop to his side. Dan could see his lips moving, but he could hear nothing. McKinley seemed detached and strangely calm amid the turmoil. Then first-aid men rushed in with a stretcher, and the president was carried off.

Dan pulled out his notebook and scribbled furiously. He looked around. At the back of the platform, a young man wearing an Associated Press armband was shouting into a telephone. Other reporters were grabbing at him, trying to pry him loose. He beat them off with his free hand.

Dan's mind was working well enough, but he felt somehow disconnected, as if he were standing outside himself and looking on from a distance.

I better get out of here, he thought. *I've got to find out where they took him—and if he's still alive. Then I'll have to find a telephone.*

The news went out, as always, in contradictory fragments. At the *Dakota Daily News,* the day's press run was finished, but the plates were still on the press and the pressmen had not yet left the building. David Currier ran into the shop to tell the foreman they'd be replating page one, then hurried back to assemble a brief story. Currier pasted up the first bulletins just as they came from the Associated Press wire, scribbled a hasty headline, and rushed the copy to the waiting printers.

M'KINLEY SHOT!

The President in Grave Condition After
He Is Shot at Buffalo by Assassin.

BUFFALO, Sept. 6—President McKinley was shot twice in the stomach here this afternoon at the Temple of Music. His condition is serious. Two shots took effect in his stomach. He is now in the hospital at the Pan-American grounds. He was shot by a stranger.

BUFFALO, Sept. 6—(Bulletin.)—President McKinley is fatally injured.

McKinley was shot by a well dressed man, who wore a high

[181]

hat, and who, while shaking hands with him, fired the shots with the left hand.

One shot took effect in the left breast, the other in the abdomen. He is under arrest and unidentified.

BUFFALO, Sept. 6—(Bulletin.)—The bullet which lodged against the breast bone, has been extracted. The president is resting easy at the Milburn house.

The name of the president's assassin is said to be Fred Nieman, and he is said to come from Detroit.

———

An unofficial dispatch reporting that the president is dead, is unconfirmed.

Currier inspected a proof of the made-over front page. "Let it go, Bill," he told the foreman. "Tell them to run about a thousand, then shut down. But hold the men for a while in case he dies."

Currier went back to his office. George Norton was waiting for him.

"We'll get some boys to sell those papers downtown," the publisher said. He glanced at a note in his hand. "Dan just telephoned. He was right beside McKinley when it happened. I told him what you were doing, and he said that was fine. He'll file for tomorrow's paper."

"Is he going to write a lead or a sidebar?"

"I told him—I know it's your decision, but you were busy and he said he couldn't hold onto the phone. I told him to give us an account of the shooting, just write what he saw, and we could use the wire services for the rest."

Just right, Currier thought. *He'll make an editor yet.*

"I told him to write a lot and not to worry about the telegraph tolls, and to stay in Buffalo as long as he needs to," George added. "We'll offer his articles to the AP for the regional wire."

"You think we can make a little money that way?"

"No, no, no. We'll give them the stories free—after we print them, of course. All they have to do is give us a credit line. Every paper in the state will run them, and I'll bet Lounsberry will use them in Minneapolis, too. It'll be wonderful promotion."

Dan called Currier near midnight to tell him he had handed the last page of his story to the telegraph operators. He was exhausted, but he chuckled at Currier's account of his conversation with Norton.

"Of course. The fall circulation drive begins in two weeks."

"I never thought of that."

"That's why he owns the paper, and we work for it." Dan felt his adrenaline draining away. "Look, I've got to eat something and go to bed. Tell George to wire me some money in the morning."

By Monday, John Milburn's big house on Delaware Avenue had become the temporary seat of government. The wounded president lay in an up-

[182]

stairs bedroom; the entire second floor had been converted into a medical ward. The stable had become the executive office, and the house next door housed clerks and stenographers sent from Washington to handle mail, telegrams, and other paperwork.

Police closed off the elm-shaded street to keep traffic and sightseers away. Soldiers patrolled the sidewalks. Across the street, two big tents sheltered a large and growing crowd of reporters.

Dan was bone-tired. He had put in a long weekend, pulling himself out of bed early Saturday morning, checking to be sure McKinley was still alive, writing both a story and a column for the Sunday paper. On Sunday, he managed to find Mark Hanna, who had also rushed to Buffalo. Hanna, stunned with shock and grief, had talked to the doctors; he gave Dan details of the president's wounds.

One bullet had caused only a superficial wound, glancing off a rib without penetrating the body. The other had gone through the stomach before lodging near the spine, and the surgeons decided not to risk further trauma by probing for it. They closed the holes in McKinley's stomach, cleansed the wound, and sewed it up.

The doctors were privately optimistic, Hanna said. By Tuesday they let their optimism show in public, proclaiming that "he is out of the woods." On Wednesday, McKinley's relatives went home, Vice President Roosevelt left for his wilderness cabin in the Adirondacks, and Hanna prepared to leave, too.

Suddenly, for the first time, Dan had time to reflect on what had happened—and how he had reacted to it.

He hadn't thought once about Grace since Saturday, when he'd sent her to the depot to catch a train for home. He hadn't thought about McKinley as a human being who felt pain. He hadn't thought about Hanna as a private person grieving for a dear friend.

Dan realized he had suspended both his own emotions and his concern for the feelings of others. That didn't make him particularly proud of himself, but he reckoned it was probably the only way he could have done what he had to do that week.

On Thursday morning the doctors gave McKinley a little food to build up his strength. At first his stomach seemed to work properly, but by afternoon he was in pain, and his condition deteriorated rapidly.

The cabinet was recalled. Mrs. McKinley was brought to the bedside for a final visit. The president mumbled, "Nearer my God to Thee," and lapsed into a coma. He died at 2:15 A.M. on Saturday. The autopsy cited gangrene poisoning as the cause of death.

By Sunday Dan thought it was time for him to go home, but George Norton would have none of it.

"I want you to go on the funeral train to Washington."

[183]

Dan was not enchanted. "George, there'll be plenty of coverage on that. I'm used up."

"No, you stay with it. We've been . . . *you've* been getting wonderful display in lots of papers. Even the *Tribune* in Minneapolis."

Good old Lounsberry, Dan thought. *I'll bet George called him.*

The publisher went on. "I really liked that story this morning about Roosevelt's crazy ride down the mountain to get back to Buffalo. The Associated Press said no one else had it."

"I got that from Hanna. I was lucky to catch him right after he heard it from Teddy. . . ." He caught himself. "From the president, yesterday afternoon."

In fact it had involved much more than luck. Dan had been looking for Hanna. He guessed he might be with Roosevelt, and he guessed Roosevelt might be at the same house where he'd stayed the first time he came to Buffalo. He was right on both counts, and caught Hanna just as he came out. Dan jumped into his carriage and got the story from him in time to make the late edition of the Sunday paper.

He knew that George was buttering him up, but it felt good. "Well, all right, I'll try to get on that train."

"Get alone with Hanna," George suggested. "I want to know what he *really* thinks about Roosevelt. Remember how he talked about him last year."

"I'll try. But I can't promise anything. He's pretty broken up, and there's an awful lot of other reporters around."

"He's not the only one who's upset." George's voice crackled over the telephone line. "Every time I think of that man in the White House, I shudder."

Dan climbed onto the funeral train early Monday morning. McKinley's flag-draped casket was in a private car at the end of the train, in full view through the large observation windows. The train also included a baggage car, a diner, and three Pullmans. One of these was occupied by Roosevelt and the cabinet; the second by Hanna and other associates of McKinley; the third by the newspapermen.

Dan noticed that the two groups—those who had served the dead president and those attached to the new one—kept apart, withdrawn and gloomy. The tension between Roosevelt and Hanna was palpable.

Dan sent a note in to Hanna as soon as they left Buffalo, asking for a few minutes of private conversation. Midday came and went with no response; while Hanna remained locked in his private room, Dan spent most of the day looking out the window at the gritty manufacturing towns and grimy cities of New York and Pennsylvania. Seeing these smoky, dirty, crowded old places, he realized how deep his own roots were in the soil of the plains.

Between the ramshackle towns and smoky cities there were farms; but they were small places, shut in between steep hillsides that shadowed the farmhouses and crowded the cornfields into narrow valleys.

There may be more hills and trees here, but our country is cleaner, and there's more light and space. We're young and still growing; these farms look run-down, worn-out, used-up.

And as for the cities, well, I wouldn't want to have to breathe the air around here. Seems to be mostly coal smoke.

It's a funny thing. I never wanted to be a farmer—but part of me is still in Nebraska, out there on the plains, and I guess it always will be.

And I sure wouldn't swap Falls City for one of these dirty old towns back here.

Dan heard nothing from Hanna for almost twelve hours; then, less than an hour out of Washington, a Pullman attendant whispered to him that Senator Hanna wished to see him in his drawing room.

Hanna was obviously exhausted, but he answered readily enough when Dan asked about Roosevelt.

"Well, he's a pretty good little cuss, all in all." Hanna pulled himself up. "He asked me to take supper with him alone in his room. After we finished eating, he said he needed me and he asked me to be his friend. And he held out his hands to me."

Hanna stopped and stared out the window for perhaps a half-minute before going on.

"I took his hands, and I said I would be his friend, but there were two conditions. One was that he carry out McKinley's policies as he has promised. The other was that I'd do everything I could to make his administration a success, but I'd make no commitment to support him in 1904."

"What did he say to that?"

"He said he understood my position perfectly, and he thanked me, and he said he was grateful to me." Hanna seemed to be struggling with his emotions, but when he spoke again it was in the familiar growl. "And I told him the third condition was would he for God's sake stop calling me 'Old Man,' and he said he would."

Hanna looked at Dan and seemed to remember something.

"Now look here, Woods. I don't know why I tell you all this, I must be losing my mind. Just remember—"

"—That you never talked to me and I can't use any of this until tomorrow," Dan interjected. He was relieved to see the shadow of a smile cross Hanna's face. "In other words, your usual rules."

They both laughed. Then Dan returned to the press car, leaving Hanna alone with his private grief.

★   ★   ★

Outside the train, all along their route, there was an outpouring of public grief. All day long, Americans stood in the warm autumn sunlight, lining the tracks, waiting patiently to watch the body of the dead president go by.

Many watched in silence; but often, in both small towns and big cities, wherever the train slowed to give people a glimpse of the flag-covered casket, they sang. Often it was a group of schoolchildren, led by a teacher. Always, adults or children, they sang the same song. It was McKinley's favorite hymn, and the newspapers had reported that the president's last words were its closing phrases:

> Nearer, my God, to Thee,
> Nearer to Thee.

At Harrisburg, thousands of people filled the huge depot shed. The train stopped there to change engines, and the people sang.

> Nearer, my God, to Thee.

After dark in the Maryland countryside, groups of Negroes stood by bonfires as the train slid past. In the firelight, Dan could see their mouths moving, though he couldn't hear the words.

> Nearer to Thee.

For months afterwards, awake or dreaming, Dan heard the words of the hymn.

> Nearer, my God, to Thee,
> Nearer to Thee.

The train finally pulled into Washington at nine o'clock that night. Dan watched Hanna as he stood silently with the other public officials while the casket was taken from the rear car.

He's done, and he knows it. It may not show for a while, but it's already happened. Roosevelt's the president, and he's running things now, and he'll have his own men.

Mark Hanna's finished.

Dan looked around at the politicians and officials gathered to pay their respects to the dead president.

They're mostly done, too. They don't know it yet, but everything has changed.

It wasn't just that Roosevelt was different from McKinley; there had been a larger change.

He's different from every president before him. He's the first one who wasn't old enough to fight in the Civil War. He didn't grow up on a farm or in a small town; he's a big-city man. He looks ahead instead of back. He's a twentieth-century man.

And that's bad news for farmers and for our part of the country, because we're too few and too far away. The rest of the country may be in the twentieth century—but we're still in the nineteenth.

And we may be stuck there.

Chapter 22

Minneapolis, Minnesota, May 1902

BEEN to any good fires lately?"

Earl Edgerton was managing editor of the *Minneapolis Tribune,* and he did not hesitate to laugh at his own joke.

Dan managed a smile. "I'm getting a little old to work outdoors on cold winter nights."

Edgerton chuckled. "Well, I guess you've grown yourself a little belly, but you still look spry enough. I remember the night you called in about that big fire over on Cedar. You were just a punk kid, and you ordered me around like you owned the paper."

Dan smiled uneasily. He found the conversation awkward; he wished Edgerton would get to the point, whatever it might be. The editor obliged.

"I read your coverage of the McKinley shooting. We used a lot of it. Pretty good stuff. And Lounsberry says you're good." He paused for just a moment. "I'd like you to come to work here."

Dan had guessed that might be the reason for Edgerton's letter inviting him to drop in the next time he was in Minneapolis. Still, the abrupt way the offer was extended threw him off balance.

When I was in college I'd have done anything for a reporter's job on the Tribune. *Now here it is . . . and I'm not sure.*

He tried to think of questions. "What would you want me to do?"

"Local and regional stuff at first. But I've got the okay from the publisher to start some national coverage, including political reporting and Washington news, and I think you'd fit into that."

"You already have a political reporter."

"That's right." The editor was coldly matter-of-fact. "But he won't do. He's past fifty, and he doesn't like to travel anymore. So that's no problem. If it's the national conventions you're thinking about, you'd go to all of 'em."

Dan listened hard. *He's dangling all the things I like best. What's the matter with me? I should be jumping up and down.*

Edgerton, perhaps sensing his hesitation, suggested he think it over for a few days before giving him an answer. "You'll probably want to talk it over at home," he said. "There's no rush."

"So he popped the question." Clement Lounsberry looked across the restaurant table at Dan. "He told me he was going to."

Lounsberry drained his glass of beer, wiped foam from his mustache, and grinned at his protégé. "You don't seem properly impressed. It isn't every day that the Earl of Edgerton takes a young fellow up on the mountaintop."

"I know, Colonel. I suppose I should've said yes right then." Dan shook his head. "But I'm not sure I want to do it."

"It's a great job, on a good paper, in a city that's going to keep on growing."

"That's all true." Dan was trying to explain something he didn't quite understand himself. "But there's a lot of things to think about. I can't just walk away from my paper—and my town, the people. The land."

Lounsberry smiled. "I know how you feel. I had my own paper once, and I know how it feels to be the editor in a place like Falls City. But this is your chance to play the big tent, and you owe it to yourself to think hard about it."

Falls City, May 1902

"I can't just walk away from George, after he's done so much for me."

Dan was trying to explain his dilemma to Grace. "The paper's just beginning to boom. My mother's here. And this is a good place to bring up children. Your folks are here, too."

"You've done more for George Norton than he has for you. And you have to live your life to suit yourself, not him or anyone else." Her voice was edged. "Including me."

She answered his arguments one by one: "We could take Eudora with us, and anyway your sister will still be here even if you move. As for my family, I married you, not them. And Minneapolis would be just as good a place for Abigail to grow up." Her voice sharpened. "And *I'm* the one who's bringing her up."

"I'd be away more," he said. "There'd be a lot of traveling in this job."

"You're already away most of the time," she retorted. "Even when you're home your mind's at the office. If you stopped being the editor, you'd be home more even if you traveled more—because when you were home, you'd really be home."

And when you were away, she thought, *there'd be more to keep me occupied in Minneapolis than there is here.*

"Well, it's not just family, and it's not just George." Dan shifted his ground. "I really think I can do more here, make more of a difference, than I could in a bigger place. Here one man can count. It's the right size. I know these people, what makes them tick, and they know who I am. If I'm the editor here, I can change things."

You like being a big frog in a small pond, Grace thought, *and you're looking for reasons to stay here.*

She prodded him again.

"Think of yourself for once. If you go with the *Tribune,* you'll be doing the things you like best. You'll have a chance to be one of the top political reporters in the whole country."

He bristled. "I think I've got a pretty good reputation already, with the people I respect. And I can do the same things if I stay here—the conventions, the trips to Washington, all that."

That's true, but it's not all of it. She saw clearly something that she had only dimly perceived before: *You think you might fail in Minneapolis. You made up your mind a long time ago that you weren't going to be a failure like your father. You know you'll succeed here, because you already have, and you can't be sure anywhere else.*

"There's another thing, too," Dan said. "My being born on the claim, knowing what it's like to live on a farm, helps me make the paper a sort of bridge between farmers and town people. And that's going to be needed more and more."

You think you've put that sod house behind you, but you haven't. You're clinging to it, and you're afraid if you go to a big city you'll lose it, lose your tie to the land.

"You have to decide," she said. "I only want to be sure you think of yourself, not just other people. If you do that, then whichever you choose will be all right."

In bed that night, Dan listened enviously to Grace's steady breathing.

He knew this was a big fork in the road. He was thirty-four years old, and Edgerton was right: he'd grown a little thick through the midsection and the first gray patches were speckling his black hair. He wasn't a kid any more.

If I'm going to move, now's the time. I'll be too old and too settled next time a chance comes along.

It wasn't easy to choose. If he went to Minneapolis he'd be the top political reporter for a big, important paper. He liked covering politics better than anything else he'd ever done. Already he had met two presidents; he'd meet more in the *Tribune* job, and senators and congressmen and men like Mark Hanna who made presidents.

I'd travel, see a lot of the country, spend more time in Washington. It's an assignment I never dreamed I could have.

It would be very different from what he was doing now.

When you're the editor, you decide what goes into the paper. You call the tune for the whole paper—for the whole community. You decide what's important.

If people think you're honest, they may disagree with you, but they'll trust you, and pay attention to what you say.

If he went, it would be a gamble; if he stayed, it was pretty much a sure thing.

I can have this job as long as I want it, and it's a good job. If I go to Minneapolis, it might not work out. Edgerton didn't quite promise. He said, "I think you'd fit in." He left himself an out.

Dan turned onto his side, trying to relax and fall asleep.

But it would be wonderful if it worked out: three-four trips to Washington every year, all the conventions, swing around the circle with presidents and candidates whenever they come west. . . .

It was not only a matter of different jobs. It was also a question of different places and different ways of life.

This is my town, these are my people. I fit in here, I know this country, I understand it. This is a good place. People know each other, they help each other. Nobody goes hungry.

He turned over again.

But maybe that's just why I should go. Maybe it's too cozy here. Maybe I need to test myself in a harder place, run on a faster track. I know I can do it if I want to.

Dan rolled onto his back and stared at the ceiling.

At least I'm pretty sure I can.

The next morning, he slipped out of bed and went out on the porch. The spring morning was clear and fresh; the sun already brightened the hillside where Dan lived, though the city below still lay in shadow. Down the street, a milk wagon moved from house to house, the horse stopping unbidden so the driver could exchange full bottles for the empties waiting on each doorstep.

A morning like this almost makes you forget winter. He squinted into the low sun, warm on his face and neck. *I'd hate to live where you weren't close to the land, couldn't feel the turn of the seasons.*

Off to the east, beyond the river, Dan could see where the farms began, the fields dark where they had already been plowed, lighter where the stubble of last year's corn still stood.

They're getting a good early start on the planting. If we get enough rain in the next month or so, we'll make another good crop.

He stood for five minutes looking down on the waking city and the farms beyond. Then, abruptly, he turned and went inside.

In the kitchen Grace poured him a cup of coffee. "You were thrashing around all night long," she complained. "I certainly hope you make up your mind about this job pretty soon."

"I just did."

She watched him. Her blue eyes were calm and appraising, but she felt her heart beat. He took a drink of coffee and looked at her.

"I've decided to stay."

So that's that, she thought. *I wish you were more adventurous. I wish just once you'd take a chance, just once do something without being so careful.*

And I wish you cared as much about me as you do about that damned newspaper.

Her heartbeat slowed.

But I made this bed, so I'll sleep in it. And no regrets.

"That's fine," she said.

The next day Dan told George Norton of the Minneapolis offer.

"I've thought pretty hard for the last couple of days—and nights," Dan said, "and I finally made up my mind."

Norton nodded but said nothing, and Dan went on.

"I've thought some about what a newspaper should be, and I guess the readers have to believe it meets their real needs, that it stands with them when the going is hard on the issues they care about." The publisher's face revealed nothing, and Dan went on. "That's the kind of paper this is. I've had something to do with that. And so have you."

Norton shrugged dismissively. "I don't have anything to do with the news."

"Except you let me do what needs to be done, which is all that really matters." Dan was surprised at the urgency he felt as the words tumbled out. "And here I can do those things for people I know, my own people. So I've decided to stay."

Both men relaxed a little, and Dan went on. "I didn't say anything to you about it before because I didn't want you to think I was trying to squeeze a raise out of you. In fact I'm not sure why I'm telling you now."

Norton stared hard at him for what seemed like a long time. When he responded his voice for once was hesitant.

"I appreciate that." He stopped. "And I appreciate your decision." His voice dropped until Dan could hardly hear him. "And I value your . . . your friendship. I really don't know what I'd do if you left."

There was an awkward silence, broken when George cleared his throat noisily. Then he spoke again, this time in his usual flat, no-nonsense voice.

"I mean there's so much work to do here, and I'd lose a lot of time if I had to break in a replacement."

Chapter 23

WHEN Will White wrote proposing a rendezvous in Washington and promising to arrange an interview with Roosevelt, Dan agreed at once. Now they were in the president's upstairs study. Sunlight flooded through two south windows, brightening the tan wall covering and reflecting off freshly varnished bookshelves.

"The old laws and the old customs were once enough to regulate the gathering and use of wealth," Roosevelt was saying. "That is no longer true, thanks to the enormous growth of industrial power. The nation must assume the power to supervise and regulate corporations that do interstate business."

"Some people call that pretty strong medicine, Mr. President," Dan said, thinking of George Norton. "Some business people think you're singling them out."

"Woods, I am no genius. The things I talk about are the plain old principles of right and wrong." Roosevelt showed his big teeth in an abrupt grimace. "I would not single out any one class; we go up or down together."

Abruptly, the president changed the subject. "Now see here, I need some intelligence from you. Senator Hanna has been perfectly loyal and completely straight with me, but he will never be my man, even if I were to entreat him, which of course I shall not do. Indeed it is not beyond the realm of possibility that he might himself become a candidate."

"Oh, I doubt that, Mr. President." Dan heard himself speaking and stopped, abashed.

"So do I," Roosevelt said. "But in any event I must have my own leaders and my own organization in every state. How do I stand in Dakota?"

"Well, Mr. President . . ." Dan hesitated.

"With the bark off."

"Frankly, you have problems in South Dakota. The farmers—you know how farmers are, they distrust all politicians. They've done well the last few years, but the Populists were always strong in South Dakota, and there's still a good deal of doubt about the Republican party."

"What needs to be done?"

"For the farmers? Well, a strong federal law to control railroad rates and prohibit rebates would certainly help. That's the main grievance. But there's the grain elevators, too. People believe they take advantage of farmers by price fixing, and cheat them with short weight and dishonest grading. They want those things stopped, and the states aren't doing the job."

Roosevelt nodded, but he seemed impatient. "Anything else?"

"Well, yes, sir. There are the grain exchanges—you know, in Chicago and Minneapolis. Farmers think it's wrong when a few men in the city can decide what every farmer gets for his crop. They think there should be a law forbidding gambling—speculation—in grain futures."

Roosevelt walked over to the window and stood for a moment, looking across the south lawn toward the gray spike of the Washington Monument.

"Of course abuses must be corrected," he said. "But I must move cautiously at first."

He reminded them he had already brought suit against the huge railroad holding company formed in 1901 by J. P. Morgan, Jim Hill, and E. H. Harriman.

"You must understand this is a struggle," Roosevelt added. "When we took that action, Morgan came in to see me. He said, 'If we have done anything wrong, send your man to see my man and they can fix it up.' Then he asked me if I also meant to attack his other interests.

"Mr. Morgan could not help regarding me as a big rival operator—who either intended to ruin all his interests or else could be induced to come to an agreement to ruin none of them."

It was not just railroads, he went on: fundamental changes were occurring everywhere. Look at the great combines recently formed, Morgan's United States Steel, Rockefeller's Standard Oil, the beef trust, the coal mines.

"That's all quite true, Mr. President," White said. "But the railroads are at the root of it. They control the state legislatures; the legislatures elect United States senators; senators control the selection of federal judges."

Dan picked up the theme. "And the judges interpret the law to suit the railroads and the other big corporations. At least that's how people look at it in our part of the country."

Roosevelt struck his desk with a clenched fist. "By George, wherever we find such a damnable alliance between business and politics, we must

[194]

break it." He paused. "But we must take one step at a time. The first requisite is knowledge of the facts."

For all the bluster, he's a careful politician, Dan thought. *He'll play it slow and safe until he's been elected in his own right.*

Once again Dan found himself drawn to this man as he never had been to any other political figure. *A fellow could even go into politics with a leader like that. He's one of a kind.*

Falls City, January 1903

Dan remembered that scene a few months later as he listened to George Norton and Amos Harper on a Saturday in midwinter.

Norton was complaining about Roosevelt. "I never did trust him, and that message to Congress proves I was right. He wants the government to stick its nose in every kind of private business. It's an outrage!"

"Now, George." Amos stopped to scratch a match on the underside of his chair and light his pipe. "You know perfectly well that he has no such idea. Far as I'm concerned he's altogether too gentle with those thieves."

"Hogwash. He thinks he's an emperor. That's why I'm for Mark Hanna."

"For president?" Dan broke in. "That's not in the cards. He's just not up to it physically. He's sick."

"He wouldn't have to campaign for it, just let his name be put in."

"Don't sell Teddy short," Dan said. "He talks about morality and reform, but he's no goo-goo. He's hard as nails. And he can count."

"He's not really much of a radical," Amos chimed in. "He's strong for the things people are already strong for. He talks reform, but only when he knows he's got the crowd with him."

Norton shook his head. "He doesn't have *me* with him, I guarantee you that."

Amos laughed. "I'm sure he doesn't. But he's doing what I said someone would do: he's stealing the Populist platform—at least those parts of it that most everybody else already supports."

"There's more to him than that," Dan protested. "He says up to now the national government hasn't done much for anyone except the biggest and strongest, and they don't need help. Roosevelt thinks government should look out for the general interest, not the special interests—and the president has to make sure it does."

Norton was not persuaded. "People have to look out for themselves."

"Roosevelt believes that too," Dan insisted. "But he thinks government has to help people who *can't* help themselves."

"I just hope he doesn't forget the farmer," Amos said.

"Well, I admit that worries me. I think he may." Dan described his

White House exchange with Roosevelt—and the president's apparent lack of interest in farmers' troubles. "I don't think he understands what the farmers are really mad about, and why the government has to help them get a fair deal."

"Well, I hope you're wrong," Amos rumbled. "It would be nice to have a real president for a change. But you can't tell yet."

"It's not too soon for me to tell." Norton was emphatic. "I know what he's for, and I know I don't like it."

"Well, I only know one thing for sure." Dan stood up. "Teddy's sure to make one of you mad, no matter what he does."

Chapter 24

Washington, D.C., March 1905

GRACE was surprised and delighted when Dan invited her to go with him to Roosevelt's inauguration. She had never been to Washington, and it pleased her to have him ask her along. The fact that the trip would let her escape from winter for a couple of weeks made it all the more enticing.

She accompanied Dan to all kinds of festivities and events—including a White House reception where she met Theodore Roosevelt for the first time.

"What did you think of him?" Dan asked when they were alone in their hotel room that night. He was lying on the bed, watching her as she sat in front of the mirror taking down her hair.

Grace thought for a moment. "Well, first of all, up close he's shorter than I expected. I suppose he seems bigger because he never stands still and talks all the time. And you never told me how small his hands and feet are."

"No, Grace, I never did." Dan sighed. "I meant, what's your *opinion* of him?"

"It's not as if I'd had a chance to study him." She pulled pins from her hair. "It was like being in the middle of a stampede. There must have been five hundred people there."

"You must have gotten some impression."

She hesitated. "I know you think a lot of him, but if you really want to know, I didn't care for him. I think he's a prig."

Dan was suddenly irritated: she was criticizing him for thinking well of Roosevelt. The thought sharpened his voice.

"A *prig?* Why?"

"Well, for one thing, I think he's old-fashioned about women. He'd put us on a pedestal—and then put the pedestal in a closet, and let us out only for breeding and raising children."

"I don't know how you can say that." Dan was astonished. "Look at the way he stopped you and took the time to talk with you when we went through the receiving line."

"Oh, that was just playacting." She extracted the last hairpin and her hair fell over her shoulders. "He wouldn't have spent five seconds with me if I weren't married to the editor of the biggest paper in South Dakota."

"What makes you think that?"

Grace was surprised to hear the irritation in his voice: *Why, he really likes that man. He's never been so defensive, even about Hanna.*

"Sometimes I don't think you have the sense to come in out of the rain." She picked up her hairbrush as she spoke. "While he was talking to me he kept looking at you, to make sure you saw how much attention he was paying to me."

"I didn't notice anything like that." Dan searched for an explanation; he wanted her to change her mind about Roosevelt. "Maybe it's sort of an unconscious attitude, because women can't vote."

"Well, he could do something about *that.*" Grace was unrepentant. Her eyes widened, and she brushed harder. "Anyway, I'm not sure I'd vote for him if I could. I just don't like him."

Dan sat up on the edge of the bed. Her back was to him as she sat at the dresser, but he could see her face in the mirror.

"You don't have to like him," Dan said. "That's not important. What counts is whether you like what he does."

"You're quite right, and I hope you remember it, too." Grace looked at him in the mirror. "I think you're too quick to make excuses for politicians you like. Mark Hanna, for example."

"I'm sure you're right." Dan's voice softened at the mention of Hanna, who had died the previous year of typhoid fever. "But this man is different. I think he's going to be a great president, because he understands the country has changed, and he's not afraid to do the right things."

Grace came across the room and stood beside the bed. "I hope you're right. You usually are," she said. "All I want is for you to judge him by what he does, not by whether he makes good stories."

Dan talked about Roosevelt again in a column a fortnight later.

> In his inaugural address, President Roosevelt spoke of the changes that have occurred since the Civil War, changes that have brought both great progress and great problems. He made it clear that he wishes to control these forces of change so they will nourish, and not disrupt, the nation.
>
> The President did not offer details of his program in his

inaugural. But he has made clear that he believes railroads must be regulated by the national government—to control rates and rebates, so as to end abuses by railroads and powerful shippers.

In an earlier speech in Philadelphia, the President stated in plain language why regulation is needed: "We do not intend that this Republic shall ever fail as those republics of olden times failed, in which there finally came to be a government by classes, which resulted in either the poor plundering the rich or in the rich exploiting the poor."

There, in one sentence, is the essence of the Roosevelt program: To enact remedial measures, thus preventing the violent struggles that would inevitably occur if abuse of great economic power is not curbed.

The President's critics say his proposals are revolutionary, but in fact his program is *conservative;* it is designed to preserve the best by eliminating the worst. That is not revolution; instead it is the most useful kind of reform. . . .

Grace put down the paper. "Now I see why you're so strong for Roosevelt. It's not just what he's *for,* it's what he *is.* You finally found a politician who thinks like you—not a wild-eyed Populist, but not a thief or a plutocrat either."

She saw her husband more clearly now. *You're not farm, not city, but small-town. And your politics is in-between, too: not reactionary, not radical, but more or less liberal.*

"I just think he makes sense." Dan didn't like being analyzed, by Grace or anyone else. "You know I never liked the way Bryan always tried to set class against class. Well, Roosevelt is trying to *prevent* class war."

"Oh, I see," she said, sarcasm edging her voice. "The great war hero is really a peaceful man, the Rough Rider is a respectable reformer—just right for the middle class."

"Well, what's wrong with that?" He was fed up with her needling. "The middle class is most people, so it's up to them, storekeepers and farmers and teachers, and maybe even editors"—now there was an edge to his voice, too—"to see that the world's goods are shared fairly. Otherwise there'll be a big blowup someday, and the middle class will get squashed between the rich and the poor."

He's found his political hero, she thought. *A reformer but not a radical. And a reporter's dream to boot, full of color and always saying outrageous things.*

Dan had stopped. "I'm sorry. That sounded like a sermon. You kind of set me off."

"Don't apologize," she said. "I like you when you get mad. You should let go that way when you write your editorials. You'd convince more people."

Dan shook his head. "I don't think preaching works, except in church. It's better to make people think for themselves."

"Maybe so." She thought a moment. "You know, you might be right about your president, but I still think he's more interested in getting power than in using it."

"No, you're wrong there." Dan was quick to answer. "He has to build up the presidency. For forty years this government has been run by Congress, and that's why the big interests have had things their way almost all the time. Roosevelt has to get the upper hand over Congress."

"How can he do that?"

"By stirring people up. By fighting for his railroad rate bill."

"People always talk about the railroads," Grace said. "I remember Pa being angry about them even when I was a little girl. But why is this particular bill so important?"

"Because both sides have decided to make it a test of strength." Dan paced back and forth, hands jammed in his trouser pockets, as if to reinforce his argument by movement as well as words. "If Roosevelt beats them on this one, he'll be on top, and he'll get the railroad bill and most of the rest of his program too. If he loses, the big corporations will still run the country."

Grace was caught up by her husband's intensity. "How's it going to come out?"

"I don't know." Dan looked at her, then laughed. "That's what makes it such a good story."

Chapter 25

ROOSEVELT'S reform proposals cast shadows all the way from Washington to South Dakota. Congressional approval of his railroad rate bill, passed in 1906 after a knuckles-down struggle in the Senate, rekindled political wildfire on the plains. But this time the angry farmers had allies in towns and cities, and for once Dan Woods and Amos Harper were on the same side of the fence.

"I don't feel right agreeing with you," Amos told his son-in-law one Saturday afternoon as they sat with George Norton in the publisher's office. "It doesn't feel natural."

"I like it—for a change," Dan retorted. "It won't do any harm as long as it doesn't get to be a habit."

"It just means you're both wrong." Norton growled. "I'm used to you, Amos, but I hate to see a younger man go so far astray."

As usual Norton would have nothing to do with reformers, even though this time they were inside the Republican party—a circumstance that greatly enhanced their political power in a dyed-in-the-wool Republican state. An alliance between the state's nascent progressive movement and liberal Republicans put a reform-minded governor and legislature into office in 1906.

That led to an avalanche of reform legislation: not only the outlawing of free railroad passes, but direct primary elections, antilobbying laws, a prohibition on corporate campaign contributions, public disclosure of campaign funds, establishment of a pure food and drug commission, provision for free public school textbooks—and even a law requiring a bona fide one-year residence for divorce.

It was a heady time for Dakota reformers. Amos, acting half his age, organized precincts and townships and counties, planned legislative strategies, lobbied at the state capitol. Dan wrote editorials and columns explaining and endorsing the reform bills. He spent considerable time persuading a reluctant and skeptical George Norton to let him give the movement full editorial support.

"You must be putting something in George's coffee," Amos joked one Sunday. "How else could you get him to go along so much?"

"Well, he really does try to keep out of editorial decisions most of the time," Dan said. "And even though he'd never admit it to you, he's in favor of some of those bills."

"If he is, he sure does a good job of keeping it a secret."

"He doesn't talk a lot," Dan said. "He surprises me sometimes when he comes out with something. But he's usually thought about it."

"Huh." Grace included both her father and her husband in the sound of disapproval. "Maybe he talks less and thinks more than some men I know."

Norton surprised Dan again a month or so later.

"I have concluded that we have to do something about patent-medicine advertising," he announced one morning. "I believe both the products and the advertisements for them are fraudulent."

Dan was startled. "Well, you're probably right about that, George. But won't we lose a hell of a lot of money if we stop taking those ads?"

"We will forgo a substantial amount of revenue, yes."

"Are you talking about dropping all of them? Do you think they're all bad?"

"Can you think of a way to tell the good from the bad?" Norton lifted his hands in frustration. "I can't."

Dan had always been embarrassed by the patent-medicine ads, with their blatant and transparently overblown appeals to the gullible and the suffering, especially women. But he felt uneasy about accepting some kinds of ads but rejecting others.

And what got George all worked up about this, anyway? He seems to have his mind made up. My God, that'll cost us thousands of dollars a year.

Norton's next remark provided at least a partial answer.

"There's another reason. Several of the big ones—Lydia Pinkham's is one—are trying to force us to sign contracts that would let them cancel if we printed anything they didn't like." Norton fixed Dan with his unblinking stare. "If we give in to one, we'll have to do the same for all of them. I didn't think you'd want me to agree to that."

"I wouldn't."

"Neither would I, and I thought we should make that clear." Norton shook his head ruefully. "I hate to lose the revenue, but even if they backed down on the contracts, I'd still be uneasy about the ads." He spoke with finality. "So I've decided to drop them."

Dan expressed his amazement to Grace that night. "I don't understand it. It can't just be the contracts—it'd be more like George to sign them and not say anything to me, then let them cancel if we ran something they didn't like. But to pick a fight, that's not his way. Maybe he's thinking about the post office regulations, that somehow we might be excluded from the mails if we publish false ads."

Grace disagreed. "No, there's more, and I think I know what it is. I've heard Margaret talking to Abigail about all the bottles in her mother's bedroom. Mary Norton uses all kinds of medicines."

"So do a lot of women."

"Yes, but not many of 'em have husbands as smart as George. I'll bet he's kept track of what she takes and figured out that none of it cures anything, and the painkillers are mostly alcohol—or opium, or morphine. They stop the pain, but pretty soon you want them all the time. I think that's what's happened to Mary."

"That may be. But George would never admit it. He always pretends it's just good business when he does something that's right."

"I don't care, and you shouldn't either." Grace's tone was brisk. "What matters is what he does, not how he explains it. And I think he's doing this because of his wife."

Norton admitted mixed motives in making another advertising decision that year. It began when the paper gave editorial support to a proposed reduction in the hours that saloons could be open. A delegation of saloon keepers, accompanied by a couple of whiskey salesmen, came in to see the publisher. Their spokesman suggested that unless the paper changed its stand, they would withdraw their advertising.

"I'm afraid you can't do that," Norton said quickly.

"Why not?" one of the saloon keepers asked.

"Because I have just removed all liquor and saloon advertising from the *Dakota News*," Norton snapped. "Good day, gentlemen."

Afterward he minimized the affair, telling Dan that "we don't carry much liquor linage anyway." But he made sure that the Falls City Ministerial Association heard about it, and the paper was warmly praised from the city's pulpits for its high moral tone and civic conscience.

George was delighted. "People who go to church also subscribe to newspapers. I'll take the subscriptions and let the street sales go," he told Dan. "Those people are more likely to think of us as a family member if we turn down liquor ads. I want the reader to think it's *his* paper, not 'Norton's paper.' "

The publisher favored Dan with one of his once-in-a-decade winks. "Besides, it was a perfectly sound business decision. We can get along much better without the saloons than they can without us."

[203]

Chapter 26

HARRISON NORTON had a fresh-looking bruise on his cheekbone. The frame of his eyeglasses was bent, and the buckle below one knee of his knickers was hanging loose. But despite the damage, the publisher's twelve-year-old son was calm and composed.

"Are you busy?" he asked as he came into Dan's office. "Can I ask you a question?"

The editor laughed. "That's two questions, and the answer to both is 'yes.' So make it fast." Dan was used to Harry's questions. The boy had dropped in on his way home from school one day the previous winter, and had turned up almost every day since.

"I've been wondering about something."

"For a change."

Harry paid no attention to the remark. He was like his father: it took a lot to divert him once he got launched on a subject.

"You know President Roosevelt."

"Just a little bit. He wouldn't know me."

"Well, what I want to know is, did he wear his glasses when he charged up that hill in Cuba?"

Dan considered the question.

"I don't know for a fact, Harry. But he must have, because he can't see beyond the end of his nose without 'em."

"That's what I thought." The boy seemed pleased.

Dan grinned at him. "Now it's my turn. Why did you ask?"

Harry scuffled his feet in embarrassment.

"Um. Well, you see, James and I were playing San Juan Hill, and we had an argument about who would be Teddy. And he said he should because he's older and bigger. But I said I should because I wear glasses just like Teddy.

"Then he said even if Teddy does wear glasses he wouldn't wear 'em in a fight. And I said why not, and he said because here's what would happen, then he hit me and that's how my glasses got bent."

He's not mad at his big brother for hitting him, Dan thought, *as long as he knows that he was right and James was wrong. Funny kid.*

Harry thanked Dan and disappeared. Dan found himself once again wondering about this solemn, slightly built child with regular features and dark hair that tumbled over his forehead. He was physically unremarkable, except for his eyes: he looked at the world through large, round glasses, with an unwavering gaze that he fixed directly on whatever he was examining at the moment. His usual expression was grave, his countenance that of an adult who had somehow been trapped in a child's body.

He was quite different from his older brother. James, now nearly fifteen, was big for his age, athletic, blond, and handsome. These days he was interested primarily in baseball, though he had begun to notice girls, too. He showed no interest whatever in the *Dakota News,* a fact that pained his father.

Harry more than made up for it. He was fascinated by the newspaper and by everything connected with it. He poked into every corner of the plant, trying to find out how everything worked. He got the printers to show him how they set type by hand; then he memorized the type case so he could do job work and set headlines for the paper. He crawled over and around and through the press until he was ink from head to toe—and knew how it worked. He learned how to write up a classified advertising order; he made the rounds of the downtown stores with the ad salesmen; he rode the wagon that hauled bundles of papers to the railroad stations.

Most of all, he asked questions until he drove everybody nearly crazy. Not that they were dumb questions; far from it. They were the kind that grownups would ask, *smart* grownups. It was just that he asked so many of them.

Harry's special favorite was Dan, and the editor returned the compliment—partly because he knew George Norton favored his older son, and partly because he sensed that Harry, not James, would be publisher someday. Dan knew there was another reason, too: a boy whose father didn't pay much attention to him had something to offer to a man who had no son of his own.

So Dan took Harry under his wing, giving him time and attention and patience, trying to keep him out of other people's hair, and teaching him whatever he could about news and the newspaper.

He'll learn all he needs to know about the business end from his father, Dan thought. *I've got to teach him about news, and the sooner we start the better. I do believe he's going to run this place.*

* * *

[205]

There was plenty of news to teach him about. By 1907 Falls City had over twelve thousand residents and was growing again after a long hiatus during the decade of depression and recovery. Despite the forebodings of the conservatives, Theodore Roosevelt had calmed the country in the first shocking days after McKinley's death, taken Hanna's advice to "go slow," and kept the economy on an even keel. The prosperity of the McKinley years continued unchecked.

Beyond the city line, there was no frontier any more, and the little land that was left was now overrun by a final wave of homesteaders. In South Dakota, that meant taking more Indian land.

"Three years ago the government grabbed off a big chunk of the Rosebud Reservation and gave it away to white settlers," Grace complained to Dan. "Now they're at it again."

"Grace, there's just so much pressure for land. A hundred thousand people signed up for that Rosebud land lottery—for twenty-four hundred homesteads. They've got to find more, and the reservations are the only places where there's good land left."

"So they'll do it again this year." Indignation tinted her voice. "The frontier may be gone, but we're still stealing from the Indians, same as ever."

The *Dakota News* prospered with the city and state. Total weekday circulation was now more than eleven thousand, a little over half of it in the city, the rest out around the state. Some subscribers lived more than a hundred miles away. Sunday circulation had reached about seven thousand; it still lagged behind the daily edition because they could not yet promise same-day Sunday delivery to rural customers.

It wasn't that the farmers couldn't afford a Sunday paper. For a change, they were sharing in the good times. High prices and ample rainfall for several consecutive years allowed them to pay down their debts and still have something left over to spend. That meant merchants were thriving, too, and that in turn meant more advertising and fatter papers—sixteen, twenty, sometimes even twenty-four pages a day. George had just approved Dan's request to hire two more reporters and another copy editor. The new newsroom, which had seemed so roomy when they first moved in eight years earlier, was filled up.

Despite the steady growth in city circulation, which was easier and cheaper to deliver, Norton kept pushing country sales. "We'll have good roads sooner than you think," he explained. "Meanwhile we have to make that daily reading habit so strong it will seem natural to the farmer to take the Sunday paper, too, when we offer same-day delivery."

George and Dan talked a lot about better roads. The post office department's rural free delivery, begun as an experiment in 1896, had been an instant success. Within a year or two it was so firmly established—and

[206]

so popular—that there was no chance it would be stopped, regardless of the cost.

The expense was considerable, as city members of Congress liked to point out. It was not so much the mail service itself; what cost more in the long run was improving country roads so the postal service would certify them as mail routes. Rural mail service improved the life of farm families in many ways, but none was more significant than its role in reducing the loneliness and isolation of farm families by making it easier for them to get to each other—and to town.

The *Dakota News*, to no one's surprise, came out strong for good roads, arguing that farmers needed them not just to receive mail but to get their produce to market promptly and cheaply. The fact that better roads also made it easier to deliver newspapers was not mentioned in editorials, but George Norton made no bones about why he supported good roads.

"Just because farmers live in the country doesn't mean they don't deserve a newspaper just as much as any city fellow. And I want to be able to fulfill that desire for every farmer in the state."

Dan's views on the subject had more to do with his own family than with his newspaper. Though Grace's parents lived close to town, there were still times every spring when the road to the Harper farm was impassable, hub-deep in mud. And Dan could still recall the isolation and loneliness of the Nebraska claim, where the only road was a rutted wagon track and you had to drive fifteen miles to Grand Island to pick up the mail.

He also remembered a spring day when his mother had walked five miles cross-country, hauling two little children along, to call on a new neighbor.

She was the first white woman Ma had seen in eight months. They took one look at each other and never said a word, just grabbed each other and cried.

Dan didn't think it was doing too much to make it easier for the farmer's wife to see another female once in a while.

One farmer's wife who had more companionship these days was Dan's mother-in-law. Charlie Harper had finally proposed to Laura Hanson, a neighbor girl he'd been courting for more than two years, and Charlie built a little house for them on a rise in the south pasture of the Harper farm.

"It's my favorite spot on the whole place," Charlie explained to Dan. "You can look farther and see less than anywhere else I know."

Amos was relieved to have Charlie put down roots on the home place. He was ready—well, almost ready—to turn the place over to his son. He thought about that as he watched Charlie and Laura exchanging vows at their wedding.

It's time he took over. He wants to, and I ought to get out of his way. There's only one thing bothers me: he's impatient. He thinks I'm too old-fashioned, too cautious, the way I keep so much land in grass and don't plant more corn.

He sees the other fellows plowing up their pasture and planting right up to the fence line, and he thinks we ought to do the same thing.

I taught him all I could about caring for the land, and he paid attention and does it my way, and I guess he will as long as I'm around. But that won't be forever, and I'm not sure what he'll do to the place after I'm gone, if he starts to feel pinched when times get bad again.

And times will get bad again.

They always do.

Chapter 27

Falls City, November 1908

GEORGE NORTON was delighted with the election of William Howard Taft as president. "I don't even mind that he was Roosevelt's choice," he told Dan and Amos. "He's a real conservative. We've finally got the country back in safe hands."

"Oh, come off it, George." Amos Harper was sixty-one now, but his rumbling voice was as strong as ever. "The country's done pretty well under that crazy radical Roosevelt. And so have you."

"I'm surprised to hear you defend him."

"Well, I have to admire him." Amos grinned at Dan. "He's an accomplished thief. He's stolen enough planks from the Populist platform to stock a lumberyard."

Dan spoke up. "I think George has it right. I believe Roosevelt's misjudged his man. Taft's heart is with the old guard, and that's what counts; the platform's just window dressing. I think he'll change a lot of Teddy's policies."

"I certainly hope so," Norton snapped.

"Well, I don't." Dan was emphatic. "Roosevelt's the best thing that's happened to the Republicans since Lincoln. If Taft doesn't keep on in the same direction, there'll be some hell raised."

Amos was surprised by the fervor in Dan's voice. *He really cares about Teddy. That's the first time I've ever heard him talk that way about any politician.*

"Who's going to raise hell?" Amos asked.

"There's some in Congress, Republicans from this part of the country. They call themselves 'insurgents,' and they look out for farmers." He held up two fingers. "The best of the bunch are Senator LaFollette from Wisconsin and Congressman Norris, George Norris, from Nebraska."

Robert LaFollette was a national figure; as governor of Wisconsin, he had made his state a proving ground for reforms, and there was talk he might run for president. Norris was less well known; he was the leader of a bipartisan group of House members struggling to break the absolute power of Speaker Joseph Cannon.

"I really like Norris, he's an easygoing fellow, and we've become pretty good friends," Dan said. "LaFollette is cold, but he's smart and he's a fighter. I think they'll both play big parts."

And so will Theodore Roosevelt, he thought. *He may step out for now, but he'll only be fifty-five in 1912.*

He'll be back.

The Woods family was at Sunday dinner a week later, and Dan's eleven-year-old daughter had just interrupted him for the fifth time in five minutes.

"Abigail, mind your manners," he scolded. "Stop interrupting your mother."

The child was indignant. "I wasn't interrupting Mama, I was *talking* to *you.*" Her face flushed. "You never listen to me."

She burst into tears and ran from the table and up the stairs. The door to her room slammed shut.

Dan looked at Grace. "What on earth is the matter with her?"

"If you paid more attention to her you wouldn't need to ask." Grace's answer was quick and sure. "You barely know her, you talk to her once a week—and then you shout at her about her manners. She sees you so little that naturally she wants to talk all the time when she's with you."

Dan looked across the table at his wife. She stared back coolly, her blue eyes unforgiving.

"I'm sorry," he said. "I'm sure you're right. I'll go tell her I'm sorry and make up with her."

Grace watched him start up the stairs. *I've tried to tell you a dozen times,* she thought, *but you don't listen to me, either.*

Maybe I should try crying once in a while.

Falls City, December 1908

George Norton and Dan stood on the sidewalk in front of the *Dakota News* building one cold morning, inspecting a shiny new automobile.

"Ugly, isn't it?" Dan said. "They say you can get any color you want as long as it's black." The brand-new Ford Model T had a seat, an engine, and four wheels—and not much else. It was tall and gawky, its canvas roof a good seven feet above the ground.

"It's not ugly at all," Norton said. "It's beautiful. Look at that clearance, it'll be perfect for country roads. It's simple. And it's cheap. Farmers will love it. It'll change everything."

"They do say it's wonderfully easy to repair." Dan leaned in to inspect the area around the steering wheel. There were no instruments or gauges, just an ignition key in the dashboard. "Sure looks simple enough. And it even sounds simple." They listened for a minute to the subdued putt-putt-putt of the four-cylinder engine as it idled easily along.

"This machine is going to make a lot more difference around here than all the politicians you'll ever meet, and as soon as they make a truck model I'm going to buy three of them." Norton gestured at the machine. "There's the future of newspaper distribution in South Dakota."

And it's going to connect the farmer to the rest of the world, too, Dan thought, remembering the lonely weeks and months on their Nebraska homestead. *Fifteen miles to town, it took all day in the wagon. This thing would have done that in a half-hour.*

Ma and Pa were born too soon.

Dan had reason to think of his parents again a fortnight later when Benjamin Woods died. Uncle Benjy was a bachelor, and Eudora Woods had taken him in when the store failed. One morning he didn't come down for breakfast; his sister-in-law found him dead in his bed. He was sixty-seven.

He didn't make a mark on the world, Dan thought as he stood by the grave on a steel-gray December afternoon. *But he rescued us from that godforsaken soddy on the claim by asking Pa to be his partner, and I'll always be in his debt for that.*

Chapter 28

G OT a minute, Dan?"
Harry Norton looked different, almost grown up, in a dark suit with long pants instead of knickers and a dark green tie knotted snugly against the stand-up collar of his white shirt. He seemed even more solemn than usual. Then Dan remembered Harry was leaving for the East today; he must have come to say good-bye.

Dan leaned back in his chair. "Well, well. Off to the wars, eh? Don't worry, you'll do fine. You're as smart as any of 'em. Smarter'n most."

Harry nodded silently. *He's scared to death,* Dan realized, *but he's damned if he'll let it show.*

"You'll probably feel funny for a few days," Dan said. "Just remember, so does everyone else who's starting there."

"I'll be all right." The uncertainty in Harry's voice belied his confident words. He took off his glasses and wiped them on his shirttail. "I'll write you. I've subscribed to the paper so I can keep up on things here."

"You do that." Dan, looking at him, knew he was seeing the last of the boy who had come to seem almost a son to him. The next time they talked, he'd be someone else. Dan searched for something cheerful to say. "If you write and tell me what you think of the paper, I'll write you all the *real* news—the stuff we can't print."

Harry didn't respond. As usual, he had his own agenda.

"Please look out for Margaret." He was fiercely protective of his little sister. "I told her you'd show her how things work here if she wanted to know."

"I hope she doesn't ask as many questions as her big brother." That made Harry smile for a moment. Then he drew himself up.

"Well, I guess I better go. John's waiting outside with my trunk. We have to check it through at the depot."

"Your folks going to see you off?"

"No. I said good-bye to Mother at home, it'd be hard for her to go to the train." He paused. "And I spoke to Father just a minute ago."

Dan stood up and held out his hand. "So you're on your way. Well. You'll be all right."

Neither man nor boy could find more words, so they just shook hands. Dan watched Harry go out through the newsroom to the street.

You'll be all right. And if you're not, no one will ever know it, at least not from you.

Dan had another thought.

I'm glad girls don't go away to school.

Dan was in fact largely responsible for Harry's departure. A year or so earlier, he had suggested to George Norton that he consider sending the boy away to school. Dan, forever watching and studying people as he traveled, had concluded that hard work and native intelligence were no longer enough to assure success. In a more complicated world it was essential to be well educated—especially for a boy whose life had been bounded by the cornfields at the edge of a remote Midwestern town.

In Harry's case there was another reason. *He needs to get off on his own,* Dan thought, *someplace where he won't be told all the time that he's second-best.* Going away would get Harry out of the long shadow of his older, bigger, more athletic, better-looking brother.

Somewhat to Dan's surprise, George Norton took to the idea at once. "I've heard about those schools. Some of the men I know in Minneapolis send their boys out East. Costs a lot, but they say they learn a lot, too," he said. "Harry would find out there's more to the world than South Dakota. That would be good, since he's probably going to have to move somewhere else, what with James taking over the paper."

Dan didn't debate the publisher's assumption. Norton had fixed it in his mind the day his elder son was born, and there was no disputing him—even though it was Harry, not James, who was interested in the paper.

Norton looked at Dan. "You pay a lot of attention to Harry, I know. I hope he doesn't get in your way. I do appreciate it."

"He's a fine boy. It's no trouble having him around." Dan was embarrassed by Norton's acknowledgment. "If he went away to school, I'd miss him. But I think it'd do him a world of good."

George had wasted no time. He sought advice from banking and business friends in Minneapolis and Chicago, and within two months Harry was entered for the following fall at Phillips Exeter Academy in New Hampshire.

* * *

A week after Harry boarded the train for the East, his older brother took a much shorter trip to enroll as a freshman at the University of Minnesota in Minneapolis. James had graduated that year from Falls City High School, where he distinguished himself on the athletic field if not in the classroom. Both father and son thought Minnesota was the right choice: George liked the idea of his son being close enough to keep him conscious that his future was at the paper; James liked the prospect of being far enough away so that his father couldn't monitor his social life.

Dan hardly had time to miss Harry. He was fully occupied keeping track of the political fratricide that was once again ravaging the Republican party. As always, the conflict divided region and class: Midwestern Republicans still felt the shame of Eastern dictation, the weight of Wall Street domination, the oppression of small farm and small town by big city and big business.

To these traditional grievances were added new ones. President Taft, surrendering to the old guard as Dan had expected, had accepted a high-tariff bill that made a cynical mockery of the Republican platform. It also enraged farmers, whose self-interest lay with free trade. "The president," said Iowa's insurgent senator Jonathan Dolliver, "is surrounded by good men who know exactly what they want."

By 1910 there was open war between the insurgents and the old guard. The Republican Congressional Committee refused to provide campaign funds or backing to insurgent candidates; so the insurgents turned to their old political hero for help, and Theodore Roosevelt responded with a cross-country speaking tour to help his hard-pressed friends.

The former president arrived at Falls City on the first Saturday in September. The downtown streets were festooned with patriotic bunting, national flags, and portraits of Roosevelt; visitors poured in from the countryside; there was a triumphal parade.

More than ten thousand people crowded into a huge circus tent to hear him. Several thousand more stood in the late-summer sun outside, peering under the rolled-up sides of the tent to see him even if they couldn't hear him.

Dan found the speech to be mostly standard stump oratory, but there was one new idea—something Roosevelt called the "New Nationalism":

> The New Nationalism puts the national need before sectional or personal advantage. It is impatient of local legislatures trying to treat national issues as local issues. It is still more impatient of the impotence which springs from overdivision of governmental powers.

Roosevelt explained how he would cure that diffusion of power.

The New Nationalism regards the executive power as the steward of the public welfare. It demands that the judiciary shall be interested primarily in human welfare rather than in property; it demands that the legislative body shall represent all the people rather than any one class or section.

A man shouted from the crowd: "That's the stuff! You know how we feel up here!"

Roosevelt took the cue. "Of course I know how you feel, because that's the way I feel myself." He went on to recall his days on his Dakota cattle ranch. "I know how the man that works with his hands and the man on the ranch are thinking, because I have been there and I am thinking that way myself."

He won more cheers when he explained another concept that echoed longstanding Populist sentiments.

I stand for the square deal. But when I say that, I mean not only that each man should act fairly and honestly under the rules of the game as it is now played, but I mean also that if the rules give improper advantage to some set of people, then let us change the rules of the game.

He's still talking sense, Dan thought, *and he's still one of a kind. I hope he runs again in 1912.*

If he does, I just might bend my own rules. He's the only politician I ever felt like working for.

George Norton was still no admirer of Theodore Roosevelt. "He talked the same old empty nonsense," the publisher complained to Amos and Dan the following Saturday. "Attacking legitimate businessmen, stirring up the radicals. He sounded just like Bryan back in '96."

"Maybe that's why people cheered so loud," Amos retorted. "He's still hedging, but he's getting there. When he talks about changing the rules of the game to give people a square deal, he's beginning to talk sense."

"And beginning to sound like a candidate," Dan added. "I think he's already decided to run."

"How could he run against Taft?" Norton was indignant. "Why, he handpicked him."

"Roosevelt's not the only one who's been disappointed in Taft," Dan said. "The party's split worse than it ever was over gold and silver. And the insurgents are stronger every day."

"I'm not so sure about that," Amos mused, knocking ash out of his pipe. "They make a lot of noise and look strong around here, but it's all in the West. There's no support in the East, and damned little in between.

[215]

It's the same old story: the farmers are marching, but no one joins the parade—even though everybody knows they're right."

That's the first time I ever heard him sound like he's giving up, Dan thought. *Maybe he's finally getting old.*

"You may be right about that," he said. "Obviously Roosevelt doesn't understand farmers or farming. I mean, he may have studied up on it, but he doesn't have any *feeling* for it."

He warmed to the subject. "On the other hand the insurgents, LaFollette and Norris and the rest, they grew up on farms, and they want to help farmers. On the surface it may look like Teddy and the insurgents are together, but I don't think they really are."

"They talk alike," Norton injected.

"I know, but that's deceptive." Dan shook his head. "The insurgents stand for the same kind of thing the Populists and Bryan did—for keeping things small, and if they get big, breaking them up so the individual doesn't get hurt."

"That's the old philosophy, back to Jefferson," Amos noted.

"That's right," Dan said. "But Roosevelt knows you can't turn things back—that what's already big is going to stay big, and he wants to build up the national government so it can control big business and make sure people get what they're due."

"He's obviously sold you," Amos said. "But don't forget the farmer. He's going to be left holding the short end of the stick, as usual."

Norton disagreed. "Farmers have been doing pretty well the last few years."

"That's because it's been raining. Soon as the next drought comes along, they'll be in trouble again."

"Well, you can't run the country for the benefit of the farmers any more," Norton said. "It's a different place now, cities are growing and people are moving off the farms."

"That's why Roosevelt and LaFollette don't get along," Dan said. "Teddy's a city man, never mind all his talk about his ranch. And most people nowadays live in cities, or soon will. Roosevelt is talking about that kind of country. LaFollette wants it to be the way it was when Pa homesteaded forty years ago."

"Well, there's two things Teddy and LaFollette do agree on." Norton's voice was tinged with sarcasm. "They're both against Taft—and they both want his job."

The November elections made it clear that Taft was in trouble. The Republican insurgents did well, ousting regulars in almost every state west of the Mississippi. LaFollette won reelection to the Senate easily. A few weeks later, a group of insurgents founded the National Progressive Republican League, saying they wanted to move the Republican party "beyond the control of reactionaries." The organizers made clear they believed the way to do that was to replace Taft with LaFollette. Roosevelt, for once, said nothing.

Dan was surprised and delighted to look up one December morning and see Harry standing in the office door, a self-conscious smile on his face. His dark suit was the same one he had worn the day he left, but his striped tie was new.

Red and gray must be the school colors, Dan thought as he got up to shake hands.

"Well, stranger! Welcome home. When did you get in?"

"About fifteen minutes ago, on the overnight train from Chicago," Harry said. "I thought I'd stop and say hello."

Dan was embarrassed—and pleased. "Don't you think you better let your mother know you're here?"

"I will, right away. But first I wanted to tell you that—" The boy hesitated. "That you were right."

"About what?"

"About every new boy feeling the same." Harry seemed about to say more, but did not. He straightened his eyeglasses and hefted his suitcase. "I better go say hello to Father and then get along home."

Dan saw him again two nights later. Dan and Grace were taking Abigail and her friend Margaret Norton to the Lutheran church, where a China missionary on home leave was lecturing and showing stereopticon pictures. When they stopped at the Nortons' to pick up Margaret, Harry asked if he could come along.

"Sure," Dan said. "If you'll help me keep these females rounded up."

At the church, Harry listened intently, fascinated by the photographs of dusty streets and open-air markets, family groups, camel caravans, and ancient city walls—and everywhere people, crowds of people, staring out of the pictures.

Walking home through the bright cold night, Dan asked Harry if he had some special interest in China.

"Well, yes." Harry tugged his coat collar up. "Say, it's a lot colder here than it is out East! Yes, there is a reason. I have a Chinese friend at school."

"A *real* Chinese?" Thirteen-year-old Abigail Woods was doing her best to attract the attention of this older man. "Does he wear a dress, like the people in the pictures? Does he have a pigtail?"

Harry laughed. "No, he dresses just like all the rest of us, and he cuts his hair like any other boy. His father is a rich merchant in Canton—that's a big city in China—and he's got two uncles here, in San Francisco."

"How'd you come to meet him?" Grace asked.

"We're in the same debating society. He speaks really good English, and he's awfully smart."

The new snow crunched under their overshoes as they climbed the hill toward the Norton house.

"That's one of the good things about school. You meet people from all over—even China." Harry was silent for a minute. "Someday I'd like to go visit him."

"It's on the other side of the world!" Abigail exclaimed.

"Yes," Harry agreed. "But that doesn't seem so far, now that I've been away at school."

Dan watched his daughter trying to get Harry's attention. *She already knows how to flirt,* he thought. *My God, she's growing up, and I hardly know her. I've paid more attention to Harry Norton than to my own daughter.*

I wonder if she's noticed that, too.

Chapter 29

Falls City, October 1911–January 1912

DAN STUDIED the sheet of figures that Axel Aslesen had brought into his office.

"This professor who put all this together," Dan said. "How reliable is he?"

"Everybody I talked to says he's careful, responsible, and an expert on grain grading. He's a chemist, and his specialty is wheat." Aslesen tapped the sheets. "He doesn't name the companies in the report itself, but he told me which ones were involved and showed me the government records it's based on. So it's all solid."

Aslesen, the farm reporter for the *Dakota News*, was also a careful, responsible man. Dan read over the professor's report again, his anger rising.

People have been guessing this for a long time, but he's proved it. They've been stealing from the farmers for years. He made up his mind quickly. *This is one hell of a story, and I don't want to read it in the Minneapolis papers first.*

"All right, Axel, let's go with it. Be sure you've got the figures right, double-check them all, and proofread the story after it's in type. I don't want any mistakes. There'll be enough squealing from the elevators without giving them something to get their teeth into."

Dan looked at Aslesen. "And get it written as soon as you can. When did you say the report's being published?"

"Sometime next week. I got hold of this copy by—"

Dan cut him off. "I don't need to know that. I just want to print it before anyone else does."

The story ran on the front page that Sunday:

N.D. EXPERT'S SURVEY SHOWS
ELEVATORS "DOCTORED" GRAIN
TO RAISE GRADE—AND PROFITS

Head of Chemistry Department at Fargo
Demonstrates How Big Firms Dock
Farmers, Then Treat Wheat

A new study has demonstrated how some Minneapolis grain companies earn large profits by "doctoring" wheat after they buy it from farmers at low prices.

The deceptive grading of grain so as to first lower and then raise its grade and price has long been suspected by Dakota farmers. Now a study by Professor Edwin F. Ladd, head of the Chemistry Department at the North Dakota Agricultural College, provides the first statistical proof.

Dr. Ladd's work reveals that last year one elevator at Duluth bought 890,000 bushels of grain, of which 376,000 graded No. 4 or lower. But when it sold the same grain, not one bushel graded in those categories; the entire lot was graded No. 1, 2, or 3.

The elevator apparently mixed different grades of wheat to produce a higher average grade and so sell at top prices what it had bought at discount.

Dr. Ladd publishes in his study the following table to demonstrate the operation at the Duluth elevator, which he calls typical of practices in the industry. It covers wheat received and shipped out during a single season:

Grade of Wheat	Bushels Received	Bushels Shipped
No. 1 Northern	99,711	196,288
No. 2	141,455	467,764
No. 3	272,047	213,549
No. 4	201,167	None
No Grade	116,021	None
Rejected	59,742	None
Total	890,143	877,601
On hand, estimated		12,542
		890,143

There are other tables in the study, dealing with elevators not only at Duluth but at Minneapolis and Chicago as well. They tell the same story.

The study was based on records of the Minnesota Railroad and Warehouse Commission. Dr. Ladd said they reveal numerous cases where wheat graded higher when shipped out of elevators than when taken in. . . .

"Once in a while there's something worth reading in your newspaper." Amos Harper's blue eyes twinkled.

Dan returned the favor. "Why, thank, you, Amos. I thought you'd like that story; it reinforces your prejudices."

"It proves that if you put a grain dealer and an elevator operator in a barrel and roll it down a hill, you'll always have a son-of-a-bitch on top."

Dan laughed, but Amos wouldn't quit. "Some of us have known for forty years that the grain companies were cheating us. But some professor has to say it before newspapers will pay attention."

"Or maybe they have to prove it instead of just bellyaching about it." Dan was proud of the story, and of his reporter for jumping on it, and he wasn't going to take any guff about it—not even from his favorite father-in-law.

At the turn of the year, Will White asked Dan to become an active worker for Roosevelt.

"The great big important fact is this: That this country is going Democratic as sure as November comes unless the party changes leaders," White wrote. "Someone must take the reins who can put cayenne pepper on the balky horse where it will do the most good. It's Roosevelt or bust."

White, now a member of the Republican National Committee, asked Dan to run for a delegate's seat at the Republican convention in June: "You'd have no trouble getting it, and I know you think Roosevelt's the only man. We need you. You carry more weight than you think, especially with the political writers."

Dan told Grace about it that night. "I'm really tempted. I never have been before, but this time I am."

"You've always said a newspaperman has to keep clear away from party politics." Grace was truly puzzled. "I've listened to you I don't know how many times, criticizing Will White for getting so involved. What's different now?"

"Theodore Roosevelt's different, that's what." Dan had been thinking about this all day. "He's one in a million. And this election is different, too. It's going to decide who controls the Republican party for a generation—the people, or the interests."

"But why should you get involved? You've always said it was wrong for newspapermen to go into politics."

Dan tugged at his cowlick in the old telltale gesture of uncertainty. "Well, I—I guess I've decided that once in a lifetime even an editor can give his hand to a candidate."

"Just so long as you hold onto your head." Grace's voice was measured, but inwardly she was astonished. *He's really thinking about doing it,* she thought. *He always was soft on Roosevelt, but this is different. It's not just a good story anymore.*

Dan raised another argument. "Besides, I get tired of always staying on the sideline, watching someone else play the game."

"And thinking you could play it better?"

"Well, maybe. I guess so." All at once he bridled. "You bet I do. I've spent most of my life studying politics. I think I know a little about it by now."

"Of course you do. You know a lot." *This is important,* she thought, *don't say the wrong thing.* "But there's something you're forgetting."

"What's that?"

"Your influence in this town and this state." Her eyes snapped. "People know that you know what you're talking about—but they also know you're your own man. That's why they believe what you write."

"They already know I'm a Republican."

"Of course." She stifled a giggle. "Nobody's perfect. But they also know that when a Republican does something you don't agree with, you'll say so. Even when it's your beloved Teddy."

Dan ignored the gibe. "And you think I couldn't write that way about Roosevelt if I was a delegate pledged to him."

Grace shrugged. "That would be up to you. But it would be hard. And the point is, people wouldn't be so ready to listen to you if you were working for Roosevelt at the same time."

"Well, perhaps so. But I could have a different kind of influence, maybe more. T.R. says it's the man who gets into the fight who makes the difference, not the one who just stands by and watches."

But it's your nature to stand by and watch; that's why you're a good newspaperman, she thought. *My God, he's really hooked. I don't think I'm going to be able to talk him out of it.*

Dan stood up, yawning and stretching. "I think I'll sleep on it."

He fidgeted in the straight wooden chair that George Norton kept by his desk to discourage visitors from lingering overlong. Dan had been awake most of the night, thinking, and now he had to tell the publisher what he proposed to do.

"I've been thinking some about the political situation this year."

"So have I. It's not a pretty prospect."

"That's not what I mean, George." Dan took a deep breath. *Might as well spit it out.* "I've decided to run for delegate to the national convention—as a Roosevelt delegate. Get actively involved for a change."

Norton stared at him for what seemed forever. When he spoke there was ice in his voice.

"How do you propose to square that with being editor of this newspaper?"

"Well, I guess maybe I ought not to write about the presidential election this year."

Another long silence was followed by another icy response.

"I hardly think that would be adequate."

"What do you mean, George?"

"I mean that even after the election is over, you'd always be labeled a partisan, a politician. Everything you wrote about politics from then on would be suspect."

Dan was wounded. "You know me better than that."

"I'm not talking about me, I'm talking about our readers, and about public confidence in the paper. It would be bad for the paper. Very bad."

Norton walked over to the window and stared out at the traffic on Union Avenue, seemingly lost in thought. Finally he turned to Dan.

"A long time ago you told me I was doing something that risked destroying everything I'd built up here—my standing in the community, my influence, everything." George stared at Dan. "Well, that's what you're doing now."

Dan was astonished: *He remembers every word that I said to him fifteen years ago about that woman.*

"George, with all due respect, I do think it's different. Everybody knows that most newspaper editors are partisan in politics."

"But you've not been, at least not until now, and you've criticized those who were." Norton recalled another confrontation. "Remember in '96 when you reminded me what I'd said the day I bought the paper, that our success would depend on the trust of our readers?" He shook his finger at Dan. "I did say that, and it's still true. And it applies to editors as well as publishers."

"I don't think there's anything evil about what I'm proposing to do." Dan, shaken by Norton's intensity, fell back on a platitude. "It's a citizen's duty to participate in politics."

"Some citizens are different. Newspaper editors are different, and you know it."

"I said I'd step aside from writing during the campaign—"

"That would mean nothing in terms of public trust. They'd soon forget that you stepped aside, but they'd always remember you were a Roosevelt delegate. And they'd discount everything you ever wrote on politics after that."

Norton kept reminding Dan of his own words. "As you once reminded me, a newspaper is more than a piece of private property, more than just a business. Well, the same thing is true of its editor—he's more than a private person, more than a businessman."

Dan was silent. Norton continued, now speaking slowly and carefully as if he wanted to be sure Dan heard every word.

"If you want to do this, of course you will. I can't stop you." The publisher sighed. "But if you do, you will have to resign as editor of this newspaper."

Dan was too stunned to speak. Norton sat down at his desk and picked up some papers. The discussion was over.

★　★　★

Dan went back to his own office, and a little later he typed out a letter to White.

January 10, 1912

Dear Will:

You really know how to tempt a sinner. Your proposal rattled around in my head all week until I finally nailed it down.

I would have to give up my pulpit at a time when there are important sermons to be preached, and I find I can't quite bring myself to do that. I know you'll say that such a step wouldn't be necessary, but our situations are different.

Another problem: In politics, White's rule is the right one—if you work for someone, you've got to be for him first, last and all along, right or wrong. Now, I've got into the habit of saying so when I think they're right and saying so when I think they're wrong. I'd either have to be less than loyal to my candidate or less than true to my own instincts, and neither prospect pleases.

So the short of it is I'm not going to do it. No one but Roosevelt could come so close to making me change my habits. Of course I'll argue the case for him in the paper when the time comes. I think I can be more persuasive on his behalf if I'm not personally involved.

Yr friend as ever,
Dan

Dan addressed an envelope, folded the letter and sealed it, put on his overcoat, and walked the two blocks to the post office. When he had mailed the letter he returned to the plant. He stopped at the door to Norton's office.

"George."

Norton looked up. "Yes?"

Dan ran his hand through his hair. "I believe you're right." He hesitated. "Thank you, George."

Norton cleared his throat. "Sometimes I've had reason to thank you. I guess maybe we're even now."

That night Dan told Grace of his decision.

"What did George say?" she asked.

Dan hesitated. "He said he was glad I decided not to do it."

She looked at him. *You're a poor liar. You're not telling me all he said. He must have really jumped on you.*

He read her look and guessed her thought. "Actually, he said a lot more." He hadn't planned to tell her the whole story, but now it came pouring out. Grace waited until he finished.

"Sooner or later George was bound to make you pay."

"Pay? Pay for what?"

"For making him behave when he got mixed up with that woman—and for being right about it."

"I don't believe that."

"Oh, he wouldn't do it consciously. But you passed judgment on him, and even though he knows you were right, and even though you did him a favor, something inside him wanted to make you pay for it."

Besides, she thought, *he was right. Thank you, George.*

February–June 1912

In early February, seven Republican governors asked Roosevelt to become a candidate. No one was surprised—least of all Roosevelt, whose own people had drafted the governors' statement. He said that he would "accept" the nomination: "My hat is in the ring, the fight is on, and I am stripped to the buff."

LaFollette had announced his candidacy the preceding summer, and he had the early support of a number of rich Easterners who were attracted to progressivism. But many of them had already secretly switched to Roosevelt, and now his statement just about finished LaFollette.

Roosevelt next went after Taft, baiting him into primary elections where the president's control of party machinery was no match for Roosevelt's popular appeal. Taft won New York, Indiana, and Massachusetts; LaFollette held his home state of Wisconsin and carried North Dakota. All the rest were won by Roosevelt; he even carried Ohio—Taft's home state—by a two-to-one margin.

But neither Taft nor Roosevelt could gain a decisive edge in the primaries. In early June, a fortnight before the national convention, Dan wrote to Harry Norton, who was going to the Chicago convention with him: "The contested delegates will decide the nomination. Your first convention looks like a three-ring circus."

Chapter 30

D AN MET the train bringing Harry Norton from the East. Watching him stride down the platform, Dan was struck again by how much he had grown up. He was nearly six feet tall, his shoulders and chest had filled out, and two years away from home had given him an air of self-confidence that made him seem older than seventeen.

Dan had invited Harry to join him at the Republican convention because he figured it was time he began to learn politics. He explained the arrangements to Harry as they walked to their hotel. "I managed to get us rooms at the Congress. That's where the Roosevelt people have their headquarters, and there's a good press setup there."

Harry was his usual straight-faced self, but he was excited by Dan's words. He had followed the newspaper reports on the struggle between Roosevelt and Taft, and like most of his schoolmates was an ardent Roosevelt supporter.

"Your first assignment is to learn where the back stairs are," Dan advised. "Once things get going, the elevators will be so jammed they'll take forever."

"When do things get going?" Harry asked, looking around the press room, empty at this hour of the morning except for a lone Western Union messenger dozing in a corner.

"Well, the convention doesn't officially start until a week from tomorrow," Dan said. "But everything is likely to be decided before then."

"How come?"

"Because the national committee makes up the temporary roll of delegates this week. The committee will probably decide enough of the challenges in favor of Taft to give him a majority on the temporary roll. That means he'll be able to name the chairman of the convention. And *that* means the Taft people will be in control all the way through."

"If Roosevelt is going to lose, why is he making a fight?"

"For effect—to make it seem closer than it really is."

"I see," Harry said, slowly. "But what good is that if he loses in the national committee?"

"Well, first of all, it might help him turn it around when they get to the floor of the convention itself. And if he can't do that, he can still claim he lost those 120 delegates because of theft, fraud, and highway robbery—and maybe stir up a public reaction."

Harry pondered this. Dan, watching him, thought: *He has his father's stare, and he asks questions like the Old Man, too.* Now he asked another.

"But Roosevelt won a lot more votes than Taft in the primary elections. Won't the committee pay attention to that?"

"This committee was chosen four years ago, and most of them owe whatever they've got to Taft. Especially the Southerners, they're all federal officeholders who got their jobs from Taft."

"But those states never vote Republican," Harry said. "It doesn't seem fair."

Dan laughed. "Maybe not, but Roosevelt played the same game four years ago to make sure things went the way he wanted. Only he was for Taft then."

The National Committee was meeting in a room at the south end of the Coliseum, the great auditorium where the convention was to be held.

"A lot of the Roosevelt challenges are phonies, filed just to kick up dust and make it look closer than it is," Dan told Harry. "But this bunch wouldn't give him a seat even if no one else wanted it. They don't care if they wreck the party, as long as they own the wreckage."

The committee awarded 19 contested seats to Roosevelt and 229 to Taft. The reporters calculated that on the merits Roosevelt should have been awarded about 50 more seats—the bulk of those on which there were real contests.

"If he'd gotten another fifty, wouldn't he have had a majority?" Harry asked.

"It looks that way," Dan said. "But when it's that close and the stakes are that high, you never can tell. Those bozos on the committee sure weren't taking any chances."

Roosevelt's managers saw only one way out. That night there were urgent exchanges over the long-distance telephone, and in the morning the Rough Rider announced he was on his way to Chicago.

He reached the Congress Saturday afternoon.

"How are you feeling?" a reporter shouted at him.

"Wonderful!" Roosevelt bellowed, his jaw clenching and his face twisting into the familiar grimace. "Just like a bull moose!"

[227]

He was extracted from an admiring mob by police and hustled inside. A few minutes later he reappeared, climbing through a second-floor window onto a small balcony. He leaned over the parapet and waved while the crowd gradually quieted.

> This has come down to be a fight of honesty against dishonesty. It is a naked fight against theft, and the thieves will not win.

"That's the tip-off," Dan said. "They're going to claim the delegates were stolen from them."

"Do you think he can make it stick?"

"You never can tell what will happen in a convention. But the odds are against it."

"I don't see how that can be," Harry said. "Why, everyone here seems to be for him. I've never seen so many people as there are working in his headquarters."

Dan had to agree that the Roosevelt headquarters was unlike any other he had seen. Instead of the usual political hangers-on, this one was filled with respectable, middle-class, professional people—bankers, publishers, businessmen, professors, lawyers, even an occasional doctor—leavened with a sprinkling of eager young college men.

We've come a long way since the Farmers' Alliance and the Populists, Dan thought. *These people aren't the have-nots; they're the haves. They don't have grievances, they have causes.*

They're not farmers or workers or poor people, they're people like . . . like me.

Monday night the Roosevelt forces rallied at the Chicago Auditorium. Five thousand jammed into the hall; ten thousand more filled the sidewalks and streets outside.

Dan and Harry sat near the stage in a section that had been reserved for reporters. Suddenly there were cheers from the crowd.

"Is Roosevelt coming?" Harry asked.

Dan looked around, then laughed. "No, it's just William Jennings Bryan. He always comes to Republican conventions and he always gets a hand."

The country's most famous Democrat came into the press area, waved to acknowledge the cheers, and sat down. Dan was just introducing Harry to him when a roar interrupted him and Roosevelt strode onto the stage.

The candidate began by redefining the political struggle in his own apocalyptic terms.

It is not a partisan issue; it is more than a political issue; it is a
great moral issue. If we condone political theft, not merely our
Democratic form of government but our civilization itself cannot
endure. . . .

The majority of the national committee in deciding the cases
before them have practiced political theft in every form, from
highway robbery to petty larceny.

Bryan muttered amiably into Dan's ear. "They say the Arabs have
seven hundred words which mean 'camel.' Teddy's got just as many words
for 'theft,' and I believe he'll use them all tonight."

Roosevelt spelled out his strategy for the days ahead.

We ask merely that neither set of contestants be allowed to vote on
any question before the convention until the thousand members
whose seats have not been contested shall themselves decide which
of the contested delegates are entitled to membership.

If the contested Taft delegates were allowed to vote on their own
cases, Roosevelt said, it would invalidate everything the convention did.

It is our duty to insist that no action of the convention which is
based on the votes of these fraudulently seated delegates binds the
Republican party or imposes any obligation upon any Republican.

That drew the loudest cheers yet, and Dan put his mouth to Harry's
ear. "He's saying that if they lose on the floor they should walk out and
split the party."

"Did he say that?"

"That's the message."

Roosevelt was dripping with sweat as he waved his arms, shook his
fists, and clenched his jaws, stirring the crowd to more and more frenzy.
Then, coming to the end, he lowered his voice. The crowd was so quiet
that the sound of a single woman sobbing in the balcony could be heard
throughout the hall.

It would be far better to fail honorably for the cause we champion
than it would be to win by foul methods the foul victory for which
our opponents hope. But the victory shall be ours—

He was interrupted by the loudest, longest cheering of the evening.

—and it shall be won as we have already won so many victories, by
clean and honest fighting for the loftiest of causes. We fight in

[229]

honorable fashion for the good of mankind; fearless of the future; unheeding of our individual fates; with unflinching hearts and undimmed eyes.

We stand at Armageddon, and we battle for the Lord.

For a moment the crowd was hushed. Then the room exploded in sound.

Chapter 31

Chicago, Tuesday, June 18, 1912

T HE CONVENTION opened amid rumors of riot and suggestions that
Roosevelt's people might try to take over the hall by force. The
Taft men in charge of arrangements took no chances: by the time
Dan and Harry arrived, the aisles of the Coliseum were lined with hundreds of uniformed police, with more in reserve just off the floor. The
tension was reflected in the faces and voices of delegates. As they took their
seats, they seemed unusually subdued, almost like soldiers awaiting the
opening of a battle.

Even the physical arrangements reinforced the sense of impending
conflict: a long, narrow walkway was thrust like a sword into the contentious hall. This led to the speakers' podium. On either side of the walkway,
newspapermen sat in tightly packed rows on narrow benches, elbow to
elbow and cheek to cheek, their eyes almost exactly at the floor level of
the speakers' platform.

The first question to come before the convention—approval of the
temporary roll of delegates prepared by the national committee—would
normally have been routine. But this temporary roll was full of contested
seats; the Roosevelt forces moved to substitute the names of their delegates
for seventy-two of the Taft men on the roll, and the fight was on.

Within a few minutes the huge hall was in an uproar, literally shaking
under a continuous barrage of sound. Speakers on both sides were hissed,
booed, insulted, ridiculed, or simply shouted down. Hardly a word uttered
by any speaker could be heard; the debate became a contest to see which
side was cooler under fire.

After the last speech on the Roosevelt proposal, the temporary presiding officer, a Taft man, ruled that it was out of order and so could not
even be voted on. He then declared the temporary roll approved—with the
seventy-two contested Taft men on it.

Roosevelt's people had failed to alter the balance of delegate votes. Now, looking for some other way to gain control, they tried to win the permanent chairmanship. Again the debate was long and ugly, but when it was all over and the roll was called, Taft's candidate, Elihu Root, had been elected by a vote of 558 to 502.

"I think that's all she wrote," Dan muttered to Harry as he scribbled down the tally. "That was their last chance."

Wednesday, June 19, 1912

The next morning, the Roosevelt forces renewed their motion to unseat the seventy-two contested Taft delegates. If those delegates had been barred from voting on the chairmanship, Root could not have won, and Roosevelt's men would have controlled the convention. Their only remaining hope was somehow to change enough votes to reverse the earlier actions.

The debate resumed, but for some reason the atmosphere was more amiable, as if both sides knew how it was going to come out and had tacitly agreed to have a good time in the process.

The fun began when Roosevelt delegates started jumping to their feet, laughing, shouting, climbing on chairs, waving their state standards.

"What's going on?" Harry shouted into Dan's ear.

Dan pointed to the front row of the spectator gallery. A handsome young woman in a white linen dress, her face flushed, brown hair tucked under a straw hat, was holding up a picture of Roosevelt. As the crowd began to notice her, she waved a poster in one hand and her handkerchief in the other.

Three members of the California delegation ran up into the gallery and handed her a big, golden Teddy bear. She embraced it; the crowd was transported. The Californians escorted her onto the convention floor, where she led a rapidly growing parade up and down the aisles.

Finally the woman was boosted up onto the press stand right in front of Dan and Harry. She looked down and saw the youth; before he realized what was happening, she pulled him up beside her, threw her arms around him, and planted a kiss on his cheek. Then, as a blushing Harry scrambled down off the bench, she called out: "Three cheers for Teddy!"

Ten thousand voices joined her: "Hip . . . hip . . . HOORAY! Hip . . . hip . . . HOORAY! Hip . . . hip . . . HOORAY!"

Stepping nimbly across the press benches, she reached the speakers' platform, slipped under the rope, and led another cheer from the podium. Finally she was escorted back to her seat in the gallery, blowing kisses and waving all the way.

"I know who she is," Harry told Dan as the din quieted. "I saw her do pretty much the same thing in that Florentine Room at the hotel the other night, at a Roosevelt rally."

"Oh, you know her?" Dan grinned at Harry. "Is that why she gave you that squeeze?"

Harry, blushing, fiddled with his eyeglasses. "I never even spoke to her. I got her name from another reporter." He dug through his notebook. "Mrs. W. A. Davis, 4231 Drexel Boulevard. Husband's a rich lumber man, office in the Great Northern Building."

"And she has a weakness for younger men."

"Aw, come on, Dan." Harry squirmed, but Dan realized he was enjoying the moment. *Why, there's a little bit of a sport hidden in there after all.*

"Actually, that was a good piece of work, to notice her the other night and get her name," Dan said. Harry wasn't sure whether he was still joshing him. "No, I mean it. We can use her in the story tonight. From what you saw before we know the Roosevelt crew planted her in that front-row seat to start a ruckus."

But the diversion changed nothing. When the roll was called, Taft won again. Root, urbane but unyielding, finished off the Roosevelt challenge by ruling that although contested delegates could not vote on their own seating, they could vote on all other contests. That assured Taft's control of the contested seats, and thus his majority in the convention.

Thursday, June 20, 1912

During the evening, angry Roosevelt delegates crowded into the ornate Florentine Room at the Congress, ready for anything and spoiling for a fight. Hundreds of other supporters, newspapermen, and the merely curious filled the ornate room and jammed the hallways outside.

At two o'clock Thursday morning, Roosevelt himself pushed into the room and jumped up onto a table. He had no prepared text, no careful wording, no elegant phrases; reporters scribbled frantically as his words poured out.

> So far as I am concerned, I am through. If those fraudulently seated delegates are admitted, then it is not a Republican convention, and it is not entitled to recognition as such.

It was a call to rebellion, to secession. Harry shivered despite the heat of the room as Roosevelt's supporters roared hoarse acceptance of the challenge. Something up near the ceiling caught his eye; the big crystal chandeliers were actually swaying because of the noise.

Harry glanced over at Dan, who was writing as fast as he could, his notebook jammed up against his chest. Harry himself could not at that moment have written a word to save his life; he was transfixed by the stocky

[233]

man who stood on the table, light glinting off his glasses, sweat running down his face, shaking his fists, shouting.

> If you want my advice, I advise that you do not permit yourselves to be committed in any further way, shape, or form, by further association with these men as long as they retain control of the Republican convention by means of a majority composed in an essential part of fraudulently seated delegates.

Dan tugged Harry toward the relative quiet of the press room. "That's enough. We've got work to do. I want you to do me a sidebar, about two hundred words of color on that room, the way it looked and sounded. And smelled. I've got to write a new lead for my story."

Twenty minutes later Dan handed several sheets of typewritten copy to a Western Union messenger and turned to Harry.

"How you coming with that sidebar?" Dan asked. Harry handed him a single sheet of copy. Dan scanned it, penciled in a few changes, then handed it back.

"That'll do. Put an address on top and send it. Give it to Postal Telegraph."

"Didn't you send yours by Western Union?"

"Always split your file. That way you'll get good service from both of 'em."

Harry stood up. "Was it all right?"

"Was what all right?"

"Was that story all right?"

"Oh." Dan realized he had been waiting for some signal of approval. "Yes, it was fine. It really was. You made it sound as if you knew just how Teddy's fanatics felt."

"I did." Harry shrugged. "I guess I am one."

"Not while you have that press badge on." Dan's tone was brisk, but he softened it with a tired smile. "I'm one too, if truth be told. Now send that and let's get some sleep."

Friday, June 21, 1912

Dan walked into the hotel dining room just before nine o'clock Friday morning. He sat down with James Morgan, who was nodding over a cup of coffee and a messy jumble of morning newspapers.

"Anything new this morning?" Dan asked the Bostonian.

"Oh, this and that." Morgan took a swallow of coffee. "I understand Teddy finally made up his mind about three o'clock this morning. They've taken Orchestra Hall for a rally Saturday night to launch the third party."

Now the drama was playing out, inexorable as a Greek tragedy: while

[234]

Taft moved steadily toward victory, Roosevelt plotted to turn that victory into ultimate defeat.

Roosevelt's strategists wrestled with the practical problems of a third-party candidacy. It was one thing to proclaim the crusade in ringing rhetoric; it was quite another to raise money, organize a campaign, mesh with friendly Republican organizations in some states, qualify a new party for the ballot in others, and decide where to enter separate slates of presidential electors.

But Roosevelt was not deterred. That night he climbed out on the same second-floor hotel balcony from which he had spoken when he arrived in Chicago. Looking down at a cheering crowd, he shouted: "My hat is in the ring and it's going to stay there, more than ever."

Saturday, June 22, 1912

Dan wanted to cover the Roosevelt rally at Orchestra Hall, and he knew they'd have to get there early to get in at all. When they arrived an hour before the rally was to start, the spectator seats were packed to overflowing and thousands more filled Michigan Avenue outside, pushing and shoving in a vain effort to get inside.

When Roosevelt came onto the stage there was pandemonium. As soon as he uttered his first words—"I thank you for your nomination"— the crowd began another demonstration. Finally he was able to go on.

> The time has come when not only men who believe in progressive principles but all men who believe in the elementary maxims of public and private morality should join in one movement. . . . If you wish me to make the fight I will make it, even if only one state should support me.

When the cheers finally faded, Roosevelt opened a new line of attack, one that had the reporters frantically taking notes as his words poured out:

> I am in this fight for certain principles, and the first and most important of these goes back to Sinai, and is embodied in the commandment, "Thou shall not steal."
> Thou shalt not steal a nomination. Thou shalt neither steal in politics nor in business. Thou shalt not steal from the people the birthright of the people to rule themselves.

Dan yawned as he handed his last sheet of copy to the waiting telegraph messenger. "That should hold them for one night," he said. It was after midnight.

"I don't see how you can write so fast," Harry said. "Especially when you're tired. And you have to go right on to Baltimore for the Democrats."

"Oh, that'll be easier. I'll be home by the first of July."

[235]

Chapter 32

D AN was wrong. The Democratic convention turned into an eight-day free-for-all, and by the time it finally ended it was too late for him to get home for the Independence Day picnic at the Harper farm.

Grace and Abigail were there, however, and Amos had invited the Nortons, too. George came with his wife and two younger children; James was off somewhere playing baseball.

Grace drove the young people out from town in the family Model T, the girls in the back and Harry sitting beside her in front.

"It's too bad your Pa's not here today," Margaret told Abigail. "He's nice to talk with."

Abigail cupped her hand so her mother wouldn't overhear. "It seems like he's never home on holidays. He's always working, or out of town at some old political meeting."

"My father's always here," Margaret said, "but he's not much fun. He's always criticizing us for something."

"At least he's home." Abigail pouted. "You can't have *any* fun with someone who's not there."

A rooster tail of dust trailed out sideways as the car bounced along under the relentless July sun. Meadowlarks and orioles flashed in the hedgerows; red-winged blackbirds cavorted in sloughs and potholes. Here and there, high up, a hawk circled effortlessly, riding the warm air above the corn-fields. Off to the west, huge white clouds piled up along the horizon like great sailing ships in line of battle.

"Oooh! Be careful, Ma!" The girls shrieked and collapsed in giggles as Grace steered around potholes and bumped along the rock-hard ruts dried into the road's surface.

"What do you think, Harry," Grace asked, "do I pass the test?"

"Why, sure, Mrs. Woods," Harry said. Then he laughed. "How would I know? I'm just learning to drive myself. James is teaching me. I sure don't know how to work a Model T."

"Just so you can change a flat tire . . . ooops!" Grace swerved to miss a particularly deep pothole. "I told Dan that's one thing I won't do."

"There's not many women in town can drive a car, let alone repair one," Harry said.

"There's not many women in town married to a newspaperman who's always away when you want to go somewhere." Harry heard the irritation in Grace's voice. "I don't have much choice—unless I want to be stuck at home all the time."

Baltimore, June 1912

By the time the Democrats finally finished in Baltimore, Dan would have been glad to be stuck at home. The convention seemed endless, and the humid heat of late June was a constant, oppressive presence. Like most of the political reporters, Dan had come straight from the Republican convention in Chicago, so he was already bone-tired when it began.

There were two leading Democratic candidates: Woodrow Wilson, governor of New Jersey, former president of Princeton, author and teacher, an intellectual in politics; and Champ Clark, congressman from Missouri, speaker of the House, politician, middle-of-the-road Democrat. Both were considered progressive, but Clark had more support from party regulars, especially in the South, while Wilson attracted the reform element.

Neither man was at Baltimore, where the dominant figure was William Jennings Bryan. At the Republican convention, Bryan had been merely a sentimental figure out of the past; at the Democratic convention he was a delegate and a man of influence, the party's most famous leader, three times its candidate for president. He brushed aside suggestions that he run again, but he thrust himself into the fight from start to finish.

"I tell you, Dan, I don't understand why Bryan's so popular with the party," James Morgan complained as they clambered to their seats in the press stand for the opening session. "He's a Jesus-shouter, he's a country bumpkin, and he's lost three times. He's about twenty years behind the times. But *he* still thinks he's the Peerless Leader."

"You city slickers think you're so damned smart." Dan knew he was taking Morgan's gibes personally, but he was tired enough not to care. "You know he's no bumpkin."

"Oh, I know." Dan heard the condescension in his friend's tone. "But this time the parade's passed him by. I hope he doesn't make a fool of himself."

[237]

Bryan, of course, had no idea that the parade had passed. He had become convinced, watching the divided Republicans, that if the Democrats chose a progressive candidate they would win, but if they nominated a conservative, they would forfeit the progressive vote of both parties and put Theodore Roosevelt back in the White House.

From the first hour of the convention, Bryan preached that gospel. The fringes of his once-black hair were gray, and the familiar black sack suit was creased and rumpled, but his voice was as compelling as ever. As usual, his metaphors were biblical.

> We have been traveling in the wilderness. We have now come in sight of the promised land. During all the weary hours of darkness, progressive Democracy has been the people's pillar of fire by night. I pray you, delegates, now that dawn has come, do not rob our party of the right so well earned to be the people's pillar of cloud by day.

Clark led on the early ballots, but when the bosses of Tammany Hall switched New York's vote to Clark, Bryan attacked again. He rushed onto the floor, roaring that "a progressive candidate must not be besmirched by New York's vote." As long as New York and Tammany were for Clark, he announced, he would cast his own vote for Wilson.

From that moment, Wilson gained. The frustrated Clark camp seethed with hatred for Bryan, but Clark was finished; Wilson was finally nominated on the forty-fifth ballot.

Bryan spoke once more that night. He looked tired and old, but the marvelous baritone voice still held the entire hall rapt. Dan remembered the other times he had heard that voice over the last twenty years. It had never failed, and Bryan had never wavered, right or wrong, win or lose. Now he had fought again and won again, probably for the last time in a national convention, and now as before he flung defiance at his enemies.

> Tonight I come with joy to surrender into the hands of the one chosen by this convention a standard which I have carried in three campaigns; and I challenge my enemies to declare that it has ever been lowered in the face of the enemy.

Dan, standing and applauding, looked around at his colleagues. Every reporter was on his feet in an impromptu farewell tribute to a man who had given them so much to write about for so long—and to a time and place, a time surely past and a place that never was, except that Bryan had made it real every time he spoke.

Amos Harper wanted to hear about the Republican convention, and Harry Norton was ready to tell him more than he wanted to know. Amos was amused by the youth's self-confidence; he guessed that three-quarters of his opinions were really Dan's. But Harry's enthusiasm for Theodore Roosevelt was clearly his own.

Amos filled his pipe and scratched a match on the floor to light it. He looked out from the porch, squinting into the midday sun as he looked for the telltale ripple in the ripening grain that would signal a breeze. There was none. It was still, hot, and humid—good weather for corn, if not for people.

"Harry, you're pretty high on Roosevelt, aren't you?" Amos was curious about this serious young man.

"Yes, I guess I am," Harry said. "I really like what he stands for. He's not, well, he doesn't seem like a *politician.*"

"Oh, come now. If anyone ever was a politician, he is."

Harry was not to be put off. "Don't you think he's for the right things, Mr. Harper?"

Amos sighed and pointed his pipe at George Norton. "I've explained this to your father, and to Dan, so I might as well explain it to you. Everything that Roosevelt is for that you think is good was in the platform that the People's party—the Populists—adopted way back in '92. You should read it."

"Maybe they were ahead of their time, and there's a better chance for those things now."

"I expect you're right," Amos said. "But I wonder whether your man stands for what the real progressives stand for. LaFollette, Norris, those fellows, they're all right. Roosevelt makes a big noise, but if you listen hard you find he's just a little bit slippery. And a lot of his support comes straight from Wall Street."

Amos was warming to his lecture, but Harry shifted the subject with a question. "What do you think of Wilson?"

"I don't know about him," Amos said. "He's obviously a smart fellow, but he seems kind of cold. After all, he's a professor. I don't know how much feeling he'd have for people like farmers, regular people."

Later, in the brazen heat of afternoon, the young people went for a swim in the river. Grace and George walked down through the pasture with them and sat in the shade of the big old cottonwoods. The girls shrieked and splashed and ducked each other. Harry, ignoring them, ran down the bank and dove into the stream, swimming smoothly and purposefully against the current.

A duck and ducklings came into view, paddling along the edge of the

[239]

stream. Grace and George looked at each other, and both blushed. He broke the tension with a self-conscious little laugh and a few murmured words.

"Twenty years ago today."

Grace nodded. "A day just like this one."

"Even the ducks."

"I remember them, too." George cleared his throat; something seemed to be caught in it. "I remember everything about that day."

"I think of it sometimes, too," she said. She studied the water sliding around the river bend. "It was a nice day."

"I think of it every time I see you." There was a note of appeal in his voice. "You didn't—you don't mind?"

He touched her hand; she shook her head and pulled the hand away, but her answer came gently.

"That day I thought you weren't quite nice, but I liked—" She paused. "Well, you knew what you wanted, and you meant to have it."

"So did you."

She hesitated only a moment.

"You're quite right." Now her words were brisk—and dismissive. "But we both wanted other things more."

"And so they each lived happily ever after." George's sarcasm was belied by his wistful tone.

"Yes, I think they did." Grace stood up and brushed off her skirt. "You know, I believe I'd like a glass of Mother's lemonade, and I'm sure you would too."

He stood up too and offered her his arm. "That's a first-rate idea." He turned toward the stream and raised his voice. "Harry! You're in charge here. Keep an eye on the girls."

I'm sure he will, Grace thought, suppressing a giggle. *It runs in the family.*

Chapter 33

T HE Republicans had fought a bloody civil war; the Democrats had staged a free-swinging alley brawl. By contrast, the Progressive party's first national convention seemed more like a consecration.

"It's sort of the feeling you have when you go into church," Harry muttered to Dan as they watched the delegates filing into the Coliseum on the first day.

"Well, a camp meeting, maybe." Dan's voice was tinged with mockery. "These folks are *earnest,* aren't they?"

Harry was not amused. He had found his first political hero, and he was as serious as any Bull Moose delegate.

"Well, I suppose so," he conceded. "If you mean they don't act like politicians."

"They certainly don't." Dan laughed. "And they aren't. I think every do-gooder in the country is in this hall today."

He'd never seen a convention like this one: it was made up almost entirely of successful-looking professionals, businessmen, professors, preachers, doctors, clergymen. And women: this was the first major national convention to allow female delegates, and there were lots of them.

They've come back to Armageddon to battle for the Lord, he thought. *They're not zanies, but they still have illusions and high ideals.*

And you don't have to be as young as Harry to get caught up in it.

The whole business baffled most of the reporters. Except for a few like Dan who had covered Farmers' Alliance and Populist meetings in the late '80s and early '90s, this was a new experience—a convention of serious, sober, earnest people, with very few recognizable "politicians" in the crowd.

These people are Populists in professors' clothes, Dan thought as he watched the delegates. *No, that's not quite right. They live in a different world from the Pops: big cities instead of little farms. And they're thinking about tomorrow, not yesterday.*

The Pops wanted something they could never have, something that maybe never was: the world as it used to be. These folks want the world as it can be.

The Coliseum was a mass of fluttering red bandannas—the Bull Moosers' convention symbol. Here and there someone waved a sign showing a hat in a ring.

The delegates sang "The Battle Hymn of the Republic," and "Onward, Christian Soldiers," and "America." Then they marched and shouted, sang again, laughed and cheered. The California delegation displayed a banner:

> I WANT TO BE A BULL MOOSE
> AND WITH THE BULL MOOSE STAND
> WITH ANTLERS ON MY FOREHEAD
> AND A BIG STICK IN MY HAND.

Dan tapped Harry on the shoulder and pointed to the gallery. There, in a front-row seat, wearing a white dress and waving a red bandanna, was the woman who had led that uproarious Roosevelt demonstration at the Republican convention.

"Your girlfriend's back for more," Dan shouted into Harry's ear. "Maybe she'll come see you again!" Harry blushed beet-red.

Of course it was not all hymn singing and bandanna waving. While the main show proceeded at the Coliseum, the party's platform was assembled in committee meetings.

"Just what you'd expect," Dan said as he and Harry looked over the final text. "Every reform anyone ever thought up is in here."

"I think it's splendid," Harry said. "I hope we'll print it all."

There it is, Dan thought suddenly. *His first "suggestion" to the editor. There'll be plenty more. I might as well get used to the idea.*

"We will," he said, a little more abruptly than he intended to. "We print 'em all and let people make up their own minds which is best."

There was a lot in the Progressive platform. Its core was a set of proposed changes in the political process: direct primaries, votes for women, direct election of senators, the short ballot, initiative, referendum, and recall.

Beyond these structural reforms were substantive proposals, all familiar verses in the scripture of political protest. They dealt with workers and workplaces, safety and health and old age, protection of children and working women, ending business abuses.

There was no debate on the platform; it was adopted by acclamation. Then Roosevelt was nominated in the same way. The delegates answered no roll calls, cast no votes, and had little voice in the writing of the party platform. But they felt free, even exalted, and as the convention closed, they burst into the Doxology:

> Praise God from whom all blessings flow;
> Praise Him all creatures here below. . . .

Harry was still studying the Progressive platform as they rode the train home the next day. Dan had had all the politics he wanted for a while; he was half-asleep, lulled by the endless flat fields of northern Iowa, cornstalks reflecting green and gold in the slanting sunlight of an August afternoon. Harry nudged him.

"You know, this says a lot more about farmers than either one of the other parties did."

Dan roused himself. "It would be hard not to say more than the Republicans. They didn't even mention farmers or farming—not once."

"And the Democrats just had one vague sentence, if I remember right," Harry said. "Isn't that an important difference?"

He's going to be smoother than his father, Dan thought, *but he's also going to have more opinions on more things—and he'll push them harder. Especially politics.*

"There is a difference, and it's real." Dan knew he had to deal with Harry's question; he'd been thinking about it himself. "But if push came to shove and it was city against farm, I think most of those delegates would go for the cities and against the farmers."

"What makes you think so?" Harry had inherited his father's stare, too. "Do you think the plank is too vague?"

"The words are fine. The trouble is this new party has its roots in the cities, not the country. Time was when the Republicans were the farmer's party. Now none of the parties is—including the Progressives."

"Why is that?"

"Because there aren't so many farmers and they don't have the political pull they used to. Now every time there's another election, the farm vote is a smaller part of the total. Politicians can count, so the farm states are losing their influence in all the parties."

Harry frowned. "But you said Bryan was the man who steered the Democratic convention, and he's always been the farmers' champion."

"Bryan did that, all right, but he didn't do it with farm votes. It was big states, like Illinois, that swung it."

Harry kept pressing. "Don't you think Roosevelt likes farmers?"

"He likes 'em all right. I don't think he understands 'em. When he's in our part of the country he talks about his ranch days in the territory, but I don't think being a cowboy taught him what farming is like."

"Don't you think he's sincere?"

[243]

"Sure I do. I admire him a lot." An idea came to Dan: *I might as well get some help from him while I'm at it, I may need it.*

"In fact," he added, "I'm going to try to persuade your father to let me endorse him in the paper. But—"

"Gosh, that's fine."

"But Teddy's attitude on farming isn't the reason." Dan pointed at the document in Harry's hand. "What's the headline on that part of the platform?"

Harry glanced at it. " 'Country Life.' "

"That's a funny word for farming. Sounds like they think it's a picnic, or maybe a place to ride your horse, doesn't it?"

That's the trouble with all three candidates, Dan thought. *None of 'em has ever lived on a real farm. They don't know that it's all hard work and damned little play. They don't know what it's like to have to depend on things you can't control, like weather and grasshoppers and the price of grain.*

The familiar anger rose in his throat again.

The parties are all the same. They give away the store to businessmen, but they say the farmer's got to take his chances.

Just then, the train passed close to a farmstead where a young woman was filling a bucket at the well. The sight pushed politics from his mind.

There's nothing prettier than a girl pumping water in the wind, he thought. *Oh my, it'll be good to see Grace.*

Chapter 34

I ASSUME you want to endorse that cowboy."

George Norton's voice was as grim and unyielding as his stare. Dan had expected this: the publisher not only liked Taft, but also despised Roosevelt.

"Yes, George, I do."

"I'm for Taft."

"Well, he can't win. And every vote he gets makes it likelier that Wilson will be elected." Dan figured a pragmatic approach might be more persuasive than an appeal based on the relative merit of the candidates.

"Wilson might be better than Roosevelt," Norton snapped.

Dan could not contain a laugh. "Next thing you'll be telling me you want Eugene Debs for vice president."

"At least Debs *admits* he's a socialist," Norton said. "Your friend Teddy pretends to be a Republican, but he's just as radical as Debs."

It's going to take some time and argument, Dan thought.

"Think it over," he said to Norton. "We ought to talk about the pros and cons, and where they stand on the issues."

"Ha!" Norton laughed harshly. "I already know your arguments."

"You haven't heard them yet."

"Oh, yes I have. I've had to listen to Harry. He talks morning, noon, and night about that man, and I know he got his opinions from you."

"You don't give either of us enough credit. He thinks for himself."

"Well, then he needs to learn how to think. He's head over heels for Roosevelt."

"He's seventeen, and he's never been caught up in politics before. It's like falling in love the first time."

"I hope he has better taste in girls than he does in candidates," George said. "All right, we'll talk again. But don't get your hopes up."

George was unmoved by Dan's arguments on behalf of Roosevelt.

"I usually go along with what you want, you know that," he told Dan one afternoon. "But not this time. Roosevelt is too much for me. He's a wild man."

In the end, the argument was decided by outside events. The Republican state convention in South Dakota, controlled by the insurgents, chose a slate of electors pledged to Roosevelt; the Taft people could find no way to get their man on the ballot.

"It doesn't make much sense to endorse a candidate who's not running here," Dan argued.

George was stubborn. "I don't care. We should take our stand on principle. I don't want to endorse Roosevelt, even if you and Harry do think he walks on water."

That conversation ended there, but early the next morning George walked into Dan's office and resumed as if it had never been interrupted.

"Taft not being on the ballot is a problem."

Dan, sensing an opening, returned to his very first argument. "South Dakota has got to choose between Roosevelt and Wilson. This is a Republican paper. If we don't come out for Teddy, we're inviting people to vote Democratic. We're really endorsing Wilson."

George weighed the point, then seemed to decide.

"I promised on the day I bought this paper that it would always endorse a Republican." He smiled grimly. "And I suppose Roosevelt *is* a Republican, no matter what he calls himself."

Dan realized the argument was over, and tried a small joke: "He must be, the way he talks about Democrats."

Norton was in no mood for humor as he rationalized his surrender. "I think Taft has been a fine president, and I'm for him. But if people can't even vote for him here, it's between the other two—and I'd rather have a Republican, even a renegade like Roosevelt, than a Democrat who'd turn the country over to the Southerners and the big-city machines."

"Sounds all right to me," Dan said.

Grace was wary.

"He gave in to you this time only because of an accident, because Taft was kept off the ballot," she said. "If that hadn't happened, he'd never have let you endorse Roosevelt."

"He was dug in pretty deep," Dan conceded.

Grace's voice was urgent. "You're skating on thin ice with George. Sooner or later he's going to insist on an endorsement you can't swallow. Then what?"

"I'll worry about that if and when," Dan said. "It hasn't happened yet."

It will, his wife thought. *And when it does, it'll hurt.*

Woodrow Wilson spoke at a big outdoor rally in Falls City, belittling Roosevelt's proposals for controlling big business.

> The third-party program is this: not to retrace a single step, but
> to take charge of the monopolies and regulate them. But by
> regulating monopoly you adopt it, you render it permanent, you
> accept all the things by which it has been established.
> Are you going to vote for a government which will regulate
> your masters, or are you going to be your own masters and regulate
> the government?
> I am not imagining these things. As a friend of mine said, I am
> not arguing with you, I am telling you.

Wilson isn't exactly a fire-eater, Dan thought. *But he comes on strong and he knows how to use the English language.*

Grace, standing with her husband and her father at one side of the crowd, put it a little differently. "I like the *way* he talks," she whispered. "He doesn't shout like your man Roosevelt."

Amos Harper winked at her as he leaned over to Dan. "He's got it about right," Amos said. "He's talking sense. Almost sounds like the Omaha platform."

That again, Dan thought wearily. *He must have talked about that Populist platform ten thousand times. He's showing his age.*

Dan turned to speak to Grace, but she hardly noticed him; her eyes were on Wilson, her face intent. She was applauding fervently.

I've seen that look before, Dan thought. *She's fallen for Wilson. Between her and George, I'm going to get a lot of argument.*

Roosevelt came charging across the northern plains in early October. Many people seemed almost to worship him. During one speech Dan noticed an old farmer, standing by the speakers' platform, reach over the edge of the stand to touch Roosevelt's shoe, gently, almost reverently.

Roosevelt finally talked about farming in one of his Dakota speeches, and Dan put a full text in the paper. He had been waiting for some evidence that his candidate cared as much for farmers as he did for oppressed industrial workers.

> The welfare of the farmer is a basic need of this nation. It is
> the men from the farms who, in the past, have taken the lead in
> every great movement within this nation, whether in time of war or
> time of peace. It is well to have our cities prosper, but it is not well
> if they prosper at the expense of the country.

That's a little obvious, Dan thought, *but it's more than the other candidates have said.*

> Everything possible should be done to better the economic condition of the farmer and also to increase the social value of the life of the farmer, his wife, and their children. The burdens of labor and loneliness bear heavily on the women in the country; their welfare should be the especial concern of all of us.

Dan liked that: *He could be talking about Ma.* He was less impressed by Roosevelt's next sentences.

> The government must cooperate with the farmer to make the farm more productive, and he should be helped to cooperate with his fellows, so that the money paid by the consumer for the product of the soil shall, to as large a degree as possible, go into the pockets of the man who raised that product.
> It is entirely possible by improvements in production, in the avoidance of waste, and in business methods on the part of the farmer to give him an increased income from his farm while at the same time reducing to the consumer the price of the articles raised on the farm.

George Norton came roaring into Dan's office, flourishing a tearsheet of the Roosevelt farm text. He had circled the last paragraph with red pencil. "That's nonsense," he growled. "He must know better. Farmers could give away their crops and livestock, and the price of food wouldn't drop that much."

"I know." Dan shrugged. "He gets carried away by the sound of his own voice. But at least he seems to *care* about farmers. That's more than the others do."

Norton shook his head. "None of them really cares about the farmer any more. They all kowtow to the cities. That's where the votes are now."

"Except in the Senate. Each state still has two votes there."

"Your cowboy would change that, too, if he could. He doesn't care a rap for the Constitution."

Dan couldn't help himself. He laughed so hard that even Norton let a smile thaw his face.

In the end what mattered was neither personality nor programs, but the simple fact that the Democrats were united while the Republicans were divided. No amount of Rooseveltian rhetoric could change that. Wilson won in an electoral landslide, carrying forty states while Roosevelt won only six (one was South Dakota) and Taft only two. In state after state, Wilson won simply because the Republicans split their vote.

[248]

"Well, you carried your own state for Roosevelt, anyway." Grace and Dan were at breakfast two days after the election. She passed him the coffeepot. "Have another cup and tell me what happened."

"The Republicans split so badly that even Teddy couldn't win," he said. "The Democrats stuck together and had a good candidate."

"They certainly did." Grace couldn't resist. "If you paid more attention to your wife, you might win more often."

They had disagreed many times over politics, and this was the first time she'd had a winner. Even Dan's reminder that Wilson didn't favor letting women vote couldn't spoil her fun.

Dan voiced his main concern about Wilson in a column that weekend:

> The election left important questions unanswered. Does the new President, a college professor who has always lived in the crowded east, understand the needs of midwestern farmers? Will either party in Congress address the problems of agriculture?
>
> Progressivism had its roots in the countryside; it was nurtured there until the cities were ready to adopt it. It would be tragic if the new progressives in their moment of victory were to turn their backs on those who plowed, seeded and cultivated the fields now so successfully harvested. . . .

"That's good stuff, Dan." Amos Harper sat in his son-in-law's office on Saturday afternoon. "I agree with you about Wilson. He's not a reactionary like Taft, and he's not a blowhard like Teddy, but I don't think he cares about farmers—or understands them, either."

"He didn't talk much about them during the campaign."

"None of them did," Amos said. "But I still feel pretty good about this election."

"Why?"

Amos hoisted his big feet onto Dan's desk and leaned back in his chair. "Think about it. Mary Lease and Leonidas Polk, and the Alliance. The Populists in '92 and James B. Weaver. Bryan in '96. Each time we lost, but we just kept coming. We never did win—but this time, our ideas did."

Dan looked at Amos. *I think he's wrong, he's fooling himself. He is getting old, and sometimes now he lives in the past.*

Dan remembered something from that past. "There was a fellow named Harper, made a pretty fair Independence Day speech back in '89."

"You didn't hear a word of it." Amos's blue eyes twinkled. "You were too busy trying to impress a pretty girl you'd just met."

"No, I even remember your best line: 'Ten-cent corn and ten-cent oats and ten-*per*-cent interest.' "

[249]

Dan saw the fairgrounds, Amos on the speaker's stand, and Grace slipping down beside him in the shade. "But you're right, that was a good-looking girl."

He stood up and looked at his watch. "And I better get home to her. It's after five."

Chapter 35

Falls City, December 1912

WHEN Harry came into Dan's office a few days before Christmas, his sister was with him. Margaret Norton was a pixie. Just fifteen, she was barely over five feet tall, quick and slender. She had her father's chestnut hair and hazel eyes; freckles spilled cheerfully across her nose and cheeks.

"We're going shopping," Harry explained as he wiped his eyeglasses, fogged up by the change from outdoor cold to indoor warmth. "Margaret's going to help me find a Christmas present for Mother. But we thought we'd stop in on the way to say hello. I just got home from school last night."

"Well, I'm glad you're here." Dan had been wondering how Harry was taking the defeat of his hero in November. "I want to hear what you think about the election."

"I thought it was terrible," Harry said. "The conservatives knew Taft couldn't win, but they voted for him anyway—just to beat Teddy."

Margaret wasn't much interested in politics. She wandered off toward the composing room.

"That's what they promised to do at the convention," Dan said. "Remember? You didn't think they really would."

"Well, they did. Worse yet, the reactionaries took the party back." He sounded grim. "I say, let them keep it."

Harry fell silent. *Just like his father,* Dan thought, *asks a question by making a statement and then waits for you to tell where you stand.* He said nothing, and in a moment Harry went on.

"I think we have to keep the Progressive party alive so we can run Teddy again in four years."

"Forget it." Dan didn't hesitate; he had thought and written about this. "You can't keep the Progressives going for four years. Not without jobs and patronage. They'll have to go home and make the fight inside the Republican party."

Harry shook his head. "You're probably right. But that doesn't appeal to me very much."

"Well, it's a while till 1916. Why don't you wait and see how Wilson does?" Dan suggested. "I'm sure your father wouldn't agree, but Wilson stands for pretty much the same things as Teddy."

Harry laughed. "I know. But if I get to liking Wilson, I'll have to keep it a secret—at least if I want Father to pay for college."

"That reminds me. Have you decided where you're going?"

"Harvard, if they'll have me," Harry said. "Most of my friends from school are going there, and anyway I think it's the best."

"I'm sure it is. But you better be careful—you'll get so used to being out East that you'll never come home," Dan said, only half joking.

"That could be," Harry replied, not joking at all. "There may not be a job for me here."

"Of course there will be."

"Not the one I want. Not if Father hands the paper over to James."

Harry's face was set. *He's serious,* Dan realized. *He doesn't like his big brother, not at all, and he's decided he won't work for him.*

Dan groped for something to say. "You should be the editor. You've got the feel for news. Let James worry about the business side."

"If I'm going to work here, I'm going to be in charge. That means being publisher. And I'd be better at it than James." The youth looked at his friend and mentor. "Besides, you're the editor, and I hadn't heard you were leaving."

Margaret Norton had slipped back into the office as they talked. Now she broke in. "Someday, *I'm* going to be the editor."

Dan looked at the girl's face; she seemed in dead earnest. It was a family habit.

"What about your brother?"

"Oh, he can be publisher. That's all he wants anyway." Her tone made it clear she regarded it as a lesser role; Dan and Harry exchanged amused glances, but neither of them presumed to laugh.

"You'd have some things to learn first," Dan suggested.

"You can teach me." Margaret gestured at her brother. "The way you taught Harry."

By God, she means it, he thought. *They all know what they want, those Nortons.*

Later that day, Dan told George Norton about his daughter's stated ambition. The publisher seemed surprised, and definitely not amused.

"I can't imagine that I'd ever allow that," Norton said. "And I don't think she'd really want it anyway. She's just playing make-believe, pretend-

[252]

ing she's going to grow up and work with her big brother."

"Which big brother?"

Norton stared at his editor. "Why, James, of course. He'll take over from me. I told you that the day he was born. And Margaret worships the ground he walks on."

"I'll tell you, if those Norton boys start fighting each other, it'll be Katie-bar-the-door." Dan was describing the day's conversations to Grace.

"Well, don't go looking for trouble. You'd be better off helping Margaret." She liked the girl, who was still one of their daughter Abigail's best friends. "She's just as smart and just as stubborn as any man in that family. Including her father. It's a family business; why shouldn't she help run it?"

"I don't think George is willing to have a woman editor. Not even his own daughter."

"Well, he's had the wrong idea about women all his life. It's time he got straightened out." Grace's eyes widened. "And just because he's wrong is no reason for you to be wrong, too."

Dan started to reply, then thought better of it and clamped his jaw shut.

Falls City, Summer 1914

Woodrow Wilson proved skillful and assertive as a legislative leader. He kept Congress in session for more than a year passing one major administration bill after another.

Dan took the measure of Wilson's first year in office after a trip to Washington in the summer of 1914.

> . . . Although he claims to be a member of the Democratic party, President Wilson is really the direct descendant of Populists like Donnelly, Simpson, Weaver, and Bryan. He is also a blood brother to Robert LaFollette and his Midwestern Insurgent allies, and at least a first cousin to Teddy Roosevelt.
>
> Mr. Wilson does not walk precisely in the steps of the early leaders. They sprang from the new western frontier, while he is of the old east. They were driven by emotions, he by intellect. They saw the world in terms of their own region and a conflict of classes, while he views both the nation and its people as a whole.
>
> But by and large he believes in the same things they fought for: a flexible national currency, an income tax, lower tariffs, regulation of business, control of monopoly, federal laws to promote social welfare, and so on.

Dan did express one important reservation about the new president:

The one area where Mr. Wilson's attitude remains in question is agriculture. He has not given the subject high priority, and he has yet to support such important measures as the farm credit bill. . . .

Dan's measured tone masked his deep skepticism about Wilson's attitude toward farmers and their problems—and a hardening conviction that no political party, and few if any national leaders, either understood or cared about them.

George is right, the parties will take care of the cities because that's the way the country's headed, that's where the votes are.

He felt the anger come over him again, but he wasn't sure why.

I don't know whether I'm mad at the politicians for lying—or the farmers for believing them.

"Well, it's about time you got here." George Norton made a show of pulling his watch out of his vest pocket, snapping the case open, and checking the time. "It's eight-thirty-nine. I've been here for more than an hour."

James Norton sighed. "I'm sure you have, Father. On the other hand, you got to bed much earlier than I did."

"You'd be more use here if you didn't stay out helling around until two-three o'clock in the morning." George stared at his son. "At this rate, you'll never learn to run this place."

This argument had been brewing since the day in June when James graduated from college. He wanted to stay in Minneapolis and go to law school. George would have none of it. He saw no need for James to study law, and he wanted him in Falls City, not off getting big ideas in Minneapolis.

James had finally agreed to come home for the summer. His father regarded it as permanent.

"Father, I keep telling you I don't *want* to run this place. Let Harry have the paper. He wants it, and he'd be good at it." James waved toward the back shop. "He spends all his time here already, hanging around the printers and pestering Dan. Now he's got Margaret doing the same thing."

"At least he wants to work."

"I'm perfectly willing to work. I just don't want to spend the rest of my life in a little town three hundred miles from nowhere."

"Well, I didn't send you to college so you could spend the rest of your life chasing girls around Minneapolis."

"There are girls here, too—as you well know." James had heard stories about his father's earlier escapades, and was secretly amused when the gibe seemed to embarrass him. "I'll have to work just as hard in

Minneapolis as I would here. Probably harder. But I want to live in the city, Father."

"Huh." George shook off his momentary discomfiture. "Can't understand why. Twenty years ago it might have been all right, but now it's nothing but crowds and dirt and noise and all those Swedes right off the boat."

"I've already lived there for four years," James shot back. "I like it. It sure beats Falls City."

Father and son finally reached a compromise: James could return to Minneapolis and go to law school—if he also agreed to take a part-time job at one of the Minneapolis newspapers to learn the business. That was easily arranged; the publisher of the *Minneapolis Journal* was a friend of George Norton and was delighted to take Norton's son on as his assistant.

The arrangement satisfied both Nortons. George thought James would forget about being a lawyer as soon as he got started at the *Journal*, and assumed his son would in time agree to come home. James planned to stay in Minneapolis; he assumed his father would eventually accept that.

James's departure at the end of July did not leave the *Dakota News* without young Nortons. Harry, home for his last vacation before college, was working in the circulation department. Sister Margaret was also at the paper, tucked securely under Dan's wing in her first real summer job.

For eight weeks, through the steaming heat of July and the furnace glare of August, Harry drove up and down dusty back roads, peddling subscriptions to farmers, often sleeping in his car to save travel time. He rode trains out of Falls City to see how the railroads handled the paper. He talked with circulation supervisors in small towns across the state, listening to their problems and their ideas. He walked with carrier boys as they delivered papers and collected money, learning how the last link in the distribution chain worked.

His father, as always, hammered at the importance of circulation. "Give me a mediocre paper with a good circulation department," he said, "and I'll drive the best paper in the country out of business if it has a poor circulation department."

Dan liked Margaret, and though she was only sixteen, he wanted to take her measure; it might prove important to the paper—and to him. So she got her first lessons in newspapering as Dan himself had thirty years before, running errands and cleaning up in the print shop, helping out in the office, and learning how to find and write the small news items that remained the mainstay of the local pages.

George Norton scolded Dan for wasting his time on the girl. "She's not going to work here, I keep telling you," he grumbled. "I'll decide that, and anyway she's too young to know what she wants. You're wasting your time and my money."

Dan had heard that argument once too often.

"Look, George, at the very least someday she's going to *own* a piece of this paper, whether she has a job or not," he said. "I'd think you'd want her to understand how it works."

"Huh." Norton's derisive snort masked grudging agreement. "All right. If you want to use your own time to work with her, that's your affair."

Abigail Woods asked her father for a summer job at the paper, too, so she could be with Margaret.

He rejected the idea out of hand. "The boss can't hire his own family."

Dan's aversion to nepotism was not shared by his daughter.

"I don't see why not," she protested. "If Margaret can work there, why shouldn't I?"

"Because she's different." He sighed. "Someday she'll be one of the owners of the business. So in a way it already belongs to her, and that means she can work there even though she's related."

"That's not fair."

"A lot of things in life aren't fair. You might as well start getting used to it."

She said nothing more, but her face was set in disagreement, and Dan felt the distance between him and his daughter widen again.

I get along easier with Norton's kids than with my own, Dan thought. *Why is that? Because they're part of the paper? Or is it something about me?*

He pushed the troubling thoughts away.

In any event, he didn't have much time to ponder such matters that summer. As June turned to July and then August, he was kept busy writing headlines that grew in both size and gravity.

June 29:	ARCHDUKE AND DUCHESS OF HOHENBERG ASSASSINATED
July 28:	WAR IS FORMALLY DECLARED BETWEEN SERBIA AND AUSTRIA
Aug. 4:	GREAT BRITAIN SENDS AN ULTIMATUM TO GERMANY
Aug. 5:	REAL FIGHTING HAS BEGUN IN WAR IN EUROPE

George thought it was madness, all those emperors and kings, all related to each other, all looking for excuses to slaughter each other's people. But he saw no reason not to take advantage of the story. He ordered a big board put up in front of the building, with news bulletins posted every hour. He contacted school supply houses in the Twin Cities, and within a week had made arrangements that resulted in this half-page Sunday advertisement:

NEW MAP OF EUROPE
26 × 36, Metal Top and Bottom
Free to Mail Subscribers with Dakota Daily News
$1.50 for 6 months, free war map, prepaid
$2.50 for 1 year, free war map, prepaid
Old or new subscribers may take advantage of this offer.
Everybody wants one of these new war maps!

In September the French stopped the German advance just outside Paris. "This thing can't go on much longer," Harry suggested to Dan as they read the news bulletins. "If neither side wins quickly, they'll have to stop."

Dan shook his head. "I don't know. They've opened Pandora's box and I'm not sure they'll ever get it shut again."

The war brought prosperity to Falls City. The price of wheat, corn, and other grains, which had been rising slowly for two years, jumped sharply. European harvests were disrupted and the great war machines had to be fed; the combination meant strong markets not only for American grain but also for hogs and beef. The Meyers Packing Company put on another hundred men, and the slaughterhouse soon was running two shifts to fill its orders.

Dan had a letter from Harry in mid-November.

> No one at Harvard seemed to care about the Congressional elections. Most of my classmates are extreme conservatives, so they tend to be just "aginners" anyway, with no use for either Wilson or Teddy.
>
> There *is* a lot of talk about the war. Things are very different here in the East; it's not at all like home. Everyone seems to be pro-British, and there's a lot of sentiment for helping the Allies with money and munitions.
>
> I am gradually becoming convinced that we should do more to help the Allies. I have had a chance here to meet men from all parts of the world, and I think we can no longer stand apart from events in Europe, or even Asia. What happens in other parts of the world will affect us.
>
> I know this is not the way most people think at home. So it is going to be up to the newspaper to educate our readers on this matter.

Now he's telling me what we ought to say in our editorials. He's growing up fast.

Dan thought of Harry as he had looked that summer, taller and more solidly built, now past his nineteenth birthday, his face more mature, no longer a boy.

If we don't keep clear of that war, a fellow my age could turn out to be glad he has a daughter instead of a son.

Chapter 36

D AN WATCHED George Norton and Amos Harper as they sat in Norton's office. *Going on twenty-five years they've been jawing at each other on Saturday afternoons, like some husband and wife, sitting there and arguing, not wanting to admit how much they respect each other.*

Neither man had changed much, Dan thought, over the quarter-century since the day in 1890 when Amos looked through the office window, saw George, and came in to talk politics. Now Amos was pushing seventy, his hair a white thatch and his midsection a little thicker, but his body otherwise still solid. And he was still the skeptical iconoclast, still the populist, still far ahead of his time in caring for the land. George, at fifty-six, had lost much of his hair, but nothing else; he was at the peak of his powers, still a deep-dyed conservative and defender of the accepted wisdom—except in publishing, where he, too, was well ahead of the parade.

Amos couldn't accept any idea without turning it over and over to look for the flaws; George instinctively championed the conventional values of the community.

There they sit, farmer and businessman. The whole story of the Great Plains is right there in those two, Dan thought. *Sometimes when they argue they're both right.*

Today, as it happened, the two men were on the same side of an argument, and both were doing the one thing they liked even better than arguing with each other: lecturing the editor of the *Dakota News*. The subject was the one everybody in town was talking about—how to keep out of the bloody slaughter in Europe.

George's prescription was absolute: "No involvement at all, period. Nothing. And most of all don't sell them any war material, no munitions, no chemicals."

[259]

Dan said he had felt that way, but was no longer certain. "I'm beginning to think we can't be completely neutral. Germany invaded Belgium, just crushed that little country, and the British went in to try to protect them."

"Well, they didn't have much success. The country is a wasteland now. You just talk that way because that damn cowboy is shouting about it." Norton had never forgiven Theodore Roosevelt for 1912. "All that talk about being 'prepared.' If we prepare for war, we'll get into it."

"I hate to agree with George," Amos chimed in, "but he's dead right on that one. One step down that slippery slope and we'll be goners. We can't let the munitions makers and the war profiteers and the English make our policy for us."

"Let's be honest," Dan protested. "Every farmer in South Dakota is better off today because of the war. There's a market for every hog and every bushel of grain they can raise."

"I know, and it's about time the farmer got a fair piece of the pie. He's been kept away from the table too long." Amos waggled his big finger at Dan. "But you know the farmers aren't getting rich; they're just catching up. The real winners are the big grain companies in Minneapolis."

"And the food processors," George chimed in, his voice edged. "Like that fine Christian citizen Bob Meyers." Meyers's meat-packing plant was now slaughtering hogs around the clock, working three shifts to fill European orders.

May 7 was a Friday, and at midafternoon Dan was finishing his Sunday column when David Currier burst in. He shoved some sheets of wire-service copy at Dan.

"The Germans have sunk the *Lusitania*." The *Lusitania* was the pride of the Cunard line, its biggest, fastest ship.

"A U-boat sank her with one torpedo, in the Irish Sea. In plain sight of the coast." Currier's voice shook with excitement. "She went right down. They're guessing more than a thousand dead, lots of them Americans. There'll be hell to pay."

The sinking took the lives of 1,198 people, 114 of them U.S. citizens. It enraged the country, and Falls City was no exception. There was general applause for the opening line of Dan's column: "The sinking of the *Lusitania* was plain, premeditated murder."

Amos Harper was angry too, but as usual for his own reasons. "They knew this could happen; the Germans warned 'em straight out, and our damfool government didn't do anything to keep Americans off that ship." Dan knew what he meant: a warning from the German Embassy in Washington had been published on the ship-news pages of the New York papers just before the *Lusitania* sailed.

"I told you something like this would happen," Amos told Dan.

"You'd better stop and think before you write too many more outraged editorials."

With Americans already choosing sides in the European war, the sinking of the *Lusitania* tipped the balance heavily in favor of the Allies. But the country didn't want war and wasn't ready to fight one. Besides, Woodrow Wilson was thinking about reelection, and for that he needed continued neutrality. The crisis simmered down to an exchange of diplomatic notes.

Falls City, September 1915

Margaret Norton worked all summer for Dan. Then, in September, she went off to Wellesley College near Boston.

Her father had been dubious about sending her to college, but Margaret insisted that she had a right to as much and as good schooling as her brothers. She got support from Dan, who was prodded by Grace but was also convinced Margaret would help run the paper and therefore needed a good education.

In the end George agreed, though he still insisted Margaret wasn't going to edit *his* newspaper just because she'd been to some fancy school out East.

On her last day at work, she brought Dan a bouquet of fall flowers—purple asters in a milk bottle. She interrupted when he started to thank her.

"I'm the one to say thank you, for the job, and for teaching me so much," she said. "And for helping about college."

Dan laughed. "You should thank your Aunt Grace. She prodded me the whole time."

"I know. But you would have spoken to Father anyway, and he pays attention to you."

"I was just being selfish." She looked puzzled, and he explained: "I happen to think you're going to be around here, and my life will be easier if you learn something first."

"I hope there's a newspaper at college I can work on."

"That'd be all right, I guess." Dan looked at her, a young woman now, almost eighteen, still slender but no longer the skinny adolescent she had been when she first started coming to the paper. "But don't bury yourself in something like that."

"Oh?" Margaret's quick smile lifted the freckles on her cheeks. "Don't you want me to learn to be a newspaperman?"

"Of course. But I want you to be a *good* newspaperman, and that means you need to let your mind run loose while you're in college. Follow your curiosity where it leads you. It'll be your last chance. There'll be time for newspapering later."

"I'll learn all I can." She was serious now.

[261]

"And have a little fun too."

"Oh, I promise to do *that.*" She hesitated. "I'm going to miss being here. And I'm going to miss Abigail. I wish she was going with me."

"Well, it's time the two of you made some other friends." Abigail was about to enter the University of Minnesota. "You can still see each other in vacations."

Margaret was ready to leave. Dan stood up. "Good luck. I'll miss you." He offered his hand; she slipped past it and hugged him.

Dan, caught off guard, looked down and saw tears in her eyes.

"Thanks for everything," she said shakily. "I'll be back."

Dan, embarrassed by her display of affection, held her at arm's length and waited for the thickness in his throat to go away. He finally managed a joke. "It's against the law to hug an editor in his office. But we'll overlook it—just this once."

"I feel sort of funny. As if I were going away forever."

The Woods family was at supper the night before Abigail's departure for Minneapolis and the university. Dan frowned at his daughter's remark.

"Why do you feel that way? You'll be home at Christmastime. That's less than three months."

"Oh, I know I'll be home for vacations." Abigail's voice was tense. "But that's not the same as *living* here. I'm really going away tomorrow for good, because I know that after I finish school I'll live somewhere else."

"Well, I sure hope you don't," he said, reaching for her hand. "I'd miss you a lot."

"Would you?" The question was as abrupt as a slap in the face, despite her teasing tone of voice. "You've always paid more attention to the newspaper than to me."

Later, Dan asked Grace about the exchange.

"Why do you suppose she would say something like that?"

"That's easy." Grace's answer came quickly. "Because it's true. And you pay more attention to Harry and Margaret than you do to her, and she knows that, and she doesn't like it."

Dan lay awake that night long after Grace was sound asleep. *Yesterday she was just a little girl but tomorrow she's a woman. And she's going away. I love her, but I don't know her. How did that happen?*

Falls City, 1916

That winter, with an election only months away, Wilson turned to his domestic political agenda. Under his prodding Congress passed a second round of reform bills, and this time there was something for farmers, too: not only the long-sought Federal Farm Loan Act to provide rural credit, but other new laws authorizing federal spending on highway construction, agricultural extension, and vocational education.

"For once they've done something for us." Amos Harper was needling George Norton and Dan on a sunny afternoon. "Why, if a fellow lives long enough, farming might even turn into a paying proposition."

Even Amos, Dan thought. *He's like all the other farmers, give 'em one good rain, one good crop, or one good piece of legislation, and they think everything's wonderful. They fool themselves because they love what they do, and they want to keep doing it.*

Norton had a different reaction. "Nonsense," he said, "this is all just election-year stuff."

"Then we should have elections more often." Amos's voice still rumbled strongly from deep in his chest. "God knows it took long enough to pass that farm loan bill. I was making speeches for it thirty years ago. That's what the Farmers' Alliance was all about."

"And now all those things are written into law," Dan said. "By those same old parties you tried so hard to knock down."

Amos Harper favored his son-in-law with a wry smile. "That just proves you can even educate Democrats and Republicans," he said. "It's like teaching a mule: all it takes is patience, sweet reason—and a two-by-four."

"That's about it," Dan conceded. He stood up and stretched. "George, I had a letter from Harry yesterday. He wants to work with me at the conventions in Chicago. With two of them going on at once, I could use the help. All right with you?"

"I guess so." Norton treated Dan to one of his humorless smiles. "So long as you keep him away from those wild-eyed reformers. He gets enough crazy ideas at college—he doesn't need any more. I suppose Roosevelt will be there."

"No, he'll probably stay home. But that doesn't mean he's not a candidate. I think he really believes he can make the Republicans take him."

Norton snorted. "I hope they have better sense."

"Good sense has nothing to do with it," Amos said. "You're talking about Republicans. But they do know how to remember, and how to nurse a grudge. They'll never take Teddy."

Chapter 37

A MOS PROVED to be exactly right. When Dan and Harry Norton arrived in Chicago, they found the Republican leaders who had rejected Theodore Roosevelt in 1912 still firmly in control.

The Progressives, diminished in numbers but not in their zeal for Roosevelt, were also holding their convention in Chicago that same week. They hoped to persuade—or pressure—the Republicans to join forces with them behind a Roosevelt candidacy. But the Republicans weren't about to give the Rough Rider the very prize they had denied him four years earlier.

"Teddy can have the Progressive nomination, but he doesn't want it," Dan told Harry. "He wants the Republican nomination, but he can't get it. *This* bunch of Republican delegates would nominate W. J. Bryan before they'd take Teddy. I think Hughes will be the nominee."

"How can Hughes win?" Harry asked. "The bosses are all against him."

Charles Evans Hughes was widely disliked by regular Republicans and party leaders. But Hughes, a Supreme Court justice and former reform governor of New York, was a popular figure, especially in the West.

Dan pursued his argument. "Harry, the first rule in the book is that you can't beat somebody with nobody. And nobody is who the Republican bosses have got, a bunch of favorite sons who can't any of 'em get a hundred votes, let alone a majority."

"That's why Teddy makes sense."

Dan shook his head. "Those Republican delegates were handpicked to be sure they'd *never* vote for Teddy. It'll be Hughes."

"But still Teddy will have the Progressive nomination."

"I'm sure he thinks the Progressives are finished as a party, that a third-party nomination is worthless. I think the only one he'll accept is the Republican."

"That's hard to believe." Harry clearly did not want to accept Dan's analysis.

"Has Roosevelt ever said he'd accept the Progressive nomination?"

"Not that I know of," Harry conceded. "But I can't believe he'd turn them down. They're here for only one purpose, to nominate him. He knows that. He wouldn't betray them."

He's still as starry-eyed about Roosevelt as he was last time, Dan thought. *But I've got a feeling that this time he'll be let down. It doesn't add up any other way.*

It was raining hard the next morning, and the lobby of the Congress Hotel was full of wet, unhappy delegates, their summer suits soggy and wrinkled. Dan and Harry withdrew to Dan's room to go over the confused situation.

The rain beat against the window, driven by a gale off Lake Michigan. Dan repeated his growing conviction that Roosevelt would turn down the Progressive nomination unless he could head the Republican ticket too. Then he explained how they would cover the two conventions.

"We'll keep an eye on both of them. But the important stuff will all be going on back at the hotels."

"As usual." Harry laughed. "I suppose you'll have me sitting on the floor outside some committee room all day and all night."

"Naturally. That's why you're here—because you've got strong legs and a young rump." He grinned at Harry. "You don't expect me to do that sort of thing at *my* age, do you?"

The rain went on for three days. The delegates to both conventions sat, marked time, listened to speeches, and complained. Meanwhile the leaders of the two parties met privately, away from the prying eyes and ears of the press. But they found no common ground: the Progressives wanted no one but Roosevelt; the Republicans wanted anyone but Roosevelt.

When the Republicans finally got down to business on Friday, their votes were split among no fewer than seventeen candidates. But Hughes was well ahead, and after an overnight recess he was easily nominated on the third ballot. Roosevelt was never in contention.

Saturday morning, the Progressives had only one piece of business to transact, and they did it quickly: one nominating speech, one seconding speech, and the convention chairman banged his gavel.

"It has been moved and seconded that the nomination be made unanimous," he shouted. "What do you say?" An avalanche of "ayes" shook the hall, and Theodore Roosevelt was proclaimed the nominee.

When Roosevelt's response finally arrived, three hours later, the chairman read it aloud.

[265]

To the Progressive convention:
I am very grateful for the honor you confer upon me by nominating me as president. I cannot accept it at this time.

There were gasps throughout the hall. In the gallery a single despairing voice rang out: "No!"

I do not know the attitude of the candidate of the Republican party toward the vital questions of the day. Therefore, if you desire an immediate decision, I must decline the nomination. But if you prefer it, I suggest that my conditional refusal to run be placed in the hands of the Progressive National Committee.
If Mr. Hughes's statements, when he makes them, shall satisfy the committee that it is for the interest of the country that he be elected, they can act accordingly and treat my refusal as definitely accepted. If they are not satisfied they can so notify the Progressive party, and at the same time they can confer with me and then determine on whatever action we may severally deem appropriate to meet the needs of the country.

Theodore Roosevelt.

For just a moment there was dead silence. Then a growl of outrage welled up from every corner of the hall. The chairman quickly called for a motion to adjourn and slammed his gavel down. The convention was over.

Around the big room, stunned and angry men rose to their feet. Some cursed. Others ripped Roosevelt badges or pictures from their lapels and threw them on the floor. Voices began to rise as the shock wore off and delegates came to a full realization of their rejection. Women, and some men, wept. Gradually they began leaving the hall.

Harry tugged at Dan's sleeve.

"He turned them down." Harry's voice was halting; he seemed dazed. "He said he won't run."

"That's what he said," Dan replied. "Don't pay any attention to that other stuff. He's out."

"I can't believe it."

Dan couldn't resist a reminder. "I told you."

"I know you did. But I still don't believe he'd betray all these people who fought for him. How could he let them keep going if he knew he wouldn't accept?"

Harry has just lost his first great political illusion, Dan realized. *Teddy turns out just like the rest of 'em, and it hurts.*

"He probably hoped that if he played it that way, it would put the steam on the Republicans. Unless they thought he'd run on a third-party ticket, he had no chance for the Republican nomination."

"But it didn't work, and he let all those people down."

Including Harry Norton, Dan thought. *And maybe Dan Woods, too, come to think of it.*

"That's politics," he said. He seized Harry by the elbow and shook him. "Come on, it's time to start writing. It's all over now, and it's Hughes versus Wilson."

Chapter 38

THAT'S IT," David Currier said, handing Dan a slip of wire copy. "Wilson has carried California. He's reelected. Hughes has conceded."

Dan read the AP bulletin. "Wilson won California by thirty-four hundred votes out of nearly a million cast. Not a hell of a lot to spare, is it?"

Currier shook his head. "Nope. But it fits the pattern. He carried New Hampshire by fifty-six votes, and he lost Minnesota by three hundred and some. We'll never see another election so close."

Hughes had campaigned hard, but he could not overcome the deep divisions within the Republican party. Wilson ran for reelection with a united party and a six-word platform: "He kept us out of war."

The Democratic National Committee put it even more bluntly: "If you want war, vote for Hughes. If you want peace with honor and continued prosperity, vote for Wilson." It worked, but barely. The count was so close that it was three days before Wilson knew he had carried California, and with it the country.

"At least the Democrats didn't fool people around here," Currier said. Hughes had won in South Dakota by a comfortable margin. "It must have been your editorials."

Dan laughed. "I don't think they were very persuasive. I know I wasn't very persuaded. I had a hard time choosing between 'em."

"Why?" Currier asked.

"Well, I think Wilson is a fine man, and he's made a damned good legislative record." He ignored Currier's snort of disagreement. "But I was put off by that kept-us-out-of-war talk. That's just dishonest, because he's headed right the other way, with all this 'preparedness.' On the other hand, Hughes obviously wants us to go in, too."

"So what decided you?"

"I really don't know. Some feeling in my stomach. Maybe it was just habit; I've always been a Republican."

"That's a good habit." Currier was still a stalwart.

"Tell that to Grace," Dan said with a sigh. "She was all for Wilson. It's been a long season."

Falls City, January–April 1917

They watched, alternating between hope and fear, as Wilson made a final effort to stop the fighting before the United States was sucked into the maelstrom. A week before Christmas, he asked the warring nations to set forth the peace terms that would "satisfy them and their people." The British laid down harsh terms—and the Germans ducked the question.

Wilson was running out of time and maneuvering room, but he kept trying.

"Here's something new," Dan said to George Norton one afternoon in late January. He handed him a wire-service dispatch describing a new Wilson proposal: if the belligerents agreed to "peace without victory," the United States "would add their authority and their power to the authority and force of other nations to guarantee peace and justice throughout the world"—by "adherence to a League of Peace."

Dan looked at the publisher. "He's saying we'd join in some kind of world organization to keep the peace. No American president has ever talked that way before. It's—it's revolutionary."

"It certainly is, and I don't like the sound of it at all," Norton growled. "Not at all. 'League of Peace'! Better call it a League of War, that's what it would lead to. We should never get involved in any foolishness like that. Never. Never."

Dan was silent for a moment. "George, I know how you feel. But I think it might be the only way to prevent another war like the one that's going on now. My God, they've killed *three million* men already, and there's no end in sight."

"I don't care how many of each other they kill, it's not our affair." Norton was adamant. "We'd be crazy to tie ourselves into some agreement that could get us involved in someone else's war."

The Germans responded to Wilson's offer on January 31—by announcing that on the next day they would begin unrestricted submarine warfare. Any ship, of any nation, armed or unarmed, that entered the waters around Great Britain would be sunk on sight and without warning.

Wilson broke off diplomatic relations and expelled the German ambassador, but still held back from the final step. Then came still another shock—the revelation that the German foreign minister had secretly urged Mexico to join in attacking the United States. Mexico, he suggested, would receive Texas, Arizona, and New Mexico as its share of the spoils of victory.

Americans were outraged, and now events began to move more swiftly. Wilson asked Congress for authority to arm U.S. merchant ships. A handful of senators led by LaFollette staged a filibuster that prevented a vote on the ship bill. Wilson ordered navy gun crews onto U.S. ships anyway, then called a special session of Congress "to receive a communication by the Executive on grave questions of national policy which should be taken immediately under consideration."

Dan hurried into George Norton's office when that news came over the wire.

"I think I ought to go to Washington," he said. "It sounds like he's getting ready to ask for a declaration of war."

Norton looked at him. "All right."

Dan was a little surprised that Norton passed up his usual expense-account lecture. The publisher seemed distracted, as if he had something else on his mind.

"I suppose you're right. They'll declare war." Norton spoke so softly that Dan could hardly hear him.

"And they'll take my boys, won't they?"

Washington, D.C., April 2, 1917

Wilson drove to the Capitol through a soft rain touched with the fragrance of early spring. A squadron of cavalry, the troopers hunched down under broad-brimmed hats and raincoats, escorted him. At the end of Pennsylvania Avenue the floodlit dome of the Capitol gleamed white against the black sky. Despite the rain and darkness, people waited along the route to watch the president drive by; many waved small flags as he passed.

Wilson was introduced to the warmest applause he had ever received from Congress. He began by speaking of the new German submarine warfare, which had already sunk a number of American ships.

> I was for a little while unable to believe that such things would in fact be done by any government that had hitherto subscribed to the humane practices of civilized nations. . . .
> The present German submarine warfare against commerce is a warfare against mankind. . . . The challenge is to all mankind. Each nation must decide for itself how it will meet it.

The great hall of the House of Representatives was hushed.

> There is one choice we cannot make, we are incapable of making: we will not choose the path of submission and suffer the

most sacred rights of our nation and our people to be ignored or violated.

The chamber shook with cheers and then fell quiet again as Wilson, his voice now ringing clearly in the intense silence, asked for a declaration of war—and the power to draft half a million young men into the army.

He's giving it to them with the bark off, Dan thought as he looked down from the press gallery. *They'll do what he wants, and God help us all.*

Chapter 39

April 1917–March 1918

G EORGE NORTON'S gloomy prediction quickly proved correct.
Wilson signed the declaration of war on a Friday afternoon.
On Monday, James Norton walked into a recruiting station and enlisted in the U.S. Marines. He informed the dean's office at the law school, was excused from taking his final examinations, and went home to tell his parents what he had done. By October, he was in France, completing training with the Fifth Marine Regiment.

Harry Norton, in his final term at Harvard, also enlisted quickly. He applied for a commission in the army, and despite his poor eyesight, he was accepted. (The medical officer who signed his papers said there were many uses for second lieutenants, few of which required perfect vision.) In July, along with hundreds of other college men, he reported to training camp at Plattsburg in upstate New York. In November he was commissioned in the transportation corps and sent to the Boston port of embarkation to await overseas orders.

That temporary assignment had unexpected consequences. Harry's sister had been invited to Thanksgiving dinner at the home of a college classmate, a Boston girl named Alice Brewer. When the family learned that Margaret's soldier brother was nearby, the Brewers invited him to join the party.

The food was wonderful, but Harry had no idea what he was eating. Mrs. Brewer sat him next to Alice, and he was simply swept away by this short, pert girl. Her voice was a throaty contralto; her face was set off by chestnut curls that tumbled down over a rather high forehead; her eyes, so dark as to seem almost black, held him hostage whenever she spoke to him.

Margaret, watching her brother and her friend, was vastly amused.

Why, old sobersides Harry's head over heels! And so is Alice. I've never seen either of them like this.

In the next three months Harry spent many evenings driving to and from Wellesley; on weekends, he and Alice visited museums and concerts, theaters, and restaurants. When the weather was decent they walked outdoors; when it was foul, which was often, it being New England in winter, they sat indoors and talked for hours on end.

By the time Harry sailed for France in March, he and Alice Brewer knew and liked each other very well indeed.

France, April–July 1918

The Norton brothers had a hard time getting together in France. Harry was assigned to the Services of Supply Headquarters in Tours, 130 miles southwest of Paris, while James was billeted in a village 140 miles on the other side of Paris. May was half gone before they managed to meet in Paris for one night. They had time only to catch up on each other's military career and the news from home, and eat one dinner together.

Despite good food and wine, it was not a happy evening. Neither passing time nor the upheaval of war had lessened the underlying tension between elder and younger brother; if anything, their new roles increased it. James, recently promoted to sergeant, barely concealed his disdain for Harry's little gold bars and noncombat job. For his part Harry was still envious of James's manner and appearance. James, big and handsome and blond, every inch a Marine, an archetypical American, was the object of admiring glances from everyone in the restaurant. By contrast Harry seemed invisible—dark, almost European, an obvious civilian in thick glasses and a uniform that didn't seem quite right on him.

James joked about Harry's job.

"I wish you people at headquarters could figure out some way to send us something besides corned beef and canned salmon. It's all we've had to eat for the last three months."

Harry returned a serious answer. "Our people are doing their best, but it's hard to keep supplies moving on these railroads. The French are, well, hopeless; they've just about given up."

"To our gallant allies." James raised his wineglass in a mock salute. "Look, if you just get us what we need, we'll show these people how to do it."

"It doesn't look like things are going too well right now." Harry could not match his brother's swashbuckling style. "The Germans are hammering the British and French. I hear headquarters is even worried about an attack on Paris."

James leaned forward across the little restaurant table and lowered his voice. "Well, that's going to change," he said. "The Marines will be in the line pretty soon, and when we get there, stand back!"

Him and his damn Marines, you'd think they were going to win the war all by themselves, Harry thought. *But who am I to criticize? He's going to be getting shot at while I sit safe at a desk behind the lines.*

"Keep your head down," he said. "Take care. Don't take chances if you don't have to."

James threw back his head and laughed. "Still the same little brother, always worrying. Well, you don't have to worry about me. The Marines take care of their own." He looked around for the waiter. "Let's have a cognac and go for a stroll. I don't know if I can get to sleep in a real bed after six months in a hayloft."

James was in combat even sooner than he had expected. The German attack broke the French lines in late May, and on the last day of the month the Marines were thrown into the gap to stop them. For almost four weeks they fought hand-to-hand at a place called Belleau Wood.

In all that time, Harry heard nothing from or about his brother. After the battle ended, what was left of the Marine brigade was pulled out of the line and trucked to rest areas scattered across the countryside. Anyone who knew the location of specific units was too busy to answer unofficial questions, and in any event Harry didn't have time to ask: his section was working eighteen hours a day trying to move the shiploads of supplies and men now pouring into French ports every day.

Then, one morning, he looked up from his desk to see a Red Cross worker standing there with a piece of paper in his hand.

NAVY DEPARTMENT TODAY NOTIFIED PARENTS JAMES KILLED IN ACTION JUNE TWENTYFIVE STOP APPRECIATE DETAILS STOP DEEPEST SYMPATHY DAN

It took Harry some time to get those details. Finally, in mid-July, he was sent to Paris for a couple of days. The first evening he was walking along a boulevard, looking for a place to eat, when he noticed a thin, tired-looking Marine officer, one arm in a sling, sitting at a sidewalk cafe.

On an impulse, Harry stepped over to his table. "Excuse me, Captain." The officer looked up at Harry. "Are you by any chance in the Fifth Marines?"

"As it happens, I am." He did not hide his disdain for this rear-echelon shavetail. "What's it to you?"

"I was wondering if you knew a Sergeant James Norton."

The Marine said nothing for a minute. Then he looked at Harry. "Why do you ask?"

Harry chose his words very carefully and tried to speak in a normal tone of voice.

"He's . . . he was my brother."

The Marine looked at him without expression. When he spoke again his voice was flat and utterly weary.

"Sit down."

It was not an invitation but an order. Harry obeyed, and the officer spoke again, his voice still as expressionless as his face.

"He was in my company. He made it through more than three weeks in that place without a scratch. He was a wild man; they put him in for the Navy Cross."

He put his good hand on Harry's arm.

"He was killed in the last charge on the last day. He was lucky, he didn't suffer. Machine gun hit him, he was dead."

Falls City, July–December 1918

Dan read Harry's letter again.

> . . . And eventually I got the Captain to talk some more. He was a platoon leader when the battle began but at the end was company commander because all the other officers were gone. James wasn't in his platoon but he knew of him, said he was an outstanding Marine and one of the very few new men to have been promoted to sergeant.
>
> He didn't talk much about the fighting except to say that they were the whole time in thick, tangled woods and broken ground, with steep slopes and deep gullies and huge boulders and trees so close together you could hardly crawl between them. And everywhere German machine guns covering every inch of ground our people had to cross.
>
> He said James was a hero "over and over again," and single-handed destroyed many machine-gun nests. The Captain said he will surely receive the Navy Cross and maybe even the Medal of Honor posthumously.
>
> But all that means nothing now, does it? I have written Father and Mother to say what I could but I fear this will be too much for Mother to bear. As for Father it will cause him great grief, which I suspect he will keep to himself, and will probably confirm all his prejudices against Wilson's peace league idea.
>
> To me, all this only makes what the President says all the more right, but I can hear Father now on the other side! We will have to try to persuade him otherwise when this is over. I wish I were there to help you argue it with him; I know where you stand.
>
> As for me, I feel like a slacker here in this safe job & would give anything to obtain a transfer to infantry, but that seems impossible. My first request was turned down by my C.O. here and the doctors say I couldn't get there even if he approved because of my weak eyes. But I still cannot forget James that night we were together, so cocky and confident and *alive*, and now he is gone.

[275]

Harry had guessed right. George Norton did keep his grief to himself. Watching him throw himself into his work, Dan remembered how the publisher had done the same thing when his first baby died.

Dan spoke a few words to George; George thanked him. That was all. They knew each other too well to want—or need—to say more.

Chapter 40

Falls City, 1918

I SWEAR I think people are just going crazy," Dan said to Grace one night in January 1918. "Seems like every time I turn around some judge or prosecutor has gone off the deep end."

"What do you expect?" Grace retorted. "War is crazy, so people go crazy when they get involved with it."

"This time it's worse than most. Remember those farmers out in Hutchinson County, the ones that wrote to the governor complaining that the draft quota for their county was too high, and asking him to fix it?"

"I read about them. They didn't sound crazy to me."

"They aren't, but I'm beginning to think the federal courts are. You remember the farmers were indicted under the Sedition Act, and the jury convicted them? Well, today the judge sentenced those good honest men to a year in prison."

"For writing a letter complaining about unfair treatment?" Grace eyed her husband. "What are you going to do about it?"

Dan pulled a typed sheet from his pocket, unfolded it, and handed it to Grace. "Make myself more unpopular, I guess. I'm running this tomorrow."

JUSTICE DENIED

Yesterday federal district judge George Davis sentenced 27 Hutchinson County farmers to serve a year in the penitentiary. Their crime was to write a letter to the governor claiming that the draft quota for their county was unfairly high, and asking that it be reduced.

We are frankly skeptical about the claim of these farmers that they are being unfairly treated in the draft. But if otherwise honest, law-abiding men are to be jailed for speaking their minds in a completely peaceful manner, for petitioning their government for redress of grievances, then the required sacrifices of this war will be in vain.

Freedom of speech is more, not less, important in difficult times. It is particularly important when the opinions it conveys are those of an unpopular minority.

We cannot preserve freedom in the world by denying it to our own people at home. It is as simple as that.

Grace handed the sheet back to Dan. "Perfect. Short and to the point. Not a wasted word."

Dan shook his head. "This is just the beginning. People will take this case as an invitation to settle scores, to get even, to work out grudges. It'll get worse before it gets better."

Dan wrote one editorial after another that summer, debunking the professional patriots and deploring their excesses. But except for getting the *Dakota News* windows smeared with yellow paint a couple of times, Dan's earnest editorials seemed to have little effect. He expressed his frustration one August day as he sat with Amos and George Norton.

"I don't think anyone's listening."

Norton disagreed. "Oh, they're listening. And a lot of 'em agree with you. But they're afraid to come out and say so."

The publisher tapped his desk with a forefinger. "You must keep it up. This is the kind of time when a newspaper earns its keep in a community."

"Oh, I'll keep it up," Dan said. "But it just seems to get worse and worse. We may be winning in France—but we're losing in South Dakota."

Amos chuckled. "You just violated the espionage law. You shouldn't say such unpatriotic things. George and I might have to turn you in."

"The way *you* talk about the war," Dan said, "you're more likely to be arrested than I am."

Amos had never wavered in his view that the United States had been lured into the war by Great Britain and the munitions makers—and he repeatedly made his opinions public.

"I kind of wish they'd do that." Amos laughed again. "I don't have much to do these days, now that Charlie's taken over the farm. It would occupy my time. I think it would be kind of fun."

"Fun!" Norton exploded. "Not my idea of fun. These self-proclaimed patriots make me sick. They don't know what—"

The words caught in his throat, and he swiveled his chair so he faced away from the other two men. After a moment he finished the sentence.

"They don't know what they're talking about."

Amos broke the silence that followed. "No, they don't," he said, his deep voice gentle. "That kind never does."

Grace almost never set foot in the newspaper office, so Dan was startled when she burst in the front door one morning in mid-October. She didn't even say hello to old Florence Berdahl, but hurried into Dan's little office.

"You and Pa thought you were so funny about him getting arrested for talking against the war." Grace's blue eyes were wide with alarm. "Well, it's no joke now. Look what they just did."

She handed him a paper. It was an indictment, signed by Peter Stone, U.S. attorney, and George Davis, U.S. district judge for the Southern District of South Dakota. It charged Amos Harper with violating the Sedition Act of 1918. There followed a list of allegedly criminal statements. Among them:

—"There is no excuse for this war."

—"We should never have gone into a war to help the Schwabs make forty million dollars a year."

—"One hundred years ago we fought out the alien and sedition law. The party back of it failed at the next election. The same struggle is on again."

—"People deserve to know if they are living in the United States or in old Russia."

Dan looked at his wife. "Why, this is nonsense. What happened?"

"The marshal came out to the farm. Pa had him drive by our house and pick me up on the way to the courthouse." She smiled briefly. "He thought they were going to lock him up. He was laughing and joking with the marshal about how dangerous he was. They took him to Judge Davis's courtroom, but then they told him he was free to go."

"What did he do then?"

"I think he's down at the lunchroom letting his friends buy him coffee while he tells them about it." Grace's voice turned intense again. "Dan, this is serious, isn't it?"

"Anytime the government charges you with a crime, it's serious, but *this* is ridiculous on its face. They'd be laughed out of court."

Dan realized his wife needed reassurance. "Everybody in the county knows Amos. There's damned few who agree with him, but even fewer dislike him. They'd never get a jury to convict him."

An hour later, as he told George Norton about the indictment, Dan was less relaxed. In fact, he was in a cold rage.

"They obviously went after Amos to get at the paper. We've criticized Stone and his office a lot, and Judge Davis too. They must have thought they'd shut us up."

Norton snorted contemptuously. "That little pissant prosecutor couldn't shut a screen door, let alone the *Dakota News.*"

"I know, and Amos will come out all right, too. But it's a bad day when a political prosecutor can go around trying to frighten people by indicting their relatives."

Norton had a ready answer. "That's what happens when you get into a war. People lose their senses. The government gets away with terrible things." He thought a moment. "I trust you'll say so in the paper."

"You can count on it." Dan was still steaming.

The publisher wasn't finished. "I want to sign that editorial. I can't write it, you'll have to. But I want my name on it."

He's never done that before, Dan thought. *He never has a kind word for anybody or anything, but when a friend gets in trouble he stands up beside him no matter how unpopular it might be.*

"That's wonderful," he said. "As long as I can sign it too."

The editorial was published two days later.

POLITICS AND PATRIOTISM

The publisher of this newspaper has known Amos Harper for more than thirty years and counts him a close friend. The editor is married to Mr. Harper's daughter. In these circumstances, neither man can claim to be an impartial judge of his character.

That said at the outset, it remains the opinion of the Dakota News that the indictment of Mr. Harper on charges of violating the Sedition Act may be the most absurd action ever brought by U.S. Attorney Stone or approved by Judge Davis.

It seeks to punish the casual conversation of a man who proved his own patriotism half a century ago at Cold Harbor and Petersburg—simply because he does not agree with the government.

While our young men are fighting to make the world safe for democracy, the supposed protectors of justice would punish this good old man for peacefully exercising his democratic rights.

Amos Harper was inciting no one. He was probably not convincing anyone, either, if it comes to that. But it ought never be considered a crime to speak your mind in a peaceful manner, and any law that says it is must ultimately fail.

George Norton, Publisher
Daniel Woods, Editor

When Amos came into the newspaper the next day to thank them, he seemed unsure of himself.

It's the first time I've ever seen him really flustered, Dan thought. *He doesn't quite know what's going on. He's a little confused. He's really showing his age.*

"I embarrassed you fellows with my big mouth," Amos said. "I suppose it'll cost you some money, too. I came down here to apologize. I'm sorry."

George Norton bristled. "Never apologize for speaking your mind, no matter what the consequences."

"I don't know that I'd go *that* far," Dan said. The remark wasn't all that funny, but it broke the mood and the three of them dissolved in laughter.

Of course Norton had to add something serious. "As for costing us money, we may lose an advertiser or two. It's happened before, and it generally costs them more than it does us." He looked at Dan. "That's one reason I insist on a good profit. It keeps us strong enough to stand up when we should."

Four weeks later the war ended. A month after that, without prior notice or public announcement, the government dropped all charges against Amos Harper.

Chapter 41

T HE FIGHTING was over, but still the war went on killing people. The armistice could not stop the great influenza epidemic that marched across the country that fall and winter. It began in late summer, apparently brought from Europe. It devastated the East Coast in September and raged through a score of Army camps, killing half as many soldiers as died in battle.

The disease spread westward. In Falls City, the worst time was November. Health authorities closed the schools, banned all public gatherings, and recruited women to help care for the sick in homes where there were no healthy adults. One volunteer was Emma Woods, Dan's schoolteacher sister. When the schools closed, she worked for five weeks as a practical nurse. She finally came down with the flu herself in mid-December. By then she was too exhausted to fight off the sickness, and she died in four days.

Dan sat with his mother in the front pew at the funeral.

When we were little, living on the claim, she looked out for me, so I wouldn't get bit by a rattlesnake or wander off and get lost.

When we moved to town, she went to school, and then she taught school, and all her life she lived at home and helped out. And then she died, and that was all there was to it.

She never had a life of her own, never had any fun or went anywhere, never had a man. It was all work, and all for other people, nothing for herself.

After the funeral, Dan wept for the first time in years. His mother, as usual, kept her emotions to herself. Eudora Woods said only that she thought the Lord was making a hard judgment when he took a daughter but left her mother alive.

The war, or rather its aftermath, also held Harry Norton in its grip. When President Wilson arrived in late December for the peace conference, the army had to provide transportation not only for Wilson but for the hundreds who came with him. Harry was assigned to the American motor pool in Paris as an escort officer.

When Dan learned that Will White was going to Paris for the conference, he wrote his Kansas friend commending Harry to him, and then wrote Harry suggesting that he look up White. The two did get together, and White not only introduced Harry to his circle of friends but also arranged to have him assigned as his escort officer when he traveled outside Paris.

The upshot was that Harry saw a good deal more of Europe than he could have otherwise. With White he toured the great battlefields, the devastated cities and villages of northeastern France, even the occupied zone of Germany. He wrote to Alice after seeing Belleau Wood.

> One cannot imagine how so many could have died in such a little place. There simply does not seem room for such slaughter. We were not allowed into the Wood itself—too many unexploded shells and leftover mustard gas and so on—but standing on one side we could tell it was less than half a mile to the far edge.
>
> Just a little way off was the cemetery for the Marine dead. I was able to find James's grave, and I stood there for a little while; but to be truthful I felt nothing except the cold. Perhaps there were just so many graves that you could not focus on any single one.

Or perhaps, Harry thought, *I still haven't forgiven him for being so big and handsome and popular—for being a hero, even in his dying.*
That's a hell of a way to feel about your brother.

He thought of James again a couple of weeks later when White took him into a meeting he had arranged for a few correspondents with Wilson.

"I should wait outside," Harry protested. "A second lieutenant has no business in a place like this."

"No, no, no," White said. A mischievous grin widened his moon face at the memory of an incident in a Minneapolis hotel a quarter-century earlier. "I specialize in taking people from your paper into places they shouldn't be."

Harry tried to look inconspicuous, but he was hauled forward by White.

"Mr. President, this is Harry Norton." Harry, totally unnerved, snapped off a salute instead of taking Wilson's extended hand. White went on. "He's a newspaperman, too. Family owns the paper in Falls City. That's in South Dakota."

"I've been there. I am glad to see you, Lieutenant." The president seemed older than Harry had expected.

"Mr. President," White went on. "His brother was with the Marines at Belleau Wood."

Wilson looked at Harry, and spoke to him gently, as if they were alone in the room. "Was?"

"Yes, sir." Harry replied automatically. "He was killed on the last day of the battle."

Wilson took Harry's hand in both of his own. "Will you tell your parents something?"

"Yes, sir."

"Tell them I shall not rest until we have a peace that will prevent their losing another son in war."

"Yes, sir. Thank you, sir."

Wilson continued to hold his hand tightly. Harry did not know what to do; White rescued him by asking Wilson a question about Senate opposition to his proposed League of Nations.

Wilson dropped Harry's hand and turned to White, his mood changed, his voice sharp.

"It is hard for me to say in decent language what I think of some people who are opposing it." He was still angry. "Of all the blind and little, provincial people, they are the littlest and most contemptible. They have not even good working imitations of minds. They remind me of a man with a head that is not a head but just a knot providentially put there to keep him from raveling out. Though why the Lord should not have been willing to let them ravel out, I do not know, because they are of no use."

Wilson stopped. His press officer slipped up to him and whispered in his ear.

"Well, certainly," Wilson said. He turned to the group of visitors. "Of course none of what I said may be attributed to me at all."

There was a respectful murmur of assent, and the conversation went on. Harry noticed that Wilson seemed tired after his initial outburst. *He's really showing the strain. I hope someone is looking after him. If anything happens to him they'll never get even a halfway decent peace treaty.*

On Memorial Day, Harry went with White to watch Wilson dedicate the huge United States military cemetery at Suresnes, just outside Paris. He also had some personal business: James Norton's body had been moved to a permanent grave in the new cemetery, and he wanted to see it. He went to the office where they kept the list showing where each man was buried, and was told how to find his brother's grave.

As he came out of the little building, he noticed a young Frenchwoman selling bouquets of flowers. Struggling with his halting French, Harry pointed at the flowers.

"Ma'm'selle, s'il vous plait, je veux acheter des fleurs. C'est pour mon frère. Il est là-bas." He gestured toward the slope and held out some money.

She glanced at him, hesitated, then seemed to make up her mind about something. She shook her head. "Non, non. Vous ne pouvez pas acheter."

Harry was irritated. "Et pourquoi pas?"

She seemed to ignore the question while she searched through her basket for the biggest bunch of flowers. She handed it to him, then explained.

"Parce-que moi aussi, monsieur, j'ai perdu mon frère." She looked at him again, and this time her eyes held his. "Moi, j'ai perdu trois frères."

Later Harry listened to Wilson speak of the men who slept on the sunny hillside. The slope was completely covered by six thousand graves, many of them so new that the grass had barely begun to soften the harsh rectangles of spaded earth.

> I beg you to realize the compulsion that I myself feel that I am under. . . . I sent these lads over here to die. Shall I—can I—ever speak a word of counsel which is inconsistent with the assurances I gave them when they came over? It is inconceivable.

Harry Norton looked across at the slope. Far up on one side, he could just make out a stone decorated with a fresh bouquet of spring flowers.

Chapter 42

Dan almost missed his daughter's college graduation. He delayed his departure from Falls City so he could supervise the handling of the big story on the signing of the peace treaty at Versailles. He had to scramble to reach Minneapolis the next morning, barely an hour before the graduation ceremony began.

Abigail had planned all kinds of activities for her parents. She was hurt, and had said as much to her mother when Grace arrived alone two days earlier.

Grace smiled wearily. "I know just how you feel."

Abigail looked at her. "I suppose you do. I guess this happened to you a lot, Ma."

"Yes, it did." Grace corrected herself: "It does."

Boston, July 1919

Harry rang the doorbell and waited. He heard footsteps coming along the hall and into the vestibule.

"Why, praise God, it's Mr. Norton, back safe from the war!" The maid who opened the door was the same one who had been there when he first started calling on Alice a year and a half ago. "Miss Alice has been holding her breath ever since you wrote you were coming back across the water." Then, remembering her place: "Do come in, sir, and please wait in the drawing room. I'll call her."

A minute later there was Alice, sweet Alice, remembered Alice of the brown curls and the shining dark eyes, merry Alice who always laughed and now was crying, too, as she came into his arms.

★ ★ ★

[286]

Harry had to get home to his parents, so he had only four days in Boston with Alice; but that was enough to convince them that they wanted only each other.

He thought about the future one afternoon when he rode the subway across the river to revisit his college. Alice was off somewhere with her mother, and he walked alone through Harvard Yard. The sunlight, filtered through the green-and-gold canopy of trees, splashed along the walks. The great quadrangle was almost empty, drowsing in the midsummer heat.

Harry sat on the steps of the dormitory where he had lived as a student.

It seems so long ago that I was here before the war. "Before the war." That's how we measure everything now: before the war, after the war. Before James was killed, after James was killed. Before Alice . . .

There's not going to be any "after Alice."

But how can I bring her to South Dakota? She's always lived here; she loves culture and art and literature. She'll hate it.

But that's where I'm going to be. That's where the paper is, and I'm going to run it. So she'll have to come.

If she will.

Harry would have been relieved to know what Alice was thinking that afternoon as she walked down a Boston street with her mother.

Harry's going back to South Dakota. He always wanted to run that newspaper, and when his brother was killed that settled it.

He's in love with me, but if he has to choose between me and the paper, he'll choose the paper.

So I'll go there, because that's where he's going to be, and I have to be with him.

Falls City, August 1919

George Norton wanted Harry to learn the business. But in the first few months, business took second place to politics—specifically, the Nortons' own version of the rising national debate over the Versailles Treaty and the League of Nations. Wilson had negotiated and signed the treaty, but it still had to be ratified by the Senate.

The argument centered on a provision that committed member nations "to respect and preserve as against external aggression the territorial integrity and existing political independence of all members of the League."

Wilson insisted this clause must be approved intact: "Without it, the League would be hardly more than an influential debating society." The opponents were led by Henry Cabot Lodge, now Senate majority leader as well as chairman of the foreign relations committee. He argued that the section was both an infringement on American sovereignty and a violation of the U.S. Constitution, since under it a president might try to commit military forces—a power reserved to Congress.

At the *Dakota News* on a hot August afternoon Dan and Harry went over the arguments, pro and con, with George Norton. The publisher had never liked Wilson, and now, embittered by his son's death, he blamed the president personally and wanted the paper to oppose American membership in the League.

Dan debated him point by point, explaining how the League would operate, answering the questions raised by doubtful senators. But George was adamant; they were getting nowhere.

"It's nothing but a trap. The Europeans will use it to drag us into their quarrels again, and spill our blood in their wars again." George pointed a finger at Harry. "I don't want to lose another son—or a grandson, if I ever have one."

Harry, who had been mostly a listener while Dan and his father debated the details of the treaty, jumped to his feet and leaned across the publisher's desk.

"Father, I have seen where James died, and I have seen his grave, and I am just as angry as you are that he had to die," Harry said. "But it's exactly *because* of what happened to him that we should be part of the League."

Dan started to speak, but Harry held out a hand to stop him. Then he went on talking to his father.

"If we pull out, stay home, leave the French and British in charge of the world, James *will* have died in vain, because there'll be another war in twenty years."

"That should be no concern of ours," George retorted. "That's where we went wrong last time, getting involved."

"The Germans didn't give us much choice. And they won't give us any more choice next time—probably less. The world is getting a lot smaller. We can't go off alone and hide any more."

Harry kept hammering at that theme, and talking about James. Dan had been trying to argue the case on its merits; now Harry was aiming at his father's emotions. It worked. By the end of the day, George agreed to let the paper endorse the treaty and the League, with only one condition: American troops could only be used if Congress approved.

Despite the reservation, Dan was pleased by the decision and glad to be able to write a pro-treaty editorial. He knew that Harry's intervention had turned the tide; still, he felt a little bruised by the abrupt way Harry had shut him out of the discussion.

Grace, as usual, noticed his unease.

"Come on," she said that night as they took an after-supper stroll. "You're not paying attention. What's on your mind now?"

[288]

He looked down at her, then waved a hand in token of surrender. "You can always tell, can't you?"

"That's why you keep me, darling." She smiled and squeezed his arm. "And I think I can guess what it is this time, too."

"Oh?"

"It's Harry. You taught him all he knows about newspapers, you stood up for him, you helped him with his father—and now he's stepping on your toes, pushing you aside."

Dan walked on a few steps before he responded. "I guess . . . yes, that did bother me a little."

"It bothered you a lot."

"Well, I suppose so." *Of course that's it: for thirty years I've been the one George Norton listened to.*

"You're right about one thing," he said. "I taught him, and I thought he ought to take over the paper. So I guess I can't complain when he does."

"Easy to say, hard to do." She stopped, stood on tiptoe and kissed him. When she spoke again her lips moved against his.

"You're something, Dan Woods. You really are." She put her head against his chest, her hair shining in the moonlight.

A breeze came up out of the north. He shivered, feeling the change of season.

September 1919

In September a frustrated president took his case for the treaty directly to the people with a cross-country speaking tour. His train came to Falls City one evening in September, and Wilson told a packed auditorium that the real issue was America's place in the world.

> They have looked to us for leadership. . . . They have built their peace on the basis of our suggestions, and now the world stands at amaze because an authority in America hesitates whether it will endorse an American document or not. . . .
> I have heard of standing pat, but I never before have heard of going to the length of saying it is none of your business, and we do not care, what happens to the rest of the world.

As he finished his talk the crowd was hushed, and there were tears in many eyes—including, Dan noticed, those of the president.

> There is one thing that the American people always rise to, and that is the truth of justice and of liberty and of peace. We have accepted that truth and we are going to be led by it, and it is going to lead us, and through us the world, out into pastures of quietness and peace such as the world never dreamed of before.

[289]

"Wilson makes a wonderful speech," Amos said, sitting in George Norton's office the following Saturday. "But he's wrong. He talks about being led by the truth, but he's really chasing an illusion. That League won't take us into any pastures of peace—it'll lead straight into war."

"You're absolutely right." George was delighted to have someone agree with him about the League—particularly someone of Amos's political bent. He turned to Dan. "The senators are on the right track. I don't know why I let you and Harry talk me into endorsing that treaty."

"Because you knew it was the right thing to do." Dan's temper was fraying as the two older men sniped at the treaty. "We can't live in isolation out here on the plains the way we could when you and Amos and my Pa came here. The world won't let us alone."

Later, alone in his office, Dan stared out the window, watching the steady stream of farm families as they went about their Saturday shopping.

Wilson's so damned sure, Dan thought, *so sure the people are with him and the Senate won't dare turn him down. I think he's dreaming. He's right, the League is the only way to avoid another war, but people around here just don't buy that.*

If even the thoughtful ones, like Amos, are against him, how can he carry the country—let alone those diehards in the Senate?

From a distant corner of his mind came a long-forgotten scene: Mark Hanna standing in a St. Louis hotel room in 1896, cursing Henry Cabot Lodge as a mean and devious man.

Wilson doesn't understand the Senate, or how to deal with it. He better watch out for Lodge.

And he better take care of himself. He may just be tired, but he looks like a sick man to me.

Wilson had been exhausted even before the trip began, and he refused to interrupt it for even one day's rest. He suffered from asthma and headaches. He could not sleep. Finally he collapsed, and his train rushed back to Washington, the shades on his car drawn, the rest of the tour canceled. Three days later he suffered a stroke.

Now his dream turned to nightmare. Sick and isolated, he was no match for Lodge, and the Senate voted down his treaty.

Dan knew that most people in South Dakota agreed with the action; they wanted no part of some visionary scheme that could drag them again into the old bloody quarrels of Europe.

They don't want to get "involved" in Europe, but of course they still want to sell their wheat and corn and hogs there, Dan thought, affection mingling with equal parts of irritation and frustration.

They're good, God-fearing people, but they're wrong. And I don't seem able to convince them of it. That's the hardest thing of all.

Chapter 43

I T DIDN'T take Dan long to conclude that this Republican convention had no idea where it was going. There were candidates, but no one seemed to know which of them would—or could—win. Most delegates arriving in Chicago seemed to be waiting to be told who they were for.

As Dan wandered the hallways and headquarters suites of the Congress Hotel in the days before the convention, three names came up most often: General Leonard Wood, Theodore Roosevelt's old Rough Rider comrade; Governor Frank Lowden of Illinois; and Senator Hiram Johnson of California.

Roosevelt had died the previous year. Wood was his chosen political heir, and he had come to the convention with the most elaborate organization.

"But he'll never get the nomination," Dan insisted to James Morgan, his old friend from Boston, as the two editors gossiped over dinner Saturday night. "The Senate gang would never stand for him."

"The Senate gang and the big interests, you mean," Morgan grumbled. "They both want someone they can control. I keep picking up Harding's name."

"So do I," Dan said. "He isn't at the top of anyone's list, but he keeps popping up as a second or third or fourth choice."

"That's what Harry Daugherty's counting on." Morgan's normally amiable voice turned cold as he spoke of Ohio Senator Warren G. Harding's manager. "He's a crook if I ever saw one, but he's no fool. He isn't asking for first-ballot votes. He's asking people to switch to his man *if* their own candidate drops out. If this convention gets tied up, Harding could have a chance for it."

"He doesn't impress me much. He's good-looking, and he can make a speech, but I don't think there's much inside his head."

Morgan sputtered through a mouthful of steak. "Huh! That's the nicest thing you could say about him. Maybe that's why the people who are in charge of this convention like him."

"Those are the same ones who drove Teddy out in '12 and kept him out again last time," Dan said. "I really wonder what's happening to the Republican party."

"It's already happened." Morgan chuckled. "You just haven't noticed out there in the sticks. The old guard and the new money—especially oil money—have taken over your party."

Morgan's breezy cynicism angered Dan. *The Republicans are always handing money to someone. First it was the railroads and the land speculators, and then it was the steel companies and the meat packers. And Wall Street. Now it's the oil business.*

"This party takes care of everybody—except the farmers," Dan sputtered. "They get patted on the head. Everybody else gets the boodle."

Morgan smiled at his old friend. "You've been saying that as long as I've known you, Dan. But it's always been that way."

"No, it's getting worse." Dan's voice hardened. "This is the greediest bunch of thieves since the railroads bought up Congress in the sixties and seventies."

"You're right about that. This convention stinks of money, oil money, and that's all those fellows care about."

"They sure don't give a damn for farmers," Dan said. "Or anybody else, for that matter."

Morgan shook his head. "Well, one thing for sure, this is a sorry bunch of delegates. They know they're going to win, but they're so gloomy you'd think they'd already lost."

"The fun went out of this party with Teddy," Dan said. "It's going to be a long week."

Harry Norton arrived Monday morning. By the time he found Dan in the press room at the Congress, he was dripping sweat; Chicago was in the grip of an unusual early heat wave, and the crowded hotel lobbies and corridors were fast becoming sticky swamps.

Dan grinned at the wilted figure standing by his desk.

"I trust you brought your long underwear. Your mother wouldn't want you to catch cold."

"I'd have been better off if I'd brought my bathing suit." Harry returned the smile, but his heart wasn't in it. "Well, chief, what do you want me to do for you today?"

Dan was amused. *He thinks I want to play by the old rules, when he was my legman and I told him what to do. But that won't work any more.*

"Why don't you walk around and get the lay of the land, check out the headquarters?" He knew what Harry really wanted to do, so he suggested it: "And maybe you'd like to keep an eye on the platform commit-tee."

"I'd like that. I'm mainly interested in the League, of course. It's absolutely vital that the platform endorse it."

He already talks like a publisher, not a reporter, Dan thought. "I don't think there's a snowball's chance in hell that this convention will endorse the League. The most you can hope for is some kind of fuzzy language, some straddle."

"That would be a great mistake." Harry delivered the judgment crisply.

"That may be," Dan said. "But this bunch may make a lot of mistakes before they're done."

The platform committee struggled to produce a League plank that every-body could accept. It wasn't easy. In the end, after two days and nights of argument, the committee finally adopted an equivocal statement drafted by Elihu Root, who strongly favored the League but believed the only way to avoid rejection of it was to straddle. Root's language put the Republi-cans on record for "agreement among nations to preserve the peace of the world . . . without the compromise of national independence"—but in such a way as to avoid entangling Americans in "a multitude of quarrels, the merits of which they are unable to judge."

"It's just awful," Harry Norton told Dan, showing him the draft platform language. "It's all over the lot, and doesn't come out for or against the League. They're just a bunch of . . . of *cowards.*"

"Now, come on." Dan was irritated. "Will White's no coward. He was on that committee, and he's strong for the League, and he says there was just no choice: they could adopt something that meant nothing—or have the door really slammed shut on the League. They knew they couldn't win today."

"There may never be another day. I think they didn't have the guts to fight."

Dan shook his head. "Those fellows know how to fight. But they're also practical politicians who know the country's sick and tired of the League and the treaty and Wilson and the war, and doesn't want to be bothered with them any more."

Harry stared at Dan. "That's a terrible way to think."

"I didn't say *I* think that." Dan bridled. "Harry, you know I'm for the League. I feel just the way you do. But you have to face facts, and the fact is that Wilson and the League aren't popular. There's a lot more people like your father than there are like you and me."

Wood was still the front runner as Henry Cabot Lodge, the convention chairman, called the delegates to order Friday morning for the nominating

[293]

speeches. There were a lot of them; it was late afternoon before the roll was called for the first ballot.

As expected, Wood started out ahead of Lowden and Johnson. But none of the three was even close to nomination, and with the signs of stalemate multiplying, the party leaders wanted to work things out. Senator Reed Smoot of Utah stepped to the podium.

"I move that the convention do now stand adjourned until ten o'clock tomorrow morning."

In the moment of surprised silence that followed, Lodge's patrician Boston voice sounded clearly: "Those in favor of the motion to adjourn will signify it by saying 'aye.' "

There was a scattering of ayes.

"Those opposed, 'no.' "

The hall resounded to a great chorus of nos.

Lodge did not hesitate for an instant. "The ayes have it, and the convention is adjourned until tomorrow morning at ten o'clock."

Dan and other reporters clambered across the press benches to reach Smoot before he could leave. "Why did you want an adjournment?" someone asked.

"Well, boys," Smoot answered, "there's going to be a deadlock, and we have to work out some solution, and we wanted the night to think it over."

The old guard had bought some time, but it still had no candidate of its own. Dan joined a pack of reporters in the fourth-floor hallway of the Blackstone Hotel, where a stream of party elders, officeholders, delegation chairmen, and others were shuttling in and out of the national chairman's suite.

All seemed sure that neither Wood nor Lowden could be nominated, but at first there was no agreement on a substitute. Then, as midnight gave way to the small hours, it began to appear that one man was at least less objectionable to more leaders than any other.

"It sounds like they're getting ready to go for Harding," Dan muttered to Morgan as yet another state chairman came out of Room 404 and spoke to the reporters.

"Well, Harding's the right age, he's from a big swing state, he's good-looking, nobody's mad at him or Daugherty, and he's a straight party man," Morgan replied.

"And the senators know he'll do what they tell him to do—especially on the League."

"Which is what they *really* care about," Morgan said. "I think you're right. They'll give him first shot at it if Wood and Lowden are still stuck after another ballot or two."

"Considering how much everybody wants to get out of this heat,

Harding will probably run away with it." Dan sighed. "Ain't democracy wonderful?"

In the morning four more ballots made it obvious that neither Wood nor Lowden could win, and the leaders issued their new orders. On the next ballot Harding, who had been gaining very slowly, suddenly got almost four hundred votes. It was all over, and Warren G. Harding, to his considerable surprise, was the Republican presidential nominee.

Dan was depressed as he talked with Morgan during the ritual hullabaloo that followed the nomination. "There goes twenty years of liberalism, onto the ash heap. There goes the progressive movement, down the drain. There goes everything Teddy and LaFollette and the Bull Moosers stood for."

He surveyed the floor demonstration; it seemed notably restrained. "These bozos aren't even pretending to be happy."

"The delegates don't think much of him, but the temperature's over ninety and they don't have a clean shirt left," James Morgan joked. "On such things, my boy, turns the destiny of nations."

The Republicans still had to nominate a vice-presidential candidate. The leaders passed the word that it would be another senator, Irvine Lenroot of Wisconsin.

That was too much for even this docile, weary herd. When an Oregon delegate stood up and nominated the governor of Massachusetts, Calvin Coolidge, there was a sudden stir in the hall.

Somewhere a man shouted "Coolidge! Coolidge!"; the cry was picked up and became a roar.

"That's torn it," Dan said to Harry. "They've had one senator too many."

Until that moment, Coolidge had been known only for his handling of a Boston police strike—and for his refusal to say one word more than he absolutely had to. Now he was about to become vice president of the United States.

"That's some ticket," Dan complained. "Harding has nothing to say—and Coolidge won't say anything."

And neither of them, he added silently, *gives a damn for the farmer. Does anybody?*

Chapter 44

THE Democrats nominated James M. Cox, the governor of Ohio, and Cox immediately stated his strong support for the League of Nations. That pleased the Republicans, who were delighted to run against the League.

But in the Dakotas, people were more worried about the price of wheat and corn than about the League of Nations. Farmers had plowed and planted to the fence lines during the war in response to good prices and government urging. Many had bought additional acreage at inflated prices. Now, with federal wartime incentives gone and European agriculture recovering, the inflated farm economy collapsed. The price of grain and livestock dropped sharply between June and August of 1920. The old, sad cycle of overproduction, low prices, failure, and foreclosure had begun again.

"We're in for hard times," Amos announced one hot August Saturday as he sat in George Norton's office. "Sometimes I think it's a damned good time to be seventy-three years old."

Dan thought his father-in-law sounded unusually pessimistic. "Will you and Charlie be all right?"

"Well, the place is paid for, and Charlie didn't run out and buy a lot more acreage at ridiculous prices the way so many of 'em did." Amos's tone was matter-of-fact. "We'll be all right—if prices come back up."

"What do you mean, 'if'?" Norton said. "Farm prices always come back up. As soon as Harding's elected and the Republicans are in control again, things will be a lot better."

"For big business, maybe, and for Wall Street. But I have a feeling that for the farmer things are going to be a lot harder for a lot longer."

Dan shared his father-in-law's foreboding. "I think you're right. The

[296]

people who have taken over the Republican party don't know what the farmer needs, and those who do know don't care."

Norton begged the question. "If that's so, why are all the farmers around here for Harding?"

"Because they don't like Wilson and his League of Nations." Amos spoke sharply. "You know, you boys ought to get off that one. You were wrong to support it last year. It's a bad idea."

"Amos, it's the only idea that makes any sense," Dan said. "And it's the only hope for a real peace."

"Listen, I believe in peace. I'm the fellow who got himself indicted for opposing the war, remember?" Amos chuckled at the memory, but his words were sober. "But if Wilson's any example, no American president can play at the same table with those Frenchmen and Englishmen. We'd get taken every time and we'd wind up paying all the bills—in money *and* blood."

"You're absolutely right, Amos." Norton thumped his fist on the desk. "That's what I've been trying to tell my son—and this stubborn editor here."

They come from completely opposite directions, Dan thought, watching George and Amos, *but on this one they wind up in the same place. It's just like the Senate: the old-guard Republicans and the old-time Populists despise each other, but they're both afraid of getting mixed up with the rest of the world.*

As if we had a choice anymore.

Dan was increasingly disillusioned with the Republicans and their relentless attacks on Wilson and the League. Nor could he forget how the convention had passed over so many first-rate men—Wood, Lowden, Johnson, Herbert Hoover, LaFollette—to deliberately select a manageable nonentity.

Theodore Roosevelt might as well have never lived, he thought sadly. *There'd certainly be no place for him in the party this year.*

Harry Norton was also saddened by the Republican rejection of the Roosevelt spirit; the Rough Rider had been his first great political hero. But he was much more troubled by the Republican attacks on the League. His wartime experience in France—the death of his brother, the Memorial Day ceremony at the American cemetery, the brutal wreckage of the battlefields, the devastation of city and countryside—had profoundly altered his thinking and had made him an ardent supporter of the League.

So the Nortons wrangled fiercely over the newspaper's position in this election. As the summer wore on, Dan found he was mostly a bystander, listening to the argument but not really part of it. In the end, father and son negotiated a compromise: the paper would endorse Harding, but with reservations. Harry insisted that the endorsement be based solely on the paper's longstanding Republican allegiance, and that the editorial include a reminder that the paper had endorsed the League a year earlier and still believed in it.

They worked all this out privately after George told his son that "the worst thing that can happen in a family business is public disagreement." Then they went together to Dan to tell him—and to ask him to write the editorial.

Sitting at his desk, he looked up at the two Nortons standing side by side, both staring at him, awaiting his answer, and in that instant he remembered two conversations from the past.

Twenty-five, twenty-six years ago Grace said this would happen. "He won't let you decide the most important things," she said. "You're not nearly so much of a Republican as he is." And when he let me endorse Teddy she said someday he'd insist on one I couldn't swallow.

Well, here we are.

Dan looked at the father, then at the son, then at the father again before he spoke.

"I believe I ought not to write this one."

"Why not?" George's tone was impatient.

"Because I disagree with the position."

"You've disagreed before and still written the editorials."

"Those other times never seemed that important, George. I feel strongly on this one." Dan sighed. "And there's another thing: I couldn't honestly endorse someone I'm not going to vote for."

Harry Norton wrote the editorial endorsing Harding.

FOR PRESIDENT: HARDING

The Dakota News has always been a Republican newspaper. It will remain so this year. Harding is the Republican candidate, and he has the support of this newspaper. Cox is a good man and a good governor, but that is insufficient reason for us to abandon the party we have traditionally supported.

We regret that the Republican convention and candidate did not support ratification of the peace treaty and the League of Nations. This newspaper supported the League a year ago and still does. It is now clear, however, that the Senate will not accept President Wilson's version of the League; and a new Republican President will be able better to negotiate an acceptable substitute.

We have had too much of President Wilson's self-righteous disregard for Congress. It is a tragedy that the inspired leader of 1917 should have turned into the embittered, sick man now isolated in the White House. That situation can best be corrected by electing a Republican President.

"That's pretty thin soup," Grace said as she finished reading it. "It doesn't exactly make you want to give three cheers for Harding."

Dan agreed. "It's certainly not strong. But neither is the case for Harding."

"I'll tell the world." Grace laughed. "It would have to be a pretty weak case to make you vote Democratic."

"It's not just the League. There's something I don't trust about Harding."

"I think you can see it in his eyes. Look at the photographs of him—his eyes are like windows with the shades down, they don't let you see what's inside. Makes you think there's nothing there." Grace put the paper down. "Anyway, I'm so glad you didn't write that editorial."

"I remember you saying a day would come when I wouldn't be able to straddle."

"Well." Grace changed the subject. "Now, are you going to write something? I think people should know you don't agree with the Nortons."

"I'll do it in a column. I thought I'd give Harry a few days before I started to argue with him."

The argument appeared the following Sunday.

The editor of the Dakota News has been a Republican all his life. This year, however, he disagrees with the decision of the proprietors of the newspaper to support Senator Harding.

The disagreement involves two subjects: The League of Nations and the relative merits of the candidates.

The League. It is worth saving and must be saved. Governor Cox is a strong League supporter. Senator Harding, by contrast, repeatedly denounced it before he was nominated, and continues to oppose it.

The candidates. For twenty years and more our politics have been dominated by three towering figures: Bryan, Roosevelt, and Wilson. Now all three are gone or going, and we are left with men of ordinary stature. We cannot expect always to find leaders like Roosevelt or Wilson, but even in the company of small men, Senator Harding seems a pygmy.

If we must choose among middling men, it is doubly important to look closely at the values for which they stand. Cox is an able governor with a progressive record. Harding has never distinguished himself in any public office, and does not have a progressive bone in his body.

Harding argues that the nation should "return to normalcy," by which he seems to mean we should take yesterday as model for tomorrow. That is not only wrong-headed but impractical. Half a century ago, when the two candidates were born, there was no transcontinental railroad; today men fly through the air at terrific speed. Then, there were no machine guns, no submarines, no poison gas, no electric lights, no telephones, no automobiles, no radio. The new world presents new problems that demand new remedies, not a return to some imagined "normalcy."

"Oh, that's just fine, darling." Grace hugged her husband as she finished reading. "I think it's one of the best things you ever wrote."

"Just because you agree with it." Dan's flip remark masked his pleasure at her reaction. "I hated to do it, arguing with George and Harry in public like that."

"You *had* to. You couldn't keep quiet; that would've been the same as lying about who you're going to vote for."

"I know." Dan looked out the kitchen window at the bright autumn morning. "But I failed. I couldn't persuade George and Harry. They just couldn't think of supporting a Democrat—even though they have no use for Harding, and Cox is for the League. It's just blind party loyalty, and that's stupid."

Grace had never heard him use that word about a Norton before. "At least that's not your problem. You endorsed a Democrat and you haven't been struck by lightning yet."

"But something has changed," he said. "This has been coming on for years—maybe ever since I went to that first Populist convention back in '92. But now I feel like I've crossed some kind of bridge and there's no going back."

"Something *has* changed, and part of it's politics. You're less of a Republican than you used to be. But it isn't just politics, and it isn't just you."

"What is it, then?"

"It's Harry."

"Harry?" Dan looked at his wife. "What do you mean?"

"I mean Harry's here to stay, and your situation will never be quite the same again."

Dan could recognize the truth when he heard it, but he didn't want to accept it. "Why not?"

"Because Harry's *family*." She leaned over him as he sat at the kitchen table. "It's going to be his paper, not yours."

"For thirty years I've been the one George relied on—"

Grace tried to make Dan understand. "He doesn't trust you any less, and you're still his friend as well as his editor. But Harry is different: he's George's son."

"And blood is thicker than water?"

"That's only part of it. The other part is that rich people see things differently than we do. They're used to having their way, being in charge, telling other people what to do."

"Do you think Harry Norton—"

"No, I don't mean he's going to order you around. He respects you very much, and he knows he owes you a lot. But it's just the way life is; he can't help it."

Dan looked at Grace. "You're right, of course. Fifty-two years old and now I'm not really in charge any more."

He sat stock-still for a moment. Then his eye fell on the paper, lying where Grace had put it down. When he spoke he seemed to be thinking out loud.

"Well, there may be compensations." He picked up the paper and waved it at her. "I might have time to write a first-rate column more than once every five years." He looked at his wife again, and this time he winked at her. "And after that I might even have time to—oooof!"

Grace had interrupted by sitting down hard in his lap. She was giggling as she kissed him.

"You talk pretty big for fifty-two years old," she whispered. "You want to be careful about making rash promises. Some fifty-year-old girl might take you up on them."

Charlie Harper hardly ever came into the newspaper, and never on a weekday. So Dan knew something was up when his brother-in-law burst into his office just after noon on a bright October day.

"Pa's gone." Charlie never was one for extra words, and he blurted it out without warning. "Dropped dead picking corn, didn't make a sound, didn't say a word." The story came rushing out. "We were picking the north field. I wanted him to drive while the boys and I picked, but he said he wanted to show them he could still outwalk and outwork them."

In the mind's eye Dan could see the tall, solid figure moving through the corn, snapping ears off the dried stalks and tossing them smoothly against the bang-board and into the wagon, his big body moving easily and steadily while he challenged his grandsons to keep up with him, voice booming, light blue eyes bright with the joy of a good harvest from his own land.

Charlie was still talking. "Then we flushed a pair of pheasants in the corn, and the kids were yelling about that and for a minute I didn't notice Pa wasn't there any more. Then I did, and I ran back, he was lying flat on his face in the row, stone dead."

Dan got up and put his coat on. "Grace doesn't know yet."

"Nope." Charlie blushed. "The boys and Laura are with Ma, and I came here first. I thought—"

"That's all right, it's probably better." *Of course he'd want me to break the news.* Dan took a deep breath. "Let's go up to the house."

Grace had often joked about her father getting old, but she never really believed it until she saw Dan and Charlie coming up to the house together. She didn't have to be told; by the time she met them at the kitchen door she was calm and composed.

She stayed that way until the funeral was over. Not until Charlie and his wife had left with Lydia Harper for the drive back to the farm did Grace allow herself to grieve.

"Oh, Dan," she began, "he was such a *man*, and I did love him so." Then she choked, and Dan got his arms around her just in time. He could do no more than hold her as the sobs shook her over and over again.

Dan wrote a short editorial for the paper the day of the funeral.

AMOS HARPER

Amos Harper was one of the last survivors of the generation that settled Dakota Territory. Sons of an older frontier, those men learned by hard experience how to farm this rich but unforgiving land. Many failed, but the best, like Mr. Harper, learned to live in harmony with nature, to respect and care for their land, and they not only survived but prospered.

Mr. Harper also personified the farmer's struggle for political as well as economic fairness. In the '80s he was a leader in the Farmers' Alliance; in the '90s he was prominent in the People's Party. All his life he fought the soft-handed, smooth-talking men who made their money by short-changing and over-charging the farmer. He was never afraid to stand alone, so long as he stood on principle.

Amos Harper will be sorely missed, but he is not really gone, for it is upon the foundation laid by him, and others like him, that this community stands today.

"It seems strange not to have him here to . . . to argue with."

George Norton was unusually subdued as he spoke to Dan and Harry the day after the election.

"Well, I think I know what Amos would say," Dan said. "He'd tell us that people get the government they deserve, and anybody who'd vote for Harding deserves him."

George signaled his agreement with one of his rare laughs. "I think you're about right. He certainly had no use for Harding."

"He really despised the people behind Harding, Lodge and his gang, the Wall Street crowd, and the speculators." Dan shook his head gloomily. "At least Amos won't have to sit here and watch what that bunch does to the country. They certainly have a mandate—imagine, 404 electoral votes."

"People were just fed up." George's voice was back to normal. "They were voting *against* Wilson, not so much *for* Harding."

"And against the League, too." Harry's disappointment was evident in his voice. "I don't think it has any chance now."

"Nope," Dan agreed. "It's finished."

The thought seemed to invigorate George Norton.

[302]

"Well, then, maybe I can get you two to pay a little more attention to business," he said, slapping his hands on his desk. "It's time we built this newspaper up."

The paper that George Norton wanted to "build up" was already healthy and growing as the new year began. A decade of generally strong farm prices, plus the economic growth spurred by the war, had made the region boom.

Falls City had grown from 14,000 residents in 1910 to more than 25,000 in 1920. Dan's hillside house, at the far edge of town when he built it, now seemed almost downtown. Three- and four-story office buildings and apartment houses reached south into the older residential areas. New subdivisions were going up to the west and north, and paving crews worked overtime to keep up with the construction of new streets.

In fact, almost everything in the city had changed in the last decade. Trucks had replaced horses; automobile salesrooms took the place of livery stables, the last of which closed that year. For the first time, Falls City did not smell of horse manure.

The war years had stimulated a construction boom: additions to the hospital and the high school, a new YMCA, a new Catholic cathedral, a new city coliseum. Two new theaters were designed especially for showing moving pictures. Almost every home had electricity, and at least some electric appliances, and a majority were hooked up to the local telephone company, which had recently been merged into the regional Bell system. The Nokomis Country Club had built a splendid new golf course. The police department had ordered three automobiles to use on patrol.

As the city grew, so did the paper's circulation: in 1921 it reached seventeen thousand on weekdays—and over fifteen thousand on Sundays, despite the continuing rural delivery problems caused by poor farm roads.

Of course George Norton was not satisfied. "Falls City has grown by eighty percent, but our daily circulation has gone up less than forty," he told Harry. "We're really losing ground, not gaining."

Harry chided his father for this typically selective use of figures: "You're forgetting that the Sunday has almost doubled, too."

"The rule here is every tub on its own bottom, and don't ever forget it." The publisher was indignant. "And that goes for the news department too. I don't understand why they always have to have more people and more space in the paper. Those things don't come free, you know."

Harry had heard this before, too; it was one of his father's favorite complaints. He also knew that nine times out of ten the publisher gave Dan Woods what he wanted.

The news department *had* grown. When Dan started in 1889, it was just himself and David Currier. By the turn of the century the regular staff had grown to 9, and there were two dozen stringers scattered across the state. Now, twenty years later, the news staff included 31 full-time people—the editor and managing editor; the news, state, and city editors; ten reporters, 2 sportswriters, a photographer, and a women's editor, plus a dozen deskmen who edited stories, laid out pages, supervised makeup, and prepared advance material for the Sunday edition. As always, Dan also had a couple of high school kids working part time, and more stringers than ever to keep up with the growing circulation area.

One continuing story that Dan followed was the effort to improve rural roads. This perennial crusade for the paper took on new urgency as bigger and better trucks became available to move grain and livestock from farm to market—or to deliver newspapers from the city to the farms.

On this issue, Dan needed no prodding from the proprietors. "I'd like to make some of those politicians drive those roads in mud season," he told Harry in April. "They'd see the light quick enough." He missed no chance to raise the issue in print:

THE MUD BLOCKADE

The entire eastern half of the state today is under a mud blockade. Farmers cannot get hogs to market or corn to the elevator. We have built the best dirt grades that can be built, and still in the spring most of South Dakota is almost untravelable.

Instead of sitting in the comfort of the Capitol, legislators ought to go out and spend a few days traveling our country roads. After they dug their vehicles out of the mud a few times they would better understand the problem.

Why are we in South Dakota blind to the facts of the situation? Why is this state, which has so much use for good roads, making a virtue of doing nothing?

But such "good road" arguments failed to persuade opponents, primarily well-to-do property owners who thought their taxes would be raised to pay for paving rural roads. They accused the *Dakota News* of supporting good roads solely to sell more newspapers in more places. Most legislators, caught between influential constituents and the state's largest newspaper, took the easy way out by doing nothing; and most country roads continued to be knee-deep in mud every spring.

There's so much we can't do anything about, so much that we can't change, Dan thought. *Now here's something we could change, one time when we could fight back, when we could even do something about the weather.*

But we won't do one damned thing.

Chapter 45

Falls City, June 1922

GEORGE was doing his best to be jolly. It didn't come easily, but on the whole he was succeeding.

"Well, Dan, it's been a great day." They had retreated to the front porch of the Woods house to get some fresh air and to escape the crowd in the parlor. "I imagine it's quite a feeling to see your child married."

Abigail Woods was the child in question. She had been living in Minneapolis since her graduation from college, working in the university library while she waited for a cheerful young man named Richard Martin to finish law school. Now at last he had both a law degree and a job, and that afternoon they had been married.

The two men stood at the porch railing. Along the street, the thick white blossoms of the horse-chestnut trees gleamed in the summer dusk. A hot breeze moved the air fitfully, but did little to moderate the heavy warmth of the June evening.

"It's a strange feeling, like something's ended but something's beginning, too," Dan said.

But what's really strange, he thought, *is that Abigail's gone and I don't feel like I ever really got to know her. I let my job, the paper, get in the way, and now it's too late to make it up.*

He turned to George, leaning toward him to emphasize his advice. "Spend some time with yours before they leave," he urged. "You'll be involved in a wedding yourself pretty soon."

George nodded. "Not with a daughter. I don't understand Margaret, she has no interest at all in getting married. But you're right about Harry. I just wish he'd hurry up and marry that girl so he can stop mooning around and pay some attention to the business."

They talked on easily, old friends at a family party, until Grace sailed out onto the porch, fixed them with a managerial look, and issued a command: "Come in and do your duty."

She turned to George. "You can't take the father of the bride away from the guests. You two can talk all you want when you get back to the office."

"I'd really rather talk to the mother of the bride."

Well, she thought, *he's in a gay mood today.* "That would be nice. But I've got to see about getting some more punch. You two come inside."

She ducked her head and glanced up as she turned away, managing to flirt with both men at once.

"Now there's a woman who's having a wonderful time at her own party," George said. "Come on, Dan, we've got our orders."

Margaret Norton may not have been interested in getting married, but her brother surely was. Through the winter and spring Harry had pursued Alice Brewer by mail and telephone; in July he had visited her. Finally in October he brought her to Falls City to meet his parents, and to see the place he hoped would be her home.

Harry was nervous, but he needn't have been. His parents took to Alice at once. George Norton had been grumbling about Harry's "high-falutin rich girlfriend from Boston," but he proved an easy victim of Alice's charm and candor.

"She's all right," he told his son. "More than all right. Smart as a whip, and sensible too. Speaks right up and makes sense." He squeezed Harry's elbow. "And she's a knockout."

Alice's college chum Margaret took her around one afternoon to meet Grace.

"Margie has mentioned you so often, Mrs. Woods," Alice said. "I almost feel as if I knew you."

Grace laughed. "Well, Harry has talked so much about you that I really think I *do* know you. Please call me Grace. Now tell me, how do you like our town?"

"Why, it's just so nice." Grace detected a note of caution in Alice's voice. "The weather is so beautiful, with the bright sun and crisp air. And the sky just seems to go on forever. There's nothing like it at home."

"It's Indian summer," Grace explained. "God gives it to us to make up for what's to come."

"Yes, I've heard you have very cold winters. But Harry says it's a dry kind of cold, so you don't feel it as much as that damp chill we have in Boston."

Oh, Harry, Grace thought, *you'll eat those words some January morning when it's thirty-five below.* "I'm sure that's so," she said evenly. "Of course, I've never been in Boston."

"I hope you'll have a chance to visit. It would be fun to show you something of the city. There's a lot to see."

Margaret looked at her friend. "Maybe we'll have an excuse to come to Boston sometime soon," she suggested.

"I certainly hope so." Alice smiled confidingly. "I can't say for sure just yet."

Certainty came after Christmas, when Alice's parents announced the engagement of their daughter to Harrison Norton, with the wedding to take place the following summer. In due course, Dan and Grace received an invitation.

"Of course we won't go," Dan said. "It's nice of them to ask us, but to go all that way just for a wedding . . ."

"Of course we *will* go." Grace had made up her mind the moment she opened the invitation. "You travel all the time, but I never go anywhere. It's been forever since we took a trip, Dan."

She had other arguments. "We can call it your vacation. And you could come back by way of Washington, so you could see some of your politician friends and write something."

He laughed. "It's not exactly on the way."

"It's near enough." Her voice betrayed her impatience. "I want to go, Dan."

He surrendered without further argument. He wanted to go, too.

Boston, June 1923

The overhead fans turned lazily above the wedding guests, barely stirring the humid air. The pastel colors of summer dresses seemed even brighter against the dark wood paneling. White-jacketed waiters circulated, offering little glasses of punch. Alice, her dark eyes sparkling, stood with Harry by the door, greeting guests with handshakes or small embraces, introducing them to her new husband.

"Watch the women," Grace murmured to Dan. "They just pretend. They kiss the air, and never touch each other."

She put her mouth close to her husband's ear again. "See how they look around the room when they're talking. They're not interested in the person they're talking to, they want to see who else is here."

Dan and Grace were standing in one corner of the big room, feeling very much alone. Except for the Norton family, they were the only people from Falls City at the wedding. Everybody else seemed to be from Boston, and they all seemed to know each other.

A tall, bony woman in a floral-print dress and a huge hat descended on them. Dan vaguely remembered being introduced to her the night before; she was a distant relative of Alice's.

"Mrs. . . . Mrs. Woods, isn't it?" Her voice was a kind of nasal bray, with broadened a's and disappearing r's. "My dear, you must feel as though you've come halfway 'round the world."

She paid no more attention to Dan than to the husband she had in tow. To Grace, she oozed condescension. "It must be quite a new experience, being in a large city."

Grace's eyes widened, but she kept her voice sunny. "Why, aren't you nice to worry about us. But everybody's being so *nice* to us, we almost forget that we're country folk so far from home."

She turned toward the woman's husband and held out her hand. "I don't believe we've met. I'm Grace Woods, and this is my husband Dan."

He took her offered hand, smiled, and started to speak to them, but his wife preempted him.

"Oh, we were introduced last night. But I suppose it's hard for you, meeting so *many* people all at once. It must be very different from what you're accustomed to."

Why, that old bitch, Dan thought, suddenly enraged. *She's treating us like a couple of hayseeds, country bumpkins.* He felt as if he were a small boy again, fresh from the sod house on the claim, being teased by the town kids. He was about to say something when Grace pinched his arm to stop him.

"Oh, I *am* so sorry." Grace's voice was sugary, but she gave the woman a look that would have peeled paint off the side of a barn. She smiled as she turned back to the husband. "I do have a time remembering names." She ducked her head and looked up wide-eyed at him.

Dan watched, fascinated. The man seemed paralyzed by Grace's voice and expression. He finally managed to remember his name.

"Harry Hooper," he said, blushing. "It's a great pleasure to have you here."

"I'm delighted to know you," Grace said, turning a little further to make it absolutely clear she was referring only to him. "Isn't this a lovely wedding?"

"Come, Harry." Mrs. Hooper grimly sounded retreat. "We have so many people to see."

"My God," Dan muttered, watching as the woman led her husband away. "What a battleship!"

Grace sniffed. "Some of these Boston ladies have nice things—and bad manners." She took his elbow. "But you know, she's right, this is a whole different world. It's art, and music, and culture. And it's so *old!* I do feel like a fish out of water."

They looked across the room at the bride and groom. Dan motioned toward the couple. "Think how she's going to feel when she comes to Falls City."

"I know." Grace's voice was thoughtful. "It's going to be really hard for her."

[308]

Dan and Grace spent a couple of days sightseeing in Boston. Then she went home, stopping in Minneapolis to visit Abigail, and Dan headed for Washington.

Preoccupied with affairs at the newspaper, he hadn't visited the capital in almost a year. But now, with the younger Nortons well established at the paper, he could spend more time reporting and writing.

He decided to begin with a new chapter of an old story: hard times on the farm. Although most of the country was doing well, farmers were falling behind again. After almost ten years of relative prosperity, topped off by the unprecedented wartime boom, grain and livestock prices had collapsed after the war.

It's partly the same as always, Dan thought. *Farmers borrow too much to buy land, and they pay too much for it, when the prices of corn and hogs and wheat are high. Then when prices drop, land values go down too—but mortgage payments stay high and taxes seem to go even higher.*

This time, however, there were some real differences. Now a busted farmer couldn't pull up stakes and go west, because there was no more free land out there. The total number of farms was falling, and more of the remaining farmers were becoming tenants instead of owners.

But there's another difference this time, too. This time they're not just complaining, or blaming the railroads or the "interests" or Wall Street.

This time they're doing what the bankers and businessmen do—they're organizing, lobbying, to pressure the government into helping.

Farm-state members of Congress had organized what was being called the "farm bloc" to push for equal treatment of agriculture: the government had always aided businessmen, they said, and now it was time to help farmers as well.

They argued that it was all right to have a tariff to help industry hold its markets—as long as farmers got equal protection for their markets, too. To achieve that, they proposed that the government support the domestic price of basic farm products.

It's a whole new idea, Dan thought as his train from Boston pulled into Washington's Union Station. *I wonder how it's going over. Better start by talking to Norris.*

George Norris, by now chairman of the Senate Agriculture Committee, was pessimistic.

"Those people in the administration just don't understand." He puffed on his cigar and shook his head. "We have abundant harvests, but farmers are more and more in economic distress. Markets are glutted, prices are low, interest rates are high—and the land is losing its fertility. And still the president opposes any relief program."

"It reminds me a little of McKinley," Dan said. "He *liked* farmers just fine, but he wouldn't *do* anything for them. He blamed all the problems on overproduction."

"Harding's about the same," Norris said. "He sounds sympathetic, and I think he is. But he's dead set against federal intervention, so nothing will pass."

Norris went on to describe various proposals (one of them his own) that would allow farmers to sell their products in a protected home market at a "fair" price—meaning one that bore the same relation to the general price index as the price of that commodity did in the prewar period. Commodities in excess of what the domestic market would absorb would be bought by a federal corporation for resale abroad at lower world prices.

"I don't know if you can get that kind of thing passed," Dan said. "But something's got to be done. The country banks are beginning to fail, dozens of them already—in the Dakotas, and Iowa, and Minnesota. That's a sure sign of disaster."

Norris saw a paradox: "Half the world is starving, and the other half is burdened with a surplus of products. If we could distribute the surplus wisely, both halves would be better off." The present situation was simply unfair to the farmer: "He developed vast acreages of new land to feed a starving world. Now his market is gone as suddenly as it came."

Later, as Dan and the senator walked through a Capitol corridor, they encountered a short, balding man. He looked grim; the ends of his mouth turned down as he stared balefully at Dan. Norris greeted him and introduced them.

"I want you to meet the smartest Democrat in the House of Representatives," Norris said to Dan. "Sam Rayburn of Texas. Sam, this is my friend Dan Woods. He's a newspaperman, but he's all right; he was born in a sod house."

"In Nebraska, I suppose." The Texan's somber face relaxed in a brief smile.

"As a matter of fact, yes," Dan said. "But I live in South Dakota now. My father was forced off the claim by drought and grasshoppers."

"Dan's interested in what's happening to farmers—and what we're going to do about it," Norris explained.

"Well, so am I." He spoke in the flat accent of northeastern Texas. "I'd like to hear how things are in your state. Do you have time for a cup of coffee?"

"Why don't you two go downstairs to the restaurant and talk," Norris said. "I've got to go to the floor for a while. I'll come by for you in ten or fifteen minutes, Dan."

In the Senate restaurant, almost empty at midafternoon, a sleepy black waiter brought them coffee. Dan quickly learned that Rayburn's own farm credentials were gilt-edged: he had picked cotton as a small boy on his father's forty-acre farm, and he still owned a small place in his district.

He clearly did not care for city life. "I feel sorry for people who have to live in cities where there's no time to know your neighbors," he said, "no chance to watch the seasons change and the plants grow."

Rayburn said he feared that continuing industrialization would pull young men off the land.

"If we don't bring them the conveniences, it's going to be pretty hard to keep them down on the farm," he said. "But if we can get all the farm houses on all-weather roads, and give them electricity, then people will stay on the farm."

"It's the same up our way," Dan said. "All the farmers really want are the things people in town have. We've been pushing hard for good roads, and that's coming along. But it'll be a long time before they get electricity out in the country, I think."

"I think you're right. The power companies won't be bothered, the customers are too far apart in the country for the kind of profits they're used to. So farmers—farmers' wives—can't have those conveniences." His face hardened again. "They haven't got the money, anyway. There's no opportunity for a man who can't sell his crops at a fair price."

Dan was impressed by this plain-talking, intense Texan. *He might be pretty important, if the Democrats ever get back in control.*

Of course the Democrats were not likely to get back in control, or anywhere near it, anytime soon. Dan asked Rayburn what he thought about Harding.

"I won't say anything disrespectful about a president," the Texan said. "I respect the office too much. But I will say I like that fellow Coolidge."

"Why?"

"He's got some brains, and some sense of humor. He once said 'a man never has to explain something he didn't say.' Now I think that's about the wisest thing I ever heard outside the Bible."

Later, talking again with Norris, Dan asked the senator where the vice president stood on farm issues. Norris shook his head grimly.

"Coolidge is worse than Harding; much worse. He believes the only law that should apply to agriculture is the law of supply and demand."

Dan remembered Norris's remark six weeks later when the stunning news came over the wire that Harding had died. He thought of it again in December when he read Coolidge's first presidential message to Congress.

A bumper wheat harvest had glutted the market, sent prices even lower, and given new impetus to the idea of an export corporation that would buy surplus wheat and resell it at a lower price in the world market. The new president dismissed the idea in three blunt sentences.

[311]

No complicated scheme of relief, no plan for Government fixing of prices, no resort to the Public Treasury will be of any permanent value in establishing agriculture. Simple and direct methods put into operation by the farmer himself are the only real sources of restoration. I do not favor the permanent interference of government in this problem.

Nothing ever changes, Dan raged, *it's just the way it was fifty years ago, they'll do anything to make big business bigger and rich bankers richer—but not one damned thing for the farmer. He's got to look out for himself because you can't have government "interference."*

He stood up and kicked his desk.

Chapter 46

ALICE came awake as the engineer sounded his whistle. They must be coming to another town. She raised the shade and peered at her watch in the dim light that came through the Pullman window.

Two o'clock in the morning. Outside, under an August moon, the corn shimmered, an endless silvery blanket that seemed to unroll westward without interruption.

We must be halfway across Iowa and there's still nothing but corn. We've been going through it all the way from Chicago. What on earth do they do with it all?

The darkened shapes of a farmhouse and its outbuildings came and went in the window.

How can they live out here all alone, with nothing around them but corn and pigs? I haven't seen a real tree since dinnertime. And it's getting flatter and flatter.

The whistle sounded again. The train rushed through a small town, clattering over switches at the elevator sidetrack. The cluster of houses and stores slid past, silent and still in the moonlight. Only the sight of the station agent, standing on the platform to witness their passage, offered evidence of life in the place.

Harry was sound asleep in the other berth, to judge from his steady breathing, but Alice was wide awake. It was hot and airless in the compartment; when she sat up, perspiration slid down between her breasts.

Funny, it didn't seem like this when I came out here last year. I guess I was too busy meeting people to notice the way the country really is. Of course it was the nice time of year, and I was thinking about Harry all the time—not about what it would be like to actually live here.

They had had a wonderful honeymoon in France: a week in Paris, where Alice introduced Harry to Impressionist art, and then a fortnight exploring the Loire valley and its lovely chateaux. Harry had been attentive and ardent, and she had been wholly happy.

So she had been taken aback by the remark of a college friend they visited in Chicago. As they were saying good-bye, Alice extended an invitation.

"I hope you'll drop in on us sometime."

Her friend eyed her in amusement. "Have you looked at the map?" she asked. "Falls City is almost six hundred miles from here. It takes a night and a day on the train. That's not a 'drop in'—it's a cross-country tour."

Now, as the stuffy Pullman rocked through the night, it seemed like even more than six hundred miles.

I wonder if anyone will come to see us. I won't know anybody there except Margaret, and all she cares about is the newspaper. Mrs. Woods is nice but she's old; she must be past fifty.

Am I going to like it?

And what will I do if I don't?

They had to wait at Sioux City for the Great Northern train that would carry them on the last leg of their trip home, and they ate their midday meal at the station restaurant. Despite a high ceiling and a battery of electric fans, the room was stifling.

"Harry, is it *always* this hot and sticky in the summer?"

He looked at her as if there was something peculiar about the question.

"Why, I suppose so." He gave the matter serious thought for a moment. "I never really thought about it, but I'd say this was an average day for this time of year. You know, as long as we have enough moisture, the heat's good for the corn."

She picked at the food on her plate. It seemed heavy and greasy. "It may be good for corn, but it's not for people."

Harry peered at her. "Are you not feeling well, Alice?"

"No, I'm fine. But roast pork seems sort of heavy for the luncheon special on a hot day."

"You'll find people eat big meals in this part of the country, especially at noontime. It's the farmer's dinner. And they serve a lot of pork, because they raise so many hogs." As was his habit, he went on to explain. "That's where most of the corn goes, into hogs and cattle, fed right on the farm where it's grown."

Well, that's one question answered, she thought. She cut a tiny piece of pork and chewed on it.

"As a matter of fact," Harry continued, "there's a very large stockyard here in Sioux City. All the major packing companies have plants here."

She managed to swallow the pork. "So that's what I smelled when we got off the train," she said. "I wondered what that was."

"There's a good-sized packing plant at home, too," Harry said. "Biggest employer in town."

Despite her foreboding, Alice tried to fit into Falls City. It was hard going. People were naturally curious about the society girl from Boston who had married young Harry Norton, and Alice was conscious—perhaps overly conscious—of being the object of such curiosity.

She reacted by being just a little outrageous whenever she could find an excuse. She made no attempt to hide the fact that she was an activist, a feminist, an Easterner, and an aristocrat. She smoked cigarettes, and did so in public. She stirred up old ladies of all ages and both sexes by talking about subjects not usually mentioned by respectable women in that community: she expressed strong opinions not only on art and politics but on women's rights, birth control, the treatment of Indians in South Dakota, and the hypocrisy of those who talked dry but drank wet.

Alice did more than talk. Within three months of her arrival she had organized and launched a free clinic in the east-side neighborhood where most of the packing-house workers lived. For many families, it provided the first easily available health care they had ever known. The clinic attracted a good deal of attention—especially when it began offering family planning advice along with more customary medical services.

This sort of thing raised eyebrows among the more conservative—including a number of Harry's advertisers—but Alice could do it and get away with it because she was not only intelligent but charming. Her voice, a surprise in so small a person, was a throaty alto that drew attention to what she was saying. She had an alert, attentive air that made her seem to focus entirely on the person to whom she had happened to be talking at the moment. Almost every man who met her liked her, and not only for her brains; her brisk step, curly chestnut hair, and shining dark eyes made her a distinctive presence.

The first winter was the worst time for Alice.

Initially she found it exciting. December and January were brutally cold, but it was a brand-new season, with plenty of sunshine and not many storms. She loved being outdoors on clear nights when the stars were so bright that they seemed no more than an arm's reach away, so thick that they filled the great black bowl from horizon to horizon. In moonlight the cold-crusted snow shone like polished silver; the night air was so clear that the sounds of trains being made up in distant freight yards seemed to come from just outside her bedroom window.

But then came February and a series of blizzards, great storms that combined high winds, heavy snow, and fast-falling temperatures. The piles of shoveled snow along the sidewalks rose as storm followed storm. On days when no new snow fell, the wind lifted the old drifts and drove them like spume over the land, obscuring everything in a gauzy white cloud. On such days men would shovel paths and sidewalks, only to return a few minutes later and find them completely packed with drifted snow.

March was not so cold, but there was even more snow, and now Alice could no longer see over the snowbanks.

It's like walking in a tunnel, or a maze, you can't see anything, she thought.

Not that there's anything to see. People all huddled down inside their coats, like turtles with their heads pulled in. And they walk in that peculiar way, stiff-legged with their feet apart so they won't slip on the ice.

The worst of it was that she knew she looked that way and walked that way, too. Sometimes she thought she'd never take her overshoes off, or her mittens or her scarf or her sweater, and she'd been wearing wool underwear so long she'd forgotten what silk felt like.

Even the buildings downtown look dead, shut up tight with all that snow piled up around them, and the frost covering all the windows so you can't see in or out.

I've never been in a place like this. There's hardly a building downtown over two stories high and every one seems uglier than the last. Maybe they build them low like that so they won't get blown away in the blizzards.

My God, will this winter never end? What am I doing here?

"I grew up in New England, and we had real winters," Alice told Harry. "But this is ridiculous."

They were lying in bed one morning in late March. Through the window, Alice could vaguely see big snowflakes being driven horizontally by the north wind. On the windowsill a tiny drift had formed next to the small opening that was cut out of the storm-window frame to let a little fresh air in.

"It's March," Harry replied sleepily. "It always snows in March."

"I'm so sick of seeing nothing but white I could cry."

Harry propped himself up on one elbow and looked at her. She snatched at the blanket. "Don't thrash around like that, you'll let the cold air in."

"I thought you were enjoying the winter." Harry was puzzled—and defensive.

"Don't take it personally," she said. "It's not *your* fault. I'm just fed up."

"Didn't you tell me just the other day that you liked it?"

"That was two months ago." She glanced at the white world outside the window. "Is this ever going to end?"

"April is usually pretty nice. There's hardly any snow then," he mumbled, "and what there is usually melts right away."

He really doesn't know any better, she thought. *All the people who live here are that way. They've always been in this godforsaken place, and they don't know it can be different.*

"I know just how you feel." Eudora Woods surprised Alice with the remark. "I can remember the winters on the claim. It still gives me chilblains just to think about them."

Grace had taken Alice to call on Dan's mother, now eighty-two but still living in the house Henry Woods had built when they came to Falls City a half-century earlier. Eudora poured tea and served the little cakes she had made for the occasion.

"Oh, yes, I remember," she repeated. "One year on the claim we had a bad blizzard on Easter, way into the middle of April. It came in the night, and the next morning we couldn't see anything out the windows. When we opened the door the snowdrifts made a wall up to my waist."

"What did you do?" Alice couldn't imagine this frail old lady keeping house in a sod hut.

"We shoveled, that's what we did. Didn't have much choice, the animals had to be fed and watered. And we had to take care of our needs, too, you know, so that was another path to be cleared. But it was all melted in a few days."

Eudora smiled at her guest and held up the teapot. "Another cup? So it doesn't really seem so bad to me nowadays. Of course I don't do my own shoveling, the boy next door is so nice. But it won't be long now 'til spring."

Alice remembered the prediction in early April, when a chinook brought warm air that melted most of the snow and perfumed the air with the damp, earthy smell of early spring. But then a few days later she awoke to find the city buried again in heavy, wet snow.

"You know, we've had snow on the ground for *five months,*" Alice said to Grace when they met on the street later that week.

"You've had an awful first winter," Grace said. "It's really not fair."

Alice thought of Eudora Woods and the sod house, and of Grace bringing her schoolchildren safely through that terrible blizzard.

"I believe I'll survive," she said. "It'll all be melted in a few days."

Grace smiled. "Now you're beginning to sound like a real South Dakotan—pretending it's not as bad as you know it really is."

They had liked each other from the start. Grace knew from her own travels—including the trip to Boston the previous summer—what it was

[317]

like to feel out of place. For her part, Alice quickly came to like and trust this woman who seemed to understand her without asking a lot of questions.

Grace was twice her age, and Alice knew they could never be intimates; but they instinctively trusted each other and without conscious purpose formed a sort of alliance. Alice was learning something Grace had long known: what it was like to have a husband who spent too much time thinking about his newspaper and not enough time thinking about his wife.

That first year Alice and Harry were renting a house not far from the Woods home. The two women both loved being outdoors, and as the weather improved they often walked together in the afternoon. One day in May they climbed the ridge west of town and looked down on the city below.

"When you get your own house, you should try to find a spot on high ground like this," Grace said. "I think publishers are like editors—they like to sit and look down on their people."

Alice laughed. "Harry *does* take his work seriously. But I thought maybe other newspaper people were different."

"Not the ones I know. They all think the country couldn't get along without them," Grace said. "Dan really believes the *Dakota News* holds this city, this whole state, together. I had to get used to his mind being somewhere else a lot of the time even when he's at home."

Alice looked up at Grace with a quick, sidewise glance. "I know what you're talking about, but I'm not sure I want to get used to it."

Grace smiled. "There are compensations."

Again the birdlike look. "For example?"

Grace walked on a few steps. "If a person is interested, she can influence what the newspaper says, and through that what the community thinks. In this part of the world, it's hard for a woman to do that directly. Men around here don't like to be told anything by women. But there are other ways to get your ideas across—especially if your husband is the editor. Or the publisher."

"I'm not sure Harry wants my ideas. He was talking the other night. He didn't say it straight out, but I know he was trying to tell me that some things I say around town make his life harder."

"What a pity," Grace snapped. "Maybe he shouldn't have married a woman with a mind of her own."

"That's pretty much what I said to him," Alice said. She thought for a moment. "But I see what you mean about getting your ideas across indirectly. Maybe a person could have more influence with a publisher by talking to him in private—instead of making public speeches."

"That's been my experience with editors." Grace's mock-innocent tone made Alice burst out laughing.

"I'll let you know if it works with publishers," she said.

"You won't have to tell me," Grace said. "I'll know."

Chapter 47

Washington, D.C., January 1924

D AN LOOKED at Calvin Coolidge, standing behind his desk as the reporters filed into the room for the president's weekly press conference.

He looks pretty young. Dan thought a moment. *Well, he ought to, he's younger than I am.*

Now that's something to make a man feel old.

Dan's melancholy musing was interrupted by the Associated Press White House correspondent, who introduced him to Calvin Coolidge.

"Mr. President, this is Dan Woods, editor of the *Dakota Daily News,* the largest paper in South Dakota." The president offered his hand and nodded, but said nothing.

Dan had come to Washington full of foreboding. The farmers of the Great Plains were in trouble again, caught in another swing of the iron pendulum that seemed to dictate their fortunes. When the war ended, grain prices had collapsed. Then came two years of drought, and small-town banks began to fail in the Dakotas and Montana, in Minnesota, and even in Iowa. As they went down, small businesses followed, toppling like dominoes. For the first time since the terrible '90s, farm families were heading east, not west, as drought and foreclosure forced them off the plains and onto the back trail.

By the end of 1923 there was a full-blown farm depression, but the rest of the country was booming, and no one seemed to care. Coolidge echoed the general public attitude when he opposed government "interference" in the farmer's problems.

Dan recalled that statement as he stood at one side of the president's office.

He ought to know better, he's lived on a farm, milking cows and shoveling manure. But he's just like the others, he doesn't understand.

One of these days everyone's going to hell in a handbasket, and the farmers may get there first, but sooner or later they'll drag everybody else along with them.

Like his predecessor, Coolidge required reporters to submit questions in writing; that way he could choose which subjects to deal with—and which to ignore. In addition, he could not be quoted without his permission, which he routinely refused. Still, the meetings offered a chance to measure the man and his ideas, so Dan had wanted to attend one during his winter visit.

Coolidge picked up a sheet from the pile in front of him. He sounded like a teacher explaining elementary economics as he began in his flat Yankee accent: "An inquiry about what the cabinet did in relation to the farm situation."

My luck he chose a farm question, Dan thought. He pulled a notebook from his pocket.

> The difficulty is particularly in the wheat belt, and in that belt where there is oftentimes an insufficient rainfall. That makes the production of wheat cost more, and the production, per acre, of course, is not so large.

Dan scribbled notes. *He makes it all sound so reasonable. I'll bet he's never seen what drought does to a stand of wheat.*

> Also there is a large production of wheat all over the world. Apparently Europe will import about two hundred million bushels less of wheat this year than it has in preceding years.
>   There is great anxiety and a great desire to do everything that we can for the relief of any of the farmers who are in distress, along sound economic lines, relieving a temporary situation perhaps, by trying to formulate a plan that would bring agriculture back on to a sound economic basis, so that we can have a balance of production.

Dan didn't like the sound of it. *Too many weasel words in there: "Along sound economic lines ... relieving a temporary situation ... perhaps ... sound economic basis ..."*

> It may be that some of those that are raising wheat would do well to engage in the raising of some other kind of agricultural products. It may be that we ought to look about and see what it is that we are importing in the way of food products, and suggest that the wheat raisers, if they can, try to provide us here in America with some of those things that are being brought in.

What on earth does he expect them to grow in that climate? Dan felt a rush of anger. *Oranges? Bananas? Coconuts?*

We had considerable discussion about the closing of some banks in the Northwest. The situation is serious, though not desperately so. They have a great many banks in the Northwest that are quite different from what we understand as a bank in the East, and with very small capital.

This man has absolutely no idea how farming works on the plains, Dan thought. *He doesn't even know what they look like.*

The government will assist in any way in which it can to furnish credit that may be needed at the present time, but of course nothing in the way of undertaking to replace losses that have already accrued. . . . I don't think the direct use of federal funds is contemplated.

Coolidge might not be thinking about using federal funds, but many in Congress were. Senator Charles McNary of Oregon and Representative Gilbert Haugen of Iowa had just proposed a bill setting up a government corporation to buy up all the wheat not needed for domestic use and sell it abroad for whatever it would bring. The idea was to raise the price farmers got by insulating the home market from the price-depressing effect of surplus production.

On Capitol Hill Dan called first on his old friend George Norris. The Nebraska senator wasn't optimistic about the administration's reaction to the McNary-Haugen plan.

"Coolidge says he's got an open mind," Dan ventured, flipping through his notes on the president's remarks.

Norris scratched a match and lit his cigar. "I don't believe his mind is open. Coolidge has never favored using federal money to help the farmer, and he never will."

"So the farmers get hit coming and going, don't they? They get wiped out by nature, by drought and low prices, and they get no help from their government, either."

Norris nodded morosely. "We just don't have the votes anymore."

"Not that it was a whole lot better when we did have them." Dan suddenly recalled Lounsberry's tales of Washington in the 1870s. "It was pretty much the same fifty years ago, when Congress was ladling out money to the railroads, but wouldn't give a dime to farmers after the grasshopper plagues."

He shook his head. "I guess nothing changes."

Sam Rayburn was embarrassed when Dan reminded him that he had praised Coolidge in their first conversation eighteen months earlier. "Well, I was wrong," the Texan confessed. "He may have brains about a lot of things, but not about farming. He lets his cabinet members argue farm policy, and he just stands there while they bite and gouge each other. He'll never support McNary-Haugen, no matter what he says."

Dan suggested that eventually some way would have to be found to control surplus production and improve farming practices. "Less corn, more clover, more money," he said. "That's what one of the farm magazines up our way is calling for."

"Huh!" Rayburn grunted. "This crowd will never go for anything like that. They hand out money to big business, but when you suggest helping the farmer, it's 'interference with the free market.' "

Dan talked to many others in Washington, and when he was done, he summed up in a column.

> Through the last quarter-century, people and political influence have moved steadily away from the farm and into the city. That may be one reason why none of the last half-dozen Presidents has really understood farmers or cared deeply about their problems. Certainly the two Republican presidents in this decade have been interested only in helping business, not agriculture.
>
> Today the farmers of the Plains are in trouble again—and again, the man in the White House seems unconcerned. The political climate here is more hostile to farmers than it has been in years; all efforts to provide relief seem likely to be stymied.
>
> The rest of the country is booming, and the President and his cabinet do not seem concerned about the farmers of the Plains. They will live to regret that neglect, because depressions are farm-led and farm-fed, and there is already a depression in the farm belt today. Its seeds may have been sown in the fields of the west—but the harvest will be reaped in the great cities of the east. . . .

June 1924

As Norris and Rayburn had predicted, the administration opposed the McNary-Haugen bill, and it was defeated in the House of Representatives in June. A week later the Republican National Convention nominated Coolidge—and adopted a platform that also rejected direct federal farm aid:

> The crux of the problem from the standpoint of the farmer is the net profit he receives after his outlay. The process of bringing the average prices of what he buys and what he sells closer together can be promptly expedited by reduction in taxes, steady employment in industry, and stability in business.

Dan was infuriated by the platform language. *That's a lot of double-talk. All it really says is that the Republican party will help business, and let a little of it trickle down to the farmer.*

Why don't they try helping farmers—and letting it trickle down from the farmers to business?

One candidate was foursquare for farmers. Robert LaFollette, as determined and uncompromising as ever at sixty-nine, was nominated for president by a farmer-labor coalition which called itself the Progressive party, and he got almost five million votes. But he ran a distant third behind Coolidge and Democrat John W. Davis; most Americans were content to "keep cool with Coolidge," vote Republican, and never mind the complaining farmer.

"That's the last time farmers are going to have a candidate for president who thinks the way they do," Dan told Grace after the election as they talked about LaFollette's last hurrah. "Someone who believes in what they do, feels the way they do. Someone who hurts when they do. There won't be any more like him."

Chapter 48

Falls City, 1925

GEORGE NORTON knew how to keep his son busy and satisfied: he named him general manager and put him in charge of all day-to-day operations at the newspaper.

His daughter was not so easily accommodated. Margaret had spent the years since college working as a reporter; now, at twenty-seven, she reckoned it was time for her to have a larger role, and she was not bashful about saying so.

Harry sat and listened while his father and sister had it out in the publisher's office one winter afternoon in early 1925. She wanted a promise that she would someday run the news side of the paper. George made it plain he was still dead set against the idea.

"It's a man's job. That's all there is to it."

"Father, that's nonsense." Margaret's face was grim under the freckles, her voice tense. "You know there are women editors. And even if there weren't, that's no reason to assume I couldn't do the job."

"You don't know the first thing about it."

"That's not true. That's not what Dan says. He says I'm as good as any man he's ever had, and a lot better than most."

"He just says that to be nice."

"He does not. He doesn't say that kind of thing to be nice, and you know it." Margaret had a quick temper and a sharp tongue, and Harry sensed she was close to losing control of both. "Talk to him. You'll see. And what I don't know, I can learn."

George was not inclined to debate his daughter. He didn't respond to her argument, but simply repeated his conclusion. "You're not going to be the editor of this paper while I'm in charge of it."

She glanced at Harry, trying to send a message: *No offense meant, dear brother, but I have to do this.* "I have just as much right to a place here as

[324]

Harry does," she told her father. "You'd let him be editor."

"That's beside the point. He's going to be the publisher."

"It's not beside the point. He might have been the editor, and I'm just as good at news work as he is—maybe better. The only reason you keep saying no is because I'm a woman."

"You're acting more like a spoiled little girl."

"Goddammit, Father, I am not. I—"

"Don't you speak to me that way." George's voice was cold. "That may be all right at that fancy Eastern college, but not in my office."

Margaret was silent for a moment, then took a deep breath. "I'm sorry, Father. I know I shouldn't talk that way. But you mustn't turn me down just because I'm a woman."

"That's nonsense."

"Is it? You think about it for a while." She waved in her brother's general direction. "Ask him." She stood up abruptly and walked out of the office.

George Norton looked at his son. "Well?"

"She's right." George started to protest, but Harry held up his hand to cut him off. "Wait a minute, Father. Think about it: Do you have any reason not to let her do it—assuming she's as qualified as anyone else around here—except that she's a woman?"

George stared defiantly at Harry. "I won't give her the job just because she's family."

"You'd have given it to me just because I was family—if James had been here to be publisher."

"That's different." George glanced at the framed photograph on his desk, and his voice dropped. "And he's not here."

Harry heard something in his father's voice. "Look, Father, you can't turn Margaret down because she's a woman. Or because . . . because she's not James." George glared, but Harry pushed on. "She's got as much right as I do to be part of this place if that's what she wants. And she's good, Father—really good. Besides, it wouldn't be hard to arrange."

The older man stared at his son. Then he grunted. "Go on."

"David Currier will be sixty-six this year. He'll be ready to retire sometime soon. He should; he's getting old and tired, and you know he's got plenty of money."

"He ought to. He still has that ten percent of our stock that he held back when I bought the paper from him." The publisher's tone was rueful. "I never could get him to sell it to me."

"Finally met your match, did you?" Harry smiled, but stuck to business. "The point is, he can retire soon. Why not let Margaret be managing editor for a while? She'd like that, and she'd do a first-rate job. We can worry about the editor's job later. Dan's not going to leave anytime soon."

"She's too young."

"She'll be twenty-eight in December. I'm only thirty, and you trust me to run the whole place."

"It's not the same." George's words were unyielding. Harry searched his face in vain for a sign of sympathy.

George Norton was not surprised at his son's views, but he was completely unprepared for his wife's reaction when he told her about Margaret's demands that night.

"Of course you're going to let her do it." Mary Norton's tone was matter-of-fact.

"No, I'm not."

"You *must.*" She put down her sewing and looked at him. "Or do you want her to turn out like me?"

George was stunned. "What in the world do you mean, Mary?"

"I mean she deserves something better than I've had. My whole life has been having babies and losing them, and having nothing to do to take my mind off my grief, and taking pills and tonics to help me forget."

"Mary . . ."

"You know it's true, George, and it was mostly because I wasn't any *use* to anyone, I couldn't do anything that was *needed.* Even here at home, there were always hired girls to do everything."

She had never said any of these things to her husband; now she could not stop talking.

"I know a lot of it's my own fault; God knows I haven't made anything of myself. But I'm not going to stand by while you do the same thing to her that you . . . that happened to me."

George stirred in his chair, but she held the floor. "I know I'm not very smart, but Margaret is, and it's up to us to make sure she gets to use her gifts. And you can do that so easily, you've got the paper, you can make her part of it too."

George could not remember Mary ever saying so much at one time. When she stopped he could think of no reply, and retreated behind his newspaper.

He didn't mention his wife's outburst to anyone. But a few days later, he asked Dan for an assessment of Margaret's work.

"She's doing fine."

"Is she competent to handle more responsibility?"

"Certainly." Dan stopped; he knew where this was leading, and he had to enter a disclaimer. "Look, George, this is family business. It's between you and Margaret and Harry. I don't have a vote, and I shouldn't."

"Yes, you should." The old man was insistent. "It's your paper, too. You've been running it for thirty-five years."

"All right, if you really want me to, I will." Dan cleared his throat. "And in the end it's my job we're talking about, isn't it?"

"Not if I have anything to say about it."

"Well, if you're set against it, I suspect you'll turn out to be wrong. She's about as good as any young reporter I've ever had. I don't know yet what kind of editor she'll make. She's smart enough to run the place, but she'll have to learn to apply herself—and to think before she talks."

"She certainly will. Can you teach her that?"

"I can try, George." Dan grinned at the publisher. "After all, I've had lots of experience with outspoken people named Norton."

It's strange, he thought, *I can talk to George and his kids easier than to my own wife or daughter. Maybe it's because it's all business, and I can be friendly without getting mixed up emotionally.*

In that moment Dan saw himself clearly.

It's easier for me to deal with people when I'm standing on the sidelines, watching them but not getting too close to them.

That's a good habit for a reporter, but maybe I'm missing something.

Later that same day George called his son and daughter into his office.

"Harry, it's time for Margaret to go to work on the business side. Start her in circulation, of course."

Margaret flushed angrily. "Father, you know I want to work on the news side. Why are you—"

George Norton held up a warning hand. "You must learn to listen before you speak, Margaret," he said, and then continued his instructions to Harry:

"You'll need to teach her as quickly as you can, because Dan will want her back in a year or so to start learning editing work."

He turned to Margaret. "That means you won't have much time to learn the business. You'll have to apply yourself." He stared poker-faced at his daughter. "And remember, you're going to have to work harder and be better than anyone else if you want to help run this place someday."

"I'll try to remember that, Father." Margaret bit off the words. She was about to say something more to him, but instead spoke to Harry: "I'll finish the stories I'm working on. I can probably start with you tomorrow."

Then, as if remembering something, she turned back to George Norton. Her voice was ice-cold.

"Don't worry, Father. I won't embarrass you."

That winter and spring Margaret gained a good deal of firsthand experience with bad weather and bad roads as she rode the trucks that hauled the paper to communities around Falls City. Soon the word went around the *Dakota News* loading dock that the publisher's daughter was all right: she was a good sport, did her share of the heavy lifting, and was always willing to get out in snow or mud to help push a stalled truck. She asked no favors and got none, but she made a lot of new friends.

In late summer Harry moved her into the advertising department. For the next six months she walked up and down Lincoln Avenue calling on merchants; she checked proofs with advertisers, and she took her turn at the want-ad counter in the front office.

Her last assignment from Harry was to spend a week at Florence Berdahl's side, learning how to keep the books, read the ledgers, and keep track of overdue accounts.

She got a final sermon from her father the day she returned to the newsroom.

"Maybe now you know a little about how this place really works. Always remember, circulation comes first. Everything else depends on it."

How could I forget it? You say it five times a day. "I think I understand that, Father."

"We're not doing well enough. Especially on the daily."

You never let up, do you? "I think Harry's right, it's because a lot of people are taking the Sunday paper."

"Just because people take the paper on Sunday doesn't mean they don't need it the other six days of the week. We're not getting that message across."

Dan issued her marching orders. "It's time to quit playing and get to work. I'm putting you on the copy desk."

Margaret tried to hide her disappointment. She didn't quite succeed. "I hate to give up reporting."

Dan ran a hand through his shock of gray hair. "That's the way I feel about it, too, and that's why I'm always sneaking away. But if you want to run this place someday—"

"I certainly do," she interrupted. "I want your job."

"It's not open."

She blushed and stammered. "That's not what I . . . I . . . well, I mean when you decide to do something else."

He laughed at her discomfiture, but he was not really amused. "Margaret, if you want to run this place someday, you'll have to learn to let people finish what they're saying. What I was saying was that you have to work on the desk, because that's where the paper is put out, and you need to learn how it's done."

She was suitably abashed. "When do I start? And what do you want me to do?"

"You start today, and you'll do whatever David Currier wants. Sooner or later you should learn all the jobs on the desk, so you'll know what's required." Dan tilted back in his chair and smiled at her. "I think David plans to start you on the Sunday advance."

He would, she thought. *The dullest job there is, reading all that junk that goes in the back of the Sunday paper. I was better off pushing delivery trucks out of mudholes.*

She stood up. "I better get out there and get to work."

He nodded. "That was very good."

"What was good?"

"The way you didn't say what you really think about working Sunday advance copy." He grinned. "Keep it up."

She was a quick learner, and after a few months on the Sunday desk she was moved to the night shift, editing copy for the first edition of the next day's paper. Because the editor and managing editor usually weren't around, the nightside staff was looser, more irreverent, more fun than the larger daytime crew. Margaret—self-confident, quick, sarcastic, a little ribald—felt right at home. Though a few staff members resented the fact that she was the boss's daughter, most were willing to accept her at face value, especially when she made clear that she wanted to be judged on her work, not her name.

She still had trouble with her tongue and temper. One Saturday night, with a big Sunday paper to get out and every piece of copy moving late, Margaret got stuck writing a headline; the copy-desk chief kept returning it for another try. The third such rejection triggered an outburst.

"I don't know how we're ever going to get the paper out on time if you nitpick every piece of copy," Margaret said, her face flushing and her voice carrying clearly throughout the newsroom. "There's not a damn thing wrong with that head."

The slot man, a middle-aged man of infinite patience and verbal precision, replied calmly. "We'd always be on time if everybody did the job right the first time. I do not nitpick every piece of copy. Only what isn't good enough."

She threw the copy back at him. "I think that's good enough."

He looked at it for a few seconds, sighed, and dropped it in the wastebasket. Then he wrote out a new headline, counted the characters under his breath, and sent it to the composing room. He took a wire-service story from the pile in front of him and held it out to Margaret. "Let me have six inches of that, please, with a one-column three-twenty-four head on it."

She took the copy without a word.

Dan Woods happened to be working late that night, catching up on his mail and reading. When Margaret finished her shift, he intercepted her at the door.

"I'll buy you a cup of coffee."

"Oh, Dan, thanks," Margaret said, "but I think I'll go straight home. I'm tired."

"I said I'd buy you a cup of coffee." His hand clamped hard on her elbow and he steered her down the street to the all-night diner by the Great Northern depot.

Settled in one of the tiny booths, Dan looked at her.

"Margaret, you've got a wonderful future—if you learn to mind your mouth."

She squirmed and started to reply. Dan's hands were flat on the table; he lifted one finger, and she stopped.

"Your work is first-rate. The people respect you. They know you're good." He leaned forward to emphasize his words: "And they also know you aren't perfect. Everyone gets snarled up sometime."

Margaret found her voice. "I know, Dan. I shouldn't have blown up like that tonight. I was wrong."

"Yes, you were, but that's not the point. The point is, you can never allow yourself to forget who you are. You're the boss's daughter. You're one of the owners. Other people figure you could get them fired, or at least have a lot of influence with your father and your brother—and with me."

Dan took a sip of his coffee. "Remember that the next time you feel like yelling at the slot man. And if you still want to yell, do it when the two of you are alone. Other people can do what you did tonight, but you can't. If you have to criticize, never—*never*—do it in public. It humiliates people, because they can't argue back to you."

She replied instinctively. "Of course they can."

"No, they can't. You're different. You're a Norton. That means they work for you. You own the paper. You're rich. You can't even *seem* to be pushing people around."

Margaret stared at her coffee. "Me and my big mouth."

"You and your big mouth," he agreed. He offered a weary, late-night smile, and his voice grew gentler. "You're good, Margaret, very good. You can run this newspaper. You *should* run it. It needs you. I think your father will come around. So don't throw it all away."

Dan put two quarters down on the table, signaling an end to the conversation, and they walked out of the diner. Margaret shivered as she stepped into the chilly fall night.

"Dan?"

"Yes?" A freight train rumbled past on the nearby tracks, and he strained to hear her.

"Thank you. I'll try not to let you down." She put a hand on his arm. "Just one question."

"Yes?"

"Why do you take so much trouble over me?"

He looked down at her. The pixie face was rounder now, but her wavy chestnut hair still reminded him of the young George Norton.

I wonder that myself, he thought. *Partly for your father; he's a hard man but we've come a long way together, and I can't let him go wrong now.*

But mostly for the paper. It's my life, and I want the next editor to take care of it. It looks like you're going to get the job, so we'd best try to make it come all right.

"Oh, I don't know," he said, the tired smile sliding onto his face again. "Maybe because you told me you wanted my job, and the sooner you get ready to take it, the sooner I can go back to being a newspaper-man."

Chapter 49

Falls City, 1925

THE FARMERS were in trouble, but for the moment Falls City remained relatively prosperous. With a population over thirty thousand, it was the largest city in the state and still growing. Its multiple rail connections made it a transportation and distribution center as well as a manufacturing town, so it was at least partly insulated from the agricultural depression already ravaging smaller cities and towns across South Dakota.

Besides, the legislature finally began to put up money for improving rural roads, and that made it easier for farm families to spend what money they had in Falls City. And of course every mile of grading and graveling helped the *Dakota News*.

Harry Norton established delivery routes on rural roads as they were designated for improvement. Meanwhile his father, inventive as ever, suggested adding a farm magazine to the Sunday paper; Dan and Margaret soon had a three-man staff at work producing a monthly *Dakota Farmer*. The magazine became part of a continuing emphasis on farm news that persuaded many farmers to buy the Sunday paper even in hard times. Sunday circulation rose to twenty-four thousand, for the first time exceeding the daily figure. Weekday circulation was now nearly twenty-one thousand, more than half of it in outlying communities and farms; in Falls City itself, almost every household took the paper.

Harry also sensed there was money to be made in radio. He applied for a broadcast license, and that autumn station KDDN went on the air from a rented studio in Falls City.

"Someday, we'll be broadcasting to the farmer milking in his barn before sunrise," Harry told Dan. "We'll give him market reports with his dinner at noon, and a little music in the house after supper."

"First you'll have to get electricity onto that farm," Dan reminded

[332]

him. "The power companies don't want to serve farmers because they're spread too thin for big profits."

"I'm counting on you and your friends in Congress, Norris and that fellow Rayburn," Harry said. "Sooner or later the government will make sure that farmers get electricity."

Dan was not persuaded. "I hope those farmers are still there to use it," he grumbled. "The way things are going now, there may not be any of 'em left to buy power even if it gets there."

October 1926

Several events during the fall and winter only served to deepen Dan's foreboding. One was Harry Norton's trip to Washington with a group of South Dakota businessmen. They hoped to persuade the administration to do something—almost anything—for the state's farmers.

"Well, hello, boss," Dan said when Harry walked into his office. "I heard you fellows got home last night. How did it go?"

"It was all bad. We might as well have stayed home. We got no encouragement from anyone, and the administration's not interested."

"Did you get to see Hoover?" Dan knew Harry had planned to call on Herbert Hoover, the secretary of commerce.

"Yes, I had some time with him alone. I decided I should speak frankly to him. So I told him I thought the Republicans might lose all the farm states next time if they don't do something to raise farm income soon."

"What did he say?"

"He looked at me as if he hadn't heard one word I said. I tried again to explain what was going on out here, and he cut me off. He said he'd grown up in Iowa and understood agriculture. I said I hoped the president would sign McNary-Haugen when it passes. He said it's a very bad bill."

"And merry Christmas to you, too."

"That's about it."

When Congress finally passed the McNary-Haugen bill a month later, Coolidge did veto it. In a scathing message, he said it would increase wheat production, reduce consumption, fix prices, be unworkable, and create a new federal bureaucracy. And, he added, he considered it unconstitutional.

November 1926

"They say Coolidge won by a landslide. They say Hoover *will* win by a landslide next time." Will Harper's voice was harsh. "Well, landslides bury people, and you know who gets buried the deepest. Farmers, that's who."

Grace's eighteen-year-old nephew—Charlie Harper's son Will—sat

[333]

in her kitchen a few days before Thanksgiving, drinking coffee and smoking a hand-rolled cigarette.

He talks the way Dan's been talking, she thought. *As if the world's coming to an end.*

"You're the only one in the family who understands how I feel, Aunt Grace. Pa doesn't pay any attention to politics. Neither does Ma, and my brother's still too young to understand."

"I guess you and I take after your grandfather." Grace tried to sound casual, but she was worried about Will. He was so angry about so much that he seemed perpetually enraged. He looked like his grandfather—tall and solidly built, with light blue eyes gleaming in a tanned face—but he lacked Amos's saving sense of humor and detachment.

Now Will Harper sighed. "I miss Grandpa something awful. You know, I've read all his political books, about the Alliance and the People's party and all. They're pretty interesting."

Grace nodded. "He really cared about all that, even though he tried not to let it show."

"I know. I remember a lot of things he said. Especially about how they lost all the battles but won the war—how their *ideas* won even if their candidates lost." Will's voice turned hard again. "But he was wrong about that. I've been reading the Socialists and the Communists, and they show how the Populists and people like them were bamboozled by the old parties and the Wall Street bankers."

Will rolled another cigarette, twisted the ends, and lit up before going on. "I think the Communists are right. The only hope for the future is an alliance of workers and farmers, to unite all the laboring masses in a common front."

Grace was amused by his glib use of radical vocabulary, but kept a straight face. "You won't find too many hereabouts who agree with you."

"I know. The reactionaries control everything here." He took a long pull on the cigarette, coughed, and leaned forward confidingly. "That's why I'm going to Minnesota. They've got a Farmer-Labor party, one with real political power, and I'm going to work with them until it's time for the Communist party to take over."

"What do your father and mother think about that idea?"

The youth was momentarily discomfited. "I haven't talked to them about it." He hesitated. "They wouldn't understand, so why bring it up?"

"Have you thought about what you're going to do?"

"I just said. I'm going to Minneapolis or St. Paul."

"I mean for your work, your life. Don't you want to farm?"

"Pretty soon there'll be no place to farm." The rage came into his voice again. "Pa has plowed up just about all the land that Grandpa kept in grass. He planted it all to corn, trying to make up for low prices, but with the drought there's been no crop, and pretty soon there won't be any

[334]

soil either. Pa's so ashamed of what he did to Grandpa's land, he can hardly talk about it. But he's no worse than the others—it's the same all over the state, they're plowing fence row to fence row."

Will dropped the stub of his cigarette in his saucer. "I don't think I'm cut out for farming anyway. Let Edward have the place. He's like Pa, he loves animals and growing things. I'm more interested in *changing* things."

"You *are* like your grandfather."

"Not really." Will's voice was quiet, but sure. "I believe in the revolution."

She said nothing, and he stood up. "Thank you for the coffee, Aunt Grace. And for listening." He hesitated. "Please don't say anything about my plans. You're the only one I've talked to."

Right after Christmas, Will Harper left for Minneapolis. He told his parents where he was going, but not what he was going to do.

March 1927

Eudora Woods died toward the end of the winter. She had gone into old age as she did everything else, with good humor and self-effacing grace; when she could no longer keep house for herself, she insisted on moving to a place where she could be cared for along with a couple of other old ladies—and not be a burden on her son and daughter-in-law.

When her time came she was content to go. "There's nothing wrong with me except that I am eighty-four years old, and I don't recommend it," she told Grace in February. A few weeks later, she chided a familiar nurse who brought her lunch: "I don't know who you are. Go away, I'm busy dying." That evening, her body just quit working.

At the funeral Dan read from the thirty-first chapter of Proverbs.

> Who can find a virtuous woman? For her price is far above rubies.
> The heart of her husband doth safely trust in her. . . .
> She will do him good and not evil all the days of her life.

She always backed Pa up, even when she knew he was wrong, even when she knew he was going to fail. "It'll come all right," she always said, and she never complained.

> She riseth also while it is still night, and giveth meat to her household.

I'd wake up in that sod house and she'd be moving around, lighting the stove so it would be a little warm when we kids got up, making breakfast so it'd be ready when Pa came in from chores.
She always got up in the dark, and she never complained.

[335]

She girdeth her loins with strength, and strengtheneth her arms.

She was strong, all right. She had to be. She lived in a house full of rattlesnakes, and she couldn't keep it clean no matter how she tried. It showed in her face, even a little boy could tell. She was always tired, right through to the bone. She worked and worked, and she never complained.

Strength and honor are her clothing; and she shall rejoice in time to come.

An hour later, Dan stood beside his mother's grave as the minister read the old final phrases of the committal service. But Dan wasn't listening; he was looking off to the west, down the slope of the hillside cemetery, beyond the edge of town, out onto the snow-covered plains that ran to the far horizon.

It's all coming apart, isn't it? Ma gone, Amos gone. The ones that made this country all gone or going.

But it's not just the old people. Will Harper's gone to the city to make a revolution. Abigail's gone to the city to make a life. Pretty soon we'll be fresh out of young ones around here.

Now the government's turned its back on the farmers again, the same way it always has.

Pretty soon even the good farmers, even the ones that don't have a lot of debt, are going to get ground down. There doesn't seem to be any way to get them help.

And it hasn't rained for two years.

Chapter 50

Falls City, 1928

G EORGE NORTON had often said that he wanted Harry to succeed him as publisher of the *Dakota News,* but he had never matched action to talk. Now, finally, he was ready.

On a bitterly cold January morning he asked his son to come into his office.

"I'm getting old, I really feel the cold this winter," George said. "I woke up this morning and thought it would be nice to be in Florida or someplace like that."

Harry laughed. "You? Take a vacation?"

His father, as usual, replied in a voice that was dead serious. "No, not a vacation. Something more permanent. I'll be seventy in July. It's time for me to get out and for you to become publisher. I want to announce it right away."

Harry was surprised—George had not mentioned the matter for months—but he didn't show it.

"Thank you, Father. I hope I can manage things in a way that satisfies you."

"You've been managing things around here for several years, in case you hadn't noticed. And doing it quite well."

"Thank you again." Harry had a thought. "But seriously, what are you going to do with yourself?"

"Oh, I'll come in to the office every day, just as I always have. After all, I still own a majority of the stock in this company." He favored his son with a small smile. "I have an obligation to keep an eye on my investment."

Meaning he'll keep his fingers in our finances and his nose in everything else, just the way he does now, Harry thought. *Nothing is simple.*

He raised another issue. "I assume the publisher will continue to have the final say on editorial matters."

"That's between you and Dan. You fellows will decide what goes into the paper. I'm all through with that." George stared at his son. "I may have opinions."

"I expect you will, Father," Harry said, "and I'll need all the advice you can give me. Of course I'll have to be responsible for decisions about editorial policy." He paused. "And who does what on the paper."

George Norton's face was expressionless. "Of course."

The announcement of generational change was contained in a one-paragraph news item:

NEW PUBLISHER NAMED

Harrison Norton has been appointed Publisher of the Dakota News. George Norton, who has held the post since 1889, will retire, but will maintain an office at the newspaper and will pursue various business interests.

"I'll bet he'll pursue his interests," Grace said to Dan when she read the item. "He'll be looking over Harry's shoulder every minute—and meddling."

"There's bound to be some of that." Dan shrugged. "But Harry's a big boy now. He can take care of himself."

A month later David Currier told Dan he wanted to quit.

"It's past time. Mr. Norton's retired, and I'll be sixty-nine in the fall. I'm getting too old for these winters." He smiled. "Tell the truth, I've always been too old for them."

Dan reported Currier's decision to Harry Norton.

"That means we'll need a new managing editor," Harry said. "Do you think my sister's ready?"

"I'm sure she is." Dan eyed his new publisher. "Do you think your father's ready?"

Harry chuckled. "I'm sure he's not. But that's my problem, not yours. I'll deal with Father."

"He's all yours. But if you think I can help, let me know."

George Norton listened in stony silence as Harry told him he had decided to make Margaret managing editor of the *Dakota News.* He sat still for several moments when Harry finished; when he did respond, his voice was cold.

"It's a mistake, Harry. It's a bad idea. A very bad idea. It's not a woman's job. She won't be accepted by the business community. And she's too young, anyway."

He stared at his son, then sighed wearily.

"But I put you in charge, and I knew when I did it that you would probably ignore my advice on this subject."

By God, he's given up, Harry thought. *I wonder why.*

He found out a moment later.

"I hope you'll change your mind about Margaret," Harry said.

"I hope I'll have reason to."

"All I ask is that you judge her on the basis of her work, not because she's a woman."

"That's what your wife said."

"My *wife?*"

"Alice spoke to me. I assumed you put her up to it."

"I did nothing of the kind." In fact Harry was astonished: he had told Alice about the argument, but he had not suggested she talk to her father-in-law about it.

"Well, she talked to me." George's abrupt tone masked his conciliatory language. "She said she knew Margaret better than either of us did, and she asked me to give her a fair chance."

"What did you tell her?"

"I told her I thought she was probably right." His face twitched in a brief, bleak smile. "Then I told her to take it up with you because I don't have anything to say about those things any more."

Harry told Dan about the conversation, including his father's reference to Alice. Dan told Grace. Grace smiled and said nothing.

September 1928

"I don't see how we can endorse Hoover." Dan leaned across Harry Norton's desk. "This is a farm state, and Hoover's just as wrong as he can be on agriculture. He'll give us four more years of Coolidge policies, and I don't think our farmers can survive that."

Harry Norton peered up at Dan through his big, round eyeglasses. "Dan, you have to look at the whole picture. I know farmers are in trouble, but overall the country's in good shape. I know Hoover. He may not be so good on farm policy, but he's sound, and he's right on most issues. And he certainly has more experience than Smith."

Once again Dan found himself disagreeing with the Nortons over a presidential election. He knew he had no chance of persuading them to endorse the Democrat, Al Smith, but he hoped to convince them to make no endorsement at all.

In the event, however, even that proved impossible: both father and son were for Herbert Hoover; they were Republicans, he was the Republican nominee, and the paper would support him. So Dan used his column, as he had eight years earlier, to air his disagreement.

He argued the case for Smith primarily on the agricultural issue.

. . . Governor Smith has declared his support for the McNary-Haugen bill. That means that at the very least he will not veto legislation to help farmers—legislation that the next Congress will surely enact no matter who is in the White House. Secretary Hoover, on the other hand, has made it clear that he will follow the policies of President Coolidge.

On the day that Mr. Coolidge first vetoed the McNary-Haugen bill, he also raised the tariff on imported pig iron by 50 percent. Thus on the one hand he refused to raise the income of farmers, and on the other he raised the cost of every plow, every tractor, every implement they must buy. That is the policy Secretary Hoover promises to continue. Like Mr. Coolidge, he favors tariffs, which are taxes levied to help industry, but opposes the McNary-Haugen equalization fee, which would be a tax to help agriculture.

All the American farmer has ever asked is to be treated fairly, to be given the same benefits and bear the same burdens as his city cousins. He is far likelier to get that kind of fairness this year from the Democratic candidate.

November 1928

South Dakota did not follow Dan's advice. It would have been hard enough for most of them to vote for a Democrat of any sort, but Smith was a big-city man, a Tammany politician, a New Yorker with a derby hat and a funny accent. He was for repeal of Prohibition—and, most of all, he was a Roman Catholic. The farmers voted Republican, and so did almost everyone else: Hoover won in his party's third landslide of the decade.

The result left Dan deeply pessimistic. He vented his frustration in a post-election column.

> . . . People who talk about the "danger of radicalism" are aiming at the wrong target. Radical arguments don't sell here or anywhere else in this country, no matter how loudly agitators proclaim them. This nation is not going to be overthrown; but it may well be put to sleep—by the greedy profiteers who have taken over the government in Washington and the speculators who reign in Wall Street. Both types are more interested in filling their own pockets than in building a sound, fair and truly prosperous society.
>
> The sad fact today is that there is no Roosevelt, no Bryan, no Wilson, no LaFollette to lead the liberal fight, to stand again at Armageddon. We need new leaders, but we see none. That, rather than the shrill polemics of the far left, is the real danger today.

"You sound as if you've given up," Grace said as she finished reading that column. "You've never written like that before."

"I've never felt that way before," Dan replied. "I think we're riding for a fall. We're in for bad times."

They were sitting in their kitchen on a cold Sunday morning. Outside, gray clouds scudded across a darker gray sky, promising the season's first snow. The wind tore at the edges of the house and rattled the kitchen windows.

"Well, I don't know about that, but I do know we're in for *cold* times," Grace said, trying to shake Dan's gloomy mood. "You better get the rest of the storm windows on today. A little fresh air and exercise might take your mind off politics and cheer you up."

"It's not just politics. It's this Wall Street binge. People have just gone crazy, borrowing all kinds of money to gamble on the market. It's got to end sometime, and when it does, it'll be a mess."

Dan's words echoed a grim forecast a few days earlier from George Norton. He had told Dan and Harry that the country was headed for an economic collapse.

"This stock market's completely out of hand," George said. "Why, there's more owed on broker's loans than there is money in circulation in the whole country. It's insane."

"Well, Father, as a matter of fact I've been thinking we've got an awful lot of cash just sitting there," Harry said. "Maybe we should take some of that and buy stock—of course, nothing risky, good solid companies, not speculative."

"No!" The elder Norton was curt. "It's got to a point where stock prices don't have any relation to what a company's worth or what it produces. The whole thing is built on sand, and when the collapse comes there'll be nothing to hold anything up."

George stabbed a forefinger at his son. "What we ought to do is sell what we do have, take our profit, get out of the market."

"It's hard to walk away from ten, twelve percent gain a year," Harry said. "That's what stocks are returning."

"Huh!" George snorted in derision. "Don't be greedy. Better to walk away from it now instead of holding on for more and losing your whole investment when the market collapses. There's going to be a crash, and when it comes, the good companies will go down right alongside the bad."

"Don't you think Hoover would take some action if that kind of thing started?" Dan asked.

"Well, I certainly hope so. I believe he'd try to help." George was pleased with Hoover's big victory, and he genuinely respected the man. "But I have a feeling that this next depression will be the worst we've ever seen, and nothing he could do would help much."

June 25, 1929

Dan had just begun reading the overnight wire-service dispatches when Margaret came into his office and shut the door. Dan was startled: her eyes were red and puffy, her face pale and drawn. He stood up.

[341]

"What's wrong?"

"Mother took a lot of pills last night. Father woke up this morning and she was lying there beside him." Margaret's voice shook, then broke. "Dead."

"My God, how awful." Dan stopped. "But why . . . ?"

Margaret got hold of her emotions and the words came more steadily. "I don't know for sure, but today is June 25." She saw Dan's puzzled look and realized he didn't remember. "The day James was killed in France. Eleven years ago today."

Dan thought of Mary Norton living through all those twilight years, withdrawn into herself.

It wasn't just James. Mary Norton went away a long time ago, after that first baby girl died, but she came back when Margaret was born. Then when James was killed she went away again, back to the pills and the medicines, and that time she never did come back.

"Oh, Margaret. I'm sorry."

"Don't be sorry for her." She tried to sound matter-of-fact. "She's better off where she is now, believe me."

Mary Norton was buried in the city's old cemetery. The gravesite was close to a huge oak tree which shaded the mourners from the relentless sun and heat of late June. Margaret clung to Harry's arm, but George stood a little apart, as always showing no emotion.

Dan and Grace went to him after the service: Dan simply took his hand; Grace embraced him. None of them could find words for the moment.

October 1929

When the market did crash that fall, the Nortons and their newspaper didn't suffer nearly as much as most. Harry told Dan that his father deserved the credit: George had persuaded him to get out of the stock market when it was still rising.

"He pestered me twice a day every day until I agreed," Harry said, "and he had it just right. We sold in August, and the market topped out in September. We'd have taken an awful bath if I hadn't done what he told me to do."

"He did the same kind of thing in '93," Dan said. "He started putting cash away, so when the Panic hit we were in good shape. In fact he handled things so well that we actually came out of the depression better off than when we went in."

Harry shook his head. "I'm afraid that may not happen this time. It's going to get a lot worse before it gets any better. I think this will make '93 look like a joy ride."

[342]

Chapter 51

D AN STEPPED on the accelerator, trying to get up enough speed to create a breeze inside the car. His young reporters called it "doing a four-forty"—rolling down all four windows and driving forty miles an hour. Dan decided that it might work at night, when the kids did their joyriding, but it didn't help much at high noon.

It was so hot and dry that the sky was more white than blue, a great concave lens that seemed to focus the sun's glare on each person below. A plume of dust pursued Dan's car; loose topsoil from adjoining fields coated the road and swirled up behind every passing vehicle.

That morning, he had decided it was time for a firsthand look at the countryside. He had driven the back roads for three hours. He was hot and thirsty, and thoroughly depressed.

It's flat-out awful, and getting worse. The whole country's burning up and ready to blow away. There aren't a dozen farmers in the whole county will make a crop this year.

He realized he was within half a mile of the Harper farm. *Might as well stop in and get a drink of water—if the well hasn't gone dry.*

Dan was right: it was getting worse. Every time things started to level off, every time there was a sign of recovery, the bottom fell out again. As George Norton had predicted, when the stock market went down, it took everything and everybody with it, solid businessmen as well as bucket-shop stock speculators. The whole country was down, way down, and there was no bottom in sight.

In the past, the underlying strength of American industry had brought the economy back onto an even keel when Wall Street panicked. *Not this time,* Dan thought as he drove along. *Consumers quit buying, so business laid off workers, who had less to spend, so even more businesses died.*

There's eight million people out of work, and a hundred thousand more losing their jobs every week.

The farmers of the Great Plains were hit even harder, because they were already deep in depression when the rest of the economy came crashing down on them. Wheat growers who sold their crop for $1.44 a bushel in 1925 got only $1.04 in 1929—and now it was down to 40 cents per bushel. Corn had been 80 cents a bushel in 1929; now it was 32 cents, and still falling.

Low prices are bad enough, but what really's breaking their backs is the drought. It hasn't really rained in two years. And that damned hot wind never seems to stop blowing, either. The ground is baked so hard that when it does rain, it runs off without soaking in. Even the buffalo grass is burning up this summer.

Under the double hammer of low prices and drought, more and more farmers were failing. On his morning drive Dan passed a lot of abandoned farmsteads, the empty houses sagging, barns and sheds silvered by sun and wind and blowing dirt.

Some of those who quit were taking the back trail, moving in with relatives in Minnesota or Iowa or Wisconsin, hoping that their children at least would have a better chance there. Others came into the towns and cities of the Dakotas, looking for any kind of work; but there was no work to be found. From the Canadian border to the Texas panhandle, small country towns were simply drying up, their businesses and banks failing as their farm customers went broke. Merchants and druggists and implement dealers moved to larger towns or to cities not so dependent on farm trade.

Dan's little car bounced over ruts as hard as iron. A large insect splattered against the windshield. *That's all we need,* he thought. *Now the grasshoppers are back.*

He looked for a patch of shade to park in but found none, so he pulled up to the side porch of the Harper house. The yard was bare and sunbaked; house and outbuildings were uniformly coated with fine brown dust. Behind the barn a windmill spun in the relentless wind.

Laura Harper came from the kitchen onto the porch.

"Why, Dan." She put her hand to her head, smoothing the gray hair. "What a surprise."

"I was out driving around and got thirsty," he said, giving his sister-in-law a hug. "I thought maybe I could beg a drink of water from you." He spoke casually but his mind was racing.

She looks awful, just like . . . just like Ma used to look when we were in Nebraska, all sunburned and wrinkled and leathery. This country still marks up women the same way it always has.

"Come inside," she said. "The house is full of dust but at least it's

[344]

out of the sun. I'll get you some water. I'm sorry I don't have any lemonade made. But at least our well's still got water in it, and it still tastes all right."

Dan suspected that the Harpers weren't buying lemons these days just on the off chance that some visitor might want lemonade. Grace's brother Charlie was better off than many farmers—the place was his, paid for, no mortgage—but he hadn't had any better luck than his neighbors in the last two or three years.

"I've been driving around, taking a look," Dan said. "Things are pretty bad."

"Seems like every day this summer has been a dirt-baker, hotter and windier than the day before. And we get so much dust! My white setting hen in the barn looks like she's brown." She filled a glass at the pump beside the sink. "There you are."

Dan drank off half the glass. "That tastes fine," he said. "Amos sure picked the right spot when he dug that well, it's been giving sweet water for sixty years."

It's a good thing Amos can't see the place today, see how Charlie's plowed up the pasture Amos kept in grass all those years. The old man knew what would work in this climate and what wouldn't. Charlie forgot what his Pa taught him, and the farm is paying the price.

"Where's Charlie?" Dan asked.

"Gone to town." Laura's voice was weary and defeated. "Took a load of steers to the stockyard. He's selling off most of the cattle. He won't get even a halfway good price, they're so scrawny, but we can't keep 'em any longer. There's nothing to feed 'em, and no pasture left."

That's just it, Dan thought. *Charlie plowed up the grass to plant more corn. The drought killed the corn, and now he doesn't have grain—nor grass either.*

He remembered to solicit family news for Grace. "How are the boys?"

"Well, Edward's all right, he went to help Charlie this morning. He'll be twenty-one this fall, he's talking about fixing up the little house for his own. It's been empty ever since Mother Lydia died."

"How about Will? Is he still in the Twin Cities?"

Laura sighed. "I really don't know. We don't hear from him hardly at all. Every two or three months, maybe, he turns up." Dan saw puzzlement as well as pain in her face. "He talks politics all the time, all that farmer-labor talk. I can't really make out what he's doing, except he's awful angry about these hard times."

Dan thought about that last remark as he drove north toward town a few minutes later. *That boy's always been angry about something. And now, every time he sees his mother's face, or his father's farm, or even if he's away and just thinks about them, he's got plenty to be angry about. . . .*

Driving through the oven heat, Dan remembered what he had seen in Laura Harper's face.

... Because his mother looks just the way my mother did. And his father's farm's burning up.

Just like my father's did.

Sixty years and not a damned thing's different.

Dan realized he was gripping the steering wheel of his car so hard that his knuckles were white.

Old George Norton really kept them going. The crash jarred him out of the apathy which had held him since his wife's death; now, at seventy-three, he came back to the newspaper as if he were thirty years younger.

To signal his return he revived a favorite aphorism. He had the composing-room foreman set it in two-inch type and pull enough proofs so he could tack one up in every office in the building:

THINGS DON'T JUST HAPPEN,
SOMEONE MAKES THEM HAPPEN.

Then the old man went from room to room, day after day, pestering people to "make things happen." He drafted Dan as his partner in this exercise, and soon the two of them were setting the pace for the rest of the staff, bringing the lessons they had learned in earlier crises to bear on this one.

Dan was particularly surprised by one aspect of George's return to active duty.

"He's managed to get involved without stepping on your brother's toes," he told Margaret. "Ten years ago I'd never have believed that."

Margaret chuckled. "Neither would I, but you're right. And he hasn't even tried to tell *me* how to do my job. I think he's really worried that everything he's built here could go down the drain."

Certainly there were plenty of bad omens. Advertising was way off; merchants were doing little or no business, or actually going out of business. Meanwhile a growing number of readers were deciding they could no longer afford to take the paper.

At George's suggestion, Harry told his circulation and advertising people to revive the old hard-times practice of "trading out" ads and subscriptions for usable goods. They took eggs, vegetables, corn or oats, garden truck from farm subscribers, goods or due bills from advertisers. Some of this barter was used in the business or shared out among employees, but a good deal of the food wound up in the homes of Falls City folk who were destitute. Dan often dropped off a sack of cornmeal or a bag of potatoes where he knew it was needed.

Harry welcomed his father's return. He turned over to him the job

[346]

of controlling costs, something George was very good at. Soon he was checking every bill just as he had forty years earlier, and once again none could be paid without his initials. Harry managed to avoid laying off any full-time employees, but for the first time since George bought the paper they went three years without adding to the staff.

They actually increased their circulation. No one could quite explain that, though constant pressure from the Nortons, father and son, had a lot to do with it. No one, not even newspaper delivery boys, could afford to lose a job in those days.

Still it was a near thing, and Harry Norton often wondered if they could stay in the black. One night he told his wife that he sometimes wondered if they'd survive.

Her answer took him by surprise.

"I've got a fair amount of money of my own," she said. "I listened to your father in 1929 and got my own money out of the market. I'd be glad to put some of it into the paper if that would help."

"You never told me you were selling your stocks."

"I didn't think what I did with my money was any concern of yours, darling." Alice softened the remark with a quick smile. "But if the paper's in real trouble, that's different."

Harry looked at his wife for perhaps half a minute, and when he responded his words were as surprising to her as hers had been to him.

"That's very good of you, Alice. I really appreciate it. But hold onto your money. We might want to buy another newspaper in a year or two, and it might come in handy."

Alice was astounded. Here was her usually cautious husband, in the middle of the worst depression ever, talking about buying another newspaper. Then she understood: he was his father's son, willing to take a chance, to gamble, to swim against the current, if he thought something was a good bet.

"That sounds very interesting, Harry." Her quick glance fixed on him. "Do you have something specific in mind?"

He hesitated, peering at her through his thick eyeglasses.

"Come on, dear," she persisted. "If you want me as an investor you'll have to provide a prospectus."

Harry Norton would not be pushed, even by his wife. "I've been looking around, quietly, but I haven't seen anything yet that looks quite right. It's too soon, anyway; Father would have a fit if I suggested it now."

Alice could add two and two. "That's why you've made all those trips to Minneapolis."

Harry smiled and barely nodded, but said nothing. Alice looked at him, dark eyes dancing wickedly.

"You really ought to tell me these things sooner. You've been to

Minneapolis so many times this year that I'd begun to wonder if you were keeping a mistress up there."

But beneath the banter her mind was racing. *Minneapolis would be nice, I'd like that. And Harry would, too. I do believe he's as frustrated as I am by this little place.* The thought cheered her, and she spoke briskly.

"Harry, I think I'd like a drink before dinner. Is there anything left of that bootleg Scotch you brought back from your last Minneapolis trip?"

The summer produced one happy surprise. For years Margaret Norton had devoted herself entirely to her work, and she seemed completely the career woman. Then, at thirty-two, she fell in love. Alexander Campbell was a local lawyer whose wife had died several years earlier of cancer. Margaret got to know him when he was hired to represent the paper. They began to see each other outside the office; acquaintance became friendship, which ripened into a love affair. They were discreet enough so that when they announced their marriage in July, nearly everybody who knew them was flabbergasted.

"The nicest thing about it," Margaret told Alice, "is that Alex doesn't feel threatened by my money or by me."

"The nicest thing about it," Alice retorted, "is that you fell in love with a man strong enough to make you want to be gentle."

August 1931

Will Harper looked tired, but his voice was vigorous—and, as usual, angry.

"The whole country's dying, and the government's just watching it go down, not doing anything. What does Hoover think he's running—a Sunday-school picnic?"

By now Dan and Grace were used to having their nephew appear at the kitchen door in the middle of the night. He never said where he had been or where he was going; they had learned never to ask.

Now, as Grace moved quietly around her kitchen, slicing meat and bread for a sandwich, Dan answered the young man across the kitchen table.

"Things *are* getting worse," Dan agreed. "I was out in the country last week, and it looks like nobody's going to make a crop. By the way, I stopped at your family's place. I think your mother would give about anything to see you."

Will shook his head.

"I can't go there. I can't stand to see the place with Grandpa's pastures all plowed up and ready to blow away. Pa looks like death warmed over. He's beat, finished, just waiting to die. And Ma!" He slammed his hand down on the table. "She looks a thousand years old!"

"I've seen her." Dan spoke quietly, as if to calm Will by example.

[348]

"Still, they'd like to see you. They love you and they worry about you."

Again the thin, tired man shook his head. This time he spoke so softly that Dan had to strain to hear him.

"I love them, too. That's why I'm not going out there if I can't do anything to help." His voice grew louder, harsher. "It makes me so mad I can hardly talk, and then I say things they don't understand, things that upset them."

Grace put the plate of food down in front of him. Then she stood behind him, her hands on his shoulders, kneading the taut muscles. "Oh, Will, why don't you come home, just for a little while. It'd mean so much to them, and it—"

"Aunt Grace." Again he spoke softly, but this time there was an iron finality in his voice. "There's no use talking about it. My work takes me other places. If I go home I'll have to leave again anyway, and it'll be worse than if I stay away. And there's nothing can be done for the farm now. It's finished, ruined. Done for."

"What work are you talking about?"

Will Harper wouldn't have answered if it had been Dan who asked, but he couldn't refuse his aunt.

"We know that farmers want to stand up to the Wall Street bankers and the exploiting classes." The weary figure straightened and seemed to take on new energy. "But they don't know how. We're going to organize to stop the bankers and the crooked judges and sheriffs who try to sell farms out from under their owners."

"How can you stop those sales?" Grace asked. "They're all according to the law."

"The law!" Will Harper scoffed. "The law of the jungle, that's the only law those bloodsuckers believe in. We follow a higher law, and we work to unite all the laboring classes, to unite workers and farmers against the exploiters."

Dan knew what Will Harper was talking about. He had recently begun to hear of incidents—most in Iowa, a few in Minnesota and the Dakotas—in which crowds of farmers had prevented the auctioning of the land or machinery of bankrupt neighbors. And there was talk of concerted action to stop the shipment of farm products to city markets unless prices were increased.

"Is it what that fellow Milo Reno down in Iowa has been talking up?" Dan asked. "That farm holiday idea?"

"That's as may be," Will said. "But Reno's all talk. We're going to . . ." He stopped abruptly. "Better not say. You'd have to put it in the paper, Uncle Dan."

He finished his sandwich and stood up.

"Time to go. I've got a train to catch."

"Can't we at least drive you to the station?" Grace asked.

[349]

Will laughed. "The trains I ride don't leave from stations, Aunt Grace." He seemed vastly amused. "I'd better go alone. Then if the sheriff asks, you won't know which way I went."

He shook hands with Dan, then wrapped Grace in a sudden, almost desperate embrace. "Thanks for—for everything," he whispered. "Tell Ma I love her."

He picked up his small suitcase, slung his blanket roll over his shoulder, and was gone into the summer night.

"I'm not sure what he's up to," Dan said. "Sounds to me like he's in with the Farmer-Labor people for sure. And he talks like the Communists."

Grace remembered what Will had told her four years earlier, and how he had ended: *You're the only one I've talked to.* Now she merely shrugged. "Whatever, it sounds dangerous."

"Yes." Dan rubbed his hand through his cowlick. "If they keep trying to stop foreclosure sales, they're likely to run into state police or the National Guard sooner or later. Then people are going to get hurt."

Chapter 52

Chicago, July 2, 1932

RANKLIN D. ROOSEVELT came through the doorway at the back of the platform. He wore a blue suit with a red rose pinned to its lapel. Instead of waving—his hands were occupied with his canes—he threw his head back and smiled. The klieg lights reflected off his pince-nez glasses as he looked around the crowded hall.

He came to the podium slowly, leaning on his son's arm. As he moved forward the applause grew, crested, and grew again. Scattered boos from diehard Al Smith supporters were quickly drowned out by cheers. The band blared out the new Roosevelt campaign song, "Happy Days Are Here Again." Again the nominee tossed his head back, unleashing a smile so wide it was almost a grimace.

Finally the crowd quieted. Roosevelt arranged the pages of his speech, adjusted his glasses, looked around the hall, and began. Greeting the delegates as "my friends," he began by referring to his break with tradition in making a personal appearance before the convention.

> Let it be from now on the task of our party to break foolish traditions. We will leave it to the Republican leadership, far more skilled in that art, to break promises.

The crowd guffawed and cheered.

"He knows how to make a speech, doesn't he?" Dan leaned close to Harry Norton, next to him in the press section. "He's got a rhythm that kind of takes hold of you."

Roosevelt adopted an earnest schoolteacher's tone as he moved into the body of his speech.

> A resentment against the failure of Republican leadership may degenerate into unreasoning radicalism. To meet by reaction that

danger of radicalism is to invite disaster. Reaction is no barrier to the radical. It is a challenge, a provocation. The way to meet that danger is to offer a workable program of reconstruction.

That's just what his cousin Teddy said thirty years ago, Dan thought. He leaned over again. "That's for people like you, Harry. Sensible Republicans. He's trying to convince you he's no bomb thrower."

Harry smiled and put his mouth to Dan's ear. "I don't know if he's trying to scare me—or soothe me. What I want to know is whether he's competent."

Now Roosevelt was talking about farmers' problems. His words set Dan to scribbling furiously.

> The practical way to help the farmer is by an arrangement that will, in addition to lightening some of the impoverishing burdens from his back, do something toward the reduction of the surpluses of staple commodities that hang on the market . . . and in exchange for this immediately increased return I am sure that the farmers of this nation would agree ultimately to such planning of their production as would reduce the surpluses.

Roosevelt, his voice rising and falling in a steady cadence, called for refinancing of farm mortgages and other "immediate emergency measures" to help farmers. He promised to be guided by "whatever the responsible farm groups themselves agree on."

No presidential candidate has ever talked that way. Dan was amazed. *He's promising emergency help, direct from Uncle Sam, in return for controls on production. And he's going to let them write their own program.*

> One-half of our population, over fifty million people, are dependent on agriculture; and, my friends, if those fifty million people have no money, no cash, to buy what is produced in the city, the city suffers to an equal or greater extent. . . . The purchasing power of that half of our population dependent on agriculture is gone.

Dan felt like cheering. *By God, he's talking sense. I never thought I'd hear an Easterner say things like that. Let alone a presidential candidate. Why, he sounds like Bryan or LaFollette. Or Amos.*

> Republican leaders tell us economic laws—sacred, inviolable, unchangeable—cause panics which no one could prevent. But while they prate of economic laws, men and women are starving. We must lay hold of the fact that economic laws are not made by nature. They are made by human beings.

Roosevelt grasped the podium with both hands and threw back his head again as he finished by promising "a new deal for the American people." When the thunderstorm of applause faded, Harry Norton turned to Dan.

"You're quite right," he said. "He's one hell of a speaker. He almost makes you think he could actually do something about this depression."

"At least he makes you think he'd try." Dan got in his reply before the band struck up again. "He called it a 'new deal.' Not a bad line, is it?"

Falls City, August 1932

Roosevelt's words won him the support of a great many farmers. But for some, words no longer sufficed in that long, despairing summer of 1932.

Groups of grim, silent farmers in work clothes began to turn up at bankruptcy sales, surrounding the men who came from town to bid on land or machinery.

"And if the sheriff goes to a sale to protect the auctioneer and the bidders, he may see a shotgun or two—not pointed at him, of course, just there—and he'll generally decide to go back to town."

Dan was explaining the new phenomenon to Harry Norton.

"Sometimes they let them start the sale, then one of the farmers will bid ten cents, and he and his friends stare down anyone who tries to put in a real bid on the place. So the farm is knocked down for a dime, and the farmer gets it back from his friends."

The publisher was definitely not pleased. "Well, that's a good start down the road to anarchy."

"They don't do anything against the law, they just stand there and watch, and they have a right to bid." Dan grinned. "They say they can't help it if those mortgage company agents from town don't feel like they're welcome."

"I hear they've started sending mobs into courtrooms, too."

"I wouldn't call it a mob when a bunch of farmers, clean and neat, comes into a courtroom to learn how the judicial system works." Dan obviously admired the farmers' ingenious tactics. "And they're orderly, they keep still."

"But they only go to courtrooms when a judge is hearing motions to order farms sold for delinquency on payments." Harry was not amused. "It's plain intimidation."

"Of course it is." Dan was serious now. "And I think there's rougher times coming. There's a lot of talk about a farm holiday."

"What's that?"

"Some fellows are talking about stopping shipments to city markets and creameries and packing plants. I hear little bunches of men have already been turning up at intersections on some of the main country roads. Now they're just watching, keeping track of trucks, but I think pretty soon they'll try to stop 'em."

"If they do that, there'll be people hurt."

Both Dan and Harry turned out to be right. In mid-August bands of militant farmers began stopping trucks and turning them back, returning hogs or cattle to the farm from which they had come, pouring milk out onto roads or into ditches.

Some drivers tried to force their way through the blockades. Soon nail-studded boards were puncturing the tires of such trucks, and some drivers were beaten. Police and sheriff's deputies were called out to convoy trucks; here and there they used tear gas on the blockading farmers. Drivers began carrying weapons. So did pickets. There was gunfire; inevitably, people got shot; inexorably the situation hardened and became more violent.

The three men from the *Dakota News* parked two blocks away and walked along the fence toward the main gate of the Meyers Packing Company. Behind the fence, livestock pens normally full of hogs stood empty on this August morning.

Dan Woods and the reporter stopped and waited while the photographer climbed up on the fence to get a shot of the vacant yards. Then they continued toward the gate, where men in overalls and work shirts stood or sat in little groups. Dan counted quickly: there were about thirty-five of them. Beside the gate, a tarpaulin had been stretched over poles to provide some shade. Two long planks, studded with spikes, were propped against the fence, ready to be thrown down to puncture the tires of any would-be blockade runner.

The pickets had been there for five days, and in that time no livestock had entered the Meyers yards. Dan had written editorials appealing for peaceful resolution of the Meyers blockade, and this morning he had decided he needed to see for himself—and to talk firsthand with the men who had shut down Falls City's biggest employer. So he rode over with the reporter and photographer assigned to cover the blockade.

Five men detached themselves from the group of pickets and came toward the newspapermen. When they got close, one of them spoke.

"Looking for someone?"

It was not so much a question as a challenge, and Dan suddenly felt cold despite the morning's heat. But he introduced himself and his companions. The photographer was already at work, snapping pictures of the men lounging around the gate.

"Say, Bo, we don't want no pictures taken 'round here." The picket's voice was edgy. "They might wind up in the sheriff's office." The photographer said nothing; he glanced at the man, shrugged, and took another picture.

The picket reached out and knocked the camera to the ground, then swung his fist at the photographer. Dan jumped forward to intervene; the next thing he knew someone pulled his jacket over his head, pinning his

[354]

arms, and a blow to his stomach drove the air from his lungs. As he struggled to draw breath, another punch knocked him to the ground.

He grunted in pain as a heavy work shoe slammed into his ribs, and he curled up instinctively, expecting another kick even as he struggled to get untangled from his jacket. But there was no second blow; instead there came a shout, followed by curses and the sounds of a scuffle. Dan was gasping for breath and his vision was blurred, but he realized someone was standing over him protectively.

"Touch him again and I'll kill you." Dan was too dazed to tell who it was.

"That old man is the only editor in South Dakota who understands what's happened to farmers," Dan's rescuer raged, his voice distorted with anger. "And how many times do I have to tell you chumps not to give them an excuse by starting a fight? If there was a cop here you'd be on the way to jail by now."

Dan thought he knew that voice, but by the time he sat up and shook his head clear, the man who had stopped the beating was nowhere to be seen. The attacking pickets had withdrawn to join their fellows at the gate. Dan and his colleagues limped back to their car and drove away.

He was sitting in the kitchen that night, trying to ignore the pain from his bandaged rib.

"It was bound to happen," he told Grace. "The weather's been terrible for five years, the land is blowing away, and the farmers can't do anything about it. The politicians ignore them and lie to them and double-cross them, and they can't seem to do anything about that, either. So finally they give up on politics and take things into their own hands, and they get violent."

"And they hurt people who are their friends," Grace retorted. She had been badly frightened by Dan's misadventure, and now the fright had turned to fury.

"Farmers are the last people you'd expect to do that kind of thing," Dan said. "It shows you how far they've been pushed. God only knows what'll happen if Roosevelt doesn't win and do something fast."

There was a knock at the back door. Grace opened it and Will Harper slipped in.

"I'm on my way out of town, I just wanted to be sure you were O.K."

Of course, Dan thought. *I should have known that voice, even if I was knocked for a loop.*

"Oh, I'm doing pretty well." He managed a grin. "For an 'old man.'"

"I'm sorry about this morning. I should have got there quicker." Will seemed more gaunt, more intense than ever. "I try to teach them not to use violence, but they're so desperate now that even the quiet ones some-

[355]

times go berserk. And there's some bad apples getting into the movement, too. You can't keep them all out."

"Well, thanks for rescuing me, anyway," Dan said. "Next time I go over to the east side I'll take a couple of our truck drivers with me."

Will seemed jumpy and said he had to leave, but when Grace offered him something to eat he accepted instantly. She cut thick chunks from a leftover pork roast, sliced and buttered some bread, and fried three eggs. Dan questioned him as he wolfed down the food.

"Will, let me ask you what I was about to ask those fellows this morning when I was . . . interrupted." He shifted to ease his bruises. "Do you really think these blockades will do any good?"

"I don't know, Uncle Dan." Will sighed. "But nothing else has worked, so it's time to try this. At least it makes people aware of the struggle. And the politicians have no ideas."

"Don't you think Roosevelt is talking sense?"

Will's intense eyes were cold with contempt. "You may still think the old political system can work. Well, it works for the plutocrats, but not for anyone else. Roosevelt is no different from the rest of the bloodsuckers—a rich Easterner, a Harvard boy with a bunch of Wall Street bankers for friends."

"But why do you think revolution is the answer?"

Will used a piece of bread to sop up the last of the egg. "It's the *only* answer."

Dan shook his head. "I just can't agree. It'll destroy the country."

Contempt edged the younger man's voice. "So what? The country's coming apart anyway."

Grace sat down beside Will and put her hand on his arm. "Have you seen your father and mother?"

"No." He bit off the word. Then, looking at her, he softened his voice. "The trouble is, Pa and I don't have anything to say to each other. At least nothing that I could repeat to you, Aunt Grace."

Then, remembering his last visit, he smiled as he stood up. "I've got a train to catch."

He embraced her, and again was gone into the steamy summer night.

Franklin Roosevelt campaigned hard. He was met almost everywhere by big and enthusiastic crowds as he preached his "New Deal" and promised action to stop the economic slide. President Hoover also attracted large audiences—but little enthusiasm, particularly in the farm belt, where men stood silent and hostile as he drove past them on his way to speaking engagements.

At the *Dakota News* the proprietors were divided. George, predisposed to support any Republican, thought Roosevelt was not only misguided but dangerous with his talk of new federal programs. Harry was impressed by Roosevelt's personality and energy—and by his promises, however vague, to act, to do *something*—but he was a Republican by habit, and moreover he knew and liked Hoover. As for Margaret, she had no doubt: Roosevelt might be an unknown quantity, but Hoover wasn't. He had failed, and the country should turn him out.

All three sought Dan's help in persuading the others to their position. He refused to get involved in the debate.

"They're going to wind up endorsing Hoover," he told Grace, "and there's no way on earth that I'm going to agree with that. I'm for Roosevelt. So I might as well stay clear away from their argument."

"That'll be three out of the last four elections you've supported the Democrat." Grace could still put on that mock-innocent look. "Do you think maybe you're not a Republican any more?"

Dan smiled ruefully. "I guess it may be time to change the label. Let's say I'm an independent."

"And you're tired of backing losers."

"I'm tired of the loser we've *got*. At least Roosevelt sounds like he'll do something."

"You don't have to persuade me." Grace could still giggle, too. "And I promise not to tell anyone that you've turned into a Democrat like your wife."

Dan turned out to be right. Harry cast the deciding vote for Hoover, and the *Dakota News* once again endorsed a Republican. But the closing paragraphs of Harry's editorial reflected the family disagreement:

> It can be argued that President Hoover has not yet found answers to the nation's economic problems. But we believe he is better qualified than Franklin D. Roosevelt.
>
> Mr. Roosevelt says he will take decisive action to aid the national economy. He is vague about what he would do, but it is clear he would enlarge the role of the federal government and seek new powers to intervene in state and local affairs. That is precisely the wrong way to go.
>
> As for experience, one need only recall the judgment of the writer Walter Lippmann that Mr. Roosevelt is "a pleasant man who, without any important qualifications for the office, would like very much to be President."
>
> The Dakota News believes that is not a sufficient reason to make a man President, and so favors the re-election of President Hoover.

Margaret marched into Dan's office the day the editorial was published. "I certainly hope you don't agree with that . . . that slop my dear brother put in *your* paper this morning."

Dan ignored the implied criticism. "As a matter of fact, I don't agree," he said. "I'll make that clear Sunday."

"Good for you. Just don't be namby-pamby."

"I won't be," Dan replied. He chuckled. "It's easier for me than it was for Harry. In my case, there are no doubts—and no division of opinion."

George Norton came in a few minutes after Margaret had left.

"I presume that you plan to disagree with our endorsement."

"Yes, sir, in the Sunday paper." Dan waved him toward a chair. "You'd be disappointed if I didn't."

George sat down. "I'd be surprised, but hardly disappointed. In fact I'd be delighted." He smiled briefly. "I could use some support. When it comes to politics, my children won't take my advice."

Dan tapped the paper on his desk. "They did on this one."

"Yes, but I think it's the last time." The old man seemed to shrink a little inside his buttoned-up jacket and high stiff collar. "I wouldn't have had my way this time except that Harry happens to know Hoover, and likes him personally."

"I suspect you're right. Harry was very impressed with Roosevelt's speech at the Chicago convention." Dan laughed. "So was I. He reminded me of Teddy."

"You never did understand what a fraud Teddy was." George shook his head in mock amazement as he stood to leave. "I'm afraid this cousin of his is even worse."

Dan, watching him walk stiff-legged down the hall, recalled how thirty years earlier George had let him endorse Theodore Roosevelt instead of Taft.

You were always more practical than you'd admit, George, and generally right, too. And you're right this time: your children are in charge now, and you—and I—are just about done.

Dan turned to his typewriter. *But not quite. Not until I get through telling people why they should vote for Teddy's cousin.*

On election day, they did vote for Teddy's cousin, in South Dakota and nearly everywhere else. Hoover carried six states, all in the Northeast. Roosevelt carried the rest, including every farm state.

The day after the election Harry Norton wrote another editorial. It was short:

> The people have spoken, and the message is clear. We accept the verdict so decisively given, we congratulate Governor Roosevelt, and we wish the new President a most successful administration.

He's as practical as his father, Dan thought, reading the little editorial. *And he's a whole lot more diplomatic, congratulating all those readers who ignored his advice.*

Two days later, just before noon on Armistice Day, a choking black cloud of dust rolled in from the west. There had been almost no rain for three years, and at last the country was really beginning to blow away.

Chapter 53

Washington, D.C., March 4, 1933

DAN WAS awakened by the ringing of the telephone in his hotel room.

"Dan Woods? This is Sam Rayburn." The flat Texas voice brought him wide awake. "I just got home. The doorman gave me the message. You *did* say to call no matter how late it was, didn't you?"

"Yes, I did." Dan glanced at his watch. It was 2:43 A.M. "Thank you, Mr. Chairman."

"Any sane man would be asleep. What do you want?"

Dan had not planned to do any spot-news reporting on this trip. He had come to Washington to see Roosevelt inaugurated, and to talk with old friends like George Norris and Sam Rayburn about the new administration.

But on the day before the inauguration, Washington was seething with rumors that Roosevelt's first official act would be to close every bank in the country to halt withdrawals and prevent the collapse of the entire financial system. Dan knew that Rayburn, as chairman of the House Commerce Committee, would be informed in advance of any such action, and his reporter's reflexes took over.

"I'm working on a story for tomorrow's—today's—paper, and I thought you could help me."

"Go ahead."

"I hear Roosevelt is going to declare a national bank holiday."

Rayburn hesitated just long enough for Dan to notice. "If he was, and I knew it, I couldn't say."

"Look, Mr. Chairman—"

"Sam to you."

"Look, Sam, I won't put your name in the paper. I just want you to tell me if I'm wrong."

There was another pause, longer this time. "I've been at the May-flower all evening." Dan knew what that meant: Roosevelt's preinaugural headquarters were at the Mayflower Hotel. "Governor Lehman is going to close the New York banks in about an hour. They expect Illinois to do the same, and maybe others."

"And then Roosevelt will close *all* the banks as soon as he's sworn in."

"You're saying that, not me."

"Does it sound right to you?"

Again a pause. "Not the timing. There'll be a cabinet meeting Sunday."

That's all he's going to say, Dan thought, *but it's all I need: Roosevelt will proclaim a national bank holiday, but not until Sunday afternoon. Now, let's just make sure.*

"You wouldn't let a farm boy make a fool of himself."

Rayburn chuckled. "No, I wouldn't."

It was confirmation enough for Dan. "Thank you, Sam. I'll come by your office Monday, if you'd have a little time then."

"Do that."

There was a click, and Rayburn was gone. Dan went into the bath-room and splashed cold water on his face. *If I put my mind to it, I can dictate this story before I go to bed.*

He winked at the face in the mirror.

Not too bad—for an old man.

Falls City, April 1933

By the time Dan left for home a week later, he had made up his mind: the *Dakota News* needed its own man in Washington, at least for the first few months of the new administration. There was no other way to get the kind of news he knew they would need—especially farm news.

"I know you think we can't afford it," he told Harry Norton. "But we can't afford *not* to do it, either."

"Why?" The publisher was skeptical.

"Because this depression is a long way from being over, and if we want to survive, readers are going to have to think we're essential. That means we have to print the news that affects their livelihood, and these days that kind of news is coming from Washington."

"Do we have to do it now? Can't it wait a while?"

"Not if we want to hold onto our country circulation."

Harry stared through his big round glasses. "We certainly want to do that."

"There's going to be more farm legislation passed in the next six months than in the whole history of the Republic," Dan said. "It's going to affect everyone in this state, one way or another. We need someone reporting that story who knows our people and what's important to them."

"Who would you hire to do it?"

"I wouldn't. We already have the right man: Dick Lawson." Richard Lawson had attracted attention as the paper's student stringer at the state university; he did so well in a summer tryout that he won a job as a full-time reporter. Now, after five years of reporting—including a lot of farm news—he had just been named city editor.

"He's a first-rate reporter, he understands farmers and their problems, and he's the kind of man who can handle Washington."

Harry frowned. "Margaret would have a fit. You'd be stealing her new city editor—and the best newspaperman in the shop."

"We need the best, because there'll be no time to learn; he'll have to go full speed from the first day. Anyway, it might only be temporary."

Harry shook his head. "No, you're wrong there. If you send Lawson to Washington he'll love it. You'll never get him back. You'd be lucky not to lose him there."

"Harry, we have to do this. Let me talk to Margaret."

Margaret Norton complained, but she agreed to give up Lawson, and Harry approved the transfer after getting some unexpected advice from his father.

"South Dakota's not being run out of the statehouse any more," the old man said. "It's being run out of Washington. We need to be there, even if it's expensive." He shook a finger at his son. "But don't forget to promote our 'exclusive' coverage; it'll sell papers."

Grace looked at her husband that night.

"You wish you were going."

"It's a job for a young man with strong legs. My legs might pass, but I fail the age test." His explanation, she thought, was not a denial.

"You wouldn't like it as a permanent thing," she suggested. "You like to go down there for a week or so. But you're like me: you belong here."

She's right, as usual, Dan mused. *I'm not a farm boy, but I'm a country boy and always will be, I guess.*

Still, it's a hell of a story and I'd love to cover it.

Grace could have been reading his mind. "You can still go to Washington the way you always have," she said. "You've got sources that young man will never catch up with."

That young man did pretty well. Lawson's first big story reported the Roosevelt administration's still-unannounced decision to propose price supports for wheat, corn, and other basic farm commodities. In the following weeks he filed other exclusive stories on the emergency farm programs being developed in Washington.

For his part, Dan continued to play an active day-to-day role, partly to help fill the gap left by Lawson's departure from the city desk, and partly because he couldn't resist involving himself in the rush of news that marked Roosevelt's first months in office.

Dan occasionally complained that he was tired, but Grace wouldn't hear of it.

"Quit complaining," she said. "You don't really mean it. Besides, you look better than you have in months."

Falls City, October 1933

If business was good for those who reported farm news, it was still terrible for farmers themselves. Franklin Roosevelt had lifted their spirits with his inaugural address, and emergency legislation stemmed the hemorrhage of farm mortgage foreclosures; but farmers simply could not earn enough to pay down their mortgages, even at lower interest rates. The problems remained, unchanged and intractable.

Dan was trying to sort out the situation as he returned to the office from lunch on a Saturday in October.

Until the farmers have money to spend, he thought, *business in South Dakota isn't going to get much better.*

He looked around as he walked down Union Avenue toward the *Dakota News* building. There was little of the hustle and bustle which for years had enlivened the downtown on Saturday afternoons. *This street used to be full up on a day like this, the farmers all in town to shop or take in a movie or buy the kids an ice-cream soda.*

But now you could shoot a cannon down the sidewalk and not hurt more than one or two people—and they wouldn't be buying anything, just window-shopping, looking at stuff they can't afford.

Dan thought the downtown looked particularly drab that day. The dust had been blowing all week, and the usually varied red brick and gray stone hues of the business blocks had merged into a uniform dull brown.

People walk around as if they had nothing to do and nowhere to go, Dan thought. *Well, that's the way it is for most of 'em.*

Those who had come to town mostly just stood around and talked. Groups of men in overalls hunkered down on street corners or sat in cafés, nursing a nickel's worth of coffee and swapping stories about the drought—and the dust.

The storm of the previous November had been only a harbinger. Now, with the drought worse than ever, South Dakota was really blowing away. In the fall of 1933 one storm followed another, the horizon darkening, black clouds rolling in from the west, housewives hurrying to close windows in what they knew was a vain attempt to keep the dust out of their homes. Drivers turned on their headlights, but they still could see only a few feet. Afterward an inch or two of topsoil, fine as powdered sugar, would be layered over everything.

Black humor was the fashion. Dan stopped to chat with a group of farmers sitting in the shade of a store awning, and one of them gestured at his neighbor. "We're real close, we're connected," he said. "The wind blows my dirt on his place all winter and it blows his dirt on my place all summer."

But jokes could not alter reality.

It's going to take time, Dan thought, *a lot of time. And even with time, there's no guarantee it'll get better.*

If only it would rain.

Chapter 54

EVEN AS he guided the *Dakota News* through the worst of the depression, Harry Norton was thinking of other places and of time yet
to come. Like his father forty years earlier, he was planning for the
day after tomorrow at a time when most people could hardly deal with
today.

For a long time—ever since he went East to school—his interests had
been national and international, not local or regional. His months in France
during and after the war had been a kind of epiphany; after that, he
traveled abroad nearly every year, and had even visited Russia and China
in the late twenties. Now he was looking for a newspaper in a city whose
people would share his interests and would read the kind of paper he
wanted to publish. It had to be a good-sized city with ties to the world
beyond. The paper itself had to be one he could remake to his own design,
so he could make his own reputation as a publisher.

The search took him down many dead-end streets before it eventually led him, in late 1934, to the *Minneapolis Telegram,* a faltering evening
paper whose owners were ready to sell out. It seemed the right kind of city
and the right kind of paper, one that had nowhere to go but up and could
be had for a very reasonable price.

George Norton, still active in the business at seventy-six, was skeptical.

"Everyone knows that newspaper is on its last legs," he grumbled. "It
has no Sunday edition, no country circulation, and no department store
advertising. And the other papers are stronger."

George added that he certainly would oppose tapping the cash reserves of the *Dakota News.* He reminded his son that the money was there
only because of his own cautious and conservative management, and that

it had enabled them to ride out the crash. Now, he said, they should hold onto it: "Never spend your last dollar."

"I don't want to spend your last dollar," Harry said. "I want to make an investment. *You* want to keep the money under the mattress."

"No, I do not," George retorted tartly. "I just don't want to throw it out the window."

When Margaret supported Harry, George declared it was merely because she wanted to take over the *Dakota News*. She ignored the gibe and went right on.

"Father, we have to face facts. Falls City has probably seen its best days. It will always be the biggest city in South Dakota, and we can keep on making a good profit here, thanks to what you've built. But the economy of this state is a shambles, and we can't depend on it for growth. If we want to build for the future—for the next generation of the family—we need to be in a bigger place, too, and Minneapolis looks like the best bigger place to go."

She hesitated a moment. "And you're right. I do want to run this paper."

The Norton children got support from a couple of other sources. One was Alice, who went to see her father-in-law on a January afternoon. Sitting in George's study as the midwinter sun slanted almost horizontally through the windows, Alice poured tea for the two of them.

"I want your advice," she began. "I'm considering putting some of my own money into this paper that Harry wants to buy in Minneapolis. What do you think about it?"

"Huh." The old man sounded surprised that she had money of her own. "I think it's a gamble."

"Of course," Alice said. "But is it a good gamble?"

George hesitated. "I'm not sure. It would depend on how good a job Harry did."

"Well, if *that's* the test, I'll put my money in." Alice's tone was confident. "I know he'd do a first-rate job. It would really test him, and he'd grow and stretch to handle it."

"There are a lot of risks. Can't he grow and stretch right here?"

"No, he can't. He needs a larger stage." She was dead earnest. "What he really cares about is world affairs, and he needs to have a bigger paper in a bigger place to deal with them. If he stays here, he'll go stale and dry up. And you don't want that any more than I do."

"No, of course not. But—"

Alice went right on. "Besides, you have Margaret here, ready to take over. She's married, she's happily settled down, she *won't* want to leave—and she could run this paper just as well as Harry."

"Maybe better. I was wrong about her before." The old man spoke as if talking to himself. "But what Harry wants to do is awfully risky."

"You've taken some pretty big risks yourself."

George stared hard at her.

The next morning he walked into Dan's office. As usual he wasted no time in small talk. "Tell me what you think of this Minneapolis business."

Dan knew all about the family disagreement, because Harry and Margaret had consulted him. He answered George exactly as he had answered them.

"I think it's the Norton family's money, and none of you need advice from me on how to spend it."

"Nonsense," George snapped. "If I didn't need advice, I wouldn't ask for it. Don't duck the question."

"Well, it's chancy." Dan leaned back in his chair. "But you know, George, it's exactly what you did during the Panic in the nineties. You invested a lot of money, almost all you had, when things were really bad, so we'd be able to break out when things got better and bury the opposition. It was risky, but it worked."

"This is a lot more money, and it's a lot riskier."

"What you put in then was about all you had. And if you don't think it was just as risky back then, you've got a bad memory."

Three days later, George called Harry into his office. He asked a great many specific and detailed questions about his proposed Minneapolis venture. Harry had answers for all of them. George made no commitment that day, but after another week—and a number of telephone calls to business acquaintances in Minneapolis—he told Harry he'd go along with the purchase.

"Remember, we're not going to take a penny more than we have to from this place," he warned. "You've got to use your own money first." He didn't mention Alice's promised investment. "And we can borrow at pretty good rates."

"I know, Father," Harry said. "Every tub on its own bottom, and you should never spend your last dollar."

The deal was closed in early April, and Harry moved to Minneapolis at once. Alice and the children (there were now two boys and a girl) would follow as soon as school ended and a proper house could be found.

"I don't want anyone to be able to say we're absentee owners," Harry told her. "How long will it take you to get ready to move?"

"I'm ready now," Alice said. To herself, she added: *Darling, I've been ready for longer than you'll ever know.*

Dan felt left out. "I know it's silly, but I feel as if Harry has . . . well . . . kind of deserted me," he told Grace. "I broke him in, trained him more or less, and now he's leaving me behind."

Grace knew what was really bothering Dan: *he wanted Harry to ask him to be his editor in Minneapolis, and he didn't, and it makes him feel old and useless.* She addressed the unspoken desire.

"If he'd dragged you up there with him, in two weeks you'd have been unhappy. You'd be reinventing the wheel. You've already been editor of a newspaper."

Dan thought about it, then tacitly conceded the point by shifting the subject slightly.

"I think Alice persuaded him to go."

"No, she had absolutely nothing to do with it." Grace was emphatic. "Oh, she complains about the weather. But he's been headed away from here for a long time—ever since he was a little boy and went East to school."

"But he came back after the war."

"He had to learn the business, and this was the obvious place. Besides, when James got killed, Harry had no choice. But then Margaret turned out so well, he decided he could leave after all."

"You may be right," Dan conceded.

"Of course I am. What's more, you had a lot to do with it. You're the one who told George to send Harry away to school, and you're the one who straightened Margaret out."

She laid her hand on his arm. "Besides, you belong here, and you know it."

In fact he had already reached the same conclusion, despite the bruises on his self-esteem.

Whatever I am today, he decided, *I am because I started in that sod hut and have lived on these plains for sixty-seven years. This country, this land, this town, they made me.*

The land is hard and it never forgives, but it nourished me. It shaped me, just like it shapes everyone who lives here, for good or ill.

It shaped George and Amos, and they succeeded.

It shaped Pa and Charlie Harper, and they failed.

It shaped Ma and Grace, and they survived.

At the beginning, there was just the land. Now the land is still here, but there's people and farms and cities. I've had a little part in making that happen.

The land put its mark on me, but I put my mark on it, too.

I'm part of this place. I belong here.

Within a month, Margaret became editor as well as publisher of the *Dakota News,* and for the first time Dan could focus all his attention on his column, which now appeared twice a week instead of once.

When Margaret asked Dan what his new title should be, he looked down at her with mock severity. "Young woman, there are only two jobs worth having in this business, editor and reporter. Reporter was good enough when I started and it'll do fine now."

★ ★ ★

Minneapolis was hard going at first for Harry. The city had all the problems of the rest of the country, plus some of its own. The business establishment was a closed corporation, and its leaders were tougher and more sophisticated than their counterparts in Falls City. They were still licking their wounds after a three-month truck drivers' strike which had ended in street warfare and had sharpened class divisions in the city; they didn't like it when Harry proclaimed that his paper would seek to reflect the interests of all citizens, not just a few.

But though that attitude may have hardened the hearts of the elite, it paid off in circulation gains; and Harry worked hard to win over the businessmen, making calls himself to sell advertising and reassure the city's elite that he was no radical.

Gradually he began to make a little progress. At Dan's suggestion, he used one of his father's old tactics—announcing he would turn down liquor advertising, which he wasn't getting anyway. That won praise from the pulpit, of course, but it also produced more concrete results: the owner of the city's largest department store, a fervent dry, shifted some of his advertising from the other papers into the *Telegram*. Other merchants decided they had to follow suit, and revenues began to go up along with circulation.

South Dakota, 1934–1935

If there were stirrings of recovery in the cities, there was nothing but deepening disaster on the farms of the Dakotas.

Late winter and early spring of 1934 brought more dust storms. The worst came in mid-April, when it seemed that all the dirt in Kansas blew south in a huge, rolling black cloud to Oklahoma and the Texas panhandle.

It didn't rain in April or May; it was the second consecutive year in which these normally wet months had been bone dry. A hot wind blew night and day, sucking what little moisture there was from the soil, pulling dust from one field to the next and back again. Blown dust drifted like snow along fence rows and at the corners of buildings, and for the first time travelers began to see sand dunes in South Dakota.

Then came a day in May when the whole of the Great Plains, from Texas to the Canadian border and beyond, seemed to be sucked up and blown east. This time there was no single black cloud; instead, brownish dust rose like steam from the fields and formed a pall that in some places reached as high as 15,000 feet. The sun faded to a pale orange wafer, then disappeared completely.

The prevailing west wind carried the dust to Falls City, to Minneapolis, to Chicago. By morning it reached the East Coast, shutting out the sun there too. Dust even filtered into the White House and settled on the president's desk. The next day ships three hundred miles out in the Atlantic reported a strange film of grit on their decks. And the great storm was only the beginning; all summer the wind lifted what topsoil remained and blew it away.

By December of 1934, 39 percent of the people in South Dakota—two out of every five—were on the relief rolls, the highest figure of any state in the nation. More than half of all South Dakota farmers were receiving emergency aid at the end of the year; in some counties four out of five farmers were on the rolls.

Charlie Harper had watched in deepening despair for five years as his farm dried up and then blew away. In an attempt to offset low yields by increasing plantings, Charlie plowed up all the grassland his father had so carefully nurtured, but the result was just what Amos Harper so often foretold: nature was punishing man's failure to take care of his land.

Now, on a July afternoon in 1935, a final scourge was laid on this tortured country. The grasshoppers came back.

Charlie sat with his wife and his younger son Edward in their kitchen, waiting for the cloud of 'hoppers that had swarmed down a half-hour earlier to finish their destruction and move on. The sounds of the feeding frenzy came through the tightly closed windows into the stuffy, silent room. There was nothing to say, nothing to do but wait; they could not drive away the voracious insects, and no matter how many they might kill there were millions more.

When the shimmering cloud finally thinned and moved off to the southeast, Charlie Harper still said nothing, but got up and walked outside. He crossed the empty farmyard, his boots crunching as they squashed the remaining 'hoppers underfoot, and continued into the cornfield beyond.

He stopped, looked around, then stared down at the hard-baked, cracked earth. Nothing remained of the spindly stand of corn that had been there. It had been devoured to the ground.

Slowly, awkwardly, Charlie Harper got down on his knees. He reached out to touch the hard, wind-scoured surface. Then, suddenly and without a word, he began to pound his fists against that hard ground, and now he was sobbing, shouting incoherently. His knuckles began to bleed, but still he pounded.

Laura Harper stood on the porch by the kitchen door and watched, her hands pressed against her mouth, horror in her eyes. Edward ran to his father and pulled him to his feet. Blood ran down Charlie's fingers and left dark spots where it dripped onto the bare ground.

Edward led his father to the water pump and gently washed his hands and face. Charlie, his outburst over, again was silent, standing still, letting his son care for him. Laura bandaged his hands and put him to bed.

[370]

The next day the doctor drove out to the farm. Charlie was completely relaxed and amiable as he examined him and gently questioned him. A week later, Charlie willingly climbed into the sheriff's car for the short drive to the state hospital.

He was, at last, perfectly content.

Chapter 55

Philadelphia, June 1936

T HE SETTING was straight out of a Hollywood spectacle. More than one hundred thousand people had jammed into a huge outdoor football stadium to watch Franklin D. Roosevelt accept his party's nomination for a second term. It had rained earlier, and a misty half-moon shone intermittently through broken clouds. A hundred klieg lights stabbed through the darkness to focus on the stage. As the president came forward into the bright white glare, leaning on his son's arm and walking slowly and stiffly in his leg braces, the applause and cheering rolled down out of the stands and washed over him.

In the press section, Harry Norton watched Dan scribbling in his notebook. *How many times have we sat together at a convention?* he thought. *I wonder how many more there'll be. This time the crowds seem to bother him. I don't know if he'll want to do it again.*

Or if he'll be able to.

A fortnight earlier, in Cleveland, they had watched the Republicans nominate Alf Landon, a middle-of-the-road businessman who had been elected governor of Kansas in 1932 despite the Democratic sweep. He was no reactionary. He had been a Bull Mooser in 1912, voted for LaFollette in 1924, and in 1933 even offered his support to Roosevelt.

Landon objected not so much to the substance of New Deal policies as to the "slap-dash, jazzy method" by which they had been carried out. "I cannot criticize everything that has been done in the past three years and do it sincerely," he said. Such candor did not endear him to the party's old guard, but he won the nomination easily—in part, perhaps, because no one else much wanted to run against Roosevelt.

★   ★   ★

In Philadelphia that night the president declared war—war on the rich. He called them the new enemies, comparing them with the royalists who opposed the American Revolution. The pejorative phrases boomed from the loudspeakers.

> Out of this modern civilization economic royalists carved new dynasties. New kingdoms were built upon concentration of control over material things. Through new uses of corporations, banks, and securities, new machinery of industry and agriculture, of labor and capital—all undreamed of by the fathers—the whole structure of modern life was impressed into this royal service. . . .

Dan was a little surprised at his own reaction. *I must have stopped being a Republican a long time ago, because he makes good sense to me. It's straight-out class war, but by God I think he's right. He's saying just what Amos used to say.*

> The privileged princes of these new economic dynasties, thirsting for power . . . had concentrated into their own hands an almost complete control over other people's property, other people's money, other people's labor—other people's lives.
> The collapse of 1929 showed up the despotism for what it was. The election of 1932 was the people's mandate to end it. Under that mandate it is being ended.

Roosevelt threw back his head and paused, as he always did when he wanted applause. The huge crowd responded with a volley of cheers.

Dan was again reminded of words from another place and a different time: Mary Lease, whipping up the crowd in an Omaha hotel lobby during the Populist convention of 1892.

Roosevelt was relentless.

> These economic royalists complain that we seek to overthrow the institutions of America. What they really complain of is that we seek to take away their power. Our allegiance to American institutions requires the overthrow of this kind of power.

Again he paused; again the crowd roared.

Harry Norton frowned. *When he starts talking about the "overthrow" of "economic royalists," I know I'm a Republican,* he thought, *because he's talking about people like our family. That man is dangerous.*

> The brave and clear platform adopted by this convention, to which I heartily subscribe, sets forth that government in a modern

civilization has certain inescapable obligations to its citizens. . . . But the resolute enemy within our gates is ever ready to beat down our words unless in greater courage we will fight for them.

Dan's mind raced as he scribbled notes.

What this election is all about is Franklin Delano Roosevelt. It's about nothing else and nobody else, no matter what anyone says. It's simple: Are you for him or against him?

There was a new alignment in the making; the traditional Democratic party was only part of FDR's strength, and perhaps not the critical part at that. The influence of the South was fading, and new groups were playing larger roles in what some called the "Grand Coalition."

The party's not what it used to be. A lot of politicians don't realize it yet, but the power's shifting—to the cities, to the labor unions, to the Negroes.

And that would be bad news for farmers.

Now neither party's going to look out for them. The Republicans are the same old bunch, no good for farmers, haven't been for forty years. And now there are these new Democrats, and they don't care much about farmers either.

The president gripped the podium to reduce the strain on his crippled legs as he moved from indictment to exhortation. Now Dan heard the echo of William Jennings Bryan in Roosevelt's invocation of "moral principle" and the ancient biblical virtues.

> In the place of the palace of privilege, we seek to build a temple out of faith, and hope, and charity.
> Governments can err, presidents do make mistakes, but the immortal Dante tells us that divine justice weighs the sins of the cold-blooded and the sins of the warm-hearted in different scales. Better the occasional faults of a government that lives in a spirit of charity than the consistent omissions of a government frozen in the ice of its own indifference.
> There is a mysterious cycle in human events. To some generations much is given. Of other generations much is expected. This generation of Americans has a rendezvous with destiny.

A crescendo of sound shook the stadium, almost drowning out his closing line.

> I accept the commission you have tendered me. I join with you. I am enlisted for the duration of the war.

Roosevelt clasped his hands triumphantly over his head, then summoned his family to stand with him. When the orchestra played "Auld Lang Syne," he led the great crowd in singing.

Finally, after ten minutes of uproarious adulation, he got back into his car, circled the stadium twice, and disappeared into the darkness.

[374]

Harry and Dan argued through much of the night on the train from Philadelphia to Chicago, sitting in the publisher's Pullman compartment with a bottle of Scotch, two glasses, and a bucket of ice cubes on the table between them.

"I went along with him when he first came into office, and we supported his recovery programs even though I had doubts about most of them," Harry said. "But I can't swallow him now. He's preaching class hatred."

Dan agreed with the diagnosis, but not the prescription.

"I know there's a class war going on, and I don't deny Roosevelt is stepping it up," he said. "Look, I was fussing about that when you were still a baby—when Bryan did it in '96, and a little later when Teddy did it. But it's different now."

"What do you mean, different?"

"The country has changed. Back then a poor boy could still get rich by working hard and using his brains, the way your father did. There wasn't so much separation between classes, and you could move up. But nowadays work and brains aren't enough, and the class lines are harder." Dan poured more whiskey, added ice, and swirled it in the glass to dilute his drink. "The reaction he got when he talked about 'economic royalists' tells you something."

"It certainly does." Harry's tone made clear he didn't like the message. "It tells me he's setting people against anyone who works hard and gets to be halfway well-off. Three years ago he was asking for our support. Now we're 'the enemy within the gates.'"

"I know you didn't like it." Dan noted Harry's use of the first-person pronoun. "But those cheers tell you there's already class division. He's not creating it."

"Huh!" Harry sounded like his father. "But he's exploiting it."

Dan shrugged. "That's what politicians do for a living."

They sat quietly for several minutes, sipping whiskey and watching the intermittent lights flash by in the night. Dan slouched in his chair, gray and rumpled, showing the wear of the past week—and of his sixty-eight years. Harry, dark and intense, eyes alert behind the big glasses, was still energetic despite the clamor of the convention. He reopened the discussion.

"There's another thing," he said. "Roosevelt is attracting all kinds of strange people. Communists, those Farmer-Laborites, Socialists, labor union agitators, Negroes, parlor pinks, professors. He's not really your kind of Democrat."

Dan smiled. "Harry, your grievance is with the world, not with Roosevelt. Sure, he's pulling new people into the Democratic tent, but they were always there for the picking. It's just that neither party ever reached out for them."

Harry stared at his old friend and mentor.

"I guess it comes down to the fact that Landon is a moderate man, and he's right about the New Deal being a bureaucratic nightmare," he said. "I just don't trust Roosevelt any more."

"Look, Harry, even if Landon's a moderate, he's as much in the minority in his own party as Teddy was." Dan hoped his evocation of Harry's first political hero might sway him. "And if by any chance he wins, he'll be betrayed by his own party, just the way Teddy was."

Harry wouldn't be persuaded, even by the magic name of the earlier Roosevelt, and after a time Dan returned to his own compartment and went to bed.

That conversation should remind me who I am and where I come from, he thought as the train rocked along in the night. *I'm not rich, and I'm different from those that are.*

I'm not a Norton, not even after working forty-five years for George and going on twenty now with Harry.

Actually, he thought, he was more like George than Harry.

At least the Old Man started out with nothing. Harry never had that advantage.

Of course, Harry backed Landon in his Minneapolis paper. Though he admitted privately that Landon didn't have much of a chance, he was a Republican and an honest man, and that combined with Harry's distrust of Roosevelt was reason enough to endorse him. Besides, Harry saw no need to go out of his way to offend the Republican businessmen who were just beginning to advertise in his paper; some of them so hated Roosevelt that they would not—*could* not—speak his name aloud.

In Falls City, Margaret Norton would have no part of Landon and the Republicans, and since she was now the publisher she had her way; the *Dakota News,* breaking with its past, endorsed Roosevelt. George Norton grumbled about "his" paper supporting a Democrat, but he predicted Roosevelt would win.

"People may be against the New Deal, but they like the president," George told Dan in his unadorned way. "He is the only issue, and more people are for him than against him."

South Dakota, August 1936

The people of South Dakota confirmed that judgment when the president visited the state on a tour of drought-stricken areas in late summer. Roosevelt smilingly insisted it was "nonpolitical," but there were big crowds at every stop and the atmosphere was that of a campaign.

Dan, once again riding a presidential train through the Dakotas, was struck by the variety of roles Roosevelt played. Sometimes he simply spoke from the back platform of his train; sometimes he drove into the country to talk with farmers and to inspect reservoirs and other conservation projects. In each state he also held a formal conference with state and federal officials, planners, and conservation experts.

He made a speech, usually off-the-cuff, at every stop. With minor variations he delivered the same messages everywhere. His talk at Bismarck was typical, and again Dan heard echoes of Amos Harper.

It really comes down to three problems: the first is the immediate one of keeping people going who have lost their crops and their livestock. The second is to keep them going over the winter until next year, when we hope we shall have more rain. The third problem relates to the future . . . to working out a plan of cooperation with nature instead of continuing what we have been doing in the past—trying to buck nature.

He put it even more succinctly in a brief back-platform talk at Aberdeen:

One of our troubles in the past has been that we have been fighting nature. Now it is time to cooperate with nature.

And everywhere the president sought to encourage his listeners, to persuade them not to give up.

I had a hunch—and it was right—that when I got out here I would find that you people had your chins up, that you were not looking forward in despair to the day when this country would be depopulated, but that you and your children fully expected to remain here.

He understands, Dan thought as he stood beside the train, taking notes. *He knows how bad it is—and how many people are about ready to give up and leave.*

Roosevelt also preached from Bryan's old text on the interdependence of country and city.

The very existence of the men and women working in the clothing factories of New York, in the steel mills of Pittsburgh, in the automobile factories of Detroit, and in the harvester factories of Illinois depends upon the farmers' ability to purchase the commodities they produce. In the same way it is the purchasing power of the workers in those factories in the cities that enables them and their wives and children to eat more beef, more pork, more wheat, more corn, more fruit, and more dairy products, and to buy

[377]

more clothing made from cotton. In a physical and a property sense, as well as in a spiritual sense, we are members of one another.

Falls City, November 1936

South Dakota, like every other state except Maine and Vermont, joined the Roosevelt landslide in November. He received the largest plurality in history, the biggest electoral margin in over a century.

"It's not just the numbers," Dan told Margaret as they sat in his office the day after election. "Roosevelt has changed the Democratic party into something completely different."

Margaret grinned at him. "You mean they're winning instead of losing."

"You and your wisecracks." Dan shook an avuncular forefinger at her. "It's not that simple. Now the Democratic party is a real national party, like the Republicans after the Civil War."

"You mean it's turned into a big-city party."

"That, and more—labor unions, Negroes, poor people, immigrants, Jews, women, young people, intellectuals—"

Margaret interrupted. "Those are all big-city people. I didn't hear you mention farmers."

"They're in there too, but only for now." Dan ran a hand through his hair. "Farmers don't really feel at home with those other folks. As soon as things get better they'll go back to voting Republican."

"Farmers aren't going to count for so much anyway."

Dan shrugged. "At least this president understands that the cities can't be prosperous unless the farmers are—and he's settled it that the government has to help agriculture."

Margaret lit a cigarette and took a long drag. "You know, *that's* the real point of this election."

"What is?"

"From now on people will expect the federal government to handle the big problems in their lives, to look out for them," she said. "Even Republicans accept that idea now."

"You're right." Dan picked up the thread of her argument. "And they'll also count on the government to keep things in balance, to protect the weak from the strong. That idea started with the other Roosevelt, and this one has made it stick for good."

Margaret nodded. "Right. And farmers know they'll never have the kind of strength that business and labor do, so from now on they'll count on the government to help them."

Dan swiveled his chair and looked out the window, watching the traffic on Union Avenue.

"That's been coming for forty years," he mused. "Bryan in 1896,

[378]

Teddy, Wilson. And LaFollette and Norris and the others in Congress. But now it's here, and here to stay."

A day or two later Dan recounted the conversation to George Norton. The old man, as so often before, confounded him with his reply.

"Of course that's right. The states are encouraging the transfer of power to the national government; in fact they're insisting on it," he said. "I'll tell you something else: if that's going to happen, it's better to have a plan for it than to let it just drift. Even if that wild man is doing the planning."

You never know what he's going to say, Dan thought. *But he still makes sense more times than not.*

That turned out to be the last political comment Dan would hear from George Norton. A few weeks later George came down with bronchitis. At seventy-eight he hadn't much resistance; after Christmas he developed pneumonia, and he died halfway through January.

Dan and Grace stood behind the family at the cemetery. In the gathering darkness of a bitter winter afternoon, the gray clouds scudding before a cruel wind, George was buried beside his wife. The mourners stood at the graveside, huddled down in their heaviest winter overcoats, as the minister said the last few words.

Margaret could not stop shivering in the bitter cold.

When I brought home the best report card I ever got, four As and one B, all he said was: "What about that B?"

With me he always seemed to have that chip on his shoulder. When he did say nice things about me, it was to other people, never to me. Why did he always fight me? Why?

Harry's memories were more mixed.

So many arguments. He was arbitrary and harsh. But he was also so shy he had to justify every good thing he did as a business decision—and he pretended to be a skinflint to hide his generosity to people in trouble.

Alice Norton clung to Harry's arm, clenching her jaw in a vain attempt to stop her teeth from chattering.

My God, it's cold. It's this kind of weather that killed him.

But what a wonderful old age he had, coming back, meeting the biggest challenge of his life.

He wasn't an explorer or an adventurer, but he was a settler and a founder, one of the men who built homes and institutions—and created a civilization.

Dan remembered a young George Norton walking into the back shop to announce he had bought the paper.

That changed my life. He had the most influence on me, a lot more than my own father. He taught me so much. He was a gambler, and a genius at newspapering, but he hid it behind all that penny-pinching talk.

[379]

Grace forgot the cold, remembering a hot July day, and a buggy ride, and being lifted dripping from the water.

He was a hard man. But he made love to me once, and twenty years later he said he still thought of it every time he saw me.

And I think he meant it.

Chapter 56

HARRY NORTON was in Europe when Dan had the heart attack. Margaret called her brother as soon as he returned to Minneapolis.

"The doctor said it was 'moderate,' whatever that means," she reported. "He's at home now, and he seems to be getting better. Grace is keeping him pretty quiet, but he'd love to see you if you could manage to get out here."

Harry arrived the next afternoon. Grace met him at the door.

"He's in the study. We made sort of an office out of it, so he could get back to work again."

Harry heard Dan's old typewriter clacking away as he approached the study.

Dan looked up from his work to see Harry standing in the doorway.

That's the way he always looked when he was a boy. He'd stand in my office door. "Are you busy?" . . . "Got a minute?" . . . *and most often,* "Can I ask you a question?"

Harry came to Dan and clasped his hand, searching his eyes and face for clues to his condition.

He doesn't look good, Harry thought. *He looks used up, exhausted. Well, he's seventy, after all.*

"Dan." Harry managed a smile. "You look fine."

"Let's not talk about me, I'm bored with that subject." Dan smoothed his cowlick in the familiar gesture. "Sit down. I want to know what's going to happen in Europe."

"I'd give odds of three to one there'll be war." Harry's voice was somber, his eyes serious and unblinking behind the thick lenses. "Chamberlain talks about 'peace in our time.' I think that'll turn out to be less than twelve months."

"Hitler won't be satisfied with as much of Czechoslovakia as he got?"

"When Alice and I first saw Adolf Hitler prancing around at the Olympic games two years ago we thought he was insane. We saw him again at some big rallies this summer, and he's getting worse. He won't stop now. There'll be a war."

"And that means there'll be another boom for farmers." Dan's voice was melancholy. "And another bust. This might be the last one, the end of the kind of farm life we've always had."

He never forgot those years on the farm, Harry thought. *If you want to understand Dan Woods, you have to know about that place and that time, because they made him what he is.*

Their talk turned to politics; Dan brought Harry up to date on the gossip about Roosevelt's plans for 1940.

"There's all kinds of talk in Washington, but no one seems to have a clue about what FDR will really do," he concluded.

"What's your guess?"

"I think he'll run again."

"Well, I've been out of touch, of course," Harry said. "But I certainly hope he won't. Not just because I don't like him; I think it would be terrible to break the two-term tradition."

Dan chuckled. "Sounds like you think he'll win if he runs."

"I'm afraid he will—unless the Republicans can find a stronger candidate than anybody that's around now."

Harry had become increasingly active in liberal Republican politics. Dan decided to do a little fishing.

"There's time enough, but do you have a candidate hidden somewhere?"

"I'm going to talk with some of my friends," Harry said. "The important thing is to find a man who understands the world, who can get across to people how dangerous this European situation is—and how important it is for us to be involved."

"In a *war?*" Dan was startled by the implication of Harry's words.

"It will come to that, sooner or later. The real danger is that after it's over we'll go back to the same kind of isolation that destroyed the League—and made the next war inevitable."

Dan remembered Harry's youthful political passions for Theodore Roosevelt, for Woodrow Wilson and for the League of Nations.

He's looking for a new Teddy. No, that's not quite it. He's really looking for a Republican Wilson. He put the thought into words.

"You're looking for someone with Teddy Roosevelt's personality and Woodrow Wilson's international outlook."

"That's it." Now Dan's fishing produced a bite. "And I think there's a fellow who might fit the prescription, a utilities executive from Indiana. He changed his party from Democratic to Republican just this year. Name's Willkie, Wendell Willkie."

[382]

"A renegade Democrat and a private power company executive to boot?" Dan laughed. "The perfect Republican candidate!"

He pulled the page from his typewriter and handed it to Harry. "I've been doing a little thinking about the next election, too. Had an idea for a column. You might be interested."

> The next presidential election is still two years away, but already political observers are thinking of little else. Will President Roosevelt run for a third term? Can the Republicans find a candidate to give him a run for it if he does? If FDR does *not* run, who will the Democrats choose?
>
> Such questions preoccupy the sages and pundits in Washington. But if you are in this part of the country—and have a little more time to reflect, as this writer perforce does these days—other thoughts present themselves.
>
> One is that whatever happens in the next election, this region seems now to have fulfilled its political destiny. The goals of the Alliance and the Populists and Progressives have been achieved by a President who, unlike his predecessors, understands farming and has mobilized new political forces to help farmers—forces undreamed-of when the struggle began in the last century.
>
> But that success also signals the end of this region's role as a major factor in national politics. It will never again swing the political weight it did in the past. Power has shifted from the country to the city, from farmers to labor union members. We simply do not have enough people here; there are no really big cities, and we will have fewer Congressmen after every census. As Roosevelt's Grand Coalition delivers the programs farmers want, it also renders them politically impotent.
>
> This writer has watched every skirmish and battle in the long agrarian struggle: from Greenbackers and Grangers to the Alliance and the Populists; from Insurgency to Progressivism; from the idealism of Wilson to the cynicism of the Twenties and the horror of the great depression.
>
> Finally, in the moment of crisis, Franklin Roosevelt improvised a new program and built a new coalition, mixing Populist and Progressive ideals with the practical politics of an urban society. Men like Senator Norris and Congressman Sam Rayburn are now finally finishing the job begun by Bryan and LaFollette and Wilson.

Harry looked up from his reading. "You've got it just right," he said.

"It's not finished, and it needs editing," Dan said.

"No, it's fine. I'd put it in the paper just as is." Harry was stirred by Dan's reflections. *He's a living link between yesterday, today, and tomorrow— between farms and cities, between Falls City and Minneapolis, between my father and my children, between farm wagons and airplanes, between Bryan and FDR.*

"You're one of the few left who lived through all the changes," Harry added, "and that's another reason why you should keep on writing: because you know it firsthand and can explain it."

"Other people can explain it just as well."

"No, they can't," Harry insisted. "You can do it better than any of those smart young columnists."

He's right, Dan thought, *because they weren't there. They never saw their fathers struggle with a new country—and fail. They never spent a winter in a sod house. They never watched grasshoppers eat the crops and drought crack the earth.*

But he shook his head. "I'm not going to be much of a reporter if I can't get out and around to check what's going on."

"Don't talk nonsense." Harry was brisk. "You're obviously on the mend."

Dan asked how things were going in Minneapolis, and for a few minutes they talked shop: Harry had recently heard from Richard Lawson in Washington, Dan wondered how the new editor was doing in Minneapolis, Harry was able to report steady circulation gains.

When Grace reappeared at the study door, Harry took the cue and stood up. "Well, Dan," he said. "I'm glad to see you doing so well. I'll look for that column in the paper this week. And I expect you to be back full time by Thanksgiving at the latest."

"Huh!" It was Grace. "It better be sooner than that. I don't know how long I can put up with having him around the house all day."

They went off toward the front door as Dan settled down by the west window. This was his favorite time of day: the brief interval when the low-hanging sun suddenly brightened, producing an intense golden glow that lit the landscape with penetrating clarity and then faded imperceptibly but inevitably into darkness.

Just like our politics, Dan realized: *They blazed up, they lit the country-side—but only for a moment.*

Watching the changing light, he could see now with equal clarity the truth about the place where he lived: it was so harsh, so powerful, that it had put an indelible imprint on the people who lived there; those people, in turn, had left their stamp on the nation's politics, on the national character.

They had to be so strong just to survive, and that carried over into politics. We were strong enough to make our mark. We had bigger men, we had more influence than we had votes, and we hit on the right ideas before the others did.

The golden light turned pink, then shaded into dusky red.

And in the end, those ideas won out. But the people didn't. The rest of the country's changed, but we're still a province. The last province. Still being exploited, still selling at wholesale and buying at retail—and still paying the freight both ways.

The sky was darkening faster now, red blurring into gray.

Some won and some lost, but either way they endured: Amos Harper. Pa and Ma. George Norton.

All gone now.

The last light faded coldly in the west. Dan was falling asleep in the big chair.

Only the middle of October, he thought, *but it's already getting dark so early.*

Epilogue

IN HIS DREAM, Dan's earliest memory came back clearer than ever.

He stood at the door of his family's sod house on the claim in Nebraska, looking down the slope, watching his father come across the creek and start up the hill. The slope was so steep and Dan so short that the wagon seemed to sink from sight; for several minutes Dan could only mark its progress by the sound of his father's voice as he urged Babe and Charlie up the slope. Then the horses' heads reappeared, and between them his father's head and shoulders, and then his hands holding the reins, and finally the whole outfit, legs and wagon and wheels and all. His father saw him across the farmyard and waved; Dan stepped out of the door and ran toward him.

"Pa, Pa, I saw you cross the creek!"

"Well, I saw you standing guard, looking out for your Ma." His father patted him on the head. "Now, help me carry things into the house." He handed Dan the jug of molasses.

Dan turned toward the house, but it was gone. He looked back to his father, and he too had disappeared.

ABOUT THE AUTHOR

Charles W. Bailey began newspaper work as a reporter for the *Minneapolis Tribune* in 1950. In 1954 he became a Washington correspondent for the *Tribune* and from 1968 to 1972 was its Washington bureau chief. He was editor of the *Tribune* from 1972 to 1982, and later served three years as Washington editor of National Public Radio.

Bailey has been chairman of the Washington Journalism Center, a member of the board of the American Society of Newspaper Editors, president of the White House Correspondents Association, and secretary of the Standing Committee of Correspondents, the governing body of the congressional press galleries.

He is the author of *Conflicts of Interest: A Matter of Journalistic Ethics,* published in 1984 by the National News Council. He is the coauthor (with Fletcher Knebel) of three other books: *No High Ground,* a history of the first atomic bomb, and two novels, *Seven Days in May* and *Convention.* He has contributed to other books, including *The President's Trip to China* and *Candidates 1960.*

Bailey is married to the former Ann Card Bushnell. They have two daughters and one granddaughter.